LATENT LAUDANUM BOOKS
Notary Rotary, Inc.
925 29th Street
Des Moines, IA 50312

LATENT LAUDANUM BOOKS and design are trademarks of Notary Rotary, Inc.

Manufactured in the United States of America

1 3 5 7 9 10 8 6 4 2

Quality Books has cataloged the Latent Laudanum edition
as follows:
Bosker, Pollyanna.
Wokinih's ghost dance : a novel / Pollyanna Bosker.
-- 1st Latent Laudanum Books ed.
p. cm.
1. Mothers and sons--Fiction.   I. Title.
PS3602.O84W64 2004
813'.6   QBI04-700553
CIP

LCCN 2004115601
ISBN 0-9747386-2-X
ISBN 978-0-9747386-2-8

Wokinih's Ghost Dance

A Novel

Pollyanna Bosker

LATENT LAUDANUM BOOKS
Published By Notary Rotary

The Lizard

It is mostly a story about dead people.
Among them was a man whom many knew and now mourn.
He was once my husband,
though I loved him much more than that.

In restless sleep, I see his eyes.
In sorrow, I hear his voice.
Like unharnessed hope, his smile follows me through life.

I miss him,
but not as much as I miss what died with him.
In every mirror, I see an old woman with no choices left.
No matter how I turn, I am empty, grey and ugly.
There's no one left to dream of me,
or pine for what could never be.

No one sees me as he saw me.
No one knows us as we were:
as perfect as youth,
as lovely as life,
as timeless as eternity.

When he died, I waltzed willingly with him
through the maze of memories,
charmed one last time
by the promise of Wokinih's Ghost Dance.

Part I

The Legend

According to legend, the Great Spirit appeared before the Indians in the form of a large bird, summoning all tribes to a location centered between the mighty Mississippi and the massive Missouri Rivers. There, standing before them atop a precipice of striated quartzite and rose-colored Catlinite, the Spirit reached down and educed from the crevasse a piece of rock in the form of a pipe. He proceeded to smoke from the pipe and as the skies above the multitude grew turbid, the Great Spirit conveyed to those gathered there that the pipe was as their flesh. They were all created from the sacred red stone, and the land and all stone taken from it belonged to them.

By smoking through pipes created from the stone, they would be performing a ceremony for Him. Through this ceremony, this intimate channel of communication, they would be forever linked to the Spirit World. The exhaled smoke was the breath of prayer, the tie that would bind all peoples to the ethereal. To protect the sanctity of the ground, where the rare pipestone lay nestled between shelves of solid quartz, the Spirit decreed that no weapon should ever be brought there, nor should any act of aggression ever occur there.

For four hundred years, the shelves were quarried by Indians who lived nearby, or by those who came from a distance to work the pits a few weeks each year. Between the spring rains that often filled the quarry trenches, the short, hot summers, and the excruciatingly cold winters, extracting the precious stone was usually difficult, and often impossible, making the carved pipes all the more valuable. From Oto and Iowa tribes in the 1600's and 1700's, to Yankton and Dakota Sioux in the 1800's, all of the rare quarried pipestone was carved into calumets. All tribes prized and traded the handmade pipes, from Northern Minnesota Chippewa, to Comanche and Choctaw in the South; from Western Shoshone to Eastern Cheyenne. That single quarry in the southwest corner of Minnesota was the only known source of the soft, malleable, soaplike rock that varied in color from marbled pink to blood red and burnt sienna. Valued by Indians and trappers alike, one pipe could be traded for several buffalo robes or a dozen iron arrow points. Three pipes could bring a trapper's Hudson Bay blanket, and four could buy most any horse. Since many ceremonies and rituals were dependent on partaking of the pipe, it became a passport of sorts to travelers, assuring their welcome and share of kinnikinnick, the tobacco and herb mixture that nearly all visitors enjoyed smoking.

All who traveled to the source of the stone honored the law of the sacred ground. As white settlers encroached on the Northern Plains, the long and tedious process of quarrying, creating, and trading pipes was no longer considered feasible or worthwhile. Few remaining tribes journeyed to the area to trade for pipes of peace. In 1849, a piece of pipestone was incorporated into the Washington Monument, but a full ten years later, only one square mile of the area had been designated as reservation or quarry by the United States government. Even into the 1900's, when the Sioux seldom bothered to work the quarry and settlers farmed all around it, not one act of aggression had ever been recorded on the sacred land of the pipestone.

By the turn of the century, negotiations provided forty acres of the area housing the pipestone for the sole purpose of Indian camping and quarrying. It was not considered property of the Yankton Sioux, who had refused to give up rights to it, yet there was no record of sale by any faction of the Sioux Nation and no indication that the Sioux had ever been compensated for any of the land. By 1929, the sacred Pipestone Quarry, with the only known source of Catlinite in the world, was no longer owned by any Indian or tribe. They were allowed limited access to the quarries to remove the stone, but the land belonged to the government of the United States. By 1938, the original designation of one square mile had been expanded to hundreds of acres and was formally declared Pipestone National Park.

. . .

The wild prairie grasses still grow there. A gentle waterfall still tumbles to the rocks below, and narrow strips of shelved quartz stand naked to the elements with the shallow layer of pipestone removed, like a favored card pulled from the bottom of a deck. Saplings struggle to survive on the tract of near-treeless plateau. Desolation seems to echo in the gusts of wind that brush the face of the cliffs where the Holy Spirit once stood, exhorting the law of the land. It is now empty space, pitiful and paltry, dependent on history to define its significance. What once held the fruits of hope for peace among many peoples is now a vacuum of ancient images, a hundred years after the last trade took place.

I am but a visitor. But I fear I am somehow too late. Since his death, I've been plagued day and night with residual memories and endless dreams. Each time I've been summoned, I've gone without question. I've faced the murky haze of clouded visions and every stranger's face with calm. I've met each call with courage, each challenge with conviction. Yet I've found neither vindication nor resolution. Whatever urged this journey and whoever called me to these ledges - to the stark reality of these barren walls and cold, quarry floors – they must be mistaken. I find heartache and humiliation, futility of the conquered and shame of the vanquished. I've searched for relief, but remain sick with sorrow.

Before taking my leave, I glance back once more. I'm startled at the sight shimmering in the light, just above the quarry ledge, the solemn, liquid image of a majestic brave. At his side, he firmly holds a bow that extends to his full height, the grip carved in the distinct form of a lean animal, stretched in stride, the color of clay. It seems as though great thought should spring from the sinew, that the world should understand, and in its mercy, nod. Ebony hair falls from his shoulders like a cape, and a bronzed, broad chest ripples and glows in a single shaft of brilliant white light.

I am keenly aware that I stand on sacred land. As promised, these open spaces, rippling waters, and tangled boskage, are still frequented by the Spirits. There is a free exchange of communication from which I am not exempt. Subconsciously, I know that I'm absorbing and being absorbed, but I don't try to qualify what's happening around me and through me.

His great-grandfather was said to have been truly magnificent, resplendent in courage, strength, and fortitude. In times of trouble, he was said to have possessed a commanding presence. I cannot be sure, but I think this is Wokinih who stands before me. Cautiously, I back away from the ledge and the eerie presence, but the looming apparition moves stealthily along with me. I'm being pulled from world to world, from perception to reality, unable to determine from which I haplessly fall, or which I should choose or refuse. Both sensibility and cynicism have escaped me.

I am drawn to the warmth and wisdom of this face. It is secure and comforting, a face of truth and integrity. I am pulled to him by a force that is greater than any I know, or have ever known. He does not look at me, yet I know he sees me as surely as I see him. I try to rejoin reality by shuffling my feet in the dusty path beneath me, but find I'm no longer grounded in the present. The stirred dust serves to do little more than distract a mirage of sheltered Pawnee ponies who crowd each other nervously, pawing the ground in a secluded corral of rock and rope.

He does not smile, but I feel the warmth of radiant approval and know I am here to bear witness to something, but nothing I could have prepared for. Ever so slowly, a small shadow moves timidly behind him. I am at ease with its presence and relieved that it knows and welcomes me, allows me to see. I sense that the small figure is protected by the warrior, as well as being camouflaged by an apparition - the flowing pinions of a great bird envelops them both.

My heart stirs as the child's dark eyes peer out at me, holding fast, with one small hand, the warrior's knee.

Voices

You must decide whose voice ...
I think you've missed the point.
Oh? ... So, what's the point?

The point is: We don't give a shit about voice.
The point is and always has been:
I/he/we were nearly inseparable.
It was often impossible to distinguish where
oneendedandtheotherbegan.

The point is: Our words are memories,
the legacy of life.
My memories are woven within her thoughts,
and his words now share my breath,
while our eyes relive the waltz.

Sometimes, the memories assume lives of their own,
so powerful that they can exist without conjured images,
so devastating that they can threaten life without ever having lived.

The point is: The story stands on its own merit.
You may lend your voice; narrate if you like.
You might assume our lives if you dare.
But you will never change
what is,
what has been,
what will be.

The point is: It will tell itself.

The Olde River Road
Eldon, Iowa

From the crest of the hill, where the Hofstedt House serves as silent overseer to the main road into Eldon, and trailing through the town along the railroad tracks, over the crossing, past depot, diner and drugstore, rounding corners at a snail's pace, they follow in serpentine formation. Creeping up and down the gentle slopes at the north end of town, onto Market Street Bridge and over Snag Creek, in a few miles, just beyond these open spaces, the cold, unyielding concrete will end. The welcoming warmth of the Old River Road will reach out and embrace us. Pausing occasionally to glance back, we find little comfort in confirmation. As far as the eye can see, there is no apparent end to the caravan of grief.

With headlights on in somber pronouncement, the interminable line of mourners back up traffic at every intersection. They inch slowly along at a staid and steady pace, vehicles of every vintage, class and color, bearing every imaginable friend and relative. Dell Collins Shaunessy is going home at last; he will not pass this way again.

This is my first time behind the wheel in such a solemn, mournful motorcade. At my grandfather's funeral, winding through these same familiar streets in a life long since forgotten, my first husband drove to the cemetery. I rode along in detached silence, staring out the window as though my youth was somehow imposed upon. More recently, my second husband has driven. I don't know if maturity or a keen sense of mortality has set in, but I've since abandoned all decorum and wept inconsolably for my brother, father, and mother - all the way out and all the way home, three inconceivable years in a row.

Now, I'm here as moral support. Prematurely, I have come as the matriarch of family remains. I ground myself in the present, gripping and regripping the steering wheel, determined to stay strong and stoic. I nod to myself in agreement that I'm merely an impartial chauffeur. I have nothing at stake, and I repeat the silent thought for good measure: *I'm just the driver here.* Each of us is drawn along by the wake of this grievous procession. Without exception, we will all sever ties for eternity. Unfortunately, that includes the frail bond only recently renewed between prodigal father and my erudite son.

In general, I don't have to respond. In particular, I don't know how to avoid it. Highly sensitive information cowers at the core of my heart, encapsulated in the protective custody of petrified tears. A shiver escapes with a warning: *Tread softly through these memories. Nothing is as dangerously deceptive as simplicity.*

As we head toward his final resting place in the shaded Valley of the Shepherd, my mind fills with disjointed images I can neither control nor ignore. The past twenty years wash over me in undulating waves, depositing seashells that bear the hollow echo of abandoned promises and treasured thoughts long refused. I shudder as white caps form in this sea of memories for I know crashing breakers will invariably follow. It had always been so. Where my dreams innocently lingered, his nightmares maliciously lurked.

Though the pavement glistens like a radiant ceremonial ribbon, decades of familiar summer sights simply vanish in sorrow, leaving the lifeless remains of rotted roadside fences and dusty driveways to serve as a barren backdrop for death and deliverance. With miles of deserted sky and little more than lonely clouds to note our passing, we slither along quietly without comment or question. The unknown stretches before us in open reception, silently coaxing along forsakened sons and loved ones, never again to travel without wondering what we've left behind and what lies ahead.

Just off to the side of the road, orange safety cones, yellow county trucks, and other telltale signs of highway crews rise directly before us and loom well into the distance. A signal worker holds a sign that pivots from STOP to SLOW, allowing several carloads of stalled travelers going in opposite directions to pass alternately pass through one open lane of traffic.

The stately, slate-grey Lincoln leading the procession signals a left turn, and we avoid miles of roadwork by exiting to Maggie's Tar Road, the secluded backroad that runs along the river. On plat maps, it was called The Olde River Road Northwest. The locals referred to it in abbreviated, familiar forms they'd created to suit themselves: Johnny ORR, or Old THORN. But to Dell Collins Shaunessy, it was just the ol' river road. And to locals, he was just Dieks. How appropriate, I thought, as I smiled sadly to myself. Of all who knew him well enough to have traveled with him a length of life, no one would've escaped the late night harrowing flights on the barren backroad.

For more years than we could remember, his life and attention had been divided between the tiny towns scattered about on the secondary roads of southeastern Iowa. The old asphalt road, where traffic was minimal and highway patrol nonexistent, made it possible for him to fly unnoticed between Eldon and Floris, Douds and Ottumwa. Dieks craved the time he spent with his old friends but seemed to spend an even greater amount of time searching for more people, more crowds, more activity. He always wanted more. He never seemed able to achieve balance in one place, never knew the luxury of staying put long enough to claim roots. It was a wanderlust of people that he was driven to, and the ol' river road made the journey memorable.

Though familiar as his own face, the road itself was ageless and formidable. It was a narrow, twenty-mile stretch filled with tar strips, patched asphalt, and menacing potholes that tended to melt together in the heat of the noonday sun. Since the curves were banked and the shoulders collared, Dieks interpreted this combination as a personal obstacle course, engineered to challenge a driver with unflinching nerve and unparalleled skill. Running wide open, he did more than just drive the road, he assumed its characteristics. He became as fluid as the landscape and it was often difficult to tell where the heat mirage stopped and the man began.

The tar strips served as outlines, housing manageable, memorable segments of his life. History was recorded in quarter-mile markers that existed only in his mind. Here was where Aunt Cher's Chihuahua would start doing backflips, knowing that unavoidable bump in the road meant they were almost home. Over there was where he stopped every year without fail after his mother's death, to cut cattails, milkweed, and maiden hair ferns for a winter arrangement of dried flowers. Just as she had, Dieks filled an old oversized, garish Mexican vase with the cuttings. But shortly thereafter, it would be abandoned in the corner of the living room where it stood only to collect cobwebs and dust throughout the winter months.

There were only a few lengths of road long enough and straight enough to serve as drag strips, but all the locals knew where they were. An impartial chauffeur could see them - even thirty years after the fact - with tire mark indicators noting yet another generation of Andretti hopefuls. As our solemn procession inched its way to the cemetery, images of drag racing on the ol' river road over the years were revisited in most of the pallbearers' minds: the unforgettable Zen Master, the Fabulous Baker Boys, and Dieks' oldest and now loneliest friend, Big Red.

The road had provided all of them with the familiar comfort of escape at one time or another. Whether the conquering hero's challenge of survival, or the freedom that came with speed and distance, it called to them and they willingly went. For Dieks, it lessened the pain and held the anger at bay. In his reality, home and hurt were the same, while the tar road offered fleeting moments of control, comfort, and hope.

Once again, he was being welcomed by the soothing sway of the willow, fern fronds, and ancient prairie grasses. The melodious call of the whippoorwill sang of his untimely passing, while the rest of us wept quietly as witnesses, along for the ride to the end of the line.

Who could possibly imagine the times we'd stopped along this very stretch, rushing hand-in-hand through wildflowers and brambles, into the backbrush, only to emerge a short while later, breathless, spent, and satiated. At forty slow miles an hour, I found the river road a little more scenic than at Dieks' customary eighty, but far less comforting. I couldn't help but think the pastoral solitude would have been so lovely and serene under just about any other circumstance.

At the wheel of virtually anything, Dieks drove this road hard, fast, and relentless. He knew every curve, crack, dip, bump, and roll, and if our intention was merely to get from point A to point B, he rarely paused for reflection. It seemed to be a race with the devil, in one direction or the other. But if we left and he had a mischievous glint in his eye, or seemed unable to keep his mind on the road, or his hands to himself, I knew we'd be screeching to a halt nearly anywhere. And soon, I'd find myself on a cushioned bed of fallen leaves, under a canopy of cottonwood, ancient oak, or elm, most likely naked, and usually, enraptured.

In the ten thousand days that comprise thirty years of driving, the number of trips he'd made in any direction on this road must've numbered in the thousands. I wonder now if he wondered then whether or not all his journeys might ultimately end here, on his favorite back road home.

When we crossed Timber Bridge, his story replayed itself with an eerie clarity. He said his dad crashed through the timber railings one night, in a Model A, back sixty, maybe seventy years before. On impact, Richard had been thrown clear, but the *Eldon Courier* reported his companion, a Miss Collins, of Zenetta, was found in the trunk, unconscious, and somewhat crumpled, but alive. The next day she was listed in stable condition by unknown sources at a local hospital.

"We were runnin' whiskey," Richard said with pride as he repeated the story for me from time to time.

The half-sprite sparkle in his eyes waved away any regret he might have had concerning the effect of the wreck on his friend's health or the effect it might have had on the child she was carrying.

"Damned lucky she didn't die," he'd add later, clearly irritated that anyone would give it a second thought.

As the story went, while Richard searched the wooded area to the east and walked the banks of the icy, shallow waters of Snag Creek, expecting to find body parts at best, concerned passing motorists and night deputies were out in force with flashlights doing some serious searching of their own. Bottles that had been hurled intact were retrieved and slipped inside coats, under front seats, and into the trunks of cars. In fact, when the ambulance finally arrived, Miss Collins was the only thing still obviously missing. There was no remaining reason to be concerned about the enforcement of prohibition. However, upon finding the young woman alive in the trunk, many of the search party declared good reason to celebrate throughout the area that evening, along with the fact that there was simply and certainly nothing left to indict.

"A few crates," he said with a sneer, " ... splintered pine and shattered glass from here to hell and kingdom come ... "

He'd smile and nod that it was so, and I'd just shake my head. I never knew who, what, or when to believe back then. There were just too many stories to sort through and too few truths to trust.

As we rounded Dead Man's Curve, I shuddered at the scene unfolding before me. The brilliant sunlight of the present simply rolled into itself and disappeared as a suffocating tunnel of darkness descended, taking me back to a hot summer's night in 1970. The fabulous Baker Boys, Quinn and Jim, are in the front seat of an immaculate, red and white, souped up '57 Chevy. At a hundred miles an hour, with the lights off and the moon on, they're totally relaxed and self-assured.

Every now and then, one of them glances back and makes yet another toast to good friends and good times, beer can held high. One mumbles a monologue, somewhat muted by the pounding high-pitched whine of the engine and the deafening roar of the wind. Perhaps they are mildly amused, or merely confused by my struggle to get their attention: waving and screaming, choking on muggy night-heated words, words the merciless wind force feeds me, while speed and gravity conspire to pin me to the backseat like the tail on the donkey.

Dieks is sitting next to me, staring stonefaced and enraged as I scream and cry, begging them to slow down.

"They knew that fucking road by heart," he told me later. "Every nuance, nook and cranny. Either one of 'em could've driven it with his eyes closed," he said while pacing, clearly disgusted by my ignorance of and disrespect for local customs.

Then he refused to talk to me or even look at me. I didn't care about or understand the concept of playing chicken with the road. I didn't trust the unparalleled skills of a deaf, dumb, or blind driver. And, I didn't know it was mutiny to try to influence my own destiny by refusing to die in the dark.   As it turned out, I was a shameful chicken, but he was the one who'd lost face. I thought it all a victory of sorts: we were, after all, alive. Dieks considered it a travesty. It had always been, and would always be, better to perish a brave hero than to emerge unscathed a coward.

. . .

Blazing sunlight revives me, penetrates my consciousness, deposits me back into the moment. Ten or twelve cars in the oncoming lane had pulled off the road at various intervals and seemed content to sit idly by and watch. Some of them pointed at us like roadside bird dogs. Designating drivers, I mused. They either recognized someone or stopped to think, wondering who they hadn't known well enough to attend the last rites. Who is it that warrants such an entourage? What famous dignitary, what prominent citizen graces the empty stillness of this country back road? It is his mother's native son, I'm thinking. He's come home - come home at last to rest.

Call Me Dieks

"He wasn't always that way, you know."

My mother tried to soothe me, but I didn't want to hear it.

"Someone made him like that," she said, trying hard to defend the indefensible. "At some point in time, he was so systematically abused that he created personalities just to help him get by. He simply assumes whatever persona they collectively decide can handle the crisis. It doesn't matter if it's real or not. That makes no difference. Reason won't work, because he's never known anyone reasonable. Attempts at logic are equally ineffective, because he's never seen a sensible outcome to anything in his life.

"Just think about what you've told me. You don't have to take this to an extreme, just consider the basics: When people love you, they'll break your heart. They'll hurt you in other ways, too, so hurt is normal. If you hurt them back, it's also normal that they should still love you. No one should object, because that would be unseemly and rude. No one should interfere with abuse because it's no one else's business and besides, no one ever did so on his behalf. To Dieks, returning and feeling pain is normal, familiar. Being familiar is secure. Being secure is safe … "

"So? He's a *secure* paranoid, violent schizophrenic, psychotic … what?"

I didn't know. Couldn't allow myself to care. I squinted my eyes and gritted my teeth to corral the rest of my thoughts into silence. I looked away, refusing to lend credence to Mother Freud's analytical and compassionate understanding of what I thought was aberrant behavior at my expense. Quite simply, it no longer mattered. All that mattered was that I knew I had to get the hell out of there.

The crazed maniac he'd become was not the man I loved. The sinister madman who often possessed him in the dead of the night was not the man I married. The malicious liar who, more often than not, forgot where he lived, was no one I'd ever be interested in. I didn't need to stay a lifetime to know I didn't like who he'd become, and I didn't need someone to do an in-depth psychological analysis to see that he'd never get any better.

"People change with age," she'd offered.

Usually for the worse, I remember thinking.

. . .

When I first laid eyes on Dell Collins Shaunessy, it was June of 1969. I was seventeen years old and had big plans. My very biggest plan had to do with working as many hours as I could beg or trade and for as long as my feet could stand working a checkout counter. By summer's end, I'd have enough set aside for the fall semester at the University of Northern Iowa in Cedar Falls. I'd meet new and interesting people, get involved, live life through new eyes, worldly eyes, and I'd become someone.

Falling in love was not in my plans. Dieks was not in my plans. But I'd made these plans before I'd ever seen the true wonder and glory of a brown-eyed handsome man. He was leaning, in all his splendor, against the register at the Williams' Drug checkout counter, talking to Lynn Canne. I was supposed to be upstairs on break, but I never got that far. After all, how could I walk when I glanced up from cosmetics and my heart stopped beating? I couldn't walk or talk. I simply couldn't move when I saw him there.

Keeping back where they couldn't see me, I watched the two of them make brief conversation a joy to behold, yet a sudden jealousy when excluded. I was intrigued by the way he looked, by the gestures he made with his hands as he talked, by the intimacy his casual smile conveyed. He was wiry, but not big in stature at just under six feet. He looked the part of a very distinguished gentleman in his beige linen slacks and the creamy off-white silk shirt that draped lazily across his shoulders. In a matter of minutes, I was mesmerized and amazed that I could be so completely overwhelmed by feelings for someone I'd never seen before.

It was incredible, like we'd been together somewhere in time, and fate was about to reunite us. He could've been an axe murderer, pimp, pusher, or pontiff. It would've made no difference to me. Whatever I'd done and whomever I'd known up to that point became irrelevant. My heart belonged to the magnetic man with the mile-wide smile, Dell Shaunessy. His name was a mental whisper of sweet, sensual promise.

Whenever he stopped to talk to anyone, he got close and personal, touching them at appropriate moments, sharing confidences and insignificant gossip with the same exuberance. He gave importance to whatever was shared with him, making mental lists of comments, storing information for another day, a future encounter where he'd casually mention your dog, or your poetry, or your mother's summer garden.

Dieks had a way about him. He exuded sincerity because he truly needed people. He could prompt anyone to talk while he listened intently and responded astutely, nearly always agreeing with some offhand remark, or the casual nod of his head. After several years of observing him, it occurred to me that he'd been at this for a long time. *How to Win Friends and Influence People* was probably the book of choice at his bedside. And although he seemed born to an effortless ease of schmooze, he worked at it tirelessly.

Impeccably dressed, immaculate, every chestnut hair in place, with piercing brown-black eyes keenly focused on potential for opportunity, the ever-smiling Dell Shaunessy was an anachronism, bringing to mind old family, old money, misplaced gentility. I fell in love with him in a heartbeat and was forever lost to his charm.

I couldn't eat for days, couldn't concentrate at work, couldn't sleep at night. Most of my time was spent trying to figure out who I was, where I was, what I was doing, where I was going, and why I wasn't there yet. I kept losing track of my plans and at every turn, saw instead, his face, his eyes, his hands, and his unforgettable radiant smile. Finally, I told Lynn of my sad dilemma.

"Oh," she said casually. "Wanna meet him? He's divorced, you know."

"Yes, I do," shaking my head up and down, and then, "No, I didn't know," shaking my head from side to side.

"Not too long ago, either. He's not real comfortable talking about it, so don't mention it or anything, okay?"

"Yeah, right. That'd make a good impression. 'Uh, say, hey there Bub, I hear ya just got dumped.'"

Lynn was sporadically "seeing" Pat Adams, a good friend of his. This was as much as she could commit to. She was "seeing" someone "once in awhile" or "every now and then," and that was as definite as she ever got. She said she was pretty sure she could find an excuse to swing by Shaunessy's place. She knew where it was, and said everybody was there all the time anyway. Maybe we'd just stop by after work the next day.

Dumbfounded, I watched as she walked away after her matter-of-fact offer. Lynn had no idea what she'd proposed. If she realized its impact on me, she made no issue of it. That was pretty much her way, though. She made little of everything and seemed removed from most things of consequence to others. She'd known and seen enough misery in her brief life to cover a half a dozen people for all time.

She lived downtown in a cramped, two-room apartment above the A & P with her grandmother, an invalid of many years. Lynn's mother had died young, leaving her illegitimate daughter in the unforgiving fifties, with few relatives and fewer hopes for a future with much promise. Everyone said her father was a prominent local politician, married, with several grown, "respectable" children. Although he had secretly provided a trust fund of sorts to help Lynn along, there was little recognition otherwise.

"Ships that pass in the day," she'd once said somewhat bitterly. He lived close to some of her friends up in the fashionable Lantern Square area, and she saw him often. She said he sometimes looked straight at her, and she was sure he knew, but he never once nodded in recognition nor uttered so much as a word one way or the other.

Lynn was tall, almost six feet, with the willowy figure of an athlete. I never saw her exercise a day in her life. She was always starving, ate in perpetual motion, and never gained an ounce over the "hundred twenty" she referred to as plenty. Straight, dark brown hair draped down around her waist, and her milk-and-honey complexion probably would have assured her a modeling career if she'd ever been so inclined. But, she wasn't.

Lindsey Louise Canne had her sights set on power and prestige. She knew what form it would take, and she knew how to take the form. She wasn't quite sure when the time would right, but she was sure that time was the one thing she had in great quantity. She was patient and thoughtful and boasted of all the things she knew how to do well. Planning, scheming, and waiting were at the top of her lists. She knew especially how to make Daddy Adams wait.

"With silver sideburns, Rolexed wrist, and Brooks Brothers, he waited with bated breath and blue balls," she'd say shamelessly, sashaying along in the aisles, flashing something new from her current twenty-four carat collection.

"Wouldn't he just die," she'd say hypothetically, pausing in her work, with eyes cast toward the ceiling. She was referring to her "sometimes" fling with Daddy Adams' son, Pat.

I shook my head in diplomatic silence. He would do more than die, I thought. If Pat ever walked in on them, nothing would save her or Daddy from the fury of possessive wrath Pat was known for. But it sure wasn't my place to say.

I went home at the end of the day and my feet never once touched the ground. I know my eyes never closed that night. The image of his face filled the darkness, and I watched an animated version of his every move, noted and stored for instant recall. Long before the alarm went off, I was up and in the shower, washing my hair, heating up rollers, and trying on every outfit I owned, searching for one that was just right. I couldn't find it, but I was sure they'd have it at The Mulberry Tree.

When they opened at nine, I was waiting at the door. By ten, I was home with three new outfits, settling on a pair of chocolate-brown knit shorts, a semi-transparent shell, and sandals with a purse to match. After all, I was going to meet the love of my life. I had to appear casual and coy, without a lot of hoopla. I had to look like an understated million - no hoopla, but a ton of pizzazz.

I had to accentuate the positive, as my mother often reminded me. That meant highlighting the striking baby blues or drawing attention to my long, sunbleached blonde hair or the shapely muscles my tomboy legs and firm bottom. Somehow, I'd have to camouflage the teacups, not C's, not B's, not even double A's. I was resigned to a lifetime of teacups.

Lynn dropped by to pick me up at eleven, and I jabbered a mile a minute all the way across town to Dieks' apartment up on Stein Way, which I thought was an absolutely hilarious address. I couldn't remember having ever been so nervous. My face was hot, my heart felt tight, my stomach knotted.

"Would you stop fidgeting! You look just fine," she laughed.

She parked at the side of the house, and I followed her through the backyard and up a couple weathered flights of stairs. As we stood at the inside door, Lynn started to knock, but her hand stopped in midair when a deep, resonant voice said, "C'mon in, Lincoln."

She shrugged, flipped back her long mane of hair, and pushed the door open. We walked slowly through the hallway, down toward the light at the end. A blender whirred from the kitchen where he was making daiquiris. Pat had called and warned him.

Lynn turned to me and whispered, "Oh, and sometimes, he calls me Lincoln, or Slinky, or ... " But her voice faded away as she moved from the kitchen and into the living room.

I stood back and said nothing. He turned and winked at me.

"Who's your friend?" he asked. "Introduce me. Soon."

She laughed and rattled off a reading, with her open palm up first in one direction, then the other. "Dieks, this is Libby, Elizabeth Anne Lewis. Libby, this is Dieks. Dell to some," she said, moving on to the other room.

"Ah, but they don't know me," he interrupted, leaning intimately closer, saying in whispered confidence, "and if you hear someone call me 'Dell,' you can say to yourself, 'They don't know him.' So, it'll just be 'Dieks' or 'DC' to you. My sis calls me 'Deedee.' That's just 'cause she couldn't say Sweetie when we were little. But you don't need to call me Sweetie, unless you want to. You'll find that most everybody calls me most anything, and it usually depends on how well they know me. I'll bet you get to know me pretty well. So, you just pick a name you like, any name, and I'll be sure to find a special one for you. Just," and he paused, as he turned back around winking, handing me a banana daiquiri, " ... don' call me Dell. Okay?" Then he smiled that mile long smile.

I rarely drank, or at least not a casual, social, adult behavioral sort of drinking. After work on Friday nights sometimes, I'd go out with the girls and get purposefully blasted. Karen, Marie, Pam, rum, sloe gin, cheap wine - for me, fodder for nonstop conversation. Once the liquor started flowing, the motor-mouth was off and running. I might never stand up straight or walk upright again, but drunken oral recitation was another thing. I'd never tried social drinking with a stranger, and had never drank before noon, so this would all be new and different. I was in completely unchartered territory.

I backed up to the card table and chairs.

"Back it on in there," he said, "and park it."

"Hey, Slinkin', does she talk?" he asked, raising his voice a bit to carry to the living room, keeping his eyes directly on mine.

I nodded and answered for her, saying, "Thank you," as I held up the drink. "It's very ... refreshing."

Oh, cripes, I thought. *It's very refreshing?* I'm an idiot.

"No, mostly she thinks," Lynn said, answering a little late from the living room.

"No," he said quietly, gently patting my hand and smiling, *"You are refreshing. That's* just a plain ol' daiquiri," he said, motioning toward the drink in my hand.

Lynn sauntered in, scooped up the daiquiri he held out for her, and headed back to the living room.

"Sorry about the spartan furnishings. As you may or may not know, my tepee was top-ended and most of my belongings fell out. So," he said, pausing to pop the top of a beer, "it'll be a while before we're warm and wigwam wonderful again." And he winked and grinned a million dollar grin.

He pulled one of the card table chairs out and moved it over, right next to me. "Still good?" he asked, motioning to my drink as he sat down and casually crossed his legs.

I nodded.

"Great! Hey, you two up for a little lunch break?"

I shook my head no, but Lynn yelled, "Yes, I'm starving!"

Naturally.

"How 'bout A & W? I got Red's car. You seen it yet?"

I nodded my head no, but Lynn said, "Yeah, it'll be a blast!"

Or a bust, I thought, biting my tongue.

"It's my week, you know. Half 'n' half. Red's bucks, my talents," and he clicked his tongue and winked again as he stood to go. Then he turned and disappeared down the hall.

Lynn looked at me and gave me a thumbs-up signal. I pointed to my mouth and put my palms up as if to say I didn't know where my words went. She just smiled and slid back into her sandals and put her finger up to her lips. "Shhhhh."

I finished my drink, but it seemed to be going straight to my knees. Between not eating, not sleeping, and not being much of a drinker, the combination started to take its toll. When I stood up, I rose very slowly, concentrating on just standing.

"Well, then," he said, gliding toward me, removing the empty glass from my hand, and setting it around the corner, "Let's go!" He clapped his hands together as if to say, "Let the games begin!"

"I need to use the ... restroom," I said.

"Okay." He turned me around by my shoulders and laughed, leaning in closely and asking, "New shorts?"

I looked at him and started to say, "No." But while my head was shaking no, my mouth was saying, "Yes."

"I thought so. Hold still." He lifted the ribbed waistband of my shell and quickly ripped the paper tag off the back of my shorts, then took the liberty of swatting me on the bottom.

"There ya go," and he pointed to the bath down the hall where I made my way on sea legs.

That became one of his standard answers to me. He'd smile, wink, shake his head no, and say, "Yes." However, he never, ever said no to me back then. The sky was the limit.

When we got down to the garage, Lynn opened the car door and motioned for me to slide in first, next to him. I shook my head and backed away, but she grabbed my arm and shoved me in. I was aware of every single point on my body that touched him - arms, hips, thighs. Every brushing movement he made shifting and turning the wheel was electric against me. I never remembered the drive.

My friend Mandi pulled in and parked next to us at the A & W. But she just sat there, staring at Red's beautiful car. The show car was a '49 Ford, done in British racing green with big, wide whitewalls and tons of gleaming chrome from bumper to bumper, sitting proudly on display for all to envy. Finally, Mandi remembered to order.

I motioned to Lynn to roll down her tinted window and I leaned over and said, "Hey! Mandi! You like?" pointing down to the car.

"Hey guys, it's Liz! She was straining to see past us, but gave up. Leaning forward, she said, "Who's that with you?"

"Dieks," I answered, squeezing back in the seat so she could see.

He leaned forward and glanced at her, winking, with a one-finger salute from his forehead.

"Ohhhh ... I see," she said, settling back into her seat and giving me the old cheerio approval.

He leaned back and tilted his head toward me, "She speaks. Not much, but she does speak," he said to Lynn.

Lynn smiled knowingly. "After mostly thinking, she talks."

I asked for fries and a Coke and pulled a ten from my purse. When Dieks got his billfold out, I put my hand over it and pushed it back. "I'm buying. My treat."

"Oh? Your treat?" He said, surprised.

"Yeah, you treated us to daiquiris and this Wow!WhattaCar! Look at the way people stare, like we're celebrities! And, Lynn's treat was taking me to meet you." The liquor's made my words as bold as my heartbeat, but I don't think he heard the thumping.

He seemed pleased just the same, even if he didn't have a comeback for me. He smiled an inscrutable smile, slipped his wallet into his back pocket, and leaned over to me, close enough for me to breathe in a hint of the British Sterling.

"Thanks, Liz B," he whispered quietly.

And that pleased me and it's who I came to be.

In Search of A Cure

"The injustice of it is almost perfect!
The wrong people going hungry,
the wrong people being loved,
the wrong people dying."

John Osborne
Look Back in Anger

I'd been in hiding for several months. It was what I did when I needed to tend to my wounded heart after my mother died. I was content with the busy work that took me away from everyday concerns, away from people, away from the real world. In fact, I was painting the bathroom when the phone rang.

I couldn't remember why. I could hardly remember when. It was in the middle of the morning on a sunny, late summer day when she called and asked me if I remembered her. As her words came floating out of a most remote blue sky, the conversation quickly became awkward and empty, and I knew it was leading up to something unpleasant. But I couldn't quite put my finger on it. Instinct told me to brace myself.

Yes, I said I remembered her. Bobbi was Big Red's wife, and she lived in a world that was a hundred and twenty miles, yet light-years away. There it was. That expected something surfaced. Had I heard about Dieks? Did I know they'd airlifted him to Iowa City? Could I find Dinky, his son? No, I hadn't heard. No, I didn't know. Yes, I could find our son and no qualifier was needed. I knew his name, their relationship, and his location as well. Though he was no longer called the Dinky Doodle. The toddler with that nickname had grown to manhood in the past twenty years. He went by the same name as his biological father. He'd married his college sweetheart, Debby. They had toddlers of their own, Chaun and Chelsea.

Although he hadn't necessarily been Dieks, "the son" for too long, he was nonetheless of the Shaunessy bloodline. I cringed at the thought. After determining that little damage could be inflicted by renewed contact with Dieks the elder after graduation from high school, I watched without comment as they began to rebuild the fragile matchstick bridges that I thought had been burned to ashes over their twelve-year hiatus.

It took nearly three years before they were comfortable with each other again. But at long last, they'd made a peace of sorts with their pasts and separate lives. Dieks had finally come to terms with the fact that his son had grown to manhood in the years he'd missed, that he was worthy of attention and attempts to right long-buried wrongs. I thought they were doing fairly well given all the potential for pitfalls they'd encountered along the way. The last contact had been pictures of the grandchildren, and they'd planned to meet, come summer.

While art shows monopolized Dieks' time, college and family monopolized his son's, and the summer was nearly over. Finally, on the babies' first birthday, they agreed to meet. By then, they'd both learned the art of consensus and concession.

The fall semester had begun at Iowa City. I remembered that. The babies were in daycare. Dieks and Debby were in classes again. Just as things seemed to be getting underway, the phone rang. I remembered the phone call and Bobbi's questions. I remembered calling Iowa City off and on, getting no answer, leaving messages. I drove to where my husband was working and told him I had to go to Iowa City, and why. I left, barely seeing the blur that was the interstate, caught sight of Cedar Rapids for a split second, and then I was there.

As I pulled into the parking lot at the University's married student housing lot at Hawkeye Court, they were just getting the babies out of their car seats. Dieks raised and turned while lifting Chaun out and watched me closely as I rolled down my window. His expression was marked with confusion and concern. I never showed up unannounced. He stood perfectly still when I asked him, "Haven't you heard the messages on your machine?"

He looked to Debby, holding Chelsea, and she shook her head no.

He shook his head and said, "No."

"Dieks was life-flighted to ICU early this morning! You'd better get up there - now!"

. . .

It now seems long ago, so very long ago, that terrible beginning of yet another dark thread that wove itself into the somber mantle of sorrow. Just as his mother had before him, Dieks experienced an explosive brain aneurysm and began the journey of the *mistai*, the ghost wandering aimlessly at the edge of life, lost and alone inside his own mind. In the darkness and solitude, he braced himself against death and all that lay beyond, knowing that he too would soon become *Tasoom*, another of the great entity of ancestral dead.

Cheyenne's journey had been brief, for in the fifties, there was little they could do to remedy her suffering. But at least they recognized it and allowed a simple, merciful passage.

Old Doc Petti cared for her as best he could with prescriptions to mask the relentless pounding in her head, but they did little more than that. He once told her he could see straight through her eyes, into troubling depths where something sinister grew without respite or chance of remission.

Richard dismissed it as the ravings of an aged country quack and refused to take his wife north to Rochester. He said he didn't need an overpaid blueblood to tell him Chey was "crazy in the head." Doc told him the injuries he'd inflicted on her over the years had developed into an irreversible condition. He told him the best anyone could do for her would be to make the last of her brief earthly stay as pleasant as possible.

So every few weeks, at six dollars a visit, Cheyenne Shaunessy drove up to the Eldon Depot where Doc Petti had his office. She went through the same examination, heard the same procedural prognosis and left with yet another shot of morphine and another refill for any one of various opiates, usually feeling as numb as she had when she'd first walked in.

She'd said he could do no more, adding that he'd done everything anyone possibly could. But Aunts Cher and Sue refused to believe it. Just as they could hardly believe their eyes when they came to visit. They insisted that she should get another opinion. They begged her to find a specialist. But Richard resisted, disputing all of Doc Petti's observations and accusations, insisting to the very end that she was just "crazy in the head."

Dieks was six or seven at the time, unable to grasp the meaning. When he got older, he told the story as an innocent bystander, just one more stranger who'd helplessly watched his mother drift away. But he always added something -- what he'd heard one man tell another as they stood behind him the day of the funeral, the day they took away the box that carried the remains of Cheyenne Lucy Collins Shaunessy.

. . .

Among Eldon's most prominent families were the socialites named Camden. They were being visited by some of their snooty friends from the great state of Texas. With fists full of diamonds and pockets full of pearls, in designer clothes and good Italian shoes, the visitors drove down Main in a lily-white Rolls, complaining loudly about the heat, the dust, and the hick mentality of a one-horse river town. They simply couldn't imagine suffering the experience longer than that day.

But when evening came and they huffed and puffed along in the heat, preparing to take their leave, the very wealthy widow Wiesenthal fell desperately ill. Not knowing what else to do, they called Doc Petti who agreed to meet them at his Depot office in ten minutes.

He arrived before them, wiry white hair in wild disarray, and patiently listened as Mrs. Wiesenthal whined her way through the waiting room and into one of his small exam rooms. There, upon examination for his customary six dollars, he gave her an injection and a bottle of sample painkillers one of his distributors had left. As she sat and waited for the drugs to take effect, he quietly told her the diagnosis appeared grave -- an apparent brain tumor was the cause of her great pain. Apologetically, he added it would probably worsen.

On hearing his words, she struggled to her feet and glared into his compassionate eyes, hissing that she'd get a competent opinion from someone other than a backwoods country quack with a dime store degree. She dropped a twenty on the table and slammed the door as she left, accentuating the pounding inside her head.

She returned to Texas, where her private physician arranged for an appointment with his dear close friends and cohorts, the Mayo brothers in Minnesota. A month later, Mrs. Wiesenthal and her entourage ventured north again, past the one-horse towns and on to Rochester, where she was presented to and examined by Mayo's most famous, world-renowned specialists. With the most technologically advanced equipment and facilities, they would surely dispute the old quack's prognosis and vastly improve her very privileged outlook on life.

A history of her family's maladies was gathered and sent, along with genetic mappings and very extensive personal files for advance review. The specialists insisted on a complete update of all tests and spent long hours conferring, poring over the massive medical information gleaned from the recent results.

Mrs. Wiesenthal sat in an overcrowded holding room and waited for Mayo's top neurological specialist to inform her of the aggregate findings. Each of the several times she'd asked, she was assured with certainty he'd be there soon. Yet she waited another hour before they finally called her name.

Led to yet another tastefully appointed, cramped room, she again sat waiting for her individual consultation. Mayo information was charted, and the papers duly signed by various doctors, specialists, reviewers, and consultants. Complete medical files from Texas were stagger-stacked on the counter in chronological order, confirmed, dated, and properly initialed with authorization codes and departmental transfer acceptance stamps.

When the door finally opened, an elderly man with chaotic white hair shuffled in. His stiffly starched physician's coat crackled as he settled feather-light into the chair next to hers. He casually crossed one spindly leg over the other, and clasped his bony hands together at the knee. Though clearly weary, he looked at her through aged eyes of wisdom, calmed by kindness and compassion.

In return, the woman looked at him and gasped, with a flurry of diamonds fluttering about on fingers that clutched her chest, shocked speechless, with her mouth hanging rudely open.

Undaunted, he began. "I've reviewed your extensive medical history, Mrs. Wiesenthal, as well as the results of all past and present testing.

"I've read the additional reports of the many and various medical personnel, and I've spoken at great length to several of my highly esteemed colleagues. Again, I am very sorry to inform you, Mrs. Wiesenthal, that your condition remains the same as when we last met. All evidence indicates a brain tumor. Given your age and its location, I fear it remains inoperable."

"But you? You! Who are you to tell me such things?"

"I am Dr. Albert Schweitzer Pettigrew, Ma'am." He answered in a plain and distinctively Midwestern tone. "I have a general family practice in a little backwater burg called Eldon, in the great state of Iowa. At my office in the Depot there, I'm sometimes called Doc Petti. Some even go so far as to refer to me as the Pet Doctor, but rest assured, they are my closest and most loyal friends and patients. However, strangers have been known to refer to me as a backwoods country quack with a dimestore degree. In Eldon, I doctor a few thousand folks a year, chargin' 'em six dollars a visit, if they have the means to pay without causin' a financial hardship, you understand.

"Here, my dear Mrs. Wiesenthal, I am a visiting neurological consulting specialist." A thick foreign accent slowly crept into his words and he became Viennese or Austrian, an important man of mysterious cultures and lofty unknown origin. "My clinic fees are set by the American Medical Association at established national standard rates, and my services may be procured by referral alone, from an exclusive list of only the most reputable physicians with extensive neurological expertise and outstanding medical credentials. And, of course, with at least two weeks' advance notice."

With that, Doc Petti stood, muttering something about the vagueries of life and wonders of the world as he opened the consulting room door, returning to the accentless Iowa lowbrow she'd so easily dismissed.

"I'm afraid we've used our allotted time. I must attend to other patients before I leave. Again, I'm so sorry, Mrs. Wiesenthal. I truly wish I could've offered a more acceptable prognosis."

Later that day, the Pet Doctor drove back home to Iowa where he continued to make his living disguised as a humble country quack until his retirement in the early sixties. Fortunately, for Cheyenne Shaunessy, one of the renowned medical minds of the day cared for her as best he could. He told her all he knew and did for her all he could do. With compassion and godspeed, she left the world with dignity.

. . .

Forty years later, Dieks would not be so fortunate. His journey would be long and arduous, humiliating and hopeless. But no one would say so until he'd been tested, prodded, panned, scanned and finally, abandoned. After all the neurologists said they knew and all the specialists thought they knew, after all the doctors did and all the nurses tried to do, he was left alone at last to die. In one hospital after another, ultimately hundreds of miles from home, away from all creature comforts, familiar faces and the consoling hands of friends, Dieks died.

It was not a killer brain tumor, nor respiratory failure. It was not pneumonia, nor some long-named, unpronounceable, insidious disease that couldn't be corralled. He died of simple, systematic starvation - just before the limits on his health insurance ran out. He died by directive and design, before health care costs would have to be paid from assets he'd accumulated in his lifetime, assets that would have to be liquidated, with proceeds handed over to hospitals to cover costs incurred by a patient in a vegetative state.

Kevorkian was not consulted. His methods were neither exercised nor considered.

"There's no hope. He'll surely die," the doctors assured his sister. "If you cut off antibiotics and cease respiratory therapy, he'll be lucky to make it twenty-four, forty-eight hours, tops."

"And what about his hydration?" she asked, parroting the medical students she'd heard. "You know, the glucose bag, that feeding tube thing, that too?"

"The new cancer is fast-growing," they declared. "It'll kill him. You may as well shut down the nutrition system, too."

"Since it's hopeless?" she prompted, questioning.

"Yes, it's hopeless," they reiterated. "You wouldn't want to prolong his misery, since it *is* hopeless."

"I guess it's time, then," she said, sighing heavily with relief, "to just 'pull the plug.'"

So, without further fanfare, the "plug was pulled" and within the hour, wingless scavengers took to the road and descended upon the site of his life's work and belongings.

"He won't be needin' these things," they assured each other as they pillaged and ransacked and came up for air briefly.

"We couldn't prolong his misery," they announced to each other as they struggled to haul out box after box in the early daylight hours and at various late night intervals.

"He shun't suffer no more," they added, straining to get oversized and heavy pieces of marble and metal sculpture out the door.

"He ain't gonna feel no pain now," they insisted.

Death does that. It stops everything with unrivaled certainty.

. . .

In 1965, just outside the door to Butch Baker's hospital room, before his body was cold and just after they'd agreed that "pulling the plug" was the humane thing to do, Dieks said the Fabulous Baker Boys set to fighting over who got to wear the dead man's burgundy wing tips and black trench coat to his funeral. His mother, Rush, was enraged, but kept her wits about her and immediately settled the dispute. She reached down and ripped the then-worthless oxygen tubing from the machine, and soundly thrashed the two of them about the head and shoulders. Now that'd be a real sight for sore eyes, I thought. Here, nearly thirty years later, no change. No class. No difference.

Up on Mockingbird Hill, all that remained of Dieks' life was invaded. Drawers were dumped, possessions rifled, and in the wake, priceless works of art, antiques, and collectibles were left cockeyed and scattered - as if they too were as worthless as his brittle bones. Looting took place with vengeance and defiance. Who would stop them? Who could stop them? No one.

No one went back. His beloved sister, the blue-eyed angel of mercy who gave the humane "go ahead," never returned to his bedside to witness the execution of her orders. I once heard someone in a lobby somewhere say that she would have to do "what was in the best interest of all involved," and I remembered thinking how memorized and rehearsed the words seemed. Silently, I wondered how "interested" or "involved" Dieks was by then.

I heard my mother's distant echo in my son's words, "I could bear to be with him when he dies. But I refuse to stand watch and wait; that's almost as if I'm encouraging him to die."

Oil-stained nails and grease-streaked arms on the countless clan that surrounded his deathbed accused the sons in their absence. Conspiring to paint them as grasping Shylocks who were merely waiting for the death knell to signal the gold rush, the overly obvious and undeniably sensitive throng of clan sneered, whispered and shook their butch-waxed heads in mock disbelief as they huddled together. But his sons kept to themselves, wrapping old wounds with new worries. Left to their own devices, the clan marched on, dividing forces so some could continue to run interference by caring very loudly, covering the clandestine operation of those who plundered very quietly.

Without an ounce of water, on a downhill one-course diet of morphine drip, Dieks' weight plummeted. The twenty-four hours doctors projected became forty-eight. Two days became a week that grew to a month. Still, the medical team insisted, the new tumor would kill him. Maybe not this minute, maybe not today, or tomorrow …

Like a fasting radical without cause or clue, his skin began to shrink into the ridges of his ribcage like wet parchment. Emaciated shoulder blades jutted out, pointing accusations of negligence at doctors, nurses and orderlies. Hipbones became peaks that saluted all who witnessed Death Valley and the starving sinkhole there. Still his eyes searched the face of the one loyal, persistent visitor and repeatedly asked, "Why?"

Alan Zendegas knew the question all too well. But he was drowned to silence in the tears that rose with the words needed to answer.

When we'd call, the day nurse reported Dieks' pupils were not dilated like those of a comatose patient. When they perfunctorily performed their minimal, billable chores at his bedside, he was aware of their presence. He was aware of their absence as well. When they left the room, he closed his eyes and retreated to the remote ruins of a warm and welcome world, carefully constructed with the remains of the disaster that had been his childhood.

His toes squirmed happily in plush pastel carpets imported from India. Silk sheets draped over him, and down comforters warmed his quaking cold shoulders and ribcage remains. He snuggled down further, into flokati throws that he knew were draped over the soft, supple leather of his living room furniture. As he stood on his back deck, quietly overlooking the sunny hillside that stretched well into the distance, he smiled and sighed. He heard the sweet morning songs of the birds and saw the most brilliant blue sky and feathery clouds he'd ever seen. He felt a soft summer breeze cool his heated brow, and when he opened his eyes, The Zen was looking in.

For a long time after we'd all been informed of his "condition" and convinced that death would overtake him before we got there, Alan said he'd stopped in between scheduled runs that took him and his semi crisscrossing around and about every location Dieks had ever been moved to. He was sure that Dieks communicated with his eyes, "up to the very end."

Slowly and painfully The Zen remembered the interminable moments that became hours in the day before Dieks' death. It was only on that day, he said, that the eyes of his childhood friend drifted past him and stared with death's peaceful glare, no longer needing him there. The quiet, brown eyes faded to nothing, saw no one - not Alan nor his wife, not one tear in the great river that rushed forth marking the end of forty years of memories.

For a full forty-six days, they'd waited for the killer tumor to take its toll. Refusing to reassess, recant, or offer a stay of execution, orders were left in place. At half his original body weight, starving and dehydrated, Dieks stubbornly waited, while his most precious memories were aided by merciful hallucinations. He relived his mother's last moments. He remembered that she trusted them to their agreements to take him safely away. He recalled her kind and gentle eyes, moist with tears, as his own hand reached up to touch her soft brown skin one last time, and he saw the slightest smile as her hand fell away from his. At last, he understood her weak sigh and final words, "Hoka hey." Resigned at death to the Indian way, her simple words translated to the most final of resolutions, "It's a good day ... to die."

His brain smiled at the memory of her sweet face while the last of his blood trickled from his parched lips. Vacant eyes stared patiently at the ceiling while he calmly waited for one of those someones, just one of those good, best, loyal, lifetime friends to come and hold his hand and calm his fears and bid him farewell. The Zen stood silently at his side, but Dieks saw no one there. He was busy waiting. It wasn't the first time. It was, however, the last.

Tasoom

The children heard them fight. It was no secret. Cheyenne delivered a dark-eyed child with cinnamon skin and floating wisps of jet-black hair. The child was not her husband's. At least, that's what he said, and that's what both children always remembered.

"That rat-faced bastard!" he'd bellow. Then he'd gulp another shot of Irish Rose and foul the room further with more accusations, more names: beady-eyed weasel, buck-toothed beaver. They stood just around the corner with their backs against the wall, quivering and ashamed that they were so small and helpless, as she'd screamed and cried, reaching up to him, begging for mercy.

Even as she fell to the floor unconscious, he'd continue to curse and kick her head from side to side, with a Bible in one hand and a shot glass in the other. In their minds, there was a degree of comfort in the terror they experienced after her death. He beat the innocent children as mercilessly as he had their sweet, soft mother. They were intimate with her memory, knowing they suffered the same.

"He got drunk and killed her," Dieks often said. Then the little boy who watched, hid, or ran helplessly to the back of the house with his sister, would straighten his shoulders and become a man stalled in time. He froze, recalling split-second images, afraid to move a muscle, fearing the consequence of a thought. He knew then, as they'd both learned early on, that if you intervene, no matter how good or noble your intentions, the victim shifts and becomes you.

So they ran hard between the fear of being beaten and a shared shame in hiding. When they would see her in the morning, her gentle smile would be misshapen by swollen lips and bruises in various stages colored her face and arms and legs. Her assuring doe-soft glance would be distant and sad. If she could walk at all, she'd move ever so slowly, pausing to lean against the doorways, or propping her frail, nearly weightless frame on chair backs as she made her way through the house. She'd probably need her temples rubbed. She always did. Then, she could bring herself to face the remains of the day, before he came home and it all started again.

Dieks would tell how she struggled to just open her eyes, how the light would hurt, and how a cold, wet washcloth helped. He saw small, moccasined feet running to the bathroom, and the image of a child's hands stretching to reach the sink spigots, straining to wring water out of the washrag that she used as a cold pack on her forehead. But mostly, he remembered how his little fingers rubbed so hard and ached so long because she always asked for more, just a little more, just a bit longer, just a minute, she'd plead.

One more time and a gentle child's tender, loving touch might soothe away the relentless pounding. He was startled when he'd look down and find the hands of a grown man. He always expected to see small hands instead, and the little fingers that knew the art of massage and how to quiet the horrible hammers beating inside her head. He'd get lost in the soft folds of her silken gowns, forever remembering those moments of trying in vain to ease away the pain … the pain … the pain that reverberated in his mind throughout time and became the ghost of childhood helplessness.

He basked in her praise. He was always such a good little boy, Mommy's helper -- knowing all the while that later in the day, even his best efforts would be for nothing. The peace of late morning and early afternoon would be all she'd have, all they ever planned on. For invariably, within moments of Richard's return, the quiet would be shattered with the first ear piercing shrieks of her heart-stopping screams.

Sometimes, he remembered hiding as far back in his bedroom as he could get, crouched down behind his bed on the outside wall. But, even with doors to both his bedroom and the bathroom shut, with both hands over his ears, and humming as loud and long as he could, the muffled yelling still sifted through. After the shuffling and pounding stopped, when her screams subsided and the whimpers were reduced to sniffles, the worst would start, silence and the gnawing pain of not knowing.

Once, Lucy ran to the edge of the fray and tried to buy her mother a night's peace with a sacrificial peanut butter jar full of coins that she'd been saving for months. She got as close as she dared and silently offered the jar, held up as high as she could reach. Richard grabbed it from her and threw it against the wall. As the children watched in horror, shattered glass ricocheted and rained down on their mother's sobbing body, where he had her pinned to the floor, his foot at her throat. They watched the pennies, nickels, dimes and quarters roll in all directions, and even before they'd stopped, their mother's screams had resumed.

He knew all of this was terribly wrong. His sister knew it too. But there was little they could do. They tolerated what they could and, after Cheyenne's death, the inevitable occurred: the hapless victims were smaller and younger, more vulnerable because the only authority they thought they might appeal to for mercy was at the end of the belt that beat them until bare arms and legs glistened with the criss-cross of raised red welts. Just as their pleas and bodies carried less weight, their tolerance was considerably less. To the neighbors' relief, small bodies fell much sooner. Where disruptive evening episodes once took hours, doors and windows could now be reopened within the same television show.

The ever-vigilant sheriff made his nightly rounds, driving on, unperturbed by the high-pitched screams of children reverberating through the otherwise calm evening air. Sometimes a very brave friend might opt to spend the night. Only a few ever stayed more than once. Most of the kids knew that overnight guests at the Shaunessy's were not privileged, but subjected to the same house rule terrorism as their hosts. But it was only when he got out the guns that they would actually run from the house.

Then, like clockwork, a diligent and dutiful next-door neighbor, Tacey Owens, would set aside her quilting or crocheting, and call the Eldon sheriff. He would pull up into the side yard and sit in the squad car for five or ten minutes, giving Dick time to gather what sobriety he might need to put on a face of civility. He'd walk cautiously to the front door, knock twice, and the door would open.

The guns would be handed over without question or comment, and the car would disappear into the night. The following day, good Sheriff Jasper would just happen to stop by Dick's Sporting Goods while making routine rounds. They'd laugh and carry on about every little thing, except how drunken bullies shouldn't shoot at their own children or threaten to maim and dismember them. Then with the arsenal returned and the confiscation duly noted, it'd be at least a couple weeks before it happened again, and then again, and yet again.

Shortly after Dieks secretly celebrated his twelfth birthday, and most observers secretly marveled at the survival of Cheyenne's children in the house of hell, Lucy ran away. No one reported her missing and no one asked where she was. No one went after her, although two of her closest friends and her abandoned brother knew of her whereabouts. The tattered remains of their not-so-all-American family were reduced to the abuse of one lone child with neither mother nor sibling to stand with him. What was left was his and his alone: a cold and lonely house, an embittered brutal drunk, and unavoidable beatings, all a young boy could bear and then some. The nightly ranting and raving increased in intensity, and the whiskey shot back faster and with more frequency.

If Dieks could bribe anyone to stay the night, they had to be alert and quick. They had to wake on command whenever a floorboard creaked or a door squeaked or the light switched on or a single word was spoken. They'd need to be adept, running at a moment's notice, or at the very least, be able to jerk their knees to their chest from a sound sleep, before a baseball bat came crashing down on unwary legs.

Dieks' guests couldn't be proud, for they might have to take to the tracks barefoot, in their underwear or pajamas. It would be advantageous if they were oblivious to pain, since the jagged cinders on the railroad embankment were particularly sharp, and running, ducking, and dodging while shots rang out overhead, was best addressed without whining complaints of some sissy's physical suffering. Some of Dieks' overnighters, the more fortunate, took the profanities and threats with a grain of salt – after all, they'd been warned, and Dieks seemed to survive each day and night. It was an unspoken rite of passage.

However, such considerations severely limited his circle of friends. In fact, there were only two brave enough to endure Shaunessy friendship requirements on a regular basis: Dirk Reddick, a huge, strapping German youth who was the first and most enduring of all the best friends Dieks had ever known, and Butch Baker, the oldest, strongest and bravest of all the boys in the family known as the Fabulous Baker Brothers.

By sixteen, Dell Collins Shaunessy had developed an attitude that even a seasoned survivalist would envy. With cunning and malice, it was only a matter of time before he stood his ground, and someday, some, brave historical day, he'd fight back and win. The

Rat, as his father called him, was growing more like the man whose abuse he suffered each day: mean, divisive, hard and unyielding. In public, they were a pair to draw to: generous to a fault, pleasant and gentlemanly. Behind closed doors, they squared off, threatened, dared and defied, bared teeth and claws, wielded knives and guns. Before long, one would push and the other would shove. One would aim to maim and miss, while the other would swing and connect.

Dieks connected. Though physically small and somewhat immature at sixteen, it was once too often that Richard bullied, not the rat, nor the boy, but the young man. For the first, last, and only time in his life, Dieks stood his ground and fought his father's abuse as he'd told Red he knew he'd have to do eventually. It was then and there that he learned how justice in a deaf, dumb, blind America worked in the sixties. If you're without defense, without connections to power or position, even good people will turn their backs on you, and the word of a malevolent bully can reign supreme. No one champions the cause of children. They've no visible means of support. They're of little value, negligible worth.

The hardest lesson Dieks ever learned was not wasted, for he never forgot. If you work very hard at growing up, and carefully watch everyone, so as to understand how things are supposed to be, you might win. If you think long and serious thoughts about justice, you might have a chance to change bad things to good. But you must note an unwritten rule: don't try to defend yourself in the process. If you're successful in your own defense, you will most assuredly lose.

Someone you're close to, maybe the only human being you know as security, no matter how shaky, can shove you away. That familiar someone can simply turn their back and destroy your life with the flick of a wrist. Into the depths of forever, the world will defy you to rise above the stigma imposed by someone you trusted as a child, with wishful innocence, to protect you, to defend you, to nurture and care for you. For Dieks, that someone went by the name of Father.

Late one fall, some thirty years after the fact, Dell Collins Shaunessy rose above the stigma his long dead, sadistic dear old dad had conveyed upon him. After being indicted for the crime of possible survival in the face of diminishing health care resources, an unrequested fast of forty-six days ensued. Abandoned and alone, Dieks languished in long, dark thoughts of youth, justice and the destiny of man. Then, he simply died, leaving it all behind to those more deserving.

Meet me at midnight, Mother.
Mistai tugs at my covers.
Meet me on The Hanging Road.
I come with love.
Tasoom

Methodical Modification

At Westwood, the training school for boys is known to be exactly what it says: a training school. It is a rudimentary course in basic criminology for young men who lean toward a delinquent life. Whatever was done to gain entry was improved upon, perfected, and conveyed to understudies who proved worthy. All who graduated learned early on how to walk the walk and talk the talk. Only the most progressive delinquents left with much more than had been admitted.

That was the nice part of the training school. That was the part that prominent people - directors, counselors, clergy and teachers - could talk about and summarize in their periodic progress reports. They'd have great intellectual debates regarding the dichotomy of nature and nurture, and whether or not these pitiful deviants were born with criminal minds and evil instincts. The most methodical and disciplined masters in corrections circles spent long, detached hours reading logged activities and second-hand summaries of their miscreant charges. They concluded, in what was described as painful consensus, that the mere feasibility, or even plausibility, of rehabilitation, restitution, or accountability for misdeeds beyond the scope of human frailty, was slight.

"When these young hoodlums are returned to society, with their penchants for crime uncorrected and methods of newly-acquired skills internalized, they are indeed wonders to behold. Some are simply out of control, like breeding rabbits. Crime begets crime, after all," one counselor was heard to say.

"They run from episode to episode, trying each facade for size. Breaking and entering, car theft, assault, petty thievery, rape. Some are blatant and daring, others quiet, unobtrusive. As they get older, most will modify this behavior and their crimes will become more tolerable, more socially acceptable, less noticeable. They'll begin the cycle of crimes that tend to blend with their environment. There will be a repetition of petty offenses, or the focus will become child or spousal abuse or neglect, sexual irresponsibility, deviations and compulsions that lead to hazardous lives, the usual. They'll pay by checks with insufficient funds, they'll skip out on unpaid bills, dabble in drug use, or try their luck as the local pusher. They'll gamble away their rent, ignore their taxes, and refuse to pay child support, or alimony, the usual. Of course their behavior will be blamed on the standard provocative factors of the day. Alcoholism, drugs, poverty, ignorance, and occasionally, environment or genetics. The usual.

"If they drank, they'll drink more. If merely mean and cruel, they'll become vicious and violent. If they smoked dope when they came here, they'll crave coke when they leave. Their hate will be heightened, their passions will be misdirected, their anger will be an indelible ache and their pain forever denied. Whatever they remember of youth, they'll remember the intrinsic value of extremes the most."

Dieks said the big joke among residents was that they never had to worry about running with the bad crowd because they were the bad crowd. At one time or another, all of the local dispossessed had taken up residency at Westwood. Because they belonged to no one and with no one, it was hard to hold them accountable for their actions. They didn't understand the notion of being part of anything. Terrors they'd experienced at home were often far greater than any threats found on the streets or in the holding tanks. So they collapsed, content to live in each other's nightmares, ramshackle shelters, constructed of used and mismatched playing cards.

Westwood was every adolescent delinquent's introduction to a microcosmic hell. Although caretakers took great pride in their ability to implement structure and impose discipline by constant observation and careful records, there was no preventing the inevitable. Boys, angry and lonely, starved for love and attention, took what they knew of affection the only way they knew how to get it, by force. It was the law of their jungle. Base instincts, distorted by abuse, corrupted by authority and overpowering adults, became weapons in a horrible game of bloody knuckles, sexual style. If their sentencing was accompanied by the thought that somewhere in society there existed something more horrible than what they'd known at home, at Westwood, their fears were realized.

They learned to look each other in the eye, to lie with the greatest courage and conviction, and to never, ever betray the sick sadness of their darkest secrets. Houseparents couldn't say what they knew -- that the weaker, oppressed boys would be punished in unimaginable ways. They never mentioned it. The only fear greater than humiliation and degradation was the fear that they'd be brutalized in conjunction with the sexual assaults, maybe disfigured, or permanently handicapped. Juvies didn't fear death. They'd already outdistanced it. They feared life, especially if it meant being even more conspicuous than they already felt. They could make their way through anything and most already had, but they could not bear to think that they'd return to the outside with some noticeable handicap. As Dieks often repeated, "Delinquency or Death" was their motto. They'd rather die than go back as a standout.

They did what they had to do and, for most, survival skills were so well honed by the time they got to Westwood, that this twist and turn was viewed not so much with contempt or revulsion, but with curiosity. Every evil had potential, every reprehensible act was merely a skill to be unraveled, internalized and reintroduced later, when opportunity or circumstance could lead to capitalization.

The night the leather shop burned, as Dieks sat alone and angry, he knew he'd lost a safe haven, his proverbial port in the storm. The shop had been his retreat. Once there, he'd been content to simply listen to a quiet he'd never known. There, satisfaction surrounded him in the form of creations that no one could corrupt, deny or take away. In the shop, he was driven by purpose and worked with diligence to standards only he could identify: examining the goods, cutting, forming, carving, staining, sealing images that he'd seen only in his dreams. Ancient inlays of silver hieroglyphics graced spirals of bloodstone, and the sleek sheen of sanded shafts seemed familiar to his hands, drifting innocently into his world from fragmented dreams that seemed to be someone else's life.

His work was meticulous, and became the antithesis of his life. For there, in the shop, he'd worked steadily and alone and found something he could truly control, something receptive to his love and care.

He detested the other training school activities. The heavy odor of sweat in the weight room made him nauseous. The constant posturing of muscle-bound weight lifters left him uneasy, and their clanging, slamming barbells thudding to the floor gave him headaches. The brutality of boxing, with its blood-splattering blows to the head, seemed too close to home to appreciate. Any spectator sport that made him cringe seemed unlikely to produce winners. By the final bell, participants in the boxing ring looked like battered abuse victims to him.

He was indignant at the suggestion of wrestling, which he saw as rolling around the floor with some sweaty guy musclin' in on your privates. Once, he thought that learning how to swim in the school's private pool would be kind of fun. Richard had never taken them anywhere to swim, and though Dieks thought it might be embarrassing, trying to learn the basics when he was so old, he was willing to give it a try. But after noon lessons one day, overhearing the boys' innuendo, he decided the privilege of learning wasn't worth the price exacted. Bigger, older boys went to lessons without fear of incident. But younger, smaller boys, like Dieks, went at their own risk.

The exception, and Counselor Greg's one big mistake, they said, had been Yuma. No one could ever second-guess what he might choose to do. He could be uncharacteristically compliant one moment, and in the next, a textbook case study of the effects of the renegade mutant chromosome trio, X, Y, Y. Yuma was the perfect example of genetic deviance, predisposed by nature to random, unpredictable outbursts of savage violence. No one was brave enough to try to figure out if there was relevance in his mood swings, if there was a cause that might be corrected somehow. That would mean having to get close enough to observe.

More than one counselor repeated the adage, "There's a thin line between tough and dumb." In skirmishes where Yuma was involved and someone might need to be rescued, no one crossed the thin line to intervene.

One day, after he'd heard Dieks talk about learning to swim, Yuma swaggered over to the pool with the regulars. He didn't know what to expect and didn't care. He was just there for the show, so he could say he'd been there.

He never read The Basic Pool Rules: Use toilet before showering and shower before and after pool use. No running along the walkways of the pool, and no jumping in where someone else was. No more than four boys in the deep end at any time per each Safety Instructor (though Counselor Greg was the only one ever present).

No spitting water, no snapping towels, no trunks or outerwear, though earplugs were allowed.

He never listened as Counselor Greg carefully read The Lesson Agenda: Begin with breathing and bobbing exercises in pairs, basic face and back floating, standard freestyle, and American crawl. With regular attendance, or for those demonstrating advanced skills and higher interest levels, Counselor Greg offered individual lessons. Timed water treading, sidestroke, butterfly, and diving were included here, as well as anal and oral penile penetration, at the presiding counselor's discretion.

Most of the young charges knew and accepted the standard rules without question. One, however, did not. Though no one ever brought the subject up for discussion, Counselor Greg was never seen on the grounds again after Yuma's day at the beach. He left in a rush, the boys said. As much as a man in such agony could, they added, laughing.

Yuma didn't mind the first part. He was trying to obey the rules and just get along. The others seemed to bear it without resistance. But there was something particularly disgusting about that slimy thing in his mouth after having just been "in the bum where the sun don't shine."

"So," as he told Dieks later, "I just clamped down on that son'bitch like a mo'fucker! I din't know the end'd come off like that. Hey! Git it? That's a joke," he said, slapping Dieks on the back as he left, laughing loudly. Swimming lessons were not offered again, for the duration of Dieks' stay at Westwood.

The pool incident convinced Dieks that the leather shop was the place to be. He loved the heavy scent of new leather. There was something primal about it that called up images of rushing stallions, blazing bonfires, and rhythmic bells. There was great warmth in the peace and solace of visions that unfolded before him, and the promise of freedom awaiting him renewed his strength each day. He didn't have to perform, compete, or be physically strong. He didn't have to fight off unwanted sex, no one ever got hurt, and no one had to be the boss. He simply liked being there.

Yuma didn't like him there. Yuma thought Dieks should want to be with him. He wanted Dieks to view him as the great protector and defender. He wanted Dieks where he could control him. He felt good when Dieks smiled at him. Dieks never mentioned that Yuma's eyes appeared to be crossed, never alluded to his nearly simian features, and he never even came close to incurring Yuma's uncontrollable rage.

But, when Dieks worked at the leather shop, Yuma's loneliness went unabated. No one volunteered to sit with him. No one spotted for him when he worked with the heaviest free weights in the room. And there was certainly no one who ever once smiled at him or laughed at his jokes. Most never even listened when he talked. They mocked him behind his back and called him "monkey man" or "jungle boy," with, "whoooh, whoooh, whoooh," monkey mimics when he wasn't looking. No matter how fast he turned around, he met silence as they all faced away or ducked their heads quickly. No, he certainly didn't like being alone.

When the sirens no longer sounded and the hoses stopped gushing their thousands of gallons into the hopeless inferno, Yuma swaggered over to where Dieks sat on the curb, silent and heartsick. He stood above him, fidgeting with an empty ink pen cartridge.

"Ain' it a shame," he said before limping away to his cottage with his rounded hunched back and his bent, bowed legs.

Picking the Bones

Lucille Colleen Shaunessy was fifteen when she ran away with Joe Bergen. She couldn't bear the thought of one more beating, or even one more threat. She couldn't stand the shame that came with another incident alone in the dark, relieved that it was not her turn. She couldn't hold her breath any longer, hoping he'd stop before she took another gulp of air while listening to the thuds drumming down on her little brother's head and back with yardstick, belt, broom, anything within Richard's reach.

She closed her eyes, ears, and mind to the horrors that would befall him once she was gone. She simply wiped from memory the deathbed promise they'd all made to her mother when she gasped her last begging plea, "Please, please, please get the boy out of here."

They all agreed to it -- Lucy, Aunt Cher, and Aunt Sue -- so kind, gentle Cheyenne Collins Shaunessy could at least die in peace, knowing her sweet son would be safe. His little fingers wouldn't need to soothe away the pain in his own head. His big brown eyes would be filled with hope instead of sorrow, fear, or longing. When they promised her and assured her that they would take her young son to safety, she smiled and sighed a weak, "Ok," they said. That was what all they remembered, just before she quietly passed away.

Then, after the funeral, they all went home. Aunt Cher and her monster child Marvelle, and Aunt Sue Ann with her early Amazon child, the lovely Daniella, all piled into their pristine cars with their giggling girls and drove a safe distance from the memory of promises they'd made to their dying sister. The children climbed into the dusty backseat of Richard's old Dodge and watched out their respective windows as their last hope faded with the sun down Maggie's Tar Road.

They went home with him, home to the emptiness and heartache and the terror they knew as life. The two children, whose removal Cheyenne Shaunessy had begged for with her dying words, were left to learn the relative absolutes of evil.

They took turns praying that their father would visit the other one's room that night, that at school the next day, the purple welts and bruises the size of a grown man's work shoe wouldn't be in any obvious or embarrassing place where someone might ask about them.

Together, they held hands and jointly prayed for at least one night's rest, or that he'd be out of Irish Rose, or that the liquor store would close, or that he'd pass out before the ten o'clock news. But they decided that God never heard their prayers for, invariably, the devil answered.

The neighbors knew, the authorities knew, the kindhearted aunts knew. Yet there they sat, huddled in the darkness each night, the frightened children of a proud ex-bootlegger/gunrunner. Separated by the length of a house between their two lonely bedrooms, Cheyenne's orphans had only their frail bodies to protect their aching hearts and comfort the sadness in their souls.

As she stood next to Dieks' casket, Lucy ran her hands along the sleek black lacquer, and her heart raced ahead. She knew what this could mean. For the first time in fifty years, Lucille Colleen would be someone with real value. She would not be the dutiful squaw, the fry-cook and bottle-washer, as she'd been to father and brother. She would not be the Injun scrubwoman and gardener, as she'd been to husband and sons.

No one would dare punch her or slap her or pinch her arms. No one would ever again point and say "greasy half-breed," or laugh and call her "the fat blob." This smooth, black runway would provide her the means to soar. She would be Lucille Colleen Bergen, a woman of substance, inheriting all her brother left behind, heretofore unclaimed.

As she'd said to Melanie, "We ain't stupid, y'know. I gots a good lawyer. You jus' need a real dirty lawyer. That's whatcha gotta start with. We gots the one Dieks talked to 'bout taxes. He knows all 'bout this stuff."

Then she'd smile her best mirror-practiced smile, the "You can trust me, I'm your friend" smile. But translation had been lost with Dieks' passing. No one would appreciate her efforts to be as he had been. They would fail to see that the crooked nubs of her blackened, decayed teeth were on display in goodwill. No one knew that her squinted eyes were efforts at intense honesty. It was too awkward and strained to get these things across. These were, after all, stressful times.

Her home in Digger's Grove had been off limits to "these people." They never got to see what bargain shoppers them smart Bergens were, with their sixty-five dollar, tax-sale house. No one would ever know. Why, who could tell just by looking that she didn't have all her brother had -- street signs, paved roads, sewers, and all that fancy uptown stuff. Why didn't she deserve all that he'd left behind? She'd lived without long enough.

She stroked the rounded, shiny edge of the casket. It felt like cold, hard cash aplenty, surely enough to chase away that ter'ble grief she'd kept tellin' herself she'd be feelin' someday, any day now.

Here, after all, was his last and greatest gift to his beloved sister. With his life he gave her what she'd craved forever -- a shot at dignity, a one-way ticket to respect. Now they would have to recognize her as a fine human being. Her worth beyond toilet scrubbing and meal prep, bed change, and canning chores would be undeniable. She'd waited nearly forty years. She'd been patient and kind, loving and persevering. Good things come to those who wait. That's what Daddy'd always said. Good things come ... and she'd waited. She'd waited on them and for them. Now, she could afford to wait a bit longer for this gracious legacy.

After all, she'd waited years to hear that someone had once welcomed her birth. She'd waited to see the friendly smile of a stranger, because at home it'd been the bared teeth of a maniac. She'd waited for her husband to draw her near with love and admiration, adoration and desire, instead of the empty duty of service sex she'd been pummeled with since she was fourteen.

She'd waited for years to be more than his little "Teddy Bear." The words fell softly, intimately sweet on the ears of strangers. But to her, they were harsh and hurtful. Over and over, she'd been told, her stuffing had all fallen to the bottom. Her once strawberry blonde mane had faded and the colorless, thinning kinks of hair that remained were snarled and nappy, like an ol' teddy bear that had been overused and become grubby and, at last, abandoned. She was round and lumpy, "wore plumb out by love," he'd drawl as he'd reach over and pinch the sagging bag of a breast. She'd been kept hidden from the world, and the words he offered her with a smile she heard most often through welled-up tears.

She'd waited a long time, and here, on the bonepile of her brother, she'd dramatically claim her winning ticket to respect and love. They would listen to her. She would no longer be frumpy or dowdy. She would be wealthy and wise, generous to a fault, perhaps, to those who saw her worth and sang her praises. For those who agreed with the rightness of her decisions, for those who encouraged the seizure of assets, for those who assured her that a brother's love for his sister is far more enduring than a father's love for his sons. But she just couldn't think of all that now. Lucy was waitin' with nothin' but time, she said, in the relative privacy of her fuzzy, frayed head.

She turned to the room, crowded and blurred. There was really no one there for whom she felt obligation or responsibility. She was neither her brother's savior, nor her nephews' keeper. She had to take care of Number One. Sober, Pops had always said, "You just look out for Number One and you'll be just fine." So she shook it off and rose above the silly, sentimental thoughts. She, Lucy Clean, the pet name Dieks had called her as a child, was about to become Lucy Clean and Rich. She stood a little taller and straightened her shoulders. She checked her new pearl earrings, necklace and bracelet, smoothed the crease in her blouse and hiked up her slip. She was very nearly perfect, with just a bit of a limp, a slight flaw, from some forgotten battle in the early years. No matter, it had long since escaped memory. Just as well, she thought.

Her introduction to the world of the *nouveau riche* would be a short but significant moment -- just a jaunt from small town to countryside and back, in fact. But within the confines of a limo, she could finally view the world through new, more knowledgeable eyes and tinted glass windows. She would savor the moment, wallow in the throes of near victory, certain success. For she, runaway daughter of a cruel bootlegger, sole daughter of one of McGurn's Gang, she, Lucy Colleen alone, had survived. Through beatings, humiliation, poverty and ignorance, she had outlived them all.

She would stand proud and tall, jubilant at their gravesides. For her children, she held her head high, and with the chalice of childhood victory, after the long war, she offered cheers. Drink to the defeated, for she'd waited too long. Humbly, patiently, she'd waited. With all that time to think, she swore that no one, nowhere, would or could ever take from her or hers their rightful legacy: her late brother's "stuff," that was once her nephews' inheritance.

...

"Youk'n hide de fier, but w'at you gwine do wid de smoke?"
Uncle Remus

"Y'know, he was such a mean ol' man, we jes' never knowed from one minute ta the nex' how much meaner he could get an' not turn inta the devil hisself right there in front o' us."

She moved over to the side of Dieks' bed. "It was jes' awful, always a wonderin' which one of us'd get it nex' an' what he'd be a find'n t'do. Use ta be that he'd tell us if you's ta rock a rockin' chair an' look at a person sayin' three times, 'I hope ya die,' that person'd die. We'd always tried ta rock that ol' chair an' whisper them words, but he'd always start ta lookin' at us an' we'd shut right up.

"But, oh, jus' let 'im get a buzz on. He'd walk over ta that ole chair, lookin' at both o'us an' he'd jes' rock the hell out of that chair sayin' 'I hope ya die, I hope ya die, I hope ya die.' Why we'd set ta cryin' an' me an' Deedee'd jus' cry and cry. The more we'd cry, more he'd keep at it, arockin' an' alaughin' at us two kids. Then he'd jes' sit down, swish some whiskey 'round an' laugh real low ta his mean ol' self, like a ol' bear growlin' an acomin' for us in the dark. An' we's his kids! He's s'pose ta be alovin' us!"

At his bedside, she patted Dieks' gnarled and twisted hand that turned a little further inward with every successive series of "thalmic storms."

"Wern't he, hon'. He's'posed ta love us. We dint know. We jes' wished sometimes that he'd die or we'd die, so's we'd jes' git it all over with."

Sometimes, if I don't listen too closely, I begin to imagine that I'm a misplaced character in the middle of an old Joel Chandler Harris story and I'm just visiting at The Brer Bear Hospital. Soon, I'll turn the page and the story will end, and it'll all be the way it was. But I don't, and it doesn't, and believing in the ghost dance didn't make it happen.

For it's just Lucille Colleen talking to her comatose brother, the formerly vain Dieks Shaunessy, with his shaven head swollen like a pumpkin and jig-jagged stitches following the contours in a horseshoe-shaped arc. Replete with tubes down his throat, straps on his arms and legs, strips of tape stickin' every other appendage together, with a flimsy hand towel over his genitals, the hell of Dell's nightmares had become the reality of the the rest of his life.

Richard finally found a way to drag his little "rat-face bastard" son down to the depths with him. This would've made Dieks' skin crawl and blood boil. If he could only see himself now, I thought. He'd have all our heads on a platter, served up to the gods of childhood dreams gone sour.

"After seein' what I saw with Butch, you could just shoot me. I'd just as soon you'd shoot me, after watchin' Baker." I heard his voice echoing from some corner of my mind, and it paraded defiantly across his parched lips. Dried blood was in his moustache, and at the corner of his mouth, and evidence of salty tears streaked across his now wrinkled, sagging cheeks, from the "episodes," they'd said. Once in an "episode," his teeth clenched together and locked shut. If unsuspecting tongue or lips were in the way, they'd stay captive during the seizure-like trance of "the storms."

I kept thinking Butch was near, somewhere in the room, looking down on all of us, wondering why we'd learned nothing from the many times we'd heard him say, "No way. Just unplug me and let me go." Maybe it was Butch after all, cooling the heat in his head, calming the pounding thuds of his racing heart, preparing him by letting him tire of the tedium and misery. *Thanks, Butch, and you too, wondrous wonder U of I ICU. Go ahead - ghost dance with our dead.*

Any phone call for "the Shaunessy family" was answered by a person identified to all who'd listen as, "Sally, his girlfriend." Please, not again, Oprah. Spare me. Or, Lucy'd answer and her first words would always be the same, "Nope, no change. But we're real hopeful."

He was as still as a stone, with not one solitary, voluntary movement. Then the storms came. With them, his shoulders hunched up into his neck, and each arm would turn inward against his sides, and his toes would arch and point downward like a foundered horse while his fingers turned into claw-like clamps unable to grasp even each other. His body quaked and convulsed with rocking seizures that rippled from the top of his head to the tip of his toes. *But we're real hopeful*, I thought.

He hated pain. Of all the things he feared, he hated most the notion of pain. He knew how to administer pain, of course. He'd learned it from the master of masters. But oh, how he hated feeling even the slightest pain -- sunburn, bug bites, slivers, paper cuts, or shots. Shots were administered with needles!

How he detested needles! He would've made a terrible junkie. He simply wouldn't have been able to abuse intravenously with such a fear of needles. So his main abuse of choice, his recreational choice, was beer. He loved beer. Richard had dumped it into everything he baked or cooked, and it was always there. It was Dieks' security blanket, comfort, and family crest. It didn't hurt that it was also the one thing that allowed him an easy escape from all the pain of living. In fact, he liked nearly anything illicit and ingestible. Hash, speed, downers, pot. Anything illegal was within some unwritten price range that had been branded into his head as an established hourly entertainment rate. He never would've appreciated the brief idiocy of crack. It wasn't an economically sound investment, measuring time and money.

In the end, it was probably curse and blessing alike, for a while anyway. He burned slowly away in the fast lane. He exited with morphine, making the pain at least tolerable, committing nothing from the agonizing months to memory.

After a couple weeks, visiting a day or so each week, I couldn't stand the sight any longer. I took the surgical scissors from his bedside and proceeded to cut the hair on the unshaven side of his head. Trauma-shocked, his once dark brown hair was silver grey with mousey brown veins running through it. He looked ancient and angry, seemingly disgusted with our insistence that he try to survive. If he could not be whole and well, vain and proud, he would not be.

He opened his eyes sporadically, but not by design, though I truly expected him to begin grousing as I moved his head from side to side, the same way I had years before in Eldon. I began remembering the last time I ever cut his hair, most notably, a dull pair of scissors, a squeaky, wobbly yellow kitchen utility chair, bad lighting, and the smell of a dead mouse somewhere.

. . .

I found out that Dieks went to have his haircut "fixed" the next day. It was there that he'd asked the beautician out for a drink. It was with her that he sat that night at The Horseshoe, while, for hours, I walked like a hooker up and down the street in front of the Water Way bars.

Drinking age was twenty-one and I was too young to go in. Even though I saw his car out front, and Red's just down the block, I couldn't get past the bouncers checking ID's. So, I waited. Then, I'd go down to the corner filling station and, using the pay phone, I'd call up the block and have him paged. I'd tell him I was waiting out front, and he'd tell me to go home, that I couldn't afford a baby-sitter anyway, and then he'd hang up on me.

Round and round I'd go, down one side of the street, and up the other, across, then down, across, then up. Over and over. As I approached the bar around midnight, a thin, miniskirted redhead came out and stood in front of Dieks' car. She held the keys up and dangled them in front of me and said, "You Shaunessy's ol' lady?"

"Yes," I answered, though I distinctly remember thinking that he was considerably older than I was. "Is he coming?"

"Naw," she said between gum smacking. "But he said I oughta drive ya home. Well, make a long story short, Babe, I'm on the rag. Gotta git home and make some changes, like pronto. So he said, 'Hey no problem!' You know the man! He just tosses me these, and says, 'Have at it.' So, here I am."

I stood in disbelief as she slid into the driver's seat.

"Well, you comin' or what? Git yer ass in if you are."

She fired up the Falcon and after putting it in gear, promptly backed into the car behind us. "Hey, (smack) not my (smack) fault, (chomp, chomp) Babe. Fuckwads just park too close, that's all. Oh, don' mind my French. Comes with the territory."

"Which territory?" I asked. "Whose come? And I think it's German, Lower German, maybe." As I looked away from her, into the night, knowing that her answer would be to the first question and she'd skip the other.

"Aw, shit, you know, doin' the bar scene, messin' with the guys, runnin' 'round. Hey, don't git me wrong. I am havin' the ever lovin' time ... of my life!"

I had to smile. It was true. She was the first person I'd ever seen who couldn't chew gum and drive at the same time. She actually paused between shifting, looking in the mirror and turning the wheel. She floored the car in front of the bar and headed east down Main, toward the poor side of town.

"Where to, Babe? Yer ol' man said anywhere, anywhere you wanna go, I can take ya, except maybe Vegas. Gotta be back before the bar closes, ya know." And her gum cracked into the night air.

"No shit. That soon? Well then, maybe I better jes' git home. Yeah, that's jes' what I'll do. Turn here. No, never mind. Just stop here. I'll git out at the light so's you can haul ass, get yer rag bags changed and charged up to git yer tits back over there for more times o' yer life."

"Whatever," she said, chomping away.

I slammed the door shut and watched my husband's car squeal out into the night. I walked the last few blocks to the corner sitter to get the baby and then two houses up the block home. Delly was heavy and deeply asleep. He didn't even notice as I took off his shoes and jeans, laid him in his crib, turned out the lights and closed the door.

I began to hate the heart of life that night. As I defiantly fought back tears, I struggled with the thoughts swirling in my head. It just wasn't supposed to be that way. But somehow, I was too far gone to climb out. All of the reasons I'd loved getting and being married were gone.

I guess he should've felt that way, too. But he never, ever suggested any kind of change was in order. Whenever he wanted me, I was there, exclusively, for rage, dinner, sex, family outings, intimate moments. A good front, all in all. He never paid us a penny of child support or alimony. Of the five or ten he sporadically left for me, he ate or drank double that amount within the next week. I never pushed the issue, I didn't feel I had the right. In fact, in 1971, essentially, I had no rights at all.

One day, a social worker named Jimmy Yoachum came by and asked if he might talk to me. To me! I was shocked. Someone knew that I was alive in Eldon, that I hadn't fallen into a rat hole and drowned.

He said I could, no, should go back to school. All I had to do was take a few tests, show the State of Iowa that I was a good risk, that I wouldn't flunk out after they'd invested in me, and I could pretty much go back to college wherever I wanted. The state would pay for my books, my tuition, child care, commuting expenses. I was stunned! I was Cinderella and he was the fairy godfather!

It was the state's way of trying to get people off welfare rolls, he said, allowing them to better themselves, to become self-sufficient eventually. They were working with a new program that held promise, one that helped children primarily, like my child, to avoid becoming second or third generation welfare recipients.

Dieks was enraged, infuriated. I told him it was mandatory, that all welfare recipients had to be tested and had to go back to school if they wanted to get any money from the state. I told him the state said I had to show interest in learning a trade or getting some kind of skill, unless I wanted to "go back to my husband" and get off the welfare rolls.

Since he didn't want to have to pay for the care of his son, or his estranged wife, and he certainly didn't want us interrupting his playboy life, and God forbid, having us move back in with him, he stepped aside. That summer, the summer of '71, I enrolled in Parsons College in Fairfield, Iowa.

. . .

It had a reputation, a couple, in fact. During the 60s, it had once been voted Playboy's Party College of the Year, so it became a good time school. It also lost its accreditation at about that same time. But it still had the most learned scholars, wooed and bribed to settle in the middle of Iowa farmland from their mostly eastern digs. My history prof had been JFK's roommate, my chemistry prof was the original Mr. Wizard and taught, among other things, Witchcraft 101. They said there was an even split of economics where the student body was concerned. Half couldn't afford a McDonald's hamburger on any given weekday, the other half could buy the franchise with the balance in their checking accounts. I was of the former, and the first true welfare recipient allowed to attend Parsons. But my caseworker said that I had the highest test scores ever recorded. Of course, they'd honor my choice of school. That was my reward.

I loved Parsons. It was just what the doctor ordered. But, by the spring semester, I had what all chauvinist husbands abhor, a basic understanding of my rights as a human being. I arranged to see a lawyer. It was my first attempt at getting a divorce.

As I explained why I needed representation, and that I would only be able to pay a little at a time, the old lawyer came around his desk and up behind me. As he responded, he put his hands on my shoulders and continued talking. Without pausing, his left hand dropped to my neck, then swiftly circled lower, resting on my breast.

I inched forward, reached down and grabbed my purse, then quickly got up and moved away from him, around to the other side of his desk. We'd talk again, I said. I'd bring him a list he might need, knowing this was a time of divorce, not dissolution. I had to have good reasons for wanting to leave my wonderful, well-paid working husband. I needed proof that my intentions were true and reasonable.

I nearly ran from the lawyer's office, and down the street to a diner where I sat stunned and confused, wondering what terrible crimes I'd committed that would make my life so irreversibly locked into madness at every turn. Everywhere I looked for help I found a hole, even in the heart of the world. My child and I were insignificant beings with nonexistent futures and regrettable, forgettable pasts.

I never went back to that office. I watched the old man's son years later at my class reunion, and realized that even seemingly insignificant happenings of years before can renew old anger and set flashfires raging. I refused to believe that men were designed as the enemies. I wanted the opportunity to respect and admire them. I wanted to choose their company, share their dreams, and be equal partners. It'd been far too long in the making.

The M is cracking.

The A weeps.

The R's cower together in silent expectation (orphaned twins).

     R

     I am falling off the wall, Humpty Dumpty.

     A

     G

     E is all that's left and I am so lonely in this age.

          Yet, alone is important.
          Lost lessons of the willow,

                 Gently swaying,

            Sightless,

              Strong,

          Resilient,

                    Singular.

Sunrise, Sunset

In the summer of '73, Parsons College went bankrupt. As they announced their economic woes and subsequent closing before students and faculty one morning, I realized immediately that the problems I'd faced longer than I could remember had just been solved. Days of anticipation were gone. Emotional replacements of anger and fear moved in and took over before I had time to dispute the inevitable. I knew it was time to move on.

Tangled images began to emerge, and I reviewed the source of contempt with which I'd begun to see my once-loving husband. Moments that had once meant loving rapture were replaced with episodes of harassment, beatings, humiliation, rape, and repulsive scenes of insanity that crept into every corner of our lives. I'd become completely numb in the process, and there was no longer a line in the sand that he was not able to step over. The straw that breaks the camel's back can take any form. For me, it was that morning, and the looming presence of a heavy cloud that said my options were limited was something I could no longer accept.

My only escape had been in the form of classes each day. No matter what, I could drive away from it all, thirty miles down the road to Fairfield, where I sat and pretended I was as normal as anyone else. In class, I nursed back to health whatever pride I could reach with the knowledge that I had good grades and potential. Every injury he inflicted in whatever strange, raging personality he'd assumed, and every threat he made and carried out with conviction, was wiped away for those few hours in the halls and classrooms of Parsons College.

One day, I thought, I'd emerge able-bodied, capable of supporting my child and myself. Someday I'd be able to say, "No, I won't be kept any longer. I'm not hiding in the shadows while you dance with the debutantes." Soon, I'd escape. It was just a dream. Shortsighted, narrow-minded, maybe. But it was *my* dream.

At that point, it was the thing I coveted and knew to be worth fighting for. No one would take it from me. I had somewhere to go. I had literature to quote and history to memorize, psychology to practice and sociology to live. He wouldn't stop or dissuade me.

In my dream, I could run, fast enough and far enough that he would never find me, catch me, beat me, or rape me. He wouldn't be able to destroy what I had, because it would be out of his reach. I could sleep in peace and live without fear and look to the future.

On that day, I found that all those thoughts were enough. So I left. I rented a U-haul trailer, went back home, and took one long, last look at poverty and despair, and decided to turn my back on it all. I loaded up all I could pack into the trailer, buckled in the baby, and headed north. Without plan, promise or hesitation, we left with all we owned in a space that became mobile for three hours. I drove 'til I ran out of gas, never once looking back.

Somehow, I figured he'd never come for me. It seemed perfectly clear that there was no other way. Our paths were so different and our love, long withered, was worthless. Much later, when I no longer watched or worried, he did come north, looking for and almost expecting open arms and relief. But it was too late. I didn't know the sober, humble person who came to my door. I couldn't remember ever having seen him the way he was that day. But he came just the same and wept great tears for "all we had," and said he'd always known that I'd leave him someday. It was just a matter of time, and he reminded me once again of my promise that I'd never leave him.

No, I said resolutely. I didn't leave him. He'd left me years before I'd ever entertained the thought. And now, not even vivid memories of his passionate kisses and sensuous touch could lure me back.

After establishing that I was no longer receptive to living with, or even near him, Dieks returned that winter to Eldon, the conquered lands and women in waiting. Inside a month or two, I met Sam. The truth of the matter is, I was transferred to him one night for a five-dollar debt Neary owed him. I thought it a reasonably civil exchange, considering the fact that I was pretty drunk and only pretending to study for Dr. Louise Forest's Shakespeare final the next morning. They assured me Sam was the man I'd been dreaming of for years, and his name was tattooed all over my ass. Thus, the bill of sloggy goods moved on. Not then exactly, but eventually. Shortly after graduation the following year, I moved, got divorced, married Sam, and was hired to teach high school English all in the same month.

Dieks came up north a few more times, to take "Little Dieks," who later became known less intimately and safely as "the boy," for the weekend. When I'd go to visit Mom and Dad in Eldon, I'd let "the boy" go see "the old boy" where he lived on Spruce, just down the road from my parents. There, I learned much later, when he was old enough to relay such information, being allowed to play or visit meant being thrust out the back door to his tricycle or the neighbors, so "the old boy" could continue to entertain the constant influx of troops without interruption.

But as often happens, the visits became less frequent, and after Dieks' third or fourth marriage, he stopped calling.

Unfortunately, that never stopped Little Dieks from sitting out front on the steps of our house on Seerley a couple Saturdays every month. Ashamed, I could hardly bear to look out the window. But I knew when he'd disappear after Scooby Doo that he'd be sitting clean and straight, watching and waiting for his father.

At first, I'd ask, "What're ya doin'?"

"Just sittin'," he'd say, then he'd fold his hands together and wait.

By noon, when I'd call him for lunch, out the back door, he'd come around back and into the kitchen. He'd climb up into his chair and eat in silence, with the empty hazel eyes staring at every bite, seeing nothing, tasting nothing, believing in nothing.

Finally, as we'd expected and half-hoped, he stopped waiting. But, one day, as we hadn't expected, Dell Collins Shaunessy called from his throne in the conquered south lands. At first, it was nervous small talk. He never asked to arrange a time for visitation. Then he said maybe it wasn't the right time. He'd just call back some other time.

"For what?" I asked

"I'll call back, some other time," he repeated.

"The right time for what?" I insisted.

"Well," he began, "I thought, maybe, since I don't really get up there as often as I should … "

"Like, ever?" I interrupted.

I heard Mandy, his most recent bride, prompting him in the background. "If … Sam would, might like … to adopt him. Well, then … he could have the same name and stuff and it would be better for you … at tax time and … "

"And you, of course, would pay up the seven years of back child support that you owe him, right?"

"Well, I'm not really set up for that right now. We're kinda short on cash … " More Mandy in the wings … " And well, if he ever wants to see the ol' man, he's sure welcome, and I'll be here for him … like when he needs cash … for college … or somethin' … "

Mandy words … lots of words, words, words … angry, hard, ugly words … in the background, slapping him into reality.

"Anyway, you know what I mean. So, if you just have the papers drawn up, I'll sign 'em and it's been real good talkin' to ya … "

Angry Mandy words, again, "and uh, well, drop by, or … " Rip his head off Mandy words and then she helped him hang up. Click.

I talked to Sam about the call. He was as enthusiastic as a near emotionless man could get. But he'd long seen himself as my son's father, and didn't care what the asshole's reasons were for relinquishing rights.

"Get on the stick, and get the papers drawn up before he comes to his senses and calls back."

We called a local attorney and arranged to meet with Dieks and Mandy, to have the papers presented and reviewed. They signed without reading them and turned to leave the law office. As he pulled the door shut, he said matter-of-factly, "Hey, psssst, Richard died."

. . .

I didn't speak to him again for twelve or thirteen years, I think. I saw him once, following me around in Sears several years after he'd signed off his son's life. I was very pregnant so it must've been the summer of '78. But he never let on that either of us knew the other was there, breathing the same air, occupying the same space. After all, I'd made major concessions as well - access to my hometown, to my family and friends - the standard spoils of war. Year in and year out, he'd left us alone, up north.

After his violent, explosive marriage to Mandy ended, I'd started sending him the old cards that I'd kept, cards he'd sent to me years before. It was my way of punishing him, I think, reminding him of the elusive joy of sentimental passion and love lost. Funny, witty, lust filled letters and cards, covering only three or four years in all, unsalvageable years of carelessly spent youth and life.

Seeing Dieks' letters, reading them, I realized we'd all been cheated. Everyone had cheated him of his life, of his chance to be normal, to love and give, nurture and receive, in any relationship.

I'd been cheated, raked over the coals. I caught only a fleeting glance of passion's fires, and then looked back in anger at the embers that became humiliation and painful remembrance. His son knew even less of what he'd been given in the gene pool, much less what he'd pass on to his own children. He would probably never even understand where the impassioned creativity and fire-fashioned intensity came from. He'd never once witnessed it in process.

I couldn't remember trust, and our son had never known it to start with. Just as Dieks was about to embark on the most challenging journey of his life, college and independence, "the old boy" swaggered in, bearing gifts, promises and stories, regaling his son with the friends' lives he'd had to settle for -- a vicarious picture of his life as seen through their pasts, complete with painted images of future-perfect promises.

He'd finally moved over and had come to embrace the notion of his son, the man. The child had been too delicate a life to interfere with. He'd had no childlife of his own; he knew nothing of its composition. But he knew the stuff capable and successful young men were made of. It was frightening to try to capture something that had been so elusive to him.

He acknowledged Sam's efforts and results, then shamelessly held out the remains of his broken heart, pieces that had long been damaged in the shuffle of wives, children, girlfriends and buddies. With that gesture, he gave his grown son the substance of fill for the void that I'd never been able to give. His father, this father, with so many friends and other obligations, had at long last returned and set time aside for him, and only him. He referred to him as "the biological father," and said nonchalantly that the biological father had a really neat show car.

"He always did," I said.

The biological father had bought his beloved grandmother's, my mother's, house. And even though it made him sad, he said he could feel her there, in the plants and bushes, in the evening breezes. He was sure only he could feel her there, walking next to him, through the biological father's yard.

Dieks, he said, was settling down in his old age, and he'd laugh that laugh they both had, and glance his father's old sideways glance. Dieks, he said, the biological father, was surprisingly good with the babies. Dieks, he said, had called, found him a second car, and would be bringing it to him at the University in Iowa City on the weekend.

Dieks was a changed man, he was sure. And the son's grades were very good. He was coming to terms with this, I told his dad. Not the biological dad, I noted mentally. The Dean's List was a good sign, I thought. He's taking his responsibilities in stride, paying attention to his wife, Debby, to the babies, coping quite nicely with the new terms and the old biological dad.

"Dieks thinks you should keep your hair long," he said to me, "like it is in the picture I sent him, the one where you're holding Chauncey, you know, at our place, after the Iowa game."

"Dieks is bringing us Grandma's blue rocker up this weekend. Dieks says he's doing the house over in navy, burgundy and forest green. Dieks is leaving the bedrooms the same, and he said what you said, that Grandma's bedroom set's too big a hassle to move out and back, so he's not going to recarpet in there."

Dieks said. Dieks called. Dieks's here. I'm at Dieks'.

. . .

"Dieks is dead." He spoke into the phone and the words raced across the wires to me. From Iowa City to Cedar Falls, they reached out of the receiver, and slapped me and made me cry. "Just a while ago. Forty-six days," they said.

So, I thought, even with a weak man, a little money, a lot of talent, a few good friends, and a faulty brain, it still takes that long. I guess he had heart, a great big heart. But I simply couldn't say it. The words refused to rise.

We continued to talk, but the thoughts traded have since been lost. I'm sure he felt something, some deep sadness, some bitter loss, but I could not think my way out of the grief in that moment. It would have been instead a grief for something so far back in the recesses of my brain, something alien to this world, reverberating in my heart with words once held in a card he'd given me.

"This is the true measure of love, when we believe that no one has loved so before us and no one will ever love this way again ... " I couldn't complete it, but knew it was important. Goethe thought it was

important. I would've called my mother, knowing that she alone would understand the desperate void in that moment. But she was gone. I would've called my brother, but he was gone, too.

So I dialed my sister's number and coldly informed her that the biological father of my firstborn son was dead. I said the words mechanically and removed, shrugging, as if such a notion transcends telephone wires.

She'd wanted to know, she'd said, so they could send flowers from "his outlaws," as he'd often called them. "Paleface outlaws" would be more accurate, I remember thinking. As I held the receiver to my ear, she turned on the TV to the channel that lists local deaths and read to me the notice as it scrolled down the screen and it still didn't register in my brain.

"He'll be buried October first," she was saying. "Family will receive friends the night before."

And so they did. His body was shipped home from some insignificant holding tank where he'd spent his last lonely hours, apart from a lifetime of carefully accumulated friends. The morphine diet had left him to die at about ninety pounds.

I stumbled back through time to my brother's deathbed. In the last days, he'd ask one question without fail each morning, "How much do I weigh?" He'd always said to watch out for eighty-nine pounds, and assured me that the average weight at death was eighty-nine pounds.

There, for all to see, at about eighty-nine pounds, they'd shipped Dieks' body -- a skeleton, dressed as a comedian, ready to host his class reunion. Although I viewed him only once, I've seen the sight a thousand times over in my mind. And though I vowed I'd leave it all behind, it skipped and flitted along with me, stored for instant recall with all the rest of the vile, unshakeable quease.

The clan had planned the dearly departed's ensemble weeks in advance, not taking into account that only partial, mortal remains would come home. Looking anything but sporty, the bones of his shoulders jutted out in awkward defiance toward the ceiling, under the ill-fitting bumblebee gaiety of a plaid rock and roll sports coat. His face was clearly pumped with air or chemical to fill the ridges of hollowed-out bones in the shrunken skull. A dashing young man's leftover dark lashes swept upward, resting on blowfish cheeks sculpted down in the morgue by some master plastician. The hands that once caressed the nape of my neck were glued together like colorless, gnarly tree roots, pencil thin and puerile. When I could no longer stand it, I turned away, and finally drew a breath that stalled somewhere in my empty chest.

He'd kill us, I thought. He would absolutely, positively, murder each and every person responsible for dressing him up like a tasteless party clown, for allowing him to be seen this way, for etching in our final memories this horrible sight - this dehydrated bonepile of a man.

The Sixth Deadly Sin

Thinking back, Dieks seemed to take particular interest in Wade and Benny. Though they were the "bad boys" of Dirty Luke and Rotten Rachel, I think he saw something in them that he'd longed for his whole life -- the carefree fun of being someone's naughty son, someone's busy little boy.

They lived across the street from me, down by the fairgrounds where every other house was run down, abandoned, or red tagged for demolition. There, in the midst of the tumbledown squalor that made up the poorest of areas, lived most of the town's retired and welfare poor. We didn't mean to be that way, it just happened. The old dream deferred finally settled into dust, and though we did our best, both efforts and outcome were, for the most part, mediocre.

Luke and Rachel lived there by choice, I think. They didn't seem to have a thing, but clearly had all they needed. I never quite figured it out, just low pay and bad money management, I concluded. Luke worked every day without fail, forty hours a week in a nearby mill. He brought his paycheck straight home at the end of the week, and they'd make a family outing of cashing the check and shopping for groceries. At the end of each month, they all piled into a nearly blue, rusted-out, '64 Chevy Bel Air. They'd take off in a cloud of dust down the old river road to the Kresge store in Ottumwa at the corner of Market and Main. There, everybody'd get one new "thang," as Rachel put it -- new jeans, or shirt, a pair of socks or shoes. Something, but only one each.

Rachel kept her kids clean, she said, doing the wash each day, hanging all their "thangs" out back to soak up the sun. Every night she cooked a huge supper that would've impressed the gluttons of Rome. Then, they'd move to the backyard, sit in their respective lawn chairs, and just poop away the evening. Week in and week out, all summer long.

She did the dishes about once a month, when they finally ran out of every pot, pan, fork, spoon, bowl, plate, and cup in the house. In her own down-home fashion, she'd line 'em up across the tiled living room floor in an assembly line that stretched from the front door to the back. Then, she'd set out to wash each one, moving each piece to the "towel train" that ran an equal distance on the opposite side of the room. By the time she got to the end of the wash line, the first pieces in the dry line were ready to be stacked and put away. It was a bit unorthodox, but she was an efficient, one-woman, dishwashing operation.

When their nephew's wife, Meggy, showed up unannounced and decided to move in along with her baby, Luke and Rachel tried very hard to adapt, to be responsible, loving relatives. But, the truth was, with hearts so big, there just wasn't much room for compliance in their souls. Meggy was a freeloader, using them and their house as she'd always used everyone, as everyone'd used her. Rachel was her personal, in-house, free baby-sitter, the kitchen was her restaurant, the kids her servants, and after closing time at the bars each night, her bedroom, at one end of the living room, became a love nest where she and her most recent straggler would bounce and groan and scream until the early morning hours when Luke would get up and go to work.

Eventually, when everyone tired of the use, they decided to take action. The response was swift, the outcome as they'd hoped. Rachel watched quietly from the living room as Meggy spread rancid mayonnaise on moldy bread with slick, rotted bologna from the Oscar Meyer package. When she noticed Rachel and looked closer at her creation, she shoved all the makings off the table and into the open garbage sack, grabbed the baby, his diaper bag and bottle, her canvas bag of bar gear and night wear, and stomped out the front door, saying she'd never, ever come back to that hell hole. Nobody could make her. Nobody asked.

Rotten Luke and Dirty Rachel were literally out dancin' in the streets that night, singin' the Lord's praises. "Thank God," they sang, "thank God Almighty, we're free, free at last! She's gone, she's gone, she's gone … "

At almost the same moment, Rachel clapped her hands and jumped up with Luke. Without another word, they flew through the front door, into the house, into the bedroom, one after the other. Within minutes, there was a racket like nothin' even tawdry Meggy had ever produced. I just stayed on the front porch steps, waiting.

As I sat there I heard the rumble of one of Dieks' cars coming in from the south. Sure enough, it pulled around the corner and came up the street where it turned into my driveway and shut down. As he opened the door, Filthy Wade popped up out of nowhere, yankin' at his pants as they nearly drooped off. With matted, sweaty hair, and his sun-browned legs and back streaked with the day's dirt, Wade jumped about and carried on, resembling a rambunctious monkey as he circled the car and kept an appropriate distance from the immaculate man stepping out of it.

He loved Dieks, and could hardly be kept at an arm's length when Dieks came. There was no explanation for his feelings, for he'd certainly never been encouraged. I decided it was body chemistry or something. He bragged up the car, kept a running conversation with absolutely nothing in return, and did everything he could to capture and keep Dieks' undivided attention. Benny appeared too, but like his mother, he was a lumbering sort of kid, heavy and slow, both physically and mentally, while Wade was willowy and rabbit-fast, as well as quick-witted.

"Hey, look what I gots, Shaunce." Wade held a chunk of something out to Dieks in his sweat-lined brown hand.

"That's real nice," Dieks said, sticking his nose over it and nodding with approval as though he' was interested. "What is it?"

"Wall!" Wade yelled with glee. "It's wall wall wall!" He was jumping up and down, encircling Dieks as he tried to walk across the street to where I sat on their front porch step.

Wade then ran to Little Dieks and stopped him from coasting any further down the hill by straddling his Big Wheel. He held the clump out to him, then snatched it back when the baby reached for it with his little grabby hand.

"I can get 'nother for you. Just wait. Right there." He ran back up to the house and through the front door, stretching the spring as far back as it could go without snapping, then letting it slam against the slate siding.

Just then, I glanced back to see thick clouds of dust drifting across the empty lot next to Luke and Rachel's. Dieks looked over and asked what was going on.

I raised my eyebrows and shrugged my shoulders. "Who knows?"

Wade came flying out the front door again with another green chunk of "wall!" that he planted into Dieks' hand.

"There ya go, Shaunce!" He was screaming again and jumping around Dieks. "She ain't comin' back now, that's fer sure! Nope, no sireeee, she ain't!"

I looked at the chunk Dieks handed me and recognized the green paint of their living room wall on the piece of plaster. I put my hands over my eyes. "M'God, they're tearing down the walls."

Dieks began to back away from the front door where he'd been looking in to see where all the commotion was coming from. He brushed away the dust that drifted out on his crisp white jeans and grinned, saying, "You won't believe this one."

I stood up and moved over to the front door, where I could barely see Luke and Rachel in what appeared to be a severe in-house dust storm. He had a sledge hammer, and she had a ball-peen and a crowbar. Together, they'd just beaten to death the wall that once stood at the end of the living room.

Electrical outlets danced like marionettes at the end of wires snaking down out of the ceiling. Piles of plaster littered the floor, and the wall that had once provided Meggy with the privacy of a tiny bedroom no longer existed. It was now a dusty rose corner of their remaining green living room.

Rachel was teetering off balance as she climbed over the debris, coming toward us. "She won't be back now," she said, grinning from ear to ear. "No place to stay. Just got a bigger living room." She slapped her hands together, brushing off dust. "That oughta do it."

"Say, Shaunce, looky here!" Wade was yelling at Dieks again as he put the arm of the record player down on an album going round and round, with lumps and chunks of plaster and dust riding along. He was the only person I'd ever heard call him "Shaunce," but it seemed to be a name Dieks accepted as something just between them.

Dieks shook his head. "Where's your bug today?"

"Don' know," Wade shrugged. "Mom!" He was yelling like she was down the block. She was really just a little lost in the plaster dust tunnel. "Did we lose my bug?"

"We'll get another one," Rachel said, laughing and brushing back an escaped piece of curly black hair with her forearm.

They were snapping bugs of some kind or other. I'd never seen anything like them, before or since. Indigenous only to Luke and Rachel's kitchen, I think.

They brought their bug over to my house for Little Dieks to see one night. On a piece of particle board about two feet square, they sat for hours on the dining room floor, watching the bug flip from its back, up two feet or more in the air, and then down to the board on its feet again. Then, they'd turn it over to its flat, hard shell back, and wait quietly and patiently for it to flip again, clapping and screaming with delight when it would right itself in midair, landing squarely on the board. Neither Dieks, both small and large, nor boys, nor bug, ever tired of the bug board show.

Though amused with the antics of the boys and the bug, they could never get Dieks to touch it. He seemed to identify with Wade, but unlike him, never got the courage to touch the creepy-crawly. No one ever mentioned it. Small and feisty, hyper, happy and carefree, he was who Dieks might have become if he'd ever been allowed to be a child.

I noticed the days that Wade seemed down, or when Benny'd been picking on him -- those were the days that Dieks seemed most attuned to him. If he'd come over and just sit on my porch, I knew that he was in a safe zone, out of Benny's or anyone's reach.

When asked what he was doin' there, Wade would always say, very seriously, "Jus' waitin' ... for Shaunce."

Sometimes he showed up, sometimes he didn't. But it never bothered Wade. He'd stay put until he'd declare he was tired of "waitin'", and then he'd cross the street to go home.

Being small and quick, he was prone to trouble. When Benny wasn't bedeviling him, Wade was looking for something to get into.

They had a mangy old dog named Ralph, but nobody could ever tell what he was or might be 'cause Wade kept cuttin' his hair off or spray paintin' him, or mud-piein' his back, or otherwise altering his boring dog features.

He just couldn't be Bingo, the big black dog on the back porch. He was always being radically modified instead to something absolutely outrageous, unacceptable to the rest of the world, but wonderful in Wade's eyes. Benny tormented the animal, teasing him just beyond the end of his rope. I often wondered if Wade wouldn't unleash him sometime to even things up a bit. But I don't think he ever did.

Whenever Wade toned down his mischievous behavior, Benny would do something mean, and he'd get "all riled up again," as Rachel put it.

"They'll be the death of me," she'd mumble every time she pulled 'em apart, but I think they're what made her tick.

As they played football in the side yard one day, Dieks watched them from my front bay window. He kept getting up and going over to check on them, every ten or twenty minutes.

After about an hour, he set down the beer he'd been drinking, and stormed out the front door, saying, "I knew it! God damn it, I knew it!"

He was stomping across the street, and I looked out to see the older boys tossing the ball just over Wade's head. His usually high spirited jumping up and down orneriness was tiring, and he'd begun to whine.

"C'mon, guys, gimme the ball … C'mon, Benny."

He'd pass it to the other kid, and Wade would turn with the direction of the ball, "C'mon, my turn, let me have it, you guys, aw, c'mon," he kept pleading.

Just then, Dieks startled all of them and walked past Wade, just as the ball soared over his head. He reached up, plucking it from the air, and handed it down to Wade.

Shaking a finger at Benny, he said, "Don' let me see you doin' that again." He turned and walked away without another word.

As he stepped back up to the curb across the street, Benny yelled, "I'm tellin' my dad!"

Dieks slowly turned around and pointed his finger straight at Benny, "You just do that, Buster," as he nodded his head up and down.

Luke shook his head as he stood in the doorway watching. I've always believed that he was relieved when Benny went 'round back instead of coming up to the front door to demand justice. There was always "somethin' simmerin'," he'd say, referring to Dieks, "somethin' jus' under the hood that could make a grown man shudder."

I knew he was right because I'd seen that somethin' boil over. Luke never had, but instinctively, he knew he didn't want to either. Benny somehow knew it, too.

Wade didn't care either way. He cradled his unexpected prize and never even considered tossing it up again. Someone might snatch it away, and he knew that Shaunce wouldn't come over and rescue him if he made the same mistake again. He eyed Dieks walking back across the street, and smiled when he thought of Dieks calling his brother, "Buster."

. . .

I parked the car at the back of the lot after letting Dieks and Debby out at the side door of the funeral home.

As I weaved my way through the cars, a man approached, walking to his own car, I figured. But then he stopped in front of me and waited.

"Liz Bee?" he asked, stringing out the "B," pointing at me.

I looked up.

"Yes?"

"I thought so. I told Dad t'was. An' he said, 'Nope.'"

He grabbed my hand and shook it way up and way down like the handle on a well pump. His black Stetson jiggled rhythmically as I looked up at him. He was still vigorously shaking my whole arm.

"I knew it! I jus' knew it!" He was so proud of himself. Then I knew who he was.

"Wade?" Shut your gaping mouth, woman.

"Yep. It's me. It sure is."

"Where's your mom 'n' dad?"

"Uhhh ... Dad's waitin' in the truck. He's wantin' t'go home. Mom's gone. She's dead."

"Oh, I'm so sorry. I didn't know."

He looked up at me and then back down at his boots, while moving a rock back and forth, shifting attention between the ground and what he was saying. "Yep, she died in ... Uhm, eighty-four. Shaunce came. Yep, he really did. Gimme this. Yep. The day she got buried and I's jus' standin' there at the hole and he comed up behin' me, and gimme this."

He thrust a closed fist in front of my nose and on his ring finger was the biggest, most garish turquoise, coral and silver ring that I'd ever seen. Should've been a belt buckle, I thought.

"Pretty neat, huh?"

"Yes, I guess it is at that. But, why'd he give ya that?"

"Jus' 'cause. We were friends, I guess. Yep. That'd be what I'd guess. Not too many came to Mom's burial. But Shaunce did. That's a friend for ya. Yep. He was a good friend. Sure hate to see him go. I really do. Welp, gotta run. Saw Little Dieks go in. Sure looks different than when I seed 'im last. All growed up now, ain't he?"

"Yep. All growed up," I agreed.

"Welp, I'll be goin' now. Nice seein' ya."

"Yep, Wade. Was nice seein' you, too." A down-home drawl had crept into my words, and I was still nodding with the flow of it as Wade walked away with the cowboy stroll that had grown up along with him. He climbed up into his pickup. Yep. Four wheel. Gunrack, too. Yessiree.

He was sad, and Dieks gave him hope. He was lonely, and Dieks went out of his way to let him know that he wasn't alone. He was insignificant, and Dieks gave him recognition. Through Wade, Dieks gave his own childhood a helluva gift.

I smiled and went in.

Part II

Cheyenne Lucy

As was often the case, Richard's drunken ramblings were riddled with active escapades. When combined with the effects of aging and the massive number of mind altering pills he took each day, an often completely different world emerged from the haze, while the world to which he woke was dull and mercifully forgotten by midday. Most of the time he was alone. Sometimes he was with other men, men he respected or even feared. To his way of thinking, there was little difference between the two. At yet other times, Chey was with him.

Once, approaching the crowded backroom of a Waterloo speakeasy, someone bumped Chey's arm as she and Richard crossed the threshold. As always, when she traveled with him, she carried a loaded derringer, concealed in her dainty white mink muff. It went off, splintering the frame of the doorway where they'd been wedged to a halt. Inside, half the patrons hit the floor, the other half pulled guns of their own.

He told the story often, but rarely the same way from version to version, and the end was always some rendition of testimony to his commanding presence: his grand entrance, the beauty that always went home with him in spite of all the sly comments made to him and all the offers made to her. He'd smile a rueful smile when remembering her, how she'd sweep through a room of crowded people, how everyone stopped and stared at her drop-dead looks. Men, women, young and old alike.

Sometimes, I thought it was the fact that he'd corrupted such a winsome woman that made the story so moving for him. At other times, I believe he found the power to corrupt exciting in itself. But more than that, I think he believed his power over her translated to power over others, especially the many men who marveled at her mysterious beauty.

No one seemed to know of her family. They never mentioned her creamy caramel complexion and aquiline nose, or the lustrous black hair and penetrating black-brown eyes she'd passed on to her son. She sometimes spoke of another family, distant and somehow different, a brother up north, with the baby. She never elaborated, just spoke wistfully of Chaunce and Coochee, her little Cowacoochee.

In quiet moments that seemed to spring from the effect of drugs Doc Petti gave her for the pain, she'd whisper words to Dieks that he couldn't understand and struggled later to remember. They were secret words. To him, a string of sentences always began with words that sounded a lot like "secret" and "coach."

Even in the earliest years they could recall, Dell Collins and Lucille Colleen never thought of where they'd come from. They thought mostly about how to make it easier. How to be quiet. How to protect Mother. How to be big enough to understand and small enough to stay out of his way. They never mentioned the relentless fear that loomed in their every waking moment when he was home. After their mother's death, they couldn't imagine asking for help from their only known relatives, Aunts Cher and Sue. For the Shaunessy children, family was an old man who dared them to find strength in each other.

Sometimes, when things were really bad, the two would whisper to each other how their wonderful plan to run away would work. They would write a letter to their aunts and they'd tell them how bad it was at home and how they simply had to run away. They would tell them they would run to the woods and they could come and find them there. They would steal food from gardens to take with them, and they would leave in the night, following the railroad tracks to the outskirts of town. In the woods, they could live on nuts and berries until Aunt Cher or Aunt Sue came to get them on the old river road.

But they never wrote the letters. They couldn't remember anyone's last names, and they'd never known their addresses. Besides, they never really believed anyone could help them anyway. So they stayed.

The names of Cher and Sue continued to be whispers that fell from the children's lips as they sobbed quietly, despairing in the darkness. When they tried to rub away the stinging welts left by his belt, or when they massaged the purple bruises that remained long after the shoe had walked away, they mouthed the names of their aunts and then closed their eyes, praying that anyone or anything would respond to their pleas. But the sacred names of known relatives were never enough, and empty silence was all they ever knew of solace.

They knew who their aunts were, but they'd only heard their names and had never seen them written. It wasn't until they happened upon a dusty, well-worn Bible in Richard's forbidden bedroom that Dell Collins and Lucille Colleen Shaunessy began to put together the pieces of their family tree that no one ever mentioned. While he was away at work, they often explored in drawers, behind doors, and in closets, whose contents were otherwise off limits to them. On that day, they stumbled on to what was by far the very best find ever.

On brittle pages, yellowed with time, the children of Cheyenne Collins Shaunessy found information they'd never known enough to ask for, a sketchy family history that began a hundred years before.

As they sat staring at the names in the front of her Bible, it became clear to them that the Bible was not only their mother's, but had been her mother's as well.

"They're Indian names," Lucy said, running her stubby index finger over the list that filled the page.

"Was Mother Indian?" Dell asked.

"Her name was Cheyenne Lucy ... Fields, or Smith, I think. But these two's crossed out and Collins is wrote behind it."

"Like me?"

"Yeah. But we knew that, din't we? Mama always said you gots her same name, and I gots one kinda the same."

"Lucille Colleen ... Lucille's same as Lucy now and Colleen is kinda Collins."

She kept moving her finger over the words and hunkered down closer to the book, as if her nose would help her read the faded writing that drifted down the page.

"Her mama's name was ... Lucy Fields ... and her daddy's name ... was Chey Se-quah ... Smith. He was a Cher-o-kee ... farmer from Tennessee ... and then Arkansas. But, Arkansas's crossed out and Oklahoma's wrote in."

Lucy was squinting to make the words more readable, fighting for better light, and at the same time, trying to see through the strands of hair that draped down the page of her mother's mother's very worn

Bible. "They had some children in Oklahoma. Here it says, 'Se-quah gone, three dash three, found, died, eleven dash eighteen, nineteen-oh-five, Roaring Cloud of Sox, nineteen-oh-six, Sox Ann, nineteen-ten ... stay with John Sauts, Woquini, nineteen-eleven, Cheyenne Lucy, nineteen-twelve ... Move to Mesquakee in Iowa."

"Us?"

"No, you big dummy. Grandma Lucy, who was Mama's Mother ... took herself and ... here, it says 'Cher-o-kee Lynn, Se-quo-ya Chauncey Yellow Robe, Sox Ann and Cheyenne Lucy, who was born at settlement lodge in nineteen-twelve.' Dede, I think these are all Indian names. They are all spelled like, like Indians spell or something. That must mean we're Indian, 'cause Mama was Indian."

"Pop's not Indian. You think we're Indian, even if Pop's not Indian?"

"Uh huh. Looky here at these names. These are all names of Indian people or places or something. Mama's name and Aunt Cher and Aunt Sue is like ... Sox. We always thought it was like Shy Ann. You know, like she was shy and didn't talk. And Sue Ann's like Oh Sues-anna, or Susanne. And Aunt Cher is really Aunt Chair, 'cause it's Cher-o-kee. Get it? All Indian stuff. All our aunts an' uncles."

"And somewhere we gots uncles called Yellow Rope and See-go-ya Chance?" Dell asked in amazement.

"No. I said 'S-e-c-o-y-a C-h-a-w-n-c-e-y' is Yellow Robe, like bath robe, with a B. See my lips. B. Robe. One uncle with lots of names, and maybe, some more ... 'cause," and she poked her nose down in the page again, "it says right here, 'Went north with Sequah's people, Indiana Nation.' I thought Indiana's a state. Hmmmm. Maybe it was a nation," Lucy said.

"We can ask Aunt Cher, can't we?"

"What if she tells Pop?" Lucy answered, closing the Bible abruptly and lugging it back to Richard's bedroom to replace it in the old drawer.

"Well, maybe we could ask her somethin' else, like where's her mom and pop."

Dieks rolled over on his back, tracing the cracks across the ceiling in the living room with a make-believe arm rifle.

"I don't think I'm Indian," Lucy announced, returning from Richard's bedroom. "I got blue eyes and my hair don' look nothin' like yours or like what Mama's did."

"You look like Pop more. That's all."

"Nope. I think what he said's true. You're not his kid, and you don't look like him is why."

"Why'd you have to go and say that?"

"'Cause it's prob'ly true. It's prob'ly why we get beat up on all the time. It's prob'ly all your fault with your ole black Indian hair and your big buck teeth and your long ol' ugly nose."

Dieks didn't say anything back to her. Tears welled up in his eyes and began to run down into his ears. He couldn't help but think about his mother, about her brown eyes and her sisters and brothers and Indian parents. He always thought about her when Lucy started being mean to him. Sometimes he'd give Lucy his piggy bank if she'd just promise to quit being mean to him. But usually, he'd just go somewhere else where he could keep thinking about his mother. It was easier than trying to figure out why his Lucy didn't like him anymore.

He rolled over and stood up. Then it came to him. The words he'd heard his mother say weren't "secret code" at all. They were names, "Sequah" and "Coho." But it was more than twenty years before Dell heard the words again and finally learned their meaning.

...

Louis Kahartt was out and about, spouting history according to Saint Luke, as usual. He sat with Dieks nursing late-night beers at Sundown, talking about the trip to California he'd just come back from, where he claimed the redwoods were bigger around than a lot of rooms he'd lived in. Luke shook his head, saying those big old trees were all mighty amazing, but sequoias were his favorites.

Dieks just nodded, going along with what he was saying, not paying much attention to it all. But then, he spun around and asked Luke to repeat what he'd just said.

"Huh?"

"What you just said, about the name."

"I said that the great sequoia trees in the Northwest were named for an Indian from the south. That's quite a tribute to any man. The guy's name was Sequoya, and he was the son of a half-blood Cherokee out of the Paint Clan in Tennessee, where the Cherokee Nation was back then. Later, he moved to Arkansas and farmed, had a son there named Chusaleta. Chusaleta took himself a Cheyenne wife, and they had a son named after his grandpa, called Chey Sequah. They were all living in Arkansas when the government came along and started taking their land and pushing all the tribes on to a big catch-all reservation called the Indian Nation.

"Later, the Indian Nation became Oklahoma, named for the tribes cause 'okla' meant red and 'homa' meant people. I don't know whose language they chose for that. But that was when they had a bunch of problems. All these different tribes were thrown together in this big heap and no one was there to try to separate the heap or teach 'em how to learn to live together on land that couldn't provide enough for any one tribe, much less many, many tribes. Then, there was a lot of inter-marriage between tribes and that started more trouble, and then the government figured out there was oil in the lands, and they just kept on shovin' 'em off to other places.

"Anyway, what made this old farmer Sequoya so great was that he put together this bunch of languages -- like English, Greek, Latin, Hebrew -- you know, a bunch of those, and then the Cherokees had their own alphabet. They were really hot shit then because they were the only Indians able to write down their histories 'cause they were the only ones -- 'sides some Mexican tribe -- that had their own letters and their own vocabularies."

"When was that?"

"Ummm, early eighteen hundreds, I think. That's when the Tribal Council gave 'em the go-ahead for it all. Then, the whole Cherokee Nation was able to read and write and do business with the white man and start schools and all kinds of shit. They even had their own newspapers and stuff that the white man thought belonged only to them. Cool, huh?"

Dieks always said that Luke was a virtual storage shed of trivial information. In school, he damn near flunked out, but if you'd just sit and shoot the bull with him, you'd hear this whole barrage of stories that came straight out of the pages of history. But they'd always have a Saint Luke twist to them, as in "the gospel truth according to," and they might be a little inaccurate, but were memorable, and sometimes seeds for discovery.

When he started talking about the words and how different tribes had words that sounded the same, Dieks listened with great interest.

"For instance," he said, "the Cherokee word for 'bird,' which was 'sequah,' sounded like 'chocteau,' which actually meant 'agricultural or peaceful,' in the Chocteau tongue. Those, however, could hardly be confused for the Yankton Sioux word, 'zitkala-sa,' which translated to Red Bird, like the son of Chusaleta whose name was Chey Sequah Smith."

"What about 'Cooch Joe' or 'Kach Hul,' or something like that? Did you ever hear words like that?" Dieks asked, leaning closer, as if the information was privileged.

"How's it spelled?"

"C-O-J-O," Dieks said, remembering the words in the Bible.

"Naw, that's not Cherokee. It's more like Cheyenne. I think it means gimpy or limping, you know. I bet it's pronounced Coe Hoe. They had a funny way of translating things down to a gnat's ass."

But Dieks wasn't listening anymore. He began to realize that his mother's pain pills had released words that she'd kept safely hidden. He backed into the past and strained to remember the words she'd said. The history of her people, his people, was starting to take shape. It was the other side of the family that he and Lucy were never allowed to know. His mother had tried to tell him of his family.

Chey Sequah was his grandfather, then, not just any man, but his Cherokee grandfather and a farmer? Dieks' ancestors, then, were farmers from the Cherokee Nation. The one married to Lucy went by the name of "Red Bird" Smith. Together, he and Lucy had two children - Cherokee and Sequoya Chauncey, named after his great-great-grandfather Sequoya, the famous Cherokee linguist. Somehow, that didn't seem right. Convinced that educated Indians were the only hope for furthering the great nation's new notion of assimilation, Red Bird Smith had reluctantly agreed to assist the United States Census Bureau.

He had agreed to visit all known reservations and register the more than forty thousand Indian inhabitants living in the Indian territory. If done satisfactorily, all registered Indians would be allotted land, money, and compensation for tribal settlement deals. Just after the turn of the century, the new U.S. citizen, Cherokee Chey Sequah Smith, had set out to do the necessary polling for his country. He never returned.

A little over three years later, the young widow, Lucy Smith, along with her two children, was befriended by a Sioux educator. He'd come to the Indian Nation to help set up schools. He gave her a Bible and taught her to read and write the white man's English, in addition to the Cherokee that her husband had taught her. Although the Oglala teacher was known only as Roaring Cloud, and stayed ever so briefly, he left behind a sister for Cher and Sequah. Lucy named her infant daughter Sioux Ann.

In the early spring of 1909, Lucy Smith was thirty-four years old. She had three young children, no husband, and no prospects. Though well educated, she had no family or connections with the world beyond the reservations of Oklahoma. She was then introduced to John Sauts, and her world looked much different -- for a few years, anyway.

A bit of a celebrity, John Sauts was welcomed wherever he went. He was the only son of Wokinih, whose English name had also been John Sauts. The legendary Sioux brave, called Roman Nose by the soldiers, led the raid on Beecher's Island in '68 and died the day following his only son's conception.

His son was proud and handsome, but restless and sometimes lost. There were no great battles to fight, and no valiant struggles to survive, except life. Assimilation had not worked. In a world that evolved to manifest destiny and White Anglo-Saxon Protestantism, John Sauts would always be a Red Native American Naturalist. Though his ancestors emerged from the house of greatness, there would never be room for him. There was neither window of opportunity nor door of definition. In the nation's great melting pot, Indians settled at the bottom.

As others before him, Sauts came with hope and left in despair. Lucy and her children were once again alone to bear the brunt of emptiness and poverty. He also left her with what would be the most tragic chapter of her family's history -- Cheyenne Lucy, last grandchild born to the name of the great and noble warrior, Wokinih.

John Sauts left a well-built lodge that kept them from the cold with an evening fire. It had wooden furniture and real beds, a year's provisions and memories that held her family together until reality took hold and reminded Lucy that she had no one and no skills in a world that was quickly closing in on her and hers. Her once handsome face was aging, and she had no argument left when One-Who-Takes-Water came with the piece of paper that mapped for her the way to her late husband's people.

If she could move the children to that place, they might find comfort in space provided by others of the Cheyenne who had been displaced, relatives who'd found comfort in Iowa after having been long-separated from blood family.

By the summer of 1912, Lucy Fields Smith and her four children arrived in the Iowa town of Tama and proceeded to the reservation of her last known blood relatives. Though Cheyenne at heart, more Sak and Fox by blood, the distant Sauts family seemed huddled near the very center of a settlement that was dwindling and dying. At least, she thought, arriving early one morning, it would be a place where they might rest a bit. That was all it promised the weary mother and children.

It was almost twenty years before Dieks pieced together the sketchy history that culminated in maternal bloodlines. It was a proud heritage, but of little use to him. He still couldn't say the words. He never believed he was anything more than the bastard son of Richard Shaunessy, a motherless, rat-faced half-breed.

His Cheyenne grandmother and Cherokee grandfather had spent nearly twenty years on the land called the Indian Nation in Oklahoma, struggling to make ends meet. Their two children, Cherokee Lynn and Sequoya Chauncey Yellow Robe were joined by two more after Chey Sequah's death, Sioux Ann and Cheyenne Lucy. A flaw in the curious scenario was the disappearance of Chauncey Yellow Robe, shortly after Lucy had taken the children to Iowa. Also, there was a child his mother had called Coochee. He was the little wildcat the Indians nicknamed Cowacoochee.

If they'd managed to get north and east, they might have been absorbed into the cultures of the newly formed "melting-pot America." Dieks realized he might have an uncle and maybe a brother somewhere. He never knew the gamble that Lucy and Sequoya Chauncey Yellow Robe had to take. He never knew the survival of Chauncey and the child depended on escape -- to live within the law and beyond the confining walls of reservation or prison, their only hope lay to the north, in the peaceful country surrounding Pipestone in southern Minnesota.

There, the banished young brave lived in isolation, intermittently working the quarry with others of various tribes that had migrated north. When the quarry closed in off-season, Chauncey Yellow Robe worked at odd jobs for the many area farmers and Pipestone residents. For himself and his nephew, Billy, the fatherless child of Cheyenne Lucy, Sequoya Chauncey Yellow Robe made a lucrative living through a labor of love.

Though two generations removed from his namesake, the silversmith, Sequoya, and a generation removed from the blacksmith, Grandfather Chusaleta, Yellow Robe became a respected craftsman in his own right. William "Billy" Collins Cohoe attended the Pipestone Indian School by day and returned each night to his uncle's side, where he assisted him in many creations born of ancestral dreams and the malleable Catlinite.

As Lucy had promised them both, their progeny would live for all time, though she would never see their faces again. Dieks never saw the face of his brother, and his brother saw Dieks just once.

Passage

The registry at the funeral home included the name of an unknown man and his wife. It was written in the flowing scrawl of an artist with what appeared to be a deep red ink, the color of blood. No one noticed the name until long after the services. No one recognized the name as friend or relative. No one saw the man and his wife as they stood next to the open casket that morning in the funeral home.

It was the same morning that both of Dieks' lovers had visited, to assure themselves that the newly received and prepared mortal remains of Dell Collins Shaunessy were a reasonable likeness.

After they left, clearly dissatisfied with the results, the casket rested open and unattended, basking in the rising sun's rays next to the window at the east end of the room. His face bore only the slightest resemblance to the man who leaned over it, scrutinizing every inch. He'd said nothing to his companion as she'd taken one look and then slipped quietly back behind him. He'd touched the securely fastened hands once. In the center of Dieks' cupped palm, he'd slipped a piece of stone -- a small, intricately carved Catlinite turtle, to encourage regeneration and renewal in the next life that would surely be better than this. On its underside, engraved in Cherokee, were the words, "Son of Black Sky."

There, on the first page of the visitor's book, after "Nicole Griffin" on the first line, and just under "Sally Ratchford" on the second, the third line went unnoticed: "Sarah and William Collins Cohoe," the names unknown.

. . .

"What's *she* doin' here?"

I heard the words. She cupped her hand as she shouted into Sally's ear. Not so I couldn't hear, but more like an announcement designed to embarrass me. It was more like we were all eavesdropping on a very private moment between two intimate friends.

Dieks' last girlfriend turned and hugged Yuma's wife, Missy, praise of sorts for her efforts to single out any culprits hidden amongst all these old, close, wonderful friends. Equally loud, she returned with, "Jus' forget she's here, makes no difference. It'll be over real soon."

Allowing them the effect they so unsubtly sought, I drifted toward the secondary room, where there were chairs and a couch, no casket, no flowers, few mingling friends and fewer family. In fact, it appeared to be where the babies had been relegated. As I watched Chaun and Chelsea, toddling and playing, I began to wonder about bloodlines -- whether physiologically, or genetically, his grandchildren were more closely related to Dell Shaunessy than his sibling. Being analytical helped me forget the general ugliness rearing its head in the adjacent room.

So many friends roamed about with somber faces. Like zombies their eyes met, but they never really saw each other. They were lost. They'd never had to stand shoulder-to-shoulder or toe-to-toe without a drink in their hands to separate likenesses or neutralize differences. They had no intermediary to run interference for them or to keep their shallow conversation afloat, as Dieks had done for years. In short, without him, they had lost their significance to each other.

This may have been Dieks' most squeamish social situation - not only the visitation, nor the required sobriety, both literally and figuratively speaking, but the breadth of his friendships - all together in the same room at the same time. He would've been scurrying to keep the criminal element away from the aristocracy, the intellectual from the illiterate, the princes from the paupers, and so on. Each clique would be whispering, "Who were *they*? How could they have known him?"

He'd had to associate with myriad types. If he hadn't, he wouldn't have had ongoing stories to supply guests with the necessary social lifeblood of divergent conversation. After all, the guys toward the back, who built and drove custom rods or raced super modifieds, they all knew each other. In fact, they knew all the stories and lived many of them. There were no great shakes there.

The artists off to one side knew the critics at the other. The lawyers in the balcony knew the clients in the foreground; the bankers mingled with their borrowers. On and on it went, I thought. On and on. But, standing alone at the closed casket, periodically touching it and then lowering his head and shaking it in disbelief, I saw that Wade had returned, a grown man paying his respects. With hat in hand, he remembered what the others forgot, that all you have to do is show up. Mark the memory in someone else's mind, and the sorrow is sawn in half. That's what Shaunce had told him. Yep. So, he remembered.

The bikers knew the boozers, the junkies knew their users. All the women knew each other, one an ex-wife, one a lover. They said there were some that knew actually everyone. Though this one knew an aunt, and that one knew a son, the first one, or the second one, or the ones known by no one. Everyone knew someone as they entered draped in a solitary sadness and the memories descended and mingled on and on.

I glanced back at the side entrance, and inching their way up the aisle as the crowd allowed the space, a middle-aged woman maneuvered an elderly man in a wheelchair. Gold bracelets graced her wrists, gold chains draped the front of her lavender silk suit, and large diamond earrings glistened at each ear. I almost heard her words float atop the din of the crowd, rolling in from the past, "planning, scheming, and waiting, power and prestige ... " Lynn Adams, nee Canne. Her dreams presented a prosperous, wealthy nursemaid to an aged, ailing husband.

She nodded at me, resigned, tired. We knew him when, she was saying. But we're not that old, I countered. She nodded like an old woman, cautious and spent, worn out with worry by cares that shouldn't have happened yet.

From one side, someone whispers loudly, and I sense that it's aimed at me. "Why's she here? After all they went through ... "

For him.

Basically, as I'd told one of his oldest friends, Fortier, it took many years for us to get beyond the damage Dieks and I had inflicted on each other. I simply chose to block memories of him -- a steadfast refusal of any thought that included him. I knew that allowing his life's memories to taint mine was overpriced. The images and emotions that resulted would inevitably destroy any hope of becoming someone's "family" or anyone's significant other. He was entirely too selfish.

When Dieks allowed his history to become woven with other people's lives, their own needs were no longer governed by personal priorities. The tragedy of his life became so overwhelming that other people's lives vanished in the rush to accommodate his recovery. Fortunately, he didn't impart his own life stories to many people. He chose to reinvent himself with his own shredded memories, embellished with more acceptable people's families, homes and pleasantries. This was only possible through friends that simply handed over their lives by way of the congenial and intimate stories that he so loved. In order to make his own life and happiness possible, their parents, siblings, children, aunts and uncles became modified members of the family that lived in his memories. It was what allowed him to get by. Without knowing or meaning to, it became the focus and goal of those who loved him, the sacrifice of their emotional souls by sharing the insides of their lives.

This was not without manipulation on his part. He was a master manipulator. I don't know if it was an acquired skill that enabled him to survive his father, or if it came with the territory and the obscene charades at the training school. The point was, Dieks knew how to make each and every conquest believe that their health and well being, the very fabric of their lives, was his only concern. While they imparted the most intimate and intricate details, he made mental notes and stored the lines for future use.

Songs have been written singing the praises of men like Dieks. For the female populous, he was ever-available to help out "ready twenty-four hours a day," prepared to do whatever needed done. No problem was too small, no price too high if he could help in any way. They gave back their concern and gratitude in spades. From broken hearts to faulty faucets, Dieks Shaunessy was Every Woman He'd Ever Met's Handy Man. Men marveled at and took lessons from the intimate after-hours stories he reinvented and relayed for their entertainment. They stood in awe as a steady stream of women called him year after year, often showing up unannounced in the middle of the night to be serviced.

It was with particular interest that I watched such a woman, standing back, away from everyone else. She was no more than five feet tall, with glistening long, dark hair and deep sad eyes that remained riveted on the casket at the end of the aisle. In a simple, somber navy dress that appeared just-purchased, the folds draped over her soft curves and hung from shoulders that stayed straight and stiff, unmoved by breath or being, blending with the sobriety of the room, the mourners, the vacuous hearts.

If she wasn't an outcast, she was at least handicapped by someone's presence there. I realized that this slight wisp of a woman had been, or perhaps, was to the end, another of his many lovers. Further, it appeared that she was the back-door, serviceable kind, where only his closest friends might know of her existence.

Standing off to one side I saw a clone of hers, a daughter that bore a striking resemblance to both her mother and to early pictures of Dieks' mother. Petite and pristine, calmly focused, conversing almost too intensely, almost too purposefully engaged and serious, I overheard her say to my son that she is Mormon.

I heard her mention that she attended Brigham Young and planned to be married in the fall. Her fiancée is studying to be a cardiologist. All the while she's carrying on a very tempered conversation with my son, the older woman's wrist was tightly grasped by her daughter's delicate but firm fingers. Those fingers were keeping her mother from merging into the flow of people walking up to the casket. She seemed to be subconsciously adrift, magnetically drawn to the aisle and the line, while her daughter kept reeling her back.

The casket had been closed for the evening, probably the only sensible solution. Dieks was regarded as so many different things to so many people. But, now, the crowd has thinned and only the closest friends remain with the few known relatives. They have stayed to view, for one last time, his mortal remains. When they see, I thought to myself, there will be more convulsive weeping, weak knees, faint hearts and moist hankies.

My stomach was churning and queasy. I couldn't decide if I wanted to look, knowing how bad he was at the end, or if I'd just as soon remember him as he was in my mind: a sweet Delly hopelessly in love with me, or a swaggering Shaunessy, vibrant and brimming with life, or perhaps the macho Indian brave with manly offering under loin cloth, a Dieks capable of pleasures beyond the known world. Maybe I'd see him and remember him as he was when we were young, a husband struggling with concepts of marriage, spouse and partnership in something he'd never witnessed or experienced -

- a handsome lover whom I'd abandoned at the very age our own son was now.

In the end, I decided that I would have to go up and look. As I walked up the aisle, I kept assuring myself that it was right and it was proper and I was doing the right thing. He would have paid me that last respect, peering down on my face and appealing in silence to Wokinih for my soul's immortal comfort and care. He would have begged for some provisional companionship so I would not be faint of heart and lose my way on The Hanging Road. It wouldn't have been as kind as those words might suggest, but he would've done it nonetheless, if it meant assuring my passage. Having seen my face and pleaded my case, he would have appeared unmoved, solemn and dignified in front of these strangers.

With straight shoulders and pursed lips, my Dieks would have walked away from this room, from death, from this place forever. He would have retreated to the privacy of darkness, to silence and the soothing feel of the worry stone, the thumbprint sculpted from the soapy pink piece of pipestone that he kept next to his bed. Through it, he seemed to convey his wishes to those he'd never seen, in a language his people had been allowed from time immemorial. They would hear him and all would be forgiven; my soul would be comforted in the ancient shadows of their love. And then, I knew what I had to do as I walked up to the casket. No one joined me there in silence or tears.

> *I have come, Wokinih. Please, hear me now. Though I am not of you, I am of him. Please hold him in safe keeping and guide his feet along the weathered path of The Hanging Road to the heart of his mother, to her empty, aching arms. Please draw him near, with the warmth of your healing hands, for he has many wounds to mend. Please know, Kind Wokinih, I have loved him pure and true. I have only his means to reach you through the Great Bird's haze, but I beg you to hear me now, for here is one of your own. For him, I seek safe passage home in the wonder of grace and peace.*

It was the only prayer I'd ever created, or needed to. I moved quietly away from the black glare, and found myself safely deposited on the other side of the room without apparent notice.

Sally started wailing away again. I stood back a safe distance to avoid catching her malady, no matter how staged the theatrics had become. He would've been absolutely appalled to see such a public display, and equally pissed to think that it was his final parade on which she rained.

She's confused, I thought. This was not for her. This casket, these flowers, these quietly controlled and dignified tears were for him. She was a simple incidental, with no right to claim any part or parcel of the grief that friends and family felt for him. Yet, she was. That was precisely what she was doing. For nine months, she'd wandered through the moribund maze and on to death.

She should've been shell-shocked at the very least, or she might've been completely numb by now, inured by time. But she reacted like she'd been slapped, and after five drama-laden minutes; she composed herself in the side room with jolting hiccoughs and sobs, inconsolable choking tears. I was not saddened in any way by this display, but embarrassed and uncomfortable. If she were a television show, I'd change channels.

My mind raced ahead, completing the analogy. She simply couldn't have been shocked at seeing the remains of skin-draped bone; she was the second signature in the guest book. She'd come that morning to see for herself the job they'd done. So, I concluded, it was for her own benefit that she was grandstanding and upstaging a corpse. What a comment on her arid existence. He would've knocked her across the room.

I was no longer queasy, at least. I was more angrily amused. At the side of his casket and then once removed to the next room, with her performance of the Wailing Wall Aria, she demonstrated to all who knew him intimately that there was indeed a stranger among us.

At the back of the room, a hand released the wrist that had so firmly held the mother in place. "Only what you can handle. Don't do anything more than you can handle," her daughter whispered.

The mother nodded. Yes, she'd do only what she could handle, but just in case, her daughter's a few short steps behind.

The room seemed to freeze or stall in intermittent slow motion. Her arms were outstretched and her daughter's moved up quickly, but it was too late. She'd already draped over the suit coat of covered bones. She'd kissed the pumped-up cheeks, and whispered her last earthly intimacies to vacant eyes behind lashes swept gaily upward.

Her grief was genuine. It emanated from currents that pulsated with each beat of her broken heart. She couldn't help it. The weight of her despair cut a wide swath across the room, and his friends declined the offer. They could not bear witness to the uncut grief that shook every body in sight. They could not endorse her final appeal to the stranger in the casket, wearing an ill-fitting class reunion ensemble that once flattered their friend and compadre, Dieks Shaunessy.

She turned and walked down the center of the room that eerily loomed in stunned silence. There was no denying that whatever they had, or whatever she perceived they had, was significant. This last payment to him was of necessity, in spite of whatever else had since transpired between them.

"Marta, I told you no more than what you could handle," and she chided her mother who appeared to be wobbling blindly toward the side door on legs of jelly, in a sea of eggshells. She didn't quite make it. I heard a rustling and then a thud.

Marta'd almost cleared the area before her knees buckled and she began a shrinking, slow descent down the tastefully flocked wallpaper, just inside the foyer, next to the umbrellas. What began as a harmless fainting spell ended in a complex pile of twisted arms, tangled legs, a couple of purses, a collection of umbrellas and a daughter terribly embarrassed that she'd so miserably disrupted her mother's quiet collapse. The funeral director rushed to their sides, and pulled the near-weightless bodies upright, while his assistant stood ready with water.

Her eyes were glassy. She went through the motion of sipping the water, but struggled as though she's seen a ghost, or worse, as if the ghost saw her. *Mistai*, I thought, and watched in silence as the area parted while the Red Sea repaired. There was something there, I thought, something important. But I couldn't quite reach it through the static, nor the maze of fail-safe nets I'd constructed over the years. But that was precisely how I knew something significant walked out into the night with Marta. Her quiet, gentle tears tugged an ancient, heavy heartache.

. . .

There was a letter from Stein Way waiting for me when I got back, and artwork that looked like a frothy mug of beer next to it. I've just returned to my dorm at UNI. Before going up to my room on the third floor, I always stop by the pigeonholed post office boxes downstairs. Dieks writes me every night in the fall of '69. His letters are witty and animated, full of courtship ritual. No one could possibly guess that those lovely letters came from that young man working each day in Hog Kill at the John Morrell Plant in the east end of Ottumwa. No one could imagine that his mesh-gloved, bloody hands could clean up and create such eloquent love poems and notes that he mails without fail each night. They're precious lifesavers that I read and memorize, caress and cradle at my breast.

They're my sustenance. Each day, I shuffle through every piece of mail until I find the beloved handwriting, the long, elegant, left handed scrawl of a converted southpaw, with shamelessly adorned edges of scrolls and leaves, hearts and flowers. Usually, elaborate pen and ink drawings grace one whole side -- priceless works of art on a penny envelope. He always makes me smile. I admire his talents, crave his passion, and depend on his intensity to keep me alive. In his mirror, at the apartment, I am sensuous, beautiful, voluptuous and perfect in my gleaming, just-bathed skin. In my own mirror at UNI, a hundred miles away, I'm colorless and dull, incomplete somehow, as I search my image for evidence of his touch.

The old fortune teller's words rang true.

"A Scorpio, you?" with the leathery, twisted fingers pointing at my face. She smirked all-knowing, and turned her frizzled grey head to look back up to him, into his eyes, slowly moving the bent pointer his way.

"And Leo?" She threw her head back like a broken doll, cackling chills down my spine. "With him, you will soar like the eagle."

He grinned, shrugging one shoulder, closing one eye, as if to say, "What else would you expect? After all, I am Dieks."

But she turned back to me, and squinting her ancient eyes, she hissed, "Let him go and you'll be thankful to find refuge in the jagged rocks as the grey lizard."

Then, she shoved our money back to us and waved us away, laughing hoarsely. It was a simple story and took no time to tell.

With him, I'd soar in ecstasy, Liz B Shaunessy. Alone, I'd slither on my belly in the dust as the lizard.

. . .

I feel the words wend and wind their way along my trembling hands, not truly sending their intended messages. I'm reading my mail, but not really. As the words soak in, it occurs to me that he's talking about being downtown in Eldon that day, seeing Jean. As he walks across the street, he says, he pulls his hat down and stands his collar up against the wind. He scrunches his shoulders and, incognito, hurries past her.

"She's huge now," he writes, and he mentions in passing that, "she's probably due any day." It is stated with apathy. It simply is, and no further mention is warranted. A caution flag should've shot up right then and there. I should've known in that moment that I was ignoring the fact that another woman would be having his child.

But I didn't care. I saw her as the loser; I was the winner. His first wife lost; I won. It was a simple fact of victory: scores of lovers, a couple of wives, the haves and the have nots.

To the victor go the spoils. And the eagle soared.

. . .

My eyes reopened and I saw Marta and her daughter being helped into a waiting car. As they drove off into the night, I knew with certainty I was subconsciously protected from myself. From the weathered pages of a book long sealed by time, I caught a glimpse of one more moment that never should've been. Yet another set of dark eyes, watching out a window, waiting patiently, wishing against the odds that "the pull" would release him, that he would come home.

I heard her say she would've gone to Utah, too, except she had a young boy. My guess would be that this was Dieks' last. Perhaps, in a passionate moment of haste or lust, or in search of a certain, elusive love, unprotected intimacy produced yet one more child. Before herpes or AIDS caught his attention and forged the way for his bottomless condom supply, he found himself a father again. Perhaps, I thought, denying again.

But I knew. Just as I knew the day I read the letter about Jean, with his cavalier announcement that she was due. I knew. There was no drum roll or brilliant shaft of light that heralded my realization. It simply was. As all such previous revelations had been known. As Marta got into that car, I knew I was watching the mother responsible for the rearing of still another of my oldest son's half-brothers.

She was an untouchable. The caste system in Eldon, Iowa, hasn't lost its appeal in the last fifty years. There are certain undisputed ramifications for carelessness. Marta had fallen into the trap -- if a woman fails to provide protection for herself and/or her lover, that woman will invariably be responsible for the rearing of resultant illegitimate children. This will be, of course, at an automatic poverty level, since the social or economic level of the lover is of little or no relevance. He will plead ignorance of your plight. You will never again be acceptable to his cadre of friends and they will, factually and frankly, find you burdensome and embarrassing.

She obviously didn't understand Dieks' Rules of Order. His rules state that he service her with great regularity, or whenever he's in the neighborhood. They state that he treats her with total respect, or complete contempt. The rules are that she will be content to entertain him at home, or not at all, that only selective lovers meet his friends, all others get ribald stories and secondhand summaries. The loyal and loving are the first to be sacrificed. A little war-torn and ragged around the edges, my guess is that Marta spends a great deal of time at home with a little doe-eyed boy that loves her gentle hands, and her tender, soft goodnight hugs and kisses.

It was the boy that gave her hope. She expected no promises, never even considered clinging or making demands. She figured her undying love and its evidence thereof in this slight boy would be enough for him to ever and always return to her. My guess is that he probably did, sooner or later, occasionally, throughout his subsequent relationships. He simply had no sense of obligation or faithfulness, for he had absolutely nothing to base it on.

I have counted the women at the funeral home. I'm surprised that the numbers are pretty even, maybe a sixty/forty split, male and female. Not exactly to his specs, mind you, but acceptable. The interesting observation was that all his friends seemed to have their wives with them. I don't think they found it particularly strange that he never shared his name with sweet, sensuous, and shy Nicki. I'm sure they all understand why he never married the dark and brooding Sally. A limited number are called, I smile to myself; a few are truly chosen. Just call us Dieks' marines.

I'm angry at them all, but pleased that I've kept it in check. All these great close friends, yet not one or one of their wives offer to help with the babies so his son can exercise his social skills.

They really didn't want to know him, I'm finding. They won't ever remember his grandchildren. They're all as selfish as they ever were. They encouraged him to let go of his families and wives; there would be more room for them in his life. Yet, they kept their own wives and their own children. They wouldn't be buried next to an abusive father, nor would they be buried next to him.

I see them as I've always seen them -- parasites, all of them, feeding off each other, unable to focus on anything except their own needs. And now, now that the hub of their sorry existence was gone, would they band together to lick each other's wounds? Not likely. He was their best friend for thirty, forty years. Yet only one, Alan Zendegas, or The Zen Master, as Dieks had called him, understood the value of a hand extended in friendship or assistance to his sons. The rest simply couldn't grasp the importance of the notion, couldn't get beyond the vacuum of their own emptiness. Then, time was gone.

I'm almost pleased, smug that it's ending this way. Every selfish act, every hour or day that they took for themselves, they took from his sons. Every memory they've stored is a memory stolen, making it easier to shake free of him and to move on with life.

Written in Our Blood, 1991

We're at Dr. Bern's office in the Ottumwa Regional Health Center. I've brought my mother for her chemotherapy and it generally takes a few hours. I don't mind 'cause I get to sit and talk to the nurses, one I've known since high school.

Mary is telling me that she just realized who my ex-husband is.

"Yeah, my brother once bought a huge pen and ink drawing from him!"

"Really?"

"Yeah. It was one of his early works, in the sixties, maybe? Named, uh ... Pretty Baby, or Lovely Lady, or somethin' like that ... "

"Green-Eyed Lady?" I asked, knowingly.

"Yes, that's it! D'ya know it? Sounds just like a song."

"It was. I'm surprised he sold that one," I said, thinking back to the night he did it.

She's lining up tubes and vials full of all the different drugs and turns to ask, "Why's that?"

"It was mine."

"Oh."

I shifted a little nervously in my chair, wondering how I could be nonchalant about the picture.

"It was a project I needed for finals in Art Appreciation at Parsons. He was so much better at the artsy stuff, so he did it. One night, after supper, he just grabbed a piece of cheap poster board, and a black, skinny felt tip, and pulled up a chair in front of me. 'Sit still,' was all he said and then he was off.

"The only color on the whole page was the palest of green for those two spooky eyes. My eyes. By the time he was done they were eyes that could look right through you as you looked at them. He just grinned and ran out for some Envirotex, framed up the sides on a piece of paneling, and poured that stuff on 'til it was about half an inch deep. It looked layered, like some watery depths of an ocean or something.

"When it was set upright, it was heavy as hell, but gorgeous? My God, you'd thought I was a model. It was almost three-dimensional, like someone was just behind that layer of varnish and the nearly-mirrored image of scrolled, flowing locks was like one of those Medusa heads, ready to come alive, slither down, and coil around around the frame."

There, it was out. And my hand went fluttering up and back as if I just remembered it in that moment, and it was of little matter to me.

The fact was: it did matter to me. It was one of the few things I had ever agreed to pose for and of all that he'd ever created, "Green-Eyed Lady" was the only piece I'd ever wanted. Knowing that, it was the one thing he hid from me when I left.

"D'ya ever see him any more?" She's injecting something into the lines that will run through my mother's arm.

"Not much. Well, when my brother got sick, and then again, when Dad died. I saw him a bit more then. Our son graduated from high school about then, and Dieks just started easing back into his life, like he does with everybody. I guess I gave him the go-ahead, so I wouldn't say it's entirely his doing."

"You did?" Mary seemed surprised.

"I s'pose ... but it wasn't as though I could stop him. Dieks was eighteen, and the ol' boy eventually would've found him anyway. Dieks just lived down the street from Mom, and my Dieks drove down to see 'em all the time. He spent a lot o' time at his Grandma's.

"Dieks did help me out one night, though. Went out of his way to give me a hand when I really needed it. He actually rounded up Mom and Dad for me and took 'em back to his house to use his phone because theirs was out of order, and I'd been calling them for hours, trying to get in touch with them, to let them know my brother had been taken to the hospital in New York and was in bad shape, without much of a chance to make it through the night. After years of silence between us, and then, that night, when I called, he acted like we'd just talked the day before and everything was like it'd always been. I guess I sorta signed off then, let my bulldog guard down, you know, left the gates open that time."

She was fixing the tubes that ran down into Mom's arm, taping them securely in place, patting her hand every now and then to assure her, comfort her.

As I settled in next to her, ready for the hours that were before us to drip-drop away, I closed my eyes, recalling the lines of a letter I'd sent to him, shortly after the night that we'd spoken for the first time in years. Yes, I thought, I suppose I gave him the go-ahead, and, as time would tell, it was none too soon.

I formally broke my twelve-year ban on communications when I sent him the letter I wrote in blood.

February, nearing the end of the winter of our discontent, 1988

For several weeks now, I've thought a great deal about all that you haven't known regarding your son. First, let me say that fate was on your side that night last month. If I'd been able to reach any other neighbors of Mom and Dad, I wouldn't have had to contend with you. But, you came through and for that, I thank you.

Over the years, I've decided that you were your own worst enemy - though it was not entirely your fault. Without dredging up Freud and his lofty insight, I'd say you demonstrated everything as an adult that you had internalized as a child. Everyone that ever loved you was driven away as mercilessly and violently as your own father did you, and you abandoned everyone who loved you - as you thought your mother had you. If you'd ever humbled yourself to acknowledge the many acts you committed, you might have sought out sound therapy and other people wouldn't have had to pay for your tragic childhood by sacrificing their own healthy pasts. However, hindsight's 20/20 vision and you've probably had plenty of self-imposed hells to deal with, excluding, of course, my lovely armchair therapy descending on you out of the blue.

At any rate (which is what your son says when he wants to preface a break from any conversation that he's not interested in), I was forced to review the last decade or so and tried to be as unbiased as could be expected from any abuse victim. I figure that'll give me as much latitude as I need to say anything that might need to be said because I am, after all, lacking certain sensitivities that might otherwise keep me from being truly vicious.

I haven't determined yet if resentment or bitterness ever die. I've tried to make sense of it over the years and decided that it was one of those indecisions that settles scores in its own time and on its own accord. There are simply some things we are never allowed to know. Among them is how a man can fail to see what he will lose if he loses the love and faith of his children. I figure you've lost more than you'll ever regain in your lifetime. There are simply too many things that are priceless and never repeated. I will, however, share shards of information that you might find valuable over time. Small, splintered pieces of a boy's life that you chose to miss.

After we left, the most difficult period of both our lives began. I was his only constant. I was all he understood and he didn't like sharing me with anyone. He conceded to my having a husband, but he never let go of what he thought were his sole rights to my life. When his brother came along, he took him to his heart immediately. I was amazed and pleased. No jealousies ... but there were almost ten years between them. I think he just saw his brother as his baby boy.

Several years after the adoption, he finally let go of your name. It had never been an issue, but always an option. He hyphenated it for a while, as if he didn't want us to think that he'd forgotten that easily. We didn't.

He was an athlete from early on, showed real promise as a runner and, in general, was a good student. But his school conferences were things a mother's nightmares are made of. He was asocial, and very nearly without conscience where his peers were concerned. Meetings scheduled to discuss his behavior included parents, teachers, aides, psychologists, principals and the Area Fifteen Learning Specialists.

Educational Development Tests always averaged around the 95 - 97th percentile and, though he hardly worked at it, his grades in school were always good. Artistically, he's quite gifted, but he doesn't particularly enjoy the work because he's too meticulous. I have a self-portrait that he did a few years ago. I suspect you'd really enjoy it. Maybe I'd consider trading it for Green-Eyed Lady ... for a few years anyway. Maybe not.

By the time Dieks was a senior he'd pretty much abandoned sports. His grades were starting to shape up, which relieved us, knowing he'd need everything he could get to qualify for scholarships. Just when we thought he was on an even keel, he fell in love for the first time. I was a little scared. I didn't think he'd ever trust anybody enough to allow himself to love them. Or for them to love him. What I found more interesting, though, was of all the kids in his high school, he'd managed to ferret out a Cherokee maiden. I thought that would sure warm your heart. What'd you tell me? The only way we allow Indians to assimilate is to marry white culture. I don't think either one of them noticed, actually. What's more, I don't think they assimilated well either. However, he did try to smother her fierce independence, I think. Always demanding, controlling, isolating ... keeping her entirely to himself. And, she walked. Sound familiar?

As he closed in on graduation I think he came to terms with a lot of anger he'd had for as long as he could remember. Got in a fight with some kid in a parking lot and it took three guys to pull his feisty hundred and sixty pounds off the poor kid, who he beat to a pulp. Between karate, weight lifting and a hair-trigger temper, he's quick and deadly. But I don't think even he knew that 'til that night. He took his college entrance exams the next morning with an untreated broken thumb and still got scores high enough to get into Harvard.

If you think this all sounds like I'm bragging, it's because I am. He has reasonable talent and an ample amount of grey matter. He has prevailed in spite of, not because of, his noble background and persevering parentage. He managed to take all he's been dealt in life and capitalize on everything he could. His childhood was riddled with emotional inconsistency and contradiction. His adolescence was a combination of intensity, anger and curious disregard. But the man I see emerging is fast becoming impressive.

I didn't want you to know these things. I wanted you to be like Edward Everett Hale - the man without a country, forever exiled from any information about what you neglected, denied, or left behind. But, instead, I think your penalty has become this: I can tell you what you missed, how you unwittingly deprived yourself of the triumphs of his youth, and his painful understanding of people who drift in and out of his life without him realizing their impact. I can tell you and you have to try to imagine the pride you'd feel if you'd been there. I can laugh and say that you will never know the simple joy of a kid on the floor next to your bed in the middle of the night, after all the macho guys go home, telling you about everything that happened while he was out that night, reflecting on all that he'd observed and asking for your opinion on this or that, as if you knew, as if you deserved to know enough about the important things in life to tell him the answers.

My son's reason and logic are infallible. He has the strength to back his convictions and understands the value of verbal debate and the difference between disagreeing with the person and disagreeing with the belief. We are bookends, Sam says, with an unsuspecting world caught in the middle.

He is his mother's son. He has never turned away from me or from Sam, never spouted that he expected or deserved better than we've been able to provide. He's never allowed anyone to control him and I think he's inherited that trait from both directions. I never thought he'd be any different than what I encouraged. I let him go through the file boxes containing cards and letters of yours. He seemed mildly interested but wanted to know if there wasn't any more of the art you did in the early years. I mentioned Green-Eyed Lady, and how I thought one of your friends had it. He couldn't understand why I didn't have it. I thought it would be unfair to try to explain to him how important your friends were to you, more than your family, in my estimation, so I never offered an explanation. Maybe you can.

If you're interested in helping him, as Dad said you are, I'd suggest that you start slowly and walk softly. He'll watch your every move, so don't take anything for granted. If you've got the time to spend, you may be one of few he'd take to heart. To my knowledge, he trusts only me, and sometimes Sam, but even then, he's guarded.

He's very perceptive. The years have not robbed him of anything and his memory is more than just accurate, it's uncanny. He mentioned that you promised him your coin collection when he was five, and later he spoke of miniature planes in a wrought iron display case. I wasn't able to confirm or deny. But I've never questioned his memory.

Dieks is not prejudiced or bigoted in any sense. He has never hesitated to bring anyone or anything home and has never felt that he couldn't call on me to help, no matter what, nor that he should have to hide whatever he'd done, knowing some things might have adverse consequences. He's always been up front with me and I wouldn't trade any part of our mutual joys and pains for anything in this life.

I'm amused to think of the parallels we've experienced. I taught him to drive a stickshift, running along beside him, yelling when to clutch, shift, brake. Do you remember who taught me? I provided for his first all-out drunk because I didn't want it to happen some night with the guys, and someone trying to drive home. Do you remember who first got me stoned? I took him down to the dog track to teach him about betting and losing. He chose the dogs, I placed the bets, and he kept track of the money. We came out way ahead. I don't think he learned the lesson until the next day when he went back alone and lost more than he was willing to admit. One of us could never admit loss.

He knows that a house can be a home, whether $15,000 or $150,000, and that the people inside make the difference. They can wipe your tears away and blow life back into your useless heart when you think it's been reduced to ashes. They can blink away the fiercest storms. He trusts home as the place that will never turn you away, never give you reason to regret going there or being there.

He's got charisma in those hazel eyes, with that good, strong Roman nose, a nice build and more brains than most people twice his age. His potential for success is very good. I can't imagine that anything will stand in his way because he's already run roughshod over the obstacle course.

He hardly drinks, at least not to excess, because he doesn't like to relinquish control. He doesn't do drugs, even refuses aspirin as a rule. I think it's all he remembers of the problems that led to the great escape north. He's terribly vain, loves fast cars and has a healthy respect for smart women, though he doesn't let many get close enough to become attached. He knows that one-night stands can result in a death sentence, and that people can and will nonchalantly plead ignorance to exposure when they're gambling with your life. I'm proud to say that he's never been unable to keep his hormones under control.

Physically, he's in pretty good health. He outgrew asthma by eight or ten, has a dashing scar at his jawline from a run-in with a piece of concrete at about that same age, and when he was in seventh grade, he experienced a hellish hernia operation for a condition that was suspected to exist since he was a baby.

He's witty, proud, defiant, bright, challenging - all the things I'd seen in him as a child, only a little more pronounced. He's promised me he'll take care of me in my old age, and I suspect he means it. But, he's also promised me the Maserati that you wouldn't part with and a hundred other dreams I dreamt along the way. It's okay, really. It's who he is. It's too bad you never got to see his wonderful journey to manhood. It's been a real learning experience.

I'm going to send this tonight because I've got to get it out of here. If he finds it, it will disappear. I'm also sending various proofs and poses of his senior pictures. I don't know where this letter will lead. I don't know if you would find him receptive to anything you may suggest. When Dad asked him if he was going to stop by to see you he said he didn't think you'd have anything to talk about. Well, now you do. At least you have a general idea of who he is, what he likes, the twists and turns your lives have taken when you weren't looking.

There are only a few things I've wanted you to think about doing for him, or with him, before he gets too far from us in life, before the tail-end of his youth is also gone. One would be for him to at least "see" the clan and that bunch. I know you don't think very much of them, but he should at least be aware of their existence and know why you feel the way you do. I don't think it's my place to take liberty with what I remember as your disdain. More importantly, I would like to see if someone could arrange an introduction - to his half brother, at least. They should be able to recognize each other on the street, exchange cards at Christmas, etc.

I hope that, whatever you decide, you act in his best interest. I am trusting that this will be your guide. Please try to keep this, and any other information I've provided, confidential. Trust is hard to come by and in this world of mine, a son's trust and unconditional love is paramount.

Ever and always, Liz B

"Isn't he married?"

"Who?"

"Who d'ya think?" Mary has her back turned to me, but I see that she's attended to another chemo patient while I've been daydreaming, and she's running full tilt, drip-drop right next to Mom.

"Dieks? Yeah, no. My son is. His dad isn't."

"Wasn't he married to Amanda Dawson?"

"Mandy? Yeah. For a while," I said. "But he's been involved with Nicki Griffin for nearly ten years. She's really nice, but I think she's a lot younger than he is."

"That long?" She seems surprised.

"Oh, I'm sure. At least that long. She's a nurse over at Deere's. I'm sure her steady income and attention keep him hoppin'."

"I know her. But, that surprises me. I mean, well, you know, some time back I was over at Keri Conner's visiting, well, she used to be Conner, anyway, she married the mayor. And, I was over at her house, and she started talking about a guy named Dell Shaunessy."

"Anybody that'd call 'im that doesn't know 'im very well ... "

"Anyway," Mary's fanning her hand at me to quiet down so she can tell me this story before she forgets. "She just kept going on and on about 'He said this,' and, 'He said that,' and I started thinking maybe she had something going with him on the side, y'know. Nobody ever sees this guy she married, and she's raising his daughter from a previous marriage, but it doesn't seem quite right. Y'know? I mean it kinda sounds like she's found somebody who makes time for her."

"Oh, yeah, Ever-ready Dieks, your local handy man. You know, it's funny that you'd mention that. One night, just last year, in fact, I was in town for a few days and just happened to bump into good ol' Dieks and he started talking about Keri, out of the blue. Only, what he was asking me was if I knew anyone who might've said anything about females in this area who might be lesbian or bi."

"No!" Mary's eyes open wide.

"Really! I mean, it's nothin' to me one way or the other. People's sex lives are certainly their own business. Jesus, if I learned nothing else in New York, I learned that. But, it seems that Dieks'd been seeing Keri. She was over at his house for a little while and then jumped up, saying she'd forgotten that she was s'pose to meet 'a friend.' If he were going to be home in a couple of hours, though, she'd stop back by.

"Well, he's telling me all this, which is news of the strange to start with, like I'm supposed to care who he's wooing and doing, when I realize that he means he's not just been running around with Keri, but that he's been going to bed with her. But as he's talking he begins to get really indignant when it occurs to him that she's probably bisexual."

"What? No!" Mary's eyes are saucer wide.

"No, really, listen. He says she comes back a couple hours later. Her hair's all messed up. Her face is flushed, she smells sweet and sweaty and her clothes are all wrinkled. He asked her where she'd been and she says Adele's. Adele had some 'gifts' for her.

"Then Dieks asked me what kind of 'gift' I can think of that would result in being all wrinkled and sweaty.

"And I told him, 'A female wrestler.' He wasn't amused. He was sure he was vying for affections with a woman, and I just howled. I told him he'd better brace himself for some real competition now. He wouldn't know whether to shit or go blind! After all, she's married to the mayor, his third marriage, her first. She's raising his grade school-age daughter, but he hasn't got the time of day for her, or them. She gets her grins and giggles in the east end with some female, and then out on the hill with some guy, and Dieks's upset that he doesn't have dibs on her body while, at the same time, he's supposedly seeing the same woman for ten years? C'mon now. Somebody's really screwed. No pun intended, of course."

I laughed a little and kept going with such a good audience.

"Is that town too much, or what? Now, let's take this a step further. He's telling this whole story, whining and complaining to, of all people, the second of his several ex-wives, and I'm supposed to sympathize because, because, I don' know why, just that I am."

"Oh, Libby," my mother said, half-groggy, with the chemo dripping into her veins. "You shouldn't be so hard on Delly. You know he's had a pretty rough life."

"Yeah, and I know I had a pretty rough life because of the very antics he's practicing now. Talk about people who just don't get it."

Mary's smiling, patting Mom's arm, calming what she fears to be my mother's distress.

"I think he got plenty," her assistant said, as she slams shut another drawer where she's replacing patient files.

"That's only Mom's opinion, and she always took his side. With 'Poor Delly this and Poor Delly that.' Poor ol' Dieks has brought more misery to more women than any of us could possibly count. He just couldn't figure out how to keep his proud personal parts in his pants. He was *so* proud … "

"How proud was he?" Mary, my mother and her assistant all chimed in together.

"So proud that he felt a compelling need to share them with a limited number of the female population, limited, that is, to all females between the ages of fifteen to fifty, anyway."

My mother's smiling slightly, with her eyes closed. Mary's laughing hard.

"I'm serious!"

"Oh no, you're not," Mom says dreamily, from wherever she's floating a mind's world away. "You're jealous."

"Oh, right. I'm jealous. I just forgot for, oh, all these years I've been off in the Crusades tending to this other life! But I'm back, by God! And," I announced, standing, "it's all clear to me now!" My arms go straight up to signal a touchdown's been made.

Mary's holding her sides. Mom's closed her eyes again, and I'm posed for a picture with mouth and eyes wide open in mock amazement.

I'm smiling, remembering, and then I return to the moment. How dare Dieks Shaunessy up and die in the middle of my amusement.

Doin' Hard Time

"They done lost 'im in the helicopter on the way to Iowa City," she was whispering. "But theys brung 'im back. We comed as fast as we could, but there just weren't much we cou'do. They gived 'im a sedative, but he jus' keeped tellin' 'em, over 'n over, 'Take the ice pick out of my head. If y'all just look, you'll see there's an ice pick here, in my head,' and he'd turn to show 'em. Somethin' he was afeelin' was causin' a terrible fierce pain ... "

Like a metal spike driven into his skull? I knew that feeling.

When we were finally admitted into the Intensive Care Unit at University Hospitals, Dieks lay comatose, under the constant vigilance of staff, hooked up to every imaginable machine. His head was swollen the size of a pumpkin and wrapped like a swami. It was probably the same as his old friend, Butch, the oldest of the Baker brothers, just after the motorcycle wreck that eventually took his life.

As I stood there, realizing how helpless we all were, I couldn't help but remember how Butch's family had said that Dieks was the only person who stayed at Butch's bedside around the clock for six days. He was waiting for the moment when Butch would open his eyes in search of a familiar face. Dieks thought his best friend's face would be as familiar as anybody could get.

But Butch never came to. Dieks said the machines breathed for him, and Butch's eyes bulged like a bullfrog. Yet he stayed, waiting to be recognized, up until the very minute that they "humanely pulled the plug."

He repeated that phrase with every painful memory of the moment. "Humanely pulled the plug," became a catch-all phrase I'd learned not to trust. Mostly I remembered that he'd always wished himself braver or stronger so he could have "humanely" smothered the indignity and futility of life's struggle from his best friend's surviving soul.

I looked at Dieks with a strange detachment. Though now a paleface like me, I knew the contours of his face, the ridges of his knuckles, the muscles in his chest, as familiar as ever. Yet, as surely as I knew the father of my son, in that moment I also knew an intimate emptiness that settles in when hope dies and strings that bind hearts are severed.

I walked out as they all murmured in whispers full of hope and positive reinforcement. I glanced at my son, and he looked straight through me with anguished eyes. Words left unsaid filled our heads with a strange, old familiar finality.

We left late that first night, while the others took their bedside vigil in the visitor's area, pushing chairs together for makeshift beds. I went back with my son to the crowded two-bedroom apartment at Hawkeye Court, just off the Iowa City campus.

We recapped for Debby our observations, refusing to say the obvious: there would be no recovery of the man as we'd known him. I slept in restless discomfort on the daybed, with intermittent dreams and nightmares, wading through the murky waters of my consciousness in hip boots, fly casting for pleasantries, reeling in memories that dared me to deny them, begged me to change them. I thought I could simply watch as a sentry, but soon found I could not turn away.

Visions unfolded before me, snippets of life, then and now. Fast-forward, then fast-fading. Silent, then crashing down with echoed reverberations of images resurfacing, rising to remembrance after being held captive for years.

One minute, I'd be smiling, lying next to him on a blanket in a thicket, just off the ol' river road. I could hear cars going by up in the gravel, and tractors in nearby fields. But he ignored all the sounds and continued to lightly trace my eyebrows and lips, then circled my breasts with his forefinger. He would tease me with his own want, pushing next to me, running his hand up the inside of my thigh, across the flat plateau of stomach. I would smile and float to dizzying heights of expectation, begging, pulling him down into me …

Then, just as the dream had come without invitation, a nightmare would rise before me in a dark, conspicuous cloud as a spectre in billowing robes stood amidst a threatening tempest. Rumbling and roaring, deafening and relentless, I would be flying, breathlessly grasping, grabbing the air, hoping to catch something to keep me from crashing, while I cradled my swollen belly, protecting the child to come. Stumbling and falling into a heap, I'd huddle in my own fetal shell shape, where the inevitable blows would rain down on me and mine. There in the darkness and shadows, in the home of the damned, the bedroom loomed before me, bearing witness to yet another generation of distorted love and disillusion.

Rising like an airy apparition after the pummeling had stopped, rising like Rapunzel lifted by my hair and then down to rest ever so gently, he would mold his front to my back. There, he would reach over my side and tenderly cradle our unborn child, who squirmed and seemed to question my discontent. It was his father's hand that soothed and calmed him, stroking the child back to rest.

With eyes wide open and lost in the nightmare, I found myself stroking his bare chest and belly, to the horror, I think, of his nephew and some nameless girlfriend. I had not seen them there; I was not there. I was twenty years behind them and the confusion, where darkness melded days with nights and years. But the child had become the man who became the child, with the deep brown eyes that danced with the beauty of love, then flashed with the horror of violence and hate. He gritted his teeth and shuddered through seizures like the hounds from hell inhabited him and the blood from my heart trickled from his lips.

Days jumped around. I tossed and turned and when the mourning doves began their songs, I felt I'd never slept. Exhausted, with deep circles under my eyes, I looked in the mirror and was startled by the hard twenty years that looked back.

It could've been in the house of hell, I thought. It could just as easily have been a night where I'd wake and find the world's weight on my shoulders. If I closed my eyes again, I was sure I'd open them to an old man shuffling through the living room with his snuff in one hand and tomato juice in the other. I would just lay and wait, I thought, keeping my eyes open just in case, and I might catch him, pulling back the curtain to verify that we were there, sleeping intertwined.

I was shaking my head, refusing again the intruding thoughts, the things that tried to trick me after I'd so cleanly abandoned them. I could feel myself slipping. I sensed danger I'd once escaped and knew it was moving in, relentless.

. . .

He was seventy-two years old the first time I saw him. The ragged brocade drapery, that divided a threadbare stretch of living room and front bedroom in Harrow's Branch, was pinned back by his gnarled, arthritic fingers. An ancient, haggard, sagging face hung behind wire glasses, mounted, it seemed, atop a gray work shirt with matching pants that leaned perfectly still against the dark, oak-framed doorway. Pretending to sleep, I kept my eyes mostly closed, watching him watching me.

The drapery appeared rotted with time, blackened by coal dust. It seemed unlikely that Richard Shaunessy had ever cleaned or replaced it in the thirty years since Cheyenne hung it there, creating a bedroom for Little Lucy from a front parlor. With no storm windows and only rolldown shades behind thin plastic curtains, gusts of mid-winter winds roared through cracks in the panes and around the sills. From the steel pipe on which they hung, the heavy drapes swayed unfettered, creating a howling, surreal room with weaving walls, and the chalky face of a ghost that appeared and disappeared with curious regularity.

Just two months before, after running out of benefits from John Morrell and unemployment pay, Dieks had decided that we'd head to Arizona, where he had friends and heard there was work. After thoroughly going through the apartment on Stein Way, we took only toiletries, our clothes and the barest essentials, packing them in a rust-colored '65 Nova, leaving everything else to the landlord and next tenant. It was just before Christmas, 1969.

Though five months pregnant, I barely showed and felt little discomfort traveling. We had only the last unemployment check to finance our journey, so Dieks insisted we get a cooler and buy food at the local A & P before we left. From Iowa to Arizona, we lived on bread, cold cuts, cheese, crackers, fruit, milk and juices. It was the first and only time I ever saw him go without beer.

To our young, optimistic surprise, Arizona turned out to be no better than home. It was not the land of Oz, but a retirement state where people went when they had money, not when they needed it. Job openings at the employment office and those listed in the paper were divided into three categories: household help, day labor, and college graduates. There was no in-between. Week by week and ad by ad, hope faded and reality set in.

Dieks never located his friends, Suzi and The Zen, and never even looked for a job, much less found one. Each day, the employment office sent me to yet another outlying area of Phoenix, as a temp with secretarial, receptionist, and customer service skills. After several weeks, I held the last and longest position of the most mindless, menial work I'd ever known - as an assistant to a travel agent for two whole weeks! In the laundry room of her home, I was equipped with a card table and folding chair, a nightstand lamp, a manual typewriter, a rolodex and a phonebook. Throughout each day, the washer and dryer ran full tilt.

For eight hours, every day, I typed and retyped card after card, incorporating penciled notations onto newer, larger rolodex cards. I looked up addresses and phone numbers, correcting them where necessary and noting who went where, transferring the information of how much they'd spent on their previous trips with her, and what they'd mentioned being interested in seeing while they were on other excursions.

There was no phone. No one came in except for the maid, who moved dirty laundry into the washer, wet clothes to the dryer, and dried clothes to the waiting baskets to be folded. I envied her freedom of movement, as I had no contact with anyone and nowhere to go. In a half an hour at noon, I ate my sandwich, drank my lukewarm milk, and used the open toilet in the corner of the room. My only escape rested with thoughts of what my mother had always told me -- you can endure just about anything if you know when it will end.

After dropping me off for the day, Dieks would return to the grim, one-room motel we shared with the world's largest known cockroaches. There, he'd lay in bed for the duration of the morning, wait for the racetrack down the street to open at noon, get up, walk two blocks, spend the rest of the afternoon watching the dogs run, and leave at closing.

At six o'clock, he'd pick me up. We'd go back to our barren room, have a cold cut sandwich, fruit, chips, and a glass of milk. We'd lie in bed 'til dark, make wild and passionate love like we had a future, then drop off to sleep in the flotsam bed, content to become flotsam beings. For nearly six weeks, that was our life.

On the last day of the second week I worked, the travel agent came in with my check. She asked if I might be interested in taking one of the puppies her dog had just weaned. Leading me through the kitchen, she opened the door to the garage full of yipping, yapping, scampering puppies. If no one took them, she said, they'd all go to the pound for extermination.

I just couldn't see how we could manage a puppy when we could hardly get by ourselves. Then I saw Yuri. He was the runt of the litter, wedged up against a wall, acting like he hoped none of them noticed him there. When Dieks came to get me that day, I had a tiny black lab/German shepherd pup in my cotton lunch bag. He threw a hissy fit, saying we couldn't afford to feed ourselves, and we sure as hell couldn't afford to feed a puppy. He'd never be able to make it back to Iowa without pissin' up the car; he'd whine and cry all night, and we'd get even less sleep than we had. I didn't say anything. I named him Yuri, shared my food with him, and cradled him when he whimpered. He was just a baby, so timid that he rarely made any noise, and Dieks' great reluctance gave way to eventual amusement as Yuri proved a welcome distraction.

When I'd shown Dieks my check for almost four hundred dollars, he was so disgusted that he said we'd just have to head back home. But not before seeing a little of Mexico, he added. It would be a shame not to, since we were so close to the border and we'd probably never get the chance again.

"After all," and he winked, "we're sorta on vacation, and we do have a little money, honey."

He had every reason and excuse to back up his charm, but it really didn't matter to me. I trusted him and went along with whatever he wanted. That next morning, we headed south, through the arid lands and dusty roads of New Mexico, down to the border at Nogales. Of the nearly three hundred dollars we had left, we spent over two hundred in Mexico, on mementos he said we'd cherish in years to come: an ugly, two-foot-tall, hollowed-out, gold, plaster-cast owl that he used later to store dope and money in; an onyx chess set that was missing a Bishop, but we never knew how to play anyway, so it didn't make much difference; some fringed cowboy boots that turned out to be ideal for kicking me senseless, and a wooden music box that played *Lara's Theme* from *Dr. Zhivago*. Such are the things memories are made of when you honeymoon in Mexico.

Through the poverty-ridden streets of Nogales, in every store, at every stand, the little black puppy snuggled and burrowed deeper into my carryall. By sunset, we left the border town with our purchases stuffed into every available inch of space in the Nova. Yuri slept soundly under my seat as Dieks drove. He took his breaks when we took ours, ate when we ate, and made so little noise that we nearly forgot he was there, from town to town and state to state.

We'd been on the road for nearly thirty hours, driving straight through from Mexico. Exhausted and discouraged, with less than fifty dollars between us and vagrancy, we went straight to Eldon. After spending weeks looking for jobs that didn't exist, fighting to make ends meet with a pittance they called wages, we returned to Iowa in need of room to breathe and time to think. Where we'd go and how we'd live once we got there was completely up in the air. If we could get to Richard's, where a night's stay wouldn't cost a dime, we could get our bearings and think.

...

The night's stay became a week. The week, a month. Depression descended on us like the soot-filled draperies that separated our despair from the old man's. From the morning I first saw the face watching us as we slept, to the day I left, no one ever could've convinced me that one person or one place could have had such a profoundly destructive influence on the lives of two people.

We ceased to be the combined force we'd become when we married. The man who left the Harrow's Branch house each day was a stranger, pulling away from the drive in the slow motion of a murky dream, and staying away as if a great wall had been constructed around me. He was at Baker's garage by noon each day and returned late at night, or early in the morning. As often as not, drunk and incoherent, someone would get him as far the front porch, where the door would open and I'd hear him drop to the floor like a sack of potatoes. He'd lie there 'til morning, where I'd find him curled up with the dog, before dragging himself into bed where he stayed 'til noon.

By February, I was huge, looking very pregnant at a hundred and forty pounds. The lonely days were nearly unbearable and I spent most of my time sleeping, just trying to get to the end. With big red X's on the Williams Drug calendar that hung in the bathroom, I marked the passing of each day. But it didn't seem to help. The loving warmth and comfort I'd once known and depended on was moving further and further away until, at last, the still of one night was broken with the beginning of our own chapter of violence.

...

My company for the length of each day was a playful puppy and an old man who sat with a stagnant stare and contemptuous sneer whenever Dieks walked out the door. Vengeance and spite seemed to define his days. With each week we spent at Harrow's Branch, I understood more and more about the hell of growing up in his presence.

Like clockwork, Richard's drinking began at noon after a light lunch and his heart pills. Just as he kept track of the number of pills taken and left, he kept a mental check of the Irish Rose. By early evening, he was belligerent and cruel, when he wasn't being lewd or suggestive. He used the phone as a tool to harass neighbors and relatives alike, and as often as not, they listened only long enough to identify him, then hung up.

When I complained to Dieks, he just shrugged, like he expected it and I could live with it. In retrospect, it was a series of events within the space of a week that marked the start of our eventual, irreversible separate lives. On one day, Yuri was hit by a car and died. A few days later, in the early morning, Dieks came home horribly drunk and unexpectedly exploded into violence. It was my first experience with being abused, and I was mortified. I had never seen or known anything like it in my entire life. After we'd smoothed over the incident and he told me how he was suffocating with nothing to do, nowhere to go and no way to help, I tried forgetting the incident, blaming tension and despair. But it never, ever went away.

Within days, he came home and informed me he was leaving with Reddick for Sterling, Illinois. With no money and no hope, he said it could only get worse, and he didn't know what would happen if he had to spend another month under Richard's stare. It was late February and the baby was close, but he never mentioned it. He packed his bags and without further discussion, just walked out the door.

I watched as they pulled out of the drive in Red's 'Vette, trying hard to believe that a job was the reason he was leaving. I was sure he'd come back to me the man I knew and loved. It was the last thing I ever remembered thinking with certainty.

...

Biting winds flapping loose plastic, the bedroom curtains shuddered throughout the night, with a chill that served as a constant reminder of where I slept. The first of a series of nightmares forced me to fight the urge to run, to remember each day what my mother had said about the virtue of perseverance. But each day the mailbox was empty, and I tried to assure myself that he was putting in long hours and had no time. Loneliness was a little better than starving, but not much. Neither food, money, nor Dell Collins Shaunessy came to my rescue as I waded through the endless days.

Richard sat each day in an old grey rocker Dieks had bought for him at a used furniture store. The once clean, well-worn upholstery on the arms was slick and black with oil from his basement shop, where he worked from time to time sharpening mower blades and rewiring power tools. The whiskey spills that ran down his arms contributed to the grime, as did the sputtered chewing tobacco, but he didn't care, never seemed to notice. He sat directly across from the TV, six feet away, and stared at game shows and soaps from early in the morning 'til late in the afternoon. With the exception of lunch, pills, and the whiskey ritual, he glanced away only long enough to spit with negligible accuracy into a rusty, filthy coffee can on the floor next to the couch beside him.

I felt as large as a whale. My breasts were like cantaloupes, my stomach a watermelon. I became my own tabletop as I sat eating dinner with my plate perched two inches in front of my mouth, on the massive mound that my stomach had become. Though I barely fit behind the wheel of the Nova, I'd sometimes escape by way of the ol' river road to Ottumwa, risking the chance of unexpected labor pains for the pleasure of a store clerk's voice, or a waitress in the Koffee Kup, or someone, anyone who didn't say "huh?" to my every third word and didn't splatter my shirt with tobacco juice, or mumble about my waddling caboose whenever I passed through the house.

I was eighteen and confident that, come hell or high water, the power of love would prevail. No one had ever told me about mental illness, the far-reaching effects of child abuse, or how cycles of madness seem to spiral through families, generation after generation. I knew nothing of alcohol and drug abuse, and was so naive that I thought only abusers suffered from the effects. No one ever warned me about uncontrollably violent people and how others usually refuse to become involved, how they'll look away, embarrassed, when they suspect it. It would be years before I fully recognized that loving someone from such a family meant a lifetime of pain, solitude, humiliation, denial, fear and defeat. Reality would always be distorted and sanity would always be compromised for the greater good and in the noble name of love.

Within a few short years, the discipline of detachment and denial became an art form. The sweetest memories could be suffocated in seconds by an irrepressible sequence of powerful, violent visions that interrupted and overrode any thought. The handsome man withering away in one hospital after another had already died a thousand deaths in my mind. This was simple ceremony. A late formality.

Like Red was so quick to point out, Richard never let the public see the monster that ruled in malicious mayhem. Neither did Dieks. The old man assumed the role of master instructor, and his lessons were undeniably effective and unalterably internalized. Dieks' violence was almost completely reserved for those to whom he professed the greatest love. Like a child without chances who returned seeking unlikely compassion or a tender word, the abused was expected to be available at beck and call, understanding and forgiving without fail.

The soft-spoken gentleman, kind-hearted neighbor, helpful friend, and loving husband his bedside visitors spoke of were all lost in the great escape I'd come to know as life on the other side.

What God Knew

"They probably pull over out of respect. I mean they're probably supposed to pull over," my son said quietly in observation, to no one in particular.

"People don't pull over for funeral processions, especially when they're not in the way, or not headed in the same direction. My guess would be they're checking out the company we're keeping," I said, as I adjusted my rear-view mirror to get a better look at the mile of cars that crawled along behind us.

There was a candy-apple-red roadster a dozen cars back, followed by a bumblebee black and yellow sedan, and a brilliant orange street rod about twenty cars behind that. I couldn't see much further than that, with the roller coaster hills and sharp turns on the old, narrow road. But in my mirror, I couldn't miss the somber headlights of every car, from Cadillacs to Cavaliers at every bend and hilltop, to Volvos and Volkswagens emerging from the low points, all crawling along in doleful compliance, with almost shameful complacence.

"I don't agree with the guy who did the eulogy, by the way," I said. "Dieks wouldn't have been surprised by the standing-room-only crowd at the funeral home. He would've expected it. What's more, he probably would've asked where 'So and So' was, or 'Didn't anyone mention this gig to someone else?' Or, 'Oh, wasn't there Some Obscure Person down the street that should be here, and hadn't someone better give 'em a call.' He would've read each and every card on each and every floral arrangement. Then he probably would've stepped back ever-so-gentlemanly to think about it for a while, with his chin resting on his closed fist, and his elbow perched on the wrist that rested at his beltline. He'd have stood there looking serious and pensive, trying to figure out if orders, net worth and degree of concern were proportionate, appropriate or something along those lines, anyway. *You* didn't get all your analytical skills at school, you know."

I looked over at my son. He was purposefully looking away from me, out the side window, but couldn't avoid wiping a tear away with the back of his hand as it raced down his cheek. "He had a really rough life … poor guy."

"He grew beyond it near the end, I think." But my heart wasn't feeling it. The statement was flat, without conviction.

David Alan Coe's on my tape player: *"So take my ashes to St. Louie. Drop 'em in the Mississippi where the current's strong. I wanna flow back through the Southland one more time. I wanna know I'm goin' home … "*

Dieks hit the eject button and said nothing as we rattled slowly across the tracks, passing a mauve mini-van pulled over to the side of the road. It came to rest opposite the parking on what remains of Richard's lot, next to the tracks that run the length of Harrow's Branch. All that was left sat at the west edge of the lot line, as forlorn as the memories of their pitiful lives: the original story-and-a-half storage shed, an old garage originally built to house the new Model A Ford. The boards no longer had any discernible color, and bore only the slightest resemblance to something that might've had purpose originally. The once smartly-designed, four-pane windows were boarded up and the doors were padlocked, protecting the sanctity of dirt floors and cobwebs. The building leaned just a little bit to the east, but steadfastly refused to fall. The walls stood in defiance, I believe, shored with the memory of the hours one small boy spent huddled in the safety of their silent darkness, praying for his mother, or anyone who might care, to come back.

The painted curb number was no longer visible. No one could read the address if they'd want to send their condolences. But anyone who'd ever known the occupants would never forget who'd lived there.

History is fraught with tales that defy anyone to forget. Ghosts of the terrors linger in the ancient blades of grass, with their lithe bodies praying as they sway in the breeze. They've been there since time began. They'll be there long after we've all turned to dust, singing the sorrows of Cheyenne's children.

The rattle on the rails at night called her name. I never heard it personally, but Dieks swore that it was so. It was a like a howl, he said. In the still of the night. The train would rumble in and the steel whine on the tracks would slither through his sleep, and screams of, "Mama, Mama, Mama," would echo with every uneven tie. The words jumped and jerked, jolting him upright in bed as it howled along, all the way down the line, and on out of town. Every night as the train faded away, he lay alone, trying to remember her soft hands, her quiet brown eyes and the voice that soothed his aching heart. But the years took away the warmth, and the memories left, in a lifetime of aching emptiness where mother-love had been.

There, somewhere on the west side of that track, buried deep in a hillock, lays the rusted remains of a machine gun. To a passerby, it would never have been suspect. To the Shaunessy family, it was known purely and truly as "What God knows." Richard claimed it was a leftover from the cleaning and oiling a nameless master machinist performed for a couple of anonymous thugs. He'd said he'd met 'em when he was bootleggin' and gun-runnin' out of Chicago, but he'd always look away quickly, as if his eyes might betray whatever else he knew. It didn't matter. We'd heard it so often, and we knew them anyway. Or so we thought.

In the top center drawer of the old dining room bureau, there was a scuff-cornered cigar box with dog-eared treasures of bygone days. Though no one was allowed to touch it, we rifled though it with great regularity, just to let him know that nothing he hid was any more sacred than what he went through of ours when we were gone.

If stain and grime were any indication of what he held most dear, then the time-yellowed clipping from the *Chicago Tribune*, describing the gruesome aftermath of the St. Valentine's Day Massacre, was surely worth a king's ransom. When he first told me of it, holding it up like a fine jewel, I laughed, and his eyes ignited with evil, and he continued to glare at me until the laughter subsided. But he never elaborated, wouldn't ever defend any of his statements. He simply said that late one night, shortly after he'd received the clipping in the mail, he went out to the side yard and down the embankment where he proceeded to dig a deep hole on the incline. There he buried the gun "they'd" left behind -- the one meant to be cleaned, oiled and repaired by the time "they" returned. But there were no survivors, and the sole evidence of responsibility rested with the missing piece.

"Rusted to hell and back by now," he'd mumble as he spit a wad of chaw. "Just enough left to know what it was," he'd add, smirking at the evil of his secret.

He'd shuffle through the newsprint and pictures, holding each one just inches from his aged eyes. Invariably, the one he'd single out was of an evil-eyed young man, with pinstripes and spats, standing with one foot up, resting on the running board of a Stutz Bearcat.

"And what'd'ya s'pose that is, Miss Know-It-All? A Stutz Bearcat I bought from a very good friend," and he stuffed the next wad of Skoal into his lower lip. "A good friend, Miss Know-It-All. That ol' car's probably worth the likes of you and me and all we own by now. But I couldn't keep it, no sireee! That's just what God knows.

"More attention'n I needed with a half-breed looker ahangin' on my arm and always abawlin' 'bout not havin' no rug rats. That's fer damn sure, I tell ya. Just wanted out, I told 'em, just out for good. And they said, 'Nobody gets out. Not alive, anyway.'"

He shook a palsied, arthritic finger at me. It quivered and quaked as clearly as if he were with me in the car. "And, God damn it!" His head flipped back quickly, then sharply forth, but I couldn't tell if it was fear, emphasis, or weakness. "He came to town. They never saw the likes of him before. Nobody. Nobody since.

"He said, 'Ya done good work, J. Richard.' Always called me that. Like I was Hoover or something,' and he was proud to be ablasphemin' him. 'Kept yer mouth shut, J. Richard.' And, God damn it, he reached out and shook my hand, and said, 'Our business is done.'"

Once he'd get through episodes like that, when he'd rattle all around about knowing Capone, running whiskey for him through Prohibition or threatening us with looking up a couple of his "old friends," he'd get completely exhausted and just check out. He may have been passed out, or just dozing, but I always felt at least part of it was fright. Not so much of what was, but what might have been.

Running the full length of both our bedroom and his, from east to west, was a shared dressing room-type closet. One day, when I'd become overtly bold and took on cleaning out the remains of rotted clothes and old books, I found a paper in the breast pocket of one of his antiquated zoot suits. I can't remember the amount, but I do remember that the oversized business check I found was written on a Chicago bank, that it was to J. Richard "Dick" Shaunessy, and the return address was a Cicero post office box. It was for "services" and was dated, February 1929.

I set it aside at the edge of the dresser and continued cleaning through books, boxes, and rotted remains of coats and dresses, until

I finally made it to the back of the closet. I finished the bottom part, thinking that the next day I'd take on the shelving that ran across the top, and with the exception of multiple bathroom breaks, I worked well into the night. Filthy and exhausted, I showered and dropped into bed. Dieks showed up several hours later.

The next morning, as I finished my toast and coffee, I remembered the check. I shuffled through the dining room and the living room, careful to tiptoe as I slipped around the corner into the bedroom. As I stood next to where I'd left it on the dresser, I realized the drapes had been moved across the rod, leaving just enough space for someone to enter the room and leave without having to slide the metal rings against the metal rod and chance waking Dieks.

I turned to glance down at the dresser and knew, in that instant, the paper would be gone. I wasn't mistaken. Worn, warped veneer and rings from drink glasses without coasters uglied the surface. The check was gone. I dropped down to my hands and knees to search the floor and saw a pair of corduroy navy bedroom slippers, standing ever so still, just on the other side of the draped doorway that separated bedroom from living room.

I reached over and yanked the heavy drape back, startling him. He quickly regained his composure, backing up quickly and shuffling over to the old grey rocker where he promptly turned and sat down, feigning great interest in the TV program that was turned down too low for even hearing people.

"What's going on?"

My heart jumped, and I turned on my knees to a position that was eye-level with Dieks where he lay on his side, watching me from the bed. I stood up and yanked the drape back over to the side of the doorframe and moved back into the bedroom, away from Richard's eyes. I sat down on the bed and crossed my arms, frustrated and angry.

"He gives me the creeps," I whispered.

"So, what else is new?"

"I found something yesterday. And he *stole* it."

"What'd you find?"

"A check. While I was cleaning the closet."

"What kind of check?"

"A check check. You know, a check for money for "services" from some place near Chicago," I answered.

"His check, then."

"But he didn't even know it was there!"

"Don't bet on it."

"Dieks, it was written in nineteen twenty-nine," I said, turning around to face him where he lay immobile, with his eyes closed.

"But it was still his check."

"But I found it."

"It wasn't lost."

"How d'you know?"

"I know the ol' man."

He rolled over onto his back, clasping his hands across his chest. "He's got things that mean somethin' t'him. Nobody else gives a shit one way or t'other. But just 'cause he don' have 'em out, or show 'em off, it don' mean he don' know they're still hangin' 'round."

"Well, you should get to the bottom of this! If I worked all day in that filthy closet, tryin' to clear some space for our clothes so the baby'll have a little room. The very least he could do is leave things alone when I finally get 'em sorted.

As I stormed through the drape, I heard Dieks sigh, "*His things.*"

I marched out to the kitchen where Richard was counting various heart and blood pressure pills as they spilled across the table. He looked at me out of the corner of his eye, but pretended not to see me as I stomped up next to him.

"So, where's it at?" I demanded.

"Don' know what yer talkin' 'bout," he mumbled and threw his head back with a swig of a water and a couple of pills.

"You do too!" I yelled.

He threw his head back again while another handful of pills was chased down by a juice-glass full of water.

"A check ... I found a check yesterday while cleaning the closet. The check was written on a Chicago bank, dated nineteen twenty-nine, right about the time of your famous St. Valentine's Day Massacre. It was written to you for 'services rendered,' whatever that means.

"You brag and brag about what you did, where you went and who you were, who you knew, and when it comes time to own up to it, to own up to anything, for Chrissakes, you slink into hiding, like some snake slitherin' down a hole. So now, Mr. Big Shot, where did it go?"

He's looking at me out the corner of his eye again, pretending not to see me there at all. "Din't see no check. You musta bin seein' things, bein' in yer condition and all."

"Why don't you just say it? What's so hot about a check that's forty years no good? Who gives a shit, anyway?" I stormed out of the room and into the bedroom where Dieks was still laying in bed. He'd moved his hands up over his eyes.

"I could've told you he'd say that," he groaned in a monotone. "He never remembers anyone or anything unless it's convenient. Al Capone, Valentine's Day, gun-runnin' and bootleggin' are all filed under 'Not Convenient to Remember.' You might think it's just a bunch of hooey, but he remembers some of his ol' buddies, and he remembers how they died. They may not've meant a helluva lot to him personally, but how they died's kinda stuck with 'im. He don' care that it's been forty years. It could be a hundred and forty, and he'd still keep his mouth shut, 'cause that alone was enough to get him out of the rackets. For Capone to tell 'im he was out, 'cause he always 'knew when to keep his mouth shut.' He sure as hell ain't goin' to come clean and tell you a shittin' thing now."

"God, I don't believe you people! You're serious! Whose side are you on, anyway?"

"It's got nothin' to do with sides. It's prob'ly got nothin' to do with anything, at least anything sane. But that don' change the fact that he still runs and hides and 'members things too horrible for us to imagine. And more'n likely will 'til the day he dies. Nothin' you can say or do that'll have any effect on the way he conducts his affairs. And that's just how he sees it. You sure as hell won't bully him into it. You're wastin' your time ... "

Exasperated, I grabbed the garbage can and pulled it back into the closet and started pulling dusty bags off the first shelf, fighting my way through the anger. Dieks finally got up, showered and stood in the doorway eating a pile of toast as I thumbed my way through papers full of names, large X's, and row after row of penciled figures. It appeared to be the remains of a business.

He leaned down and kissed my cheek. "Later," he said, and disappeared out the back door to the garage where he worked sporadically at "the noble birth" of a metal sculpture.

I kept fighting my way through the papers and wanton remains of once-classy clothes left to rot. Even the mice had left the space and contents of the closet alone. There was something about it, something stark and sinister, dead cold and abandoned for good reason. But I couldn't quite put it all together in my mind. It had clearly been off-limits to anyone for more than a good twenty years, and it didn't appear that any of Richard's clothes had been moved or worn in at least that long. Dieks had no reaction to the space one way or the other, but it made me squeamish, even if I was making headway. By late afternoon, I could see both the floor and the ceiling.

By the time the monotonous music signaled the end of the six o'clock news, Richard was rocking away into oblivion, getting drunker, nastier, and meaner. I heard threatening, growling, words gurgling up from his throat, just under his breath. He was practicing his denial or his alibi, or whatever it was, over and over, and just kept on with the constant hum of rumbling, mumbling, "Ain' seed no friggin' check."

As the Irish Rose took stronger hold, he became louder, more abrasive, more threatening in his denial, "Din' see no check, and hell no, I got no friggin' gun." He patted his right pocket. "Din' see no nickel, neither," he said with a sneering laugh.

Normally, when he was belligerently drunk by news time, Dieks'd tell him to go to bed, when he was home, or in from the garage. Richard would mumble something along the lines of, "I'll show you. The rat's gang, that's who'll show you. The hell you say. You won't wake up. You won't open your fuckin' rat-face eyes. He'll give you what for. " His eyes would turn to narrow slits of wrinkled age, and liver-spotted knuckles would fade to white as he gripped the arms of his rocking chair.

"He'll give you your nickel's worth." He'd throw his head back, and the remains of his staggered, rotted teeth would jut out as he howled a fiendish laugh. "We showed 'em their nickel's worth," and he'd cackle, slowly opening his hand, slamming the other fist into the center of it.

"Put 'er there, pal. You tell me to go to bed. You," and he'd point his bony finger at Dieks, "You? You make me laugh. We'll see who'll tell who to go to bed."

Years later, long after the check, the rat's gang and a nickel's worth had faded from my consciousness, I read an article concerning who was what in the Capone camp. As I scanned the lines my eyes rested on one name -- "Machine Gun" Jack McGurn. Attributed with more killings than just the Valentine's Day Massacre, it seemed that McGurn had always left a nickel in his victim's hand.

He would've been just a few years younger than Richard, not a big man, but a scrappy welterweight gone bad. He would've been a real asset to a whiskey and gun-runnin' opportunist. If Dieks' lessons to me were any indication of his father's teachings, it would have seemed far better to have had the most heinous and unpredictable criminal element as your friend, rather than your enemy.

From all accounts, it appeared that McGurn was conscienceless and savage, just the kind of friend Richard the Dickhead would have chosen in the early twenties. Evil, ruthless, and best of all, he would've been able to bend the ear of the big boss. Whether it was true or not, the pieces all fit neatly together. It took only the slightest stretch of the imagination to see that the vicious old man who had tortured his children could easily have been the same man who oiled the machine guns for a holiday massacre.

And the old man would eventually get up from his rocker, do a sinister shuffle with shifty side glances and sneers, and make a long, labored retreat to his bedroom like that snake slithering down his hole. Once there, he would settle in and rest easy with smug memories of years in which he claimed to be someone who knew who his friends were. He'd crank up the radio next to his bed and the late night noise would drive him to sleep. Dieks would slip in through the closet door and turn it off every night.

Richard Shaunessy may well have been the most contemptible being I'd ever known to pass for human. I couldn't imagine how such a horrible excuse for a man had kept company with the likes of Cheyenne Collins, most often described as kind, sweet, and delicate. But his Irish Rose unleashed story after story, and near the end I came to understand more than I ever wanted to know about power and oppression, poverty, bigotry, ignorance and fear.

...

Richard often mentioned that she was right beside him when he ran the route in the early years -- the supplier's route to Little Chicago. To some, Little Chicago was thought to be an area up in northern Iowa near Waterloo, because crime there was comparable to that of the Windy City. But, southern Iowans swore it was in and around Ottumwa, because of their hefty population of river rats, both two and four-legged variety.

What they called it was of little concern to Richard Shaunessy. All that lay between Iowa's northern border at Minnesota and the Missouri line in the south was indisputably his. He had buyers just east of Des Moines all the way over to the Mississippi River, but Bucky and Jug Man John claimed everything to the east of the river for McGurn. They could call it the Little Shit or the Big Road Apple, but the fact remained that all profits made on back roads running north and south through that strip belonged to Big Dick Shaunessy.

Through a few hundred miles of wide spots in the road known as the boondocks, backwater burgs, and bumpkinvilles, Prohibition made a mean, ignorant man rich when, otherwise, he would've been little more than a penniless hood.

To the truly capitalistic bootlegger, the deceptive squalor of an Indian settlement could bring more favor and fortune than most men dreamed possible. At the outskirts of Tama in northeast Iowa, just off Highway 63, the Mesquakee Settlement was cradled in the lap of Big Dick's most profitable region. To young tribal members, any form of relief from reservation misery was worth whatever cost it exacted. There, in the squalor of shacks and lean-tos, they lived on top of each other, day after week after month without end.

By the early twenties, the Annals of Iowa quoted Chief Young Bear of the Mesquakee as saying that the race would soon be gone. He had long mourned the predicted loss of Fox culture. Their language was seldom spoken, their arts were nearly non-existent and customs rarely practiced. The strength of family bonds, the legacy of his ancestors, had begun to diminish before his eyes. All remaining hope for reviving ancient and sacred mores of the tribe was lost in the flurry of activity that surrounded Prohibition.

Bootleggers brought hard liquor by the trunkload, more than all the allotment checks combined could cover, and more than all the young tribal members could consume. The more they brought, the less there was of anything that mattered. The old ways disappeared and the wisdom of the elders was shunned. Without the age-old respect for their opinions, the council could no longer exert influence or control the evils that came with the unending supply of corruption. The downward spiral of misery and poverty, combined with illiteracy, alcoholism and disease, became endemic and irreversible.

The ancestors had warned Sak and Fox that a unified Indian Nation, as proposed in the Oklahoma territory, could be readily divided and conquered. If they were never unified, if the blood of their tribe was kept pure and undefiled, unlike that of the so-called civilized tribes and their vanquished neighbors - the Sioux, the Cheyenne, Cherokee, and others who had joined forces and mixed blood -- they would not have to suffer the indignity of accommodating the white man without option. Chief Young Bear insisted that the tribal council take action. Their destiny must not rest in the shameful shadows of men without honor.

The elders were convinced that the only route left that might relieve the settlement's widespread misery was a blanket dismissal of all inhabitants who were not reservation-born, nor linked by marriage to those native to tribe and land. Waves of disbelief rippled through the reservation as announcements appeared on fenceposts and storefronts throughout the community. For many, intermarriage had been the only hope of ever escaping the oppression and denigration of racial restrictions. For others, there had never been a choice. They were born to it.

The Cheyenne wife of a humble Cherokee farmer, with four children of mixed blood, representing the noble peoples of Cheyenne, Cherokee and Sioux, were among the many banished from the reservation that year. Adding to her heartache and desperation, her youngest child, the mild-mannered daughter of a once-slated Sioux chief, carried in her womb, and in her heart, the first grandchild of Lucy Smith.

They gathered all they could carry and bound the remains of their scant belongings into manageable bundles to be taken wherever they might be allowed entry. As the aged Indian woman sat with her four grown children at the Greyhound Bus Depot on Tama's Main Street, a miracle was conveyed to them in the form of a young farmer in an old, red International pickup truck. He drove past them once and then returned, slowed and came to a halt just before reaching the wooden bench where they sat huddled together.

He hopped down out of the truck and, removing his hat as he spoke, said, "Afternoon, Ma'am."

But no one looked up and no one answered.

"Ya know, I'm hearin' that the big chiefs have set to clearin' a lot of folk off the settlement, and it set me t'thinkin' 'bout what I's to do if'n I's t'find m'self with nowheres t'go. Well, what I got t'thinkin' was I'd sure be in a purdicament, and I'm s'posin' that's what a lot of hard workin' half-breeds is thinkin' 'bout now too. Uh, no offense meant there, Ma'am."

He waited for anyone to lift a head and look at him, but not one of the group did. However, from within the huddle, the sweet, small voice of a bird seemed to chirp, "None taken, mister."

The Right Thing To Do

"The paths of glory lead but to the grave."
Elegy Written in a Country Churchyard
Thomas Gray

Her grave is marked by a common fieldstone, wedged into the soil, deeply set by rain. It is half-hidden, small and smooth, its surface clean, washed and bleached by the elements and time. The stone has a bit of a red tinge to it, but there are no inscriptions, no name, date, or identifying marks.

For forty years, she's lain beneath the morning shadow of a friendly oak and basked in the full glow of the afternoon sun. For twenty-five of those years, she was alone, visited only sporadically by one who never knew her, less by those who did. Now, next to her, a newly-turned mound of barren ground brings dolefully noted company. As summer skies smile and the heavens open wide to receive her son, sorrow settles in with the memory of her silent softness, embracing all who have released his love and laughter with reluctance.

At last, we understand there could've been no other way. As she was taken from him too soon, he returned to her with haste.

Richard is applauding his daughter's efforts with Dieks, I'm thinking. His ghost is clapping with fiendish delight at her right, her decision to destroy what he tried but never could quite do. Perhaps that's too harsh, I chide myself. Maybe she really did love him so much she could no longer bear his suffering.

But my better instincts refuse the feeble offering. She was more afraid, I believe, that he would outlive his health insurance. After a few more months of deathwatch, there simply wouldn't have been a thing left for the vultures of the clan to pick clean. If through some unknown miracle of modern medicine he survived the brain damage, or the new tumor residing there, it was altogether likely that he could easily survive without the efforts of a nursing staff, skilled or other. But even technological wizardry couldn't save him without sustenance.

After a year in limbo, just a few short months away, astronomical health care costs would begin to eat away at his assets. One after another, the equity in his home and real estate, artwork, jewelry, antiques and collectibles, all would be consumed. Lucy had discovered in the earliest stages of his coma that the entirety of his life insurance had been left to his sons and could not be changed. If he lived much longer, the clan and all their dreams could be left in the cold. That was something a tribal elder could not allow.

"My brother loved me," she repeated more than once. "He meant for this to be," she'd say, trying to be more convincing. "I had t'decide what was the right thing."

Only he didn't die as they projected. He never gave in to respiratory infection or failure, nor the fatal pneumonia they said he would. His body had simply adjusted to the vegetative state he rested in so comfortably while watching them squirm.

When his friend would come to visit each week, Dieks looked at him with recognition. He knew his sister's face as well. She leaned down, looking into the pain of his fully-cognizant eyes and announced loudly, "He jus' don' know me no more," shaking her frizzled head of hair.

To my son, to his son, she said convincingly, "It'd jus' be a big waste of time, drivin' all that way now." She'd given the order to cease all food, water, medication and therapy. She never went back to witness what she had wrought. Lucille Colleen Bergen had done her familial duty with alacrity, making the greatest sacrifice of all without fanfare. As the certain funeral of her soon-to-be-deceased brother approached, the ascent of the clan began. At long last they would be momentarily released from the death grip of poverty that they had known their entire lives.

Afterwards, she was quick to point to the absence of his sons - - those sons, she said, that did not visit. She'd moved her dying brother to Omaha, out of their reach, for without job, duty, or obligation in Digger's Grove, she was free and clear. The three hundred miles that separated them should not, she declared, have proved to be a problem. After all, she'd gone each week, between duties of "administrating the estate," the stating the administrating.

This was reason, she emphasized, to question true motives. This was important, she stated, a disappointment to her and the whole family. Perhaps the sons didn't feel responsible. Perhaps their love wasn't as great, nor their requirements as pressing.

In the great consternation and overwhelming exhaustion of which she spoke, sounding an awfully lot like a Hatfield and McCoy "law-yur" preparing a case, she said that now she had to turn her energies to protecting what was rightfully hers. No one could possibly dispute the fact that she had a right to her brother's goods, to all his goods. After all, who was the "onliest one, ever' step of the way, makin' all them hard decisions" as his assigned guardian, "holdin' his poor ol' hand," as the consoling sister. Who was "acallin' his friends," and "keepin' all them relatives aknowin'?"

Who, indeed. Who else could possibly be more deserving of reward after so closely monitoring and diligently caring for the poor, dying brother, the clan asserted. Yet no one would say the obvious: after twenty years of giving her absolutely nothing, of cringing at the thought of his detested brother-in-law laying claim to his most sacred artifacts, collections of tools, goods, and an entire life's purchases, Dieks Shaunessy, with one foot in the grave, would have to witness the pilfering of every possession he owned by the remnants of the scatter-brained tribe he felt least deserving.

The brother-in-law he'd most often referred to as "the laziest sonofabitch that ever lived" was about to capitalize on all that he owned. Poverty and desperation became the only justification needed for greed that spawned looting with no bounds. Under the cover of darkness, or in the brilliant light of day, the clan descended on everything of worth at the home he'd worked so hard to create. They picked, pulled, and stripped clean all flesh from the remaining bones of Dell Shaunessy's frail existence.

I was torn between feelings of disgust and helplessness, I would neither benefit nor suffer from their actions, but our son would once again be slighted in this base business of stealing a dead man's goods. Yet they professed such great and wondrous love for the man whose sons' inheritance they looted.

Yes, I thought, Richard the Big Dick smiles at the pile of skeletal remains. I still see the Skoal wedged between his rotting, crooked teeth as he grins and bears witness to his daughter -- acting as he'd acted, killing as he'd killed, looting, pillaging, stealing as he once did with such fierce bravado. His rheumy eyes would have gleamed with pride if he'd only seen such promise of greed and avarice as she was growing up. Why, he might've treated her with more respect while assaulting her. He would've let her watch, even invited her to help as he beat her brother half to death. She wouldn't have needed to hide from him. Perhaps she wouldn't have needed to run away.

The knotted feeling in my stomach is much the same as I felt when Dieks would break from me and fall helplessly back into a past where abuse and humiliation reigned supreme. I'm as angry as I was when I heard his stories and watched him struggle with disbelief in the realization that the someone who was supposed to love him and protect him had done all things horrible, blatant and unchallenged.

Perhaps that was the catch. What they were doing was blatant and unchallenged. In my heart, it was as wrong as the savage tortures he'd suffered at the hands of his father. It was another repeat performance of a macabre show that was held in reserve for only the closest relatives of the Shaunessy clan.

The stealing and looting were no more perverse than the broken noses, ripped-out fingernails and fractures he'd known. The knives and guns from which he'd run -- only to see Sheriff Jasper return them -- were much the same as the waves of papers filed by his sister's lawyer, allowing further intrusion and a legal thievery of all he owned, all that had been left in shambles after the slipshod investigation of an alleged burglary that took place at a time no one could pinpoint.

The lifelong friends that walked away now were no different than the only relatives a small boy ever knew, piling in their cars to go home after his mother's funeral, leaving him with the crazed maniac. They were the same as the neighbors, closing their doors and windows, and turning their backs, while lamenting that they couldn't afford to get involved. They were no different than his sister professing great love and concern for his best interests while she gave the order and signed the papers that meant death for her dependent, voiceless sibling.

The principal at the elementary school once told his fifth grade teacher that her job was teaching, not preaching, not nursing. The safety of all students, he'd said, was clearly the responsibility of their parents. He sent them both back to the classroom where she sat and wept as the young Delly winced in pain and struggled to learn how to write left-handed, since all the fingers on his right hand were broken, and untreated burns oozed with new infection and fused with the strips of bandages he'd made out of the hem of his own pillowcase that morning.

So, here we are, back to the beginning of all things. A sick rendition of the ghost dance. Back to the perfect beginning. One of the people who'd broken the promise to his dying mother, one who'd abandoned an innocent boy to torture and pain at the hands of his sadistic father, the only person who could've championed his cause in his most desperate moment, was the person who said, "In his best interests, let him die."

In southern Iowa, we grew up knowing what was often said of us: "If someone would raise the northern boundary of Missouri to include the southernmost tier of Iowa counties, the average IQ of both states would increase by ten percent."

In northern Iowa, where I live in relative obscurity, I look back in anger, smugly aware of true meaning of the insult.

Delmonico 'n' Lucas

The brothers came to the heartland wild with dreams. They found a hundred and sixty acres of prime farmland, nestled in the rolling hills of Iowa, just outside the bustling town of Zenetta, located in southern Grundy County. It was said that northeastern Iowa had certain areas, particularly in Grundy and Black Hawk counties, in which the soil was so rich that early homesteaders found better than six feet of topsoil when they first turned the land. The brothers never believed such stories until they saw the luscious land of Iowa.

When the Collins brothers left Pennsylvania, at the beginning of the century, it was with the hope of finding just such land. Outside Zenetta, they took only one look before knowing they'd reached their destination. With the money they'd saved for over five years working as farmhands back East, they purchased as many acres as they could afford at a dollar and forty cents per -- an exorbitant amount in their estimation. But, it was far better land than either of them had ever seen, or heard of, flat to gently-rolling slopes of black soil so rich with minerals and water, treeless tracts that held the deep, heavy scent of crops waiting to be brought to life. It was breathtaking and nearly unbelievable.

At the far end of the southeast corner, the well witcher's divining rod dipped, and their decision was made. Here, between a simple cottage that would be more than sufficient for the two of them and outbuildings that they'd planned to build over the course of years, they dug the water well. Just beyond it, they constructed a large barn with hayloft and corral for livestock and work horses, wagons, and implements they'd brought from home and those they'd managed to acquire along the way and since their arrival. They knew the barn was really much larger than they needed, but they agreed that the extra space was incentive to expand their operation.

Delmonico was the rounder: tall, strong, resolute in his belief that he had been sent to draw from the fertile soil all that it could provide. Though named after the Italian restaurant at which his parents shared their first honeymoon meal, there was little doubt, with his steely blue eyes and nearly translucent skin, that he continued the strong line of his mother's Norse ancestry. When his large frame filled the entire space of Danish-sized doorways in the dimly-lit roadhouses that peppered the barren back roads, he evoked ghostly visions.

Lucas was the quiet one, equally fair in coloring, on a frame a bit larger than his older brother. He was also driven to and by the land, determined to draw from it a decent living, as well as meaning and purpose. He was more pensive, and though often taken to brooding, he was thoughtful to a fault, his brother said -- too serious for his own good.

He had a tendency to stammer when he spoke and often chose to work with figures in the quiet solitude of their kitchen. He was more than content to sit in front of a roaring fire and contemplate the future, leaving the uncomfortable chore of contact to his brother. Business dealing with strangers in the all-too-public communities of Zenetta and surrounding towns was not an activity that he relished.

It was all they could do to keep up with the land. Planting and harvest were all-consuming words and notions that ate up weeks and months without end. It seemed that they no longer got the crops in and it was time to begin harvest. Once they'd managed to survive the winter, the cycle started over again. After a few short years, the brothers began to see their youth consumed in lonely labors. For one, it was destiny. For the other, it was an unacceptable sentence.

Delmonico found the short jaunts in and around the many small towns lifesavers. He always finished his chores before he took off, but he had to escape just the same. Though he knew his brother well and understood his need for studious quiet, Del longed instead for companionship and craved the simplest conversation. He lived beyond the dream and saw beyond the land.

After harvest in their third year, and before the cold, Iowa winter set in, Delmonico made fast and furious rounds. Greeting each old friend and acquaintance with a hearty hello, he managed to learn the news of the area and acted as courier, informing those at each stop of his news before traveling on. With the information he'd gained, he was determined to avoid spending another lonely winter in the cud-chewing companionship of cows.

As he'd heard in the general store at Tama, the Council of Elders had issued an order of dismissal to the many inhabitants who were not truly native to the reservation. Delmonico watched with interest as they walked the dusty back roads, their belongings tied to branches that rested on shoulders stooped in defeat. Nearly every direction out of town had at least one family of Indians trudging away in quiet desperation.

The more he thought, the more it seemed to him that there was room for others at their farm. There was always work to be done. The brothers had more than enough food and supplies to support themselves. What they didn't have were enough people to suit Del. Before the opportunity escaped, he decided to seize the moment. He drove through town and saw what appeared to be a family of five huddled together on a bench at the Greyhound Depot. There would be conversation and guests at dinner that evening on the Collins farm.

Dinosaurs

The countryside along the back roads is still alive in late summer. It holds secrets and wonders that only the farmers know. They say that they can actually hear the corn growing in the dead silence of a hot summer night, that their own joints ache with the struggle of the seed to emerge and reach up to the morning sun. They say pilfering 'coons are the world's best forecasters of the prime time for picking sweet corn. The only problem is with the 'coons' rude method -- they eat the corn when it's ready.

I can't help but smile at the remains of once majestic windmills, now. The stillness of grain augers and the looming silos are no longer painful lover's memories. The secluded country lanes fail to summon and entice, and the promise of privacy found in the fertile open spaces has now faded to only a memory with the passing of the years. The birds still sing their songs clearly and the creeks run lazily along. But the open sky spreads billowy arms, blank with wonder at how movement once witnessed so often has now ceased so completely.

. . .

My son's biting his lip. I can't decide if it's to keep from crying or if he's trying to create a distracting pain that is greater than the one now pounding in his heart.

"What was she like? His mother, my other gra'ma."

"I never knew her. She died the year I was born."

I paused and looked away. The funeral procession was so slow that my car practically drove itself. It was just as well. The road before us was not the road we were traveling anyway.

"All I ever heard about her was secondhand information. Usually biased. When he'd get really drunk, Richard would talk about her.

Sometimes he'd start talking to me like I was Cheyenne. He'd say the sweetest things, like he was an adoring, loving husband with her health and happiness as his sole concern. And then, he'd turn."

I stopped, wondering if the information I had, or light I could shed, would have any bearing on what Dieks was really wanting to know.

"How?" he asked, prompting me.

I glanced back and saw my son's wife through the rear-view mirror, sitting quietly in the backseat, her eyes staring back steadily. I couldn't tell if she was pleading with me to say it, and get it out, or if I should just let it go, or clean it up somehow.

I felt his eyes on me as he turned away from the window to face me, and once again, he asked, "How did he turn?"

I couldn't think of any way to say what I was thinking. My mind was rolling and bumping along, clicking up options like a nickel-fed slot machine, with one false start, then another, and yet another.

"He became ... the devil," I said finally. "Pure, undiluted evil. Hideous without second thought. Conscienceless. Horrible beyond my comprehension almost. His words were acidic, his eyes like raging fires, and everything from his gestures to his movement and posture changed in a heartbeat. Sometimes, it was mid-sentence. But most of the time, it was just as the booze took hold.

"In one breath, he described the beauty of her face, the brilliant shine in her hair, the joy of her voice, the welcoming music of her laughter. He'd be almost trancelike, whispering reverently about the temple of her body, how he worshipped her grace and drank from her loveliness. Her delicate ears, her sweet, slender fingers, her dainty feet. He'd say her skin was silken and her charms were mesmerizing. He'd go on and on and before he was done, I'd be envious of all she was that I knew I'd never be.

"But that fast," I said, snapping my fingers, "she was a witch. A hag, the horrible high priestess to the underworld. In the blink of an eye, she was a harpy, a shrew, a black-hearted bitch who'd tricked him into submission, stole his money, ruined his reputation, lied, cheated, whelped bastards.

"And that would go on and on, but unlike the tirade on her grace and beauty, he'd grow agitated, pace, squirm, tense up like he had to hit something, or throw something, or do something violent to assuage the pain, or maybe the grief, that came with the memory of it all.

"Just that fast, and all remnants of her beauty were gone. She became ugliness and anger, black and barren, spiteful, malevolent. And he didn't say this simply and quietly, mind you. He was no longer an old man in the remains of a body whose best years have been grossly and obviously misspent. These were the speeches of a dictator, or prison guard barking commands. It was something that more closely resembled a demented obsession.

"He'd begin with the list of all he'd do to her if he could get his hands on her again. He'd slice up her face, shave off her hair. He'd tear up her clothes, destroy her jewelry, poke out her eyes, break her legs, smash her fingers, cut off her breasts. It seemed that everything he said he'd do to her were things that would make her unacceptable in the world, a threatening world that he thought might lure her away. But, if he poked her eyes out, she couldn't see to leave. She'd have to stay. If he broke her legs, she couldn't run to escape. If she had no clothes, she'd never leave naked. If he destroyed her beauty, who would want her? Who could stand to look at her? But he never, ever once said he'd kill her. He never once implied that he'd either send or drive her away. He had no intention of letting her go."

I stopped again, staring through the back window of the hearse, crawling toward eternity on the ol' river road.

"But, I don't think she ever even thought of running away, either. I don't think she had anywhere left to go. She might've looked weak and delicate, but I think she had a great deal of strength. More than that, I think she was a courageous and proud woman. For her day, she was probably considered noble, to stay with a man so vicious and violent, to protect her children from his wrath by using her own body as their shield. I don't think she ever thought she'd actually die. And then, when it became apparent that she *was* dying, she was too doped up all the time to see beyond the moment.

"That's why there were no plans for her children's welfare. I don't think she ever believed she was going to die. For whatever reason, she felt she was condemned to life.

"I suspect that Cheyenne was a truly unique woman. But she lived with the devil, and no earthly efforts could have prevented what happened."

"What? That she died and left them to fend for themselves?"

"Not so much that she died. That was inevitable. But that no one dared to cross his path when she died. The story's been told a zillion times about how her sisters promised to get the kids out. Even in her delirium, just before she died, she knew enough to beg them to get the kids away from Richard. They all agreed to it, and she let go only when Cher swore she'd take care of it.

"And then they reneged. Why? Lucy used to mention it. She talked about the promise, but the memory of it was feather-light, idle prattle with little importance. It was an old story about a woman who died and the last thing promised was a fluke and they all knew it, except her. It was a yarn spun with invisible thread about a spineless town, well-meaning, but cowardly sisters, and a system that failed two children, resulting in their deadly destiny.

"At any rate, that's about all I know. She was full-blood Indian, Sioux and Cheyenne, I think. Both of her sisters were Indian as well, but I think they all had different fathers. Don't ask me why. I saw a picture of her once. Dieks could've been her twin, and he always swore he had this big deal Indian blood. Which would've been great as far as I was concerned. Anything would've been better than the likes of Richard's mutant genes running through your family tree. No offense intended, and I hope to hell your father was right. From all that I saw, we'd have a good chance of rubbing elbows with the likes of, God forbid, Capone, or the Boston Strangler, or even Hitler, maybe.

"In that house, I saw the remains of fur coats and expensive leftovers from more prosperous days. But really, there was little evidence that anyone was allowed to remember her. Even less of her relatives. Dieks once said that he thought there was a brother, or an uncle or two somewhere else, but I don't know if he ever tried to track anybody down. It didn't seem likely that he'd have any luck, less likely that anyone would cooperate.

"Sometimes he'd take off on the history of the Cherokee people and talk of a great-great-great-grandfather and some ancient alphabet. He said he could trace 'his people' back to Tennessee and the Trail of Tears. He mentioned a headdress or a warbonnet something or other that his grandfather owned that was supposed to have supernatural powers. He said it could stop bullets and make the wearer invisible. Later, he talked about the ghost dance of his people and how everything'd return to the perfect beginning of the world and all would be set right again. But most of the time I figured he just needed validation of sorts -- that he was a descendent of a long line of suffering, and that it was their lot in life. That made it destiny, and irreversible.

"But Lucille always denied it. She said they were more Irish, and Dieks just didn't like Pops, as she called Richard. She he made up his own family tree, and filled it full of important people who couldn't ever be found."

"What d'you think?"

"'Bout what?"

"'Bout his family tree."

"I think," and I stopped again, measuring the words. "I think that there was a lot of truth to what he said. But not just because he said it. More because a lot of times, I think he felt it. And did you ever take a good look at his face, his skin color, his body structure? All chest and no butt." I smiled. "If I was t'guess what he might be, and I did have the time and energy to spend speculating, I'd guess he was a helluva lot more Indian than anything else.

"In fact, I'd guess that he was zero percent Irish, or German, or Swedish, or any of those fair-skinned folk that Lucy likes to fancy herself being. Then again, I had a whole pocketful of experiences with Dieks that I'm pretty sure no one else had. Good, bad, or indifferent, I heard and saw sides of him that no one ever suspected. Certainly never experienced."

"Like what?"

"Hmmm, let me see. Give me a minute, here. I've spent a long time trying to forget. It'll take a bit to gather the castaways ... "

I looked at the roadside rest stop. Tucked back in between field and ditch, at a crossroads that led to nowhere in both directions, I remembered, and smiled.

"One night," I began, "we were just outside Agency. There was a gorgeous full moon, and the night was full of heat lightning and this huge, spooky moon lit everything with a soft, eerie glow. Mysterious. We turned off the main highway and went a short ways down a narrow gravel road where he pulled over. We walked up to an area that sets back from the road, where Chief Wapello's gravesite is fenced off and marked with a large granite boulder.

"And Dieks gets real jumpy all of a sudden. First he thought he heard someone in the bushes, and then he said he felt like he was being watched. That somewhere close, someone was watching us ... "

"What were you doing there?"

"You writin' a book, or listenin'?"

"Yeah, I'm listenin' so I can write a book. I'm goin' to call it *The Ghost of Wapello Hollow.*"

"Very funny. Anyway, the fact is, he couldn't do much of anything, if you know what I mean. And that was what he had on his mind when he turned off that highway. But he became real ... unsettled.

"Then, he looks up at the moon and starts singin' this really weird song. In another language, mind you. I'm thinkin' that he's havin' an out-of-body religious experience or something. He's whining and then humming for a while, then he does these low, buzzing things with his lips and dippin' and divin' all over the place. To all intents and purposes, I've disappeared, because he doesn't even acknowledge that I'm there.

"When he starts chanting, I start backing away, just kind of inching out of the picture, all the while listening, and watching all these indescribable, intricate moves by a man who can't even slow dance hangin' on to somebody. In the middle of this I realize that I can't identify anything but one word of it. And I still can't."

"That's very interesting, but what was the, you know, the never-before-I-can't-believe-I'm-seeing-this thing?"

"At the end. And after that night, many times, but at the end of this big hoopla, he falls to his knees and puts his head down on the ground and says over and over, 'Wokinih, hey!' or 'Wokinih, ho!' or something else I couldn't make out. It sounded like, you know, when people say, 'uff da,' for just about any reason when they're amazed or thrilled, thankful, or surprised. Like 'aloha' means more than just hello or good-bye, it was like it meant something else, and it was just in his subconscious, and instead of swearing or praying, he'd say, 'Wokinih,' real low and slow and breathy. Who knows? He'd say it at the strangest times, but never angry or violent, and, as far as I know, never around anyone but me."

"And? What's a Wokinih?"

"It's not a what. It's a who. And that's a whole other story, 'cause I never knew for a long time."

As I thought about what I'd come to know, I drifted away from my son. He knew I was somewhere he couldn't reach and didn't push the issue. I'd allowed myself the sweet, dangerous luxury of free-fall, back twenty years to when I was young and pretty, headstrong, and unmistakably loved. I was back to the bliss-filled months that we had together in the beginning.

...

We almost lived in his car, we were on the road so much. It was a mutually understood need, and neither of us questioned or complained of the inconvenience.

On the road we didn't have to share each other with anyone else. Since Dieks had always filled his life with as many people as he could collect, we couldn't stay at his apartment or go to a bar without someone dropping by, stopping in, sitting down -- in short, trying to monopolize his time or attention. Those were ground rules he'd established over time. He simply belonged to everyone, and vice versa.

Then he found someone he didn't want to share and was found by someone who didn't want to share him. So we had to sneak away to be left alone. So every day, as a matter of course, we headed out in another direction. Of all the times we spent together, some of the funniest and most memorable moments were spent on the back roads in search of privacy.

Once, on a trip down by the Quad cities, we decided to stop and get a bite to eat. The windows had been down, and my hair looked like it had been through a wind tunnel. I'd forgotten my hairbrush, and he said I could use his comb if I wanted.

We were just crossing a busy intersection and were making our way to a massive bridge that spanned the Mississippi when he suggested that I try to find his comb, down at the bottom of his right pocket. It sounded like a reasonable solution to me.

I reached down and put my hand in his front right jean pocket. He straightened his leg a little so it wasn't so tight, but I still couldn't reach it. I looked at his face, and it was getting a little red, kinda flushed, and I didn't understand. Then I understood completely. My fingers followed the long, rigid shaft in his pocket, and I realized it was not remotely close to resembling a comb.

His eyes stared straight ahead, and he smiled ever so slightly.

"I'm afraid I'm only going to allow you another twenty minutes to find that comb."

And as I started to withdraw my hand from his pocket, he stopped me and pressed my fingers down firmly in place. It was the first time I'd ever felt what could only be described as throbbing desire.

"Wokinih," he whispered and winked. And I translated his tone to make the word mean, "It's okay. It's good, leave it there. I'm fulfilled."

And he was right. I was perfectly content to leave my hand there and I never found the comb, and we never stopped, at least not to eat. Everything took care of itself in good time.

Another time, just before I was to leave for college, we were both getting unrealistically possessive. Fearing the worst circumstances, that we might part company and never get back together again, we took off on a back roads excursion.

After five or ten miles he said he'd been thinking about what we might do to occupy us for the day. It had to do with naming something sexually inspiring we saw along the back roads. Just normal, everyday somethings, mind you.

He pointed over to a huge silo. "Like that. I'll take that for mine. Now, doesn't that remind you of something sexually inviting? Something you might not mind getting close to?"

"Oh," I said, not quite sure what he meant.

Later, of course, much later, in fact, I learned other words, more sophisticated terms, like phallic symbols, latent desire. I was game for just about anything. I loved him to pieces, and he loved me. But of the two of us, regarding these things, I was really naive. Gullible, even, and never minded the horseplay in the beginning.

So we continued on down the road, keeping his example in mind. And at long last, I finally found my thing and pointing it out. "There. That's what I want."

"Where? What is it?" He turned his head to look out my window to where I pointed.

I smiled, and said quietly, "A dinosaur ... "

. . .

"What'd you say?" My son leaned toward me, straining to hear.

"I said, 'dinosaur.' I remember dinosaurs scattered all along the farmhouses and barns on the back roads. I don't know what they're called, grain augers, maybe. They're those giraffe-like elevators that look like they probably belt feed grain up to the top of the silo where it drops down into storage for the winter, I think. But they looked liked long-necked dinosaurs to me. And I chose the dinosaurs ... "

And, as then, my three middle fingers closed down flat over the ridge of my nose. After that, every time he ever saw one of those monsters looming in a backfield, he'd say, "Dinosaur," with his three fingers covering his nose.

"You chose them for what?"

"I chose them as my symbol, for virility, I guess."

"Oh jeez," and he's shaking his head. "I can't imagine this getting any better."

"His theory," I went on, ignoring my son's embarrassment, "was that choice, if it was, in fact, sensual, or sexually stimulating, then we should pull over at each sighting and ... "

I became exhausted all over again just thinking about it. I sighed, and kept looking dead ahead.

"Do you have any idea how many of your dad's silos and your mom's dinosaurs there are lurking along rural back roads in late summer? Everywhere. They're just everywhere."

I shook my head in disbelief. "I had no idea how difficult it was for two people to do what we did for the twenty miles back to town. It might as well have been two thousand. It took me a week to recover, and to this day, I wish like hell I'd said, 'windmills.'

"But he remembered it differently. He'd point out the dinosaurs from time to time, and he'd smile this sly dog, macho smile. Oh, he'd shake his head, too. But with pride. And in time, the 'dinosaur' whisper changed to a low, reverent 'Wokinih.'"

Grandpa Dieks

In the midst of a somewhat sputtered, spastic eulogy, I heard the words, "After grade school, he lived with his aunt, CheroLynn Palmer, where he went on to complete his high school, graduating with the Fairfield Class of sixty-six."

I watched as Dieks' cousin, Marvelle, stared straight ahead without moving a muscle. Her husband's head had quickly turned, searching her stony face for truth, but she acknowledged nothing. Let sleeping dogs die, Uncle Richard would've said. I shook my head in disgust as they rewrote the basics of Dieks' life history. It was more of an exercise in hearing what they wanted heard, and seeing what they wanted seen. If the facts won't cooperate and don't correlate, then fabricate. After all, funerals are really more for the living, I heard them agree. Not to mention the fact that it's easier on the ears and more comforting to the conscience if events were not darkened with demons, if one cousin's skewed memories translated to another's dark recollections of torment.

The lovely spray from his beloved cousins had a football cut from brown construction paper rising above the common mums and junk geraniums. I thought about it for a while, straining to remember when Dieks might have been associated with football. Then I heard shrieks of rollicking laughter as Marvelle and Daniella, the devil's delightful duo who called themselves cousins, told of how each visit to Eldon was filled with hours of teasing Dieks. Since they both managed to grow from an Amazon childhood to true Amazon greatness, tossing the football back and forth, just over Dieks' head was a game they took particular pride in when they visited.

One day, however, just as they arrived, Dieks came from behind the house, and completely out of character, offered them the ball.

"We knew there was somethin' wrong," Daniella said.

"Oh, we knew right away!" Marvelle chimed in.

"He'd peed on it."

"Yeah. He'd peed on it," the other repeated.

My heart sank as I realized there was simply no end to any level of torment in his childhood. Aunts Cher and Sue visited periodically, keeping the children in touch with their kin. I'd like to believe their intention was to provide Cheyenne's children with a reprieve from Richard's vile treatment. However, as the two cousins continued with their tales, I got the feeling that the visits were merely extensions of the nastiness that filled their lives, in watered-down forms of humiliation and mean-spirited play. Their presence provided the false front for conscience and concern.

These lovely, surviving relatives simply couldn't put it all together. They stood there, recounting every moment that they amused themselves with miseries they called visits. In every memory offered, they made Dieks the brunt of the joke, the kid with the short stick, the one left out in the cold. They never mentioned tormenting Lucy, and never stopped to think that what they did and what we heard might be considered cruel. Quite simply, it never occurred to them.

On the intermittent weekends where Dieks might have gotten relief from the continual abuse suffered at his father's hands, he had to switch gears and contend with outside forces that tormented him not out of hate, or spite, or incoherent alcoholic fury, but simply for amusement. How sad that they remembered with such delight the very antics that left him with a lifetime of disdain for ball games, or activities that required any physical performance that might be measured.

He never played basketball, baseball, or football. For the rest of his life, he remained a spectator, staying completely away from contact sports, confining himself to solitary activities where no one could control or withhold anything from him again. They couldn't mock his speed, size, or agility if he never had to demonstrate them. For the balance of his short boyhood, Delly Shaunessy defied anyone to laugh at him as his cousins had, and avoided situations where someone might jeer at his struggles or predict his defeat. He never learned humility, never imagined for a moment that even the slightest human weakness might be amusing.

Instead, perhaps unconsciously, he chose to live vicariously through others. He assumed their personae as his own and repeated their family stories as if they were his. He gave them all great strength and kindly refrained from noticing frailties. Eventually, he abandoned the ruins of the shame that he'd known as his own life, and took up residency in the safety of other people's histories.

I wondered how well any of them knew him. He had listened so long and so intently that he could recite their lives back to them in modified forms that became his own. His sad, mean past disappeared, but with it, his sense of self diminished. It was a trade-off no one seemed to notice, thus it was never disputed. It seemed perfectly acceptable that Dieks filled embarrassing gaps in his life with their characteristics -- how very flattering. They were all content to share whatever parts he needed to feel complete and fulfilled.

The adult Dieks became a conglomerate of what he perceived as successful, acceptable behavior and his lifestyle became the envy of his friends. Because he had no access to their souls, though, he never seemed to grasp the concepts of conscience, morals, ethics, or integrity. These were notions beyond his reach. He couldn't witness, feel, or see the result of something that had never existed in his world. Yet the man he became was most acceptable, and he was loved by all who knew him. It was comfortable and satisfying for all concerned, except perhaps his various wives and visiting children, who could never quite come to terms with so many elusive identities.

As I listened to the cousins' laughter, I remembered all the pain we dealt with, the constraints on our marriage, the restrictions on our stymied social life. Nearly everything he displayed as an adult was the direct result of some modified form of trauma he'd experienced as a child. As he became older he simply replaced them, one by one, with someone else's more acceptable remembrance. He became less of himself and more of them, a true enigma.

It was easy to see why they loved him so and felt cheated by his death; he was truly Everyman.

How flippant that they extolled their love and concern over his mortal remains. How arrogant that they whispered over his tortured, departed soul by whimpering of their grievous loss. They never saw the emptiness in his eyes nor bothered to sort the overlapping pieces of mismatched fabric that became his patchworked life. In the end, even his closest friends remained blind to his last, faint hope. He told me he was pretty sure he'd be able to figure out how to be something special -- a normal, simple, good and very personal standout. He'd be Grandpa.

They simply wouldn't tolerate that, I thought. The significant others turned away from an identity that seemed alien to his other assets, almost beyond comprehension. After all, those two young men who stood strangely familiar but clearly apart from each other, and those babies that toddled unaware through the visitation room, they were not theirs. They'd not welcomed the announcement, nor celebrated their safe arrival. They'd never touched them, nor held them, never quieted their fears, nor bribed a toothless grin. Those creatures that bore only the slightest resemblance to the remains in the casket were merely interfering strangers, and strangers they'd always be.

But, it was his blood that ran through their veins. The genetics of his ancestors would be forever theirs, as well. They could do nothing about their family ties. They could only visit as allowed and someday realize that he chose his friendships -- close enough to be congenial, distant enough to prove harmless. Relatives were another matter completely.

At death, he was refused the single, solitary recognition that would forever set him apart from the conglomerate. The throng of friends could not claim familiarity with the most unlikely character of all, Grandpa Dieks.

Part III

Forgetting the Rules

In mid-February of ninety-one, as she lay next to me one midnight, I listened as my mother made a certain peace with the world, succumbing at last to its veritable struggle of loneliness, poverty, and pain. Though she was only inches away, I didn't reach for her hand in the darkness. It was as though she conveyed her thoughts on motes that floated down through the thin shaft of light from the street. One by one, they settled on me like pins dropping on a threadbare blanket, and I was warmed, but not comforted when I felt her words press my skin: Don't touch me. I'll be traveling alone.

In the aftermath, the surviving daughters began the long journey of grief once again. As before, we analyzed every avenue and examined every choice. As before, we realized that the answer was and always would be that there is no answer. I sought refuge in all the old familiar places, trying desperately to drown the heavy sorrow that had seeped into all the old vulnerable spaces.

But there, in the vast wasteland of southern Iowa, I could only stand back and watch as my life began slip sliding down the unavoidable path of pain one more time. Dieks made sure he was there, just close enough to catch me if I fell, and secretly hoping that I would. He seemed to try to be whatever it was I searched for, and became increasingly determined to buy my parents' home up on Mockingbird Hill. He'd just wink and grin and say he'd wait and sooner or later, I'd be back.

While Sam kept the home fires burning up north, I kept my distance and subsequent sanity in the south. The struggle to maintain meaning and recapture what little composure I'd once known consumed my days and nights. Few understood why I stayed, drifting quietly away. But Dieks knew.

I hung around the house for a week, touching the things she'd touched, sitting at her table, staring out her window, seeing all she'd seen for that last long, lonely year. I moved from room to room, porch to yard, garage to drive and back again, fighting to imprint memories that were scattering too quickly with the late winter winds. I feared that the remains of my happiest years were dying with my mother, and there was nothing I could do to salvage anything.

Dieks checked on me periodically, content sometimes to just sit in the silence and darkness while I tried to breathe in the little that was left of my childhood and early memories. No matter what anyone says, home is home. There is nowhere else in the world that can become a substitute for the ceilings, walls, and floors that have wrapped around a family.

He nodded in agreement with whatever I said. He blended with the walls and floors, rested in the rocker, leaned against the doorways, and waited. It seemed that he always waited. I left a little more often, and eventually, after another journey from basement to backyard and back again, I knew it was time to go.

I locked up and walked out to the driveway, nodding that I'd meet him over at The Wild Stallion, knowing full well that it was a short jaunt away from the highway leading out of town. He smiled and waved as he backed out of the drive ahead of me, checking from time to time in his rearview mirror to make sure I was still following.

As I pulled into the parking lot, he leaned against his truck, with arms crossed as if to say he'd been there for hours and I was terribly late.

He opened my door and said with a laugh, "Where ya been all my life, Stranger?"

I just shook my head. He reminded me of Wade, the little neighbor kid who'd always greet him before he pulled into the driveway, and then jump and dance and jabber a mile a minute to keep his attention, all the way to the house. On the spot, unforgettable, endearing.

Once inside, he ordered a rum and coke for me, and a draw for himself. "Just like old times," he said, and then ran wild through years of memories, rattling all he ever knew of me, all that had been kept on ice for so long. "Favorite color: black. Favorite number: eight. Favorite singers: male, Jim Reeves; female, Patsy Cline. Favorite movie: *Zhivago*. Favorite book: *Hawaii*--"

"That's changed," I said, interrupting his roll. *"A Prayer for Owen Meany*, I think."

"I'll stick to what I knew. Best year?"

"Sixty-nine, Dude!" we chimed in together, laughing at the double entendre.

"Greatest joy: your kids. Greatest regret--"

"The men!" I interrupted.

"Thanks a lot! I'm, well, hurt, frankly," he said, shaking his head.

"No, you're not, and don't call me Frankly. Also, you're a liar. You knew that answer years ago. That was one that never ever changed. Only thing is, my brother informed me it was his greatest regret, too." We both howled.

"Favorite place?"

"Anywhere but here!" we screamed in unison, collapsing onto the bar while the bartender eyed us cautiously and inched her way down to our end.

That was our standard line, at any event, get together, party, movie, anywhere that we couldn't disappear and relieve the sexual tension that would invariably mount.

"'Nother, Dieks?"

"Sure," he said, turning to her with the confidence of a Don Juan and his famous, everlast smile.

"Ma'am?" she asked, nodding at me.

"Nope. Gotta go."

She looked back at him, questioning my authority. Ignoring her for what she didn't understand, I turned off the bar stool and reached down for my purse.

"Always the same," he said, his voice less confident, nearly pleading. "Don't you 'member, Liz B? You said you'd never leave me. You said so."

"Oh, yeah, I remember. You leave, then."

"Can't. Got a whole beer here," he said, holding up the evidence and waiting for reprieve.

"No problem, then. Designated and assigned, abandoning ship, sir!" I saluted crisply and turned sharply to leave.

He swiveled toward the wall of liquor bottles at the back of the bar and watched in the mirror as my reflection walked solemnly out into the night. It was that fast. In a matter of moments, his possibilities faded and abruptly died. All he knew was that we were meeting on his turf, where luck had always reigned supreme. He'd stayed with me for just the right amount of time, demonstrating his love and concern for my health and well-being, following me, sitting with me, mourning as I mourned for all that was drifting away. I'd agreed to go with him that evening. He'd recited all the correct memories. There was just no sense in it at all. Perhaps, I simply didn't understand. Maybe I'd forgotten *The Rules According to Dieks*. Maybe I'd forgotten that all else was to be forsaken and all else was to be abandoned when his needs and wants were presented. And just maybe, if he sat majestically still, I'd remember *The Rules* in a minute and I'd return.

But it was in that minute that I remembered. That was what he didn't realize. I finally remembered.

I remembered that my Sam waited, husband-heater-warm and lawn mower-familiar. I'd lost all sense of mood in the last moments in the bar, for I was preoccupied, remembering long, muscular arms and the rough, strong hands of a workingman. I remembered deeply-furrowed worry lines on his brow, and deep, dark eyes that felt like raging fires without meaning to. I remembered quietly pursed lips that disagreed with my spouting obstinacy, but held back and never opened to anger. I smiled lovingly as I remembered his foot, nonchalantly inching across the sheets in the night, searching, pausing, finally touching, and then settling down, contented, to sleep.

"Don't you 'member?"

The words echoed through solid walls that had been constructed in fear, protecting the frail young heart that had withered and wept so many years before. Oh, I remembered. I remembered screaming and begging for mercy, looking up to his face and seeing him in a dimly lit room, just before his boot connected with my temple. I remembered dragging myself across a floor, trying to get to a baby, frightened by the noise in the next room, sobbing for someone to comfort his fears while I was held back by a screaming, savagely possessed demon. I remembered a brilliant smile that rivaled the sun. Later, I remembered that same smile would flash and shine for so many other women. First one. Then another. And yet another one.

I was still remembering as I walked out the door. "Nobody ever walks out on me!" he'd screamed some twenty years before. I smiled as I remembered that, not meaning to be cruel, but savoring the moment of walking tall and resolutely out the door. As I opened the car door, I thought of what my mother would've said and shook my head. No, it was not on purpose, it wasn't my fault, and I hadn't led him down a primrose path. He did that. For one of the first times in my mind's memories, I walked away from him knowing full well that I was not responsible for the tragedy of his life. I owed him no debt and my life's path was not his. In that moment, I remembered the faint feel of freedom.

I remembered, and that was sufficient. I remembered all that he knew of me and I remembered all that I knew of him. Separate and unaffected, in that moment, the memories were no longer empowered. I was no longer entrenched. The journal in his head - - the file box full of things people loved, were proud of, avoided, reviled, detested -- was complete, but housed more than just mine. I wouldn't be duped again. Everyone that had ever happened into his world was in that file box. It was his safeguard where he kept "the goods," as Richard would've said. He had "the goods" on everybody. If you were young and foolish, you might be flattered to think that he thought so much of you that he stored all your Very Important Files away because he couldn't stop thinking about you, simply couldn't forget. But it was too late for me to be taken in by his spewing of "the goods" on me.

I'd finally figured out how he'd forever played to everyone's weakness. It was his own private game of "Gotcha!" Before leaving this world, he'd managed to modify the game and learned to play "the goods" more often to strengths. That might've been where his final turn-around began, when at last he matured and grew beyond the rage of Richard, when he let go of the beasts and the burdens of abuse, when he released the savagery that lived at a barren, childhood home at Harrow's Branch.

He no longer gravitated to weakness, nor tried to capitalize on the criminal code of the misbegotten. The thief came clean. The bully learned compassion. The charlatan paid his own way. He learned that people could like him for the composite self he'd managed to draw with the ashes left from the fires his father had set. He learned how to reciprocate, and found in giving freely a certain satisfaction more lucrative than receiving had ever proved to be.

But alas, it was too late. And at least I remembered enough not to stay.

Banshees and Bottom Feeders

My son's apartment reeked of schooling – papers, computers, books, shadowed heaps of waiting laundry, all stacked in various places, desks and counter tops, nooks and crannies. I let myself in quietly, long after visiting hours were over at the hospital, confident that I wouldn't wake anyone. But what rose to greet me was almost more than I could bear. The quiet dark conjured up some the most menacing memories of some twenty years before, and I froze in the hallway, seized by images and sounds that only I could see and hear.

...

It's late in the year, seventy-two, nearing the end of the winter session at Parsons. With finals early in the morning, I'd put Baby Dieks down for the night and had continued studying well past one. I kept hearing something, and then nothing. I finally shook it off, thinking I was becoming paranoid from living alone. So I kept trying to ignore whatever I heard, a rustling or crunching movement through the snow. Maybe a raccoon, or a rat. Too cold for a cat, too late for a dog.

Shortly after two, I turned out the lights and went to bed. Just as I started to doze off, I heard the old oil furnace in the basement groan and buzz and finally click off. I got up, went to the baby's room and put another cover on him in his crib. Then I went around the corner to the bathroom, where there was an ancient cellar trap door that, when pulled up, released to drop a flight of creaking wooden stairs down to the dirt floor of the basement.

I grabbed the flashlight from the windowsill and went down the rickety stairs into the drafty darkness. I made my way across the uneven floor to the furnace, all the while reassuring myself that I was not afraid of the dark. Nothing harmful was in that basement, and I'd just push the reset button on the furnace, then go calmly and quietly back up the stairs as the old monster heaved and sighed and unleashed a rush of recovered heat.

As I headed back up the stairs, I heard the noise again. Something was definitely outside by the back porch, but I couldn't bring myself to look out the window or even at the window. I turned out the lights, and shuffled quietly back to the living room, carefully pulling the blinds forward to see what I could out front. There was nothing. No footprints, no animal slinking along or scurrying by. No stranger's eyes peering back in at me, no arm with hook or hand hanging from my roof. As my imagination offered what-if's, my heart raced uncontrollably. I tried to calm myself, to put fear into submission, reminding myself that I was always scared of the dark, even when I knew the reason, which was probably just outside my window.

I moved toward the bedroom and carefully pulled that blind forward. There was a car parked at the edge of the alley, just next to the house. I didn't recognize the car, and I still saw no one near it or the house. Not knowing what to think or do, I sat down on the bed, half angry, half disgusted that my heart was thumping in my ears, while I pulled the covers over my lap and closed my eyes.

Just then there was a deafening crash, and in the split second it took to turn and look up behind me, the noise came through the window, into the bedroom, across my bed. A body smashed through the storm window and the inside window, with glass and window frame splintering and shattering into a million, slow-motion pieces.

A billy club led the body, slamming from side to side like a blind man's cane. As the curtain swung back into place, a shaft of light from the streetlight glistened on the ice, snow, and glass that had settled into footprints across my turquoise bedspread.

He jumped off the bed and in one sweeping motion, flicked on the light, grabbed me by the hair, and tossed me through the doorway of the living room. As I rose to my knees, he kicked me in the middle of my back, and I was sent sprawling onto the living room carpet, where he jumped on my back and yanked my head up by a fistful of hair.

"Where is he? I'll kill ya if ya don't answer. Where is he?" He released his grip and my nose hit the floor with a sickening crack.

He leaned down beside my ear, screaming like an animal, with his knee in my back, anchoring me to the floor. All I saw were his knuckles, white with rage, wrapped around the tapered end of a Billy club, repeatedly, rhythmically banging the floor just next to my head, and in an instant, I'm back in horror of it.

A million miles away I hear a baby crying, "Mama, Mama?" in the darkness. But a banshee holds me down and I can't breathe. A banshee pulls me up by my hair, stretching my throat tight, constricting my air, and silence visits me there, as the wild thing looks at me from the side. Though I try, not one sound gets by.

Something wet's trickling sideways across my cheek, and then, abruptly changing course, it slithers down the side of my face. I open one eye and next to me, a small puddle of blood has begun to bead up on the carpet. Blood splatters with the next blow of the club and I realize there's no end to his thumb, that it must have been severed by the glass when he came through the window.

He doesn't seem to notice. He's somewhere else, not of this world. Not of any world I've ever known. I was sure I'd remember to avoid a place with horrible creatures like this.

Baby Dieks is crying now. His pleas for "Mama!" have been replaced with wails of fear and the unknown. At this point, our unknowns are pretty much the same, I'm figuring. Gripping the rug, I pull myself forward, trying to get my knees under me so I can rise with a hundred and seventy pounds on my back. Dieks is surveying the room, no longer screaming, but his voice has dropped to a sinister whisper in my ear.

I'm trying to form the words, to tell him that I've got to get to the baby's room. But again, the words are choked back into my throat as he moves off me for a moment and I get to my knees. Just as I move one knee forward, he jumps on my back again.

"Come save her, you cocksuckin' coward!" while the club's banging away on the floor next to my pounding head, and the blood just keeps spraying great blotches across my pajamas, and on to the rug, the side of the couch, the bottom of mint-green walls, varnished baseboard and into empty, unreceptive airspace.

"He's downstairs, isn't he? I heard the fuckin' trap door, you moron. Did you think I wouldn't figure it out? Huh?" He's yanking my head back again, and I see long, blonde strands of some woman's hair, floating away as they're pulled out. Ride 'em, Cowboy! We might as well make the most of it.

The baby's screaming and the temperature in the house is dropping rapidly as gusts of wind wail in from the north through a full length of the missing window. From living room to bedroom, in a jagged trail across the floor, clumps of mud and blotches of blood blend with melting snow and ice, while broken glass leads back to what's left of the window: a skeletal frame with compound fractures falling in every direction, splintered remains of sill and casing strewn across the bed and floor of two rooms.

I hear a gurgling sound from my own throat. I think I'm talking but I'm not. I'm choking, maybe on one of my teeth, I think. "No ... one's ... here," I finally get out. "No one, but me, Libby ... and the baby ... " and I let my head rest in the cool blood pool as he releases my hair. He shifts his weight to the knee that's on the floor instead of in my back.

The baby's back to sobbing, "Mama, Mama, Mama," calming himself with a singsong sadness of jerks and sobs, a lamenting cry for someone who can't seem to listen.

I'm too beaten to move. I just keep looking at the trail across the rug at ground zero. "We're going to freeze now. I think this is okay," my flat, dead voice says.

He jumped up and was running from room to room, switching on light after light. In my mind, I was still pinned to the floor; he had never gotten up. I lay quiet and peacefully dead, I imagined, as he ran to the bathroom, and lifting the trap door, I heard the old stairs creak down again.

"Come on up, you sonofabitch," he growled, as he beat the club from side to side in the cavernous opening. Step by treacherous step, he descended slowly, carefully, into the darkness, roaring, "Get yer motherfuckin' ass up here!"

Just then, the furnace clicked off again. I remembered thinking I wouldn't be needing to go down and push the reset ever again, and he didn't bother. It must have startled him, though, and he appeared next to me almost immediately after slamming the door behind him. That set the baby off and he stood rocking at the end of his bed, crying the Mama song, while holding out his hand for Daddy as he passed through the baby's room in quest of the intruder.

I'd gotten up and made my way to the doorway between my bedroom and the baby's. I'd managed to get into a pair of old rubber thongs I used for bedroom slippers. But everywhere I went, pieces of glass lodged in the bottom and sides, and soon slivers were in my feet.

A trickle ran down my cheek, where my head had rested in the blood, but when I reached up to wipe it away my hand was sliced cleanly open by a sliver of glass, jutting straight out of my head just below the hairline. I couldn't seem to focus on the room or the moment. I could see the baby, but felt light, almost weightless, as I inched toward his crib.

Suddenly, the banshee was behind me, like a cat. "Whose car's outside?" he's hissing in my ear.

"I don' know."

"Well," and his voiced increased in volume again, "the cocksucker ain't goin' nowhere without a coil wire. If the sonofabitch wants to leave my ol' lady's house, he's gonna have to hoof it!" he roared into the night.

Then, as quickly as the animal reared and raged, it retreated. He lifted my face tenderly up to his and said, "Oh, Sweet Liz B, you're bleeding. Here, let me wipe this." He pulled a pair of red underwear from his coat pocket and gently blotted my head, as I thought only, those aren't mine. He stood upright and looked from my bedroom to the living room and back, and quietly said, "We'd better get out of here. Better get my little family somewhere safe and warm."

He walked ahead of me and over to Dieks' crib. He lifted him out and patted his diapered bottom, soothing his sobs and quelling his fears. He then laid him down on top of all the crib blankets and rolled them around him like protective cocoon. Every one of them. He put a gentle, guiding hand on my shoulder and moved me to my closet, wading and shuffling through glass, ice, blood, mud and snow, wood splinters and covers, and whatever else had been dragged, dropped or pulled into the one-man riot.

"Better get your big snow boots," he said sweetly, gentlemanly, as he handed me a scarf from the closet. "It's a real screamin' meemie out there tonight." He opened the front door with the still-bleeding thumb, territorially marking everything he touched. As I went through the door, he turned out the lights, locking the door from the inside, closing it tightly, leaving the bedroom curtains whipping around in the great gusts of wind that raged outside and in.

We walked for a couple of blocks and turned, heading up a steep hill. He carried Dieks rolled up in the blankets. The baby was sleeping soundly, I imagined, and though I followed in his footsteps,

I kept slipping, or maybe fainting. He was very understanding and kept slowing down, periodically stopping to help me to my feet again, coaxing me along.

When at last I saw the Nova, I turned, glancing back down the hill. There lay behind us a perfectly pristine stretch of otherwise untouched snow, with a single, winding, footprinted path made along the trek we'd just taken, and a perfect view of my house. The bedroom curtains were still waving good-bye as he tenderly guarded my head from bumping the doorframe and I eased on down and into the passenger seat.

He drove in the darkness, with not another car on the street, straight to his place, the place I called The Bordello. The baby never even stirred as he and his bedding cocoon were gathered and carried in, in through the doorway of the ugly red beads, in to the room with marbled mirrors, in to the sea of bed where we'd never taken a number, nor been called for our turn.

I stood behind him, watching not so much him as the baby, not remembering moving, or standing, or walking through doors, but doing so in a trance that seemed to follow a homing device in the baby bundle. He motioned me to lie down on the bed, next to the baby, so I did, never removing coat or scarf, boots, or blood.

He was carefully taking off a blood-soaked glove that seemed to be bonded to his coagulated thumb. A large, liver-like chunk of blood danced down like a marionette as he set the glove aside. He pulled it away from his hand and held it up to the light, looking at it with great curiosity, though never uttering a sound. He turned and bent down, and I heard water running, and the medicine chest door squeaked open and shut with a quiet click. He emerged from the bathroom in briefs, and as he reached up to turn off the light, I saw that the makeshift bandage that wrapped his thumb was a Kotex pad with red masking tape around the top and the bottom. I remembered thinking only, I've never used pads.

I was relieved when he walked past me and into the living room. Within the hour, he was sound asleep, snoring loudly. I tiptoed in to find him huddled up on the floor, just inside the front door, using his shoes as a pillow, using himself as a blockade. I no longer felt sorry for him, or me -- just the baby. In the next room, there slept a child with a wild man for one parent and a big nothing for the other. I couldn't get the door open to run, even if I could've run with a bundled baby and no courage. He'd destroyed my only refuge, and I had no means to get back across town anyway.

I missed my test the next morning. I don't think there was ever any grand design on his part. I don't think that he ever actually tried to get me to fail at any time. But, in that particular course, the final constituted thirty percent of the entire grade. I knew I'd have to tell the prof what really happened. Because, as it turned out, truth was stranger than fiction, and only truth could bail my sorry ass out of the sure failure that this would result in.

By noon, after having shared Twinkies and a Coke (the only things in his refrigerator) with him, he decided he'd better go and fix "that window," as if someone else did it. Of course, as luck would have it, he seemed to imply, he was the responsible adult here and he'd just have to be the hero. He could and would make right the wrongs of the world that would allow such awful and inexplicable things to occur.

He made a few adjustments before leaving, including a trade-off of Watkins Carbolic Salve on the missing tip of his thumb and a large band aid strip wrapped across the top, with several layers of first aid tape wrapping it. It wasn't going anywhere. He took his bloody pair of gloves from the bathroom and dropped them in the kitchen garbage; a bloody pair of women's underwear followed. He looked at them curiously, like he wasn't sure when they'd arrived on the scene, but he knew that whatever they were and wherever they'd come from, it wasn't good, and he wasn't one to sentimentalize.

He moved us from house to car to house with unerring accuracy and efficiency. If in any case I'd wanted to run, I wouldn't have had the chance. Nudged forward to the front door of my house, he reached around me and unlocked the door, pushing me in with the baby, then steering me to the couch on the right side of the room, where only a few pieces of shrapnel or poisonous gas might still be lingering from the biting cold of the battle. The entire house resembled a war zone, and I sat listening as my stomach churned with anxiety, knowing I wouldn't be able to afford cleanup, fix up, startup, or repairs of any kind to anything.

It couldn't have been more than twenty, thirty degrees at the most. But he went on, undaunted, paging through the phonebook, demanding a furnace man from the oil company over there right now, yesterday, in fact. He called the paint store, requesting their mobile glass repair over there to reframe and bring panes for a very old window. Yes, of course it was an emergency. We'd been away, he told the guy. There'd been a break-in.

As he talked to the man on the phone, a tow truck pulled up by the alley. An older man in a beige trench coat got out, and went to the late model Plymouth Fury, unlocking the trunk, taking out a suitcase and a briefcase and then relocking it. As the truck hooked his car up, another car pulled up, the man got in, and they left.

Dieks watched all of this with an uncanny detachment. The car that he'd identified as that of a midnight lover, a car with Ohio plates, and missing its coil wire, was being towed down the street. He knew nothing of it, cared nothing about it.

He hung up the phone and walked into the bedroom where he stripped the bed and brought the bundle of sheets, blankets and spread into the living room, dropping it in the chair by the front door. "Busy Bee Cleaners," he said, pointing down at it. "They've got a new one-hour drop-off now."

"And you, Shorty," he said, picking Dieks up from where he sat watching on my lap. "I'll bet you'd like a great big hug, huh?"

Dieks hugged him back, and smiled a weak, unsure smile as he looked down at me. "Maybe a new car for this big boy?" He poked a playful finger into his little boy belly and hugged him when he answered.

"Uh-huh." The cure-all for big screw-ups was to buy the little boy another shiny Matchbox car.

"Well, I'll tell ya what. We'll just go on downtown, grab a bite to eat, do some shopping. Hey, now, would ya looky there," he said, pointing out to the street.

The oil company truck pulled up and the man had opened the side storage area and was taking out his tools. Dieks opened the front door and directed him to the stairs, past the dried blotches of blood, past the refrozen glacial rivers of the night, on to the door where there lurked an invisible lover in the form of a troll, just under the fold-down stairs that creaked once again and dropped.

I stood up and moved to the table in the dining room where I looked down at the blood-splattered study guide for the final I'd missed that morning. My hand moved to the tight, crusty dried blood at my temple and down my chin and neck. I went to the bathroom and for the first time, felt the sharp pain in my feet, the ache of bruises in my back, and the despair of my life, when I turned and saw my face in the mirror. I gasped and quickly reached down to turn the faucets on.

My eyes looked like a raccoon's, with black mascara smeared around them in huge, watermarked circles. My lips were swollen twice their normal size, and where my face wasn't discolored with the black and blue of odd-shaped bruises, trails of dried blood raced up and down, forward and back, as if in search of some hidden track, some secret path on a face map. I had patches of bloody bare spots on both the top and right side of my head, where long, thick, blonde hair had once fallen to my shoulders. The necklace I always wore had served as a saw, leaving chain slices high and low, frail and futile attempts to slit my own throat.

As I began wiping away the remains of the night, I swore to the dying eyes of the victim that it was the last. I would leave somehow. I would simply walk out into the night. It would mercifully swallow me up, and the baby would be safe with my mother. I would solve the dilemmas of the world by sinking slowly into the sludge of the Skunk, unnoticed among the carp and catfish, just another of many in a simple world of scavenging bottom feeders.

Ophelia's Roll Call

He called her name. She could not speak,
for she was miles away ... and weak.
He scanned the room with pen in hand,
so professorial and grand.

She stared into the empty eyes,
raccoon, clown, and phantom-sized.
With no surprise, she brushed the hair.
When it fell out, she didn't care.

With fingernail, she numbly traced
the trails of blood that framed her face.
She softly sighed, denying
who and what was sad and dying.

And then he called her name again,
with disbelief and nervous grin.
But she sat miles and miles away,
shamed in what she couldn't say.

She's just a misplaced book, you see,
and knows that he can't tell.
He thinks she's steeped in Poetry,
when, in fact, she's shelved in Hell.

Happy, Happy Birthday, Baby

He's on the living room floor at his place on Spruce Street, sitting in front of the couch where I'm laying on my side. I collapsed there just after we got back from closing the Fool's Pair O' Dice. His head leans back on the cushion, straining to be conveniently nestled against my breasts.

Staring at the ceiling, with yet another beer in his hand, he says, "You should see Lucy's kid, Li'l Dumb Clan. He's really somethin'."

"Probably pretty big by now, I bet."

"No. He's, short, like Luce. Like I was. Her other one, The Ben Clan, got tall and lanky, you know, gangly like a beanpole and dumb as a stump. But at least he works, not like the ol' man. Has a family, does okay for himself. Li'l Clan's somethin' else. Works all week, gets his check, tops off the tank in his Lincoln, and then takes off. Goes and goes 'til it's gone. Works all week to get that check, and then drives to the nearest town to get laid. Over and over. Week after week. Sometimes it's Douds, sometimes Eldon, Floris, even as far away as Fairfield. Anywhere but Bloomfield, and he gets lucky every night!"

"Lucky? Lucky? This doesn't sound like anybody you know? You guys are so screwed up. Is this written in your DNA or somethin'?"

He turned, "You knew Richard as well as anybody. What do you think?"

"I think you're all obsessed. There's deviation running rampant in your parts. It's a compulsion that's unleashed with the first rush of hormones and never stops until it's fed, or you're dead. I've never seen people so quick to equate a good fuck with good luck. You're very sick men, you Shaunessy progeny."

"You got one of them boys too, y'know."

"Oh, I know. But I managed to get some degree of civilized restraint hammered into his head along the line."

He turned up to my face, grinning. "Which head?"

"The one on his shoulders that he thinks with, unlike the rest of you guys, so far. I don't s'pose any of ya think about all the shit that can happen nowadays. You just evolved without the contingencies, ignoring the advent of new and hideous diseases."

"Hey, if it happens, it happens. He don' care. They don' care."

"Am I to read that as you don' care?"

"Oh, I care. I jus' don' see it as a new way to punish an old vice. After all, it's what livin's all about."

"It's not what livin's about; it might be what dyin's about."

"What's livin' about then?"

"It's not about getting laid, that's for sure. Anybody can get laid. Anywhere, anytime, anyplace. You don't believe me, just go to a discount store sometime and take a good look around. You see the most incredible combinations. I'm tellin' ya, it's no big deal. Anybody can get laid."

He turned around to look at me again. "It must be what livin's about if anybody can do it. Besides, to some people that is a big deal. To some people, it's the ultimate big deal, like life!"

"What? It's a goal? You plan your life around gettin' into somebody's drawers?"

"Sometime you're gonna have to see the other side."

"I was the other side."

"No, I mean that a lot of people like gettin' laid."

"But they don't plan their lives around it. You're nearly fifty years old. When are you goin' to figure out there's somethin' else out there that translates to a good time?"

"What else is there?"

"Wow. Where to start … "

"Start anywhere. What else is there that's as good as great sex - or as great as good sex, for that matter? My worst day in the rack is as good as my best day anywhere in the world."

"Then you're severely culturally deprived."

"Ooohhh, big words. Name one, Miss Yogurt Culture. Just one. I bet you can't name even one thing you've actually experienced yourself that's even close to a good orgasm. Or something, one thing that's as much fun, or as good as sweaty sex even without an orgasm."

"Get serious. This discussion has taken a particularly disgusting turn."

"I am serious, you know I am. Twenty years ago we had sex so great I still get wet dreams thinking about it."

"You're sick."

"I'm waiting. Name one thing. See? You can't."

"Oh, yes, I can. But you won't listen and you don't know. You act like everything begins and ends at the outskirts of town. Or should I say the skirts in town? Your biggest trip's been goin' down on some visiting crotch, or getting a foreign blow job."

"So? What's better? I'll wait. I'll give you five minutes. No, ten. I'll give you ten minutes."

"I don't need ten. I can give you all the examples you want without time to pause and reflect. But you've got to search your mind for something to compare them to. Try your son. Or, try to imagine the splendor and magnificence of a New York stage, of Broadway. All the glitter and glamour of costuming and sets and--"

"You're comparing a hard-on to Broadway?"

"I'm doing my best. Bear with me. Imagine something so breathtaking that you'd pay a hundred dollars a ticket to sit through it, front and center, like *Phantom of the Opera*, with a huge chandelier descending and music pulsating ... "

"I've seen some pulsating shows that'd be worth a hundred and I'd pay a hundred for you to sit front and center," as he grabbed his crotch.

"I know this is a real stretch, Dieks. Try to imagine something so beautiful that your senses overload. Try to see sights and hear sounds that are so wonderful that you almost forget to breathe."

"Like when we used to come at the same time?"

"No, not like that. This might be out of your reach. Remember the time, about a gazillion years ago, that we went to the dump just outside Eldon, to that little town, what was it, you remember? Maybe Eddyville, or something? I don't remember exactly where it was, but I remember the guy helping at the dump. He asked if you'd ever been to Eldon, and he said he planned to go there someday. But he just couldn't imagine what it would be like. And Ottumwa? That was like Kilimanjaro. Anyway, we laughed and laughed at him on the way home, but this is all kind of like that. You act like I'm being uppity, but every time I tell you something you don't know or haven't done, you say I'm trying to get snooty. Okay, here's one.

"Imagine, in your feeble, underfed mind, holding your newborn grandchild, just moments old, and recognizing the contour of *your* face or *your* eyes. Seeing your lips in his smile or the wonder and mystery of generations passed from fingertips to toes, from mothers to sons to daughters, and on and on. Is that a wonder you might want to try to compare to sex?"

"No. That's the wonder that results from great sex."

"Does it all come back to this with you? How about sunrise and sunset? What about the simple pleasure of waking up each day and knowing you'll get one more chance to make your sorry life worthwhile and one more day to find peace with yourself? When you sit down and tally this grand life that you've led, with hundreds of women bedded and a few women wedded, d'ya think you'll find one person who'll say, 'Oh yeah, that's the life I wanted to live. That's important.'"

"Maybe I can't know all those things. Maybe you were supposed to show me those things, but instead you left me behind eatin' dust. Maybe I did all I knew how to do, the best I could do it. Maybe the Injun in my genes couldn't ever imagine those sorts of things, like the guy at the dump. Maybe, just maybe I knew that. And I was just waitin' for all those maybes to settle in your head and remind you that you had to come back and show me. I needed you to come back, 'cause I was doing the best I could without you."

"Fuck you."

"Okay. Let's go."

"You know what I mean. Twenty years ago that cock-eyed logic might've worked. But I outgrew it, along with your Neanderthal mentality. I thought you'd grow with me. I trusted you'd be there and we'd become old crab buckets together, but you couldn't resist all of those other passing asses. There just wasn't a thing as intriguing to you as a pair of long legs spread wide and inviting. Glorious sunsets didn't mean shit unless someone was comin' or goin' or comin' and comin'."

"Every woman I ever took to bed, I pretended she was you."

"You're so full o' shit. That's an insult to me and everybody you've ever been with. Every woman you took to bed you notched on your slick dick as a personal victory. After you couldn't keep track of who and how, you just needed a familiar face to assign to the notches."

"Where did you ever get those words? I can't believe you're saying those things. I always waited for you."

"I listened to you guys when you didn't think I was close enough to hear, that's where. You're beyond help. I can't carry on this conversation if you're going to keep up these sophomoric antics trying to get laid. You must have some real strip 'n' spread bimbos on the side if this is what they're buyin' into."

Dieks shook his head. "I guess I just don't have the right words anymore."

"Oh, you have 'em alright. They just aren't my kind of words."

"You outgrew me."

"That's one view. You quit growing. That's another."

"You stopped listening to what I said when you left," he said with a pout.

"No, sporto. Long before I left."

"You were all I had. When you left, you took everything with you. How was I s'posed to keep growing when I had nothin'?"

"Take a ticket, Dieks. Get in line. I took less than that with me when I went in search of another life. I had to find a new town, a new home, and new friends. I was responsible for a baby and an education without an ounce of support or a dime to call my own. My whole family was back here, everything and everyone I knew and needed were back here. You ended up with everything, every wisp and whisper that might've given me even a little strength. And you fuckin' squandered it away on cheap tricks."

"I loved you, Elizabeth Anne, from the very first."

"It was a sick, demented love. In the end, we both knew that."

"It was all I had to give."

"It was all I took. And it wasn't all you had to give. It was all you were willing to give."

"I gave you other things."

"Yeah. Black eyes, bruises, welts, promises. Hollow things that never held water."

"Do we have to talk about this?"

"No. We're done. It always comes full circle, anyway. We tried to love each other and it didn't work. So, here we are again. I get the couch and you get the floor."

"I have a bedroom," he said, motioning toward the hall.

"I have a home. And a husband," I answered, motioning toward the front door. "Besides, even if I wasn't married and was desperate,

I'd never even consider sleeping in a bed where the multitudes have come before me."

"That's very funny."

"It was meant to be. But I wouldn't quote it to anyone you might be trying to impress or undress. What time is it?"

"Four thirty-six," he answered, looking up at the digital on the stereo.

"Wanna wait up and go see the sunrise?"

"I'd sure like to ... "

"How come I hear a 'but,' lurking in the wings?"

"But, I promised Red I'd pick him up in three hours. I need at least an hour of sleep before I get cleaned up and head out again."

"To where?"

"Quad Cities. There's a show where the Benz'll just shine."

"Oh, you mean that ol' car you were goin' to give me for back alimony?"

"I don't think so. I'm pretty shot, but I think I'd remember sayin' somethin' like that."

"Oh gosh, maybe I'm wrong. Maybe it was seven years of back child support. Let's see, at two hundred a month times twelve months a year, that's twenty-four hundred, times seven years. It was seven wasn't it, when you called and offered your son for adoption, wasn't it? Are you listening?"

"What? Yes. Liz B, why're you being so mean?"

"I was just saying that since you're having all these pangs of love and remembrance, that maybe we could settle an old debt. It'd only be about seventeen thousand dollars. That's not a lot. It doesn't even include interest or penalty or any of those things the IRS would make you cough up."

"How do you feel about Cadillacs?"

"Poor White Trashmobiles. Isn't that what you called Bill's?"

"Okay, uh, what about a great limited edition Impala convertible?"

"Worse. Middle Class Wanna Be's or Has Been's."

"It's a classic."

"It's shit, and you know it. I got a better idea. How 'bout a little ol' Buick? Oh, I know. I'm confused. They're the same color, that old convertible you said I could have."

"If you'd marry me." He's turned up towards me again. "That's a standing offer, the Buick's yours, if you marry me. So, will you?"

"What?"

"Will you marry me?"

"Can't. I'm already married."

"Get divorced. You did it before."

"Oh, but I was young. I'm not as resilient anymore."

"Marry me again and all I have is yours."

"Ohhhh, righhhht. 'Sides, that's the law, you moron. And that's sure somethin' I'd really want to go through again."

"Aw, c'mon," he's whining again.

"You need one of those red circles with the line through it that says 'WHINERS'."

Struggling, he got to his feet and disappeared. I heard him rifling around in the kitchen, and the refrigerator door slammed.

"C'm'ere a minute."

"No. I'm tired. You com'ere."

"No, now come in here. Right now."

I rolled over and swung my feet down, resting on my knees with my head on my arms. I finally got up and said, "If I'm movin', I should be movin' right on down the line."

"No, now look." He was waving a blue piece of paper. "It's the title to the Buick."

"What? No Mercy Benz? Is this 'cause I'm a second-class citizen?" I moved over and looked at the paper.

"No, the Buick's more you. It's cuter. More feminine."

"Oh, boy, you are desperate. I've been called a lot of things in my life, but feminine's never been one of 'em. So, this is mine?"

"Could be."

He was walking backwards, waving it at me, like a hypnotist with a pocket watch. Edging down a short hall to his bedroom, he switched on the light and fell back into bed, laying the title at the end on the comforter.

"It's yours. All ya gotta do is one little thing, then you'll remember." He slowly raised his index finger.

I stood in the doorway, shaking my head. "I think this is the first time you've ever gotten more drunk than me. 'Cause I know you wouldn't even attempt this sober."

"It frees the senses. Fly, come fly with me."

"You're nuts."

"Say, enough of that talk. Let's see some action."

I laughed. "Boy, that'd be the most expensive lay you every had, drunk or sober."

"No, I think the most expensive lay I ever had was the brat."

"Good Ol' Screw Mandy?"

"Ooohhh, we're getting a little testy, aren't we?"

"Dieks, it was a pun, a funny little pun."

"Come on over here and I'll show ya a little pun fun."

I turned and walked to the living room waving good-bye over my shoulder. "Night, Delly Pie. Happy Birthday, have a good life."

I turned off the living room light and closed the door behind me before walking down the road to Mom's.

Birds were singing and the sun was just beginning to break through in the east. Pity he'd never see it, I thought.

The Keel

"He was very violent when you were married, wasn't he."
It wasn't really a question as much as a statement of fact.
"Yes, Suzi, he was very violent," I said curtly.
"He wasn't always that way, you know."
"So I've been told. People change, right? The only thing was, it went so far back into his life that it was impossible to know him without knowing the violence in some form or other."
"He never acted like that with anybody except wives, I guess."
"Well, I don't know for sure, but that's always been my guess, too. The more I knew of him, the closer we became, the angrier he seemed to get, maybe at the thought of it. It was a Catch-22. The more intense the love, the more determined he became to sabotage the relationship. It was as if he couldn't separate those particular emotions. Love and hate seemed synonymous.
"One moment he'd pledge never-ending love, and the next minute I'd be beaten to a pulp. For every episode I survived, he seemed to conjure up another to carry out. Only the next would be worse and longer lasting. The less I carried on about the injustice, the more cruel he became. Toward the end, just before I left, there were so many destructive things, happening so often, I knew I'd have to get out or die."
"You had nowhere to go? And a baby? No money, no job, no car, no one in your corner?"
"You been reading my mail?"
"He told me."
"Really."
I stood in what I considered casual conversation with Suzi, more cordial than intimate, I thought. "Exchanging niceties," Red would say, putting one hand up like a traffic cop, refusing the plate

of sandwiches, chips and Cheetos, refusing Hawaiian Punch served in plastic cups at his nephew's house out at the edge of town.

I'd never actually met Suzi in the years before or after my life with Dieks. Besides Butch and Red, Suzi and her husband Alan had been his other best friends in both junior high and high school before Richard had him sent away. In Phoenix, just a few months after we were married, Dieks tried looking them up, but we never found them. That always seemed a shame to me. There were only a few whose opinions he respected and insights he valued, and they seemed to have both good sense and good intentions. They knew more of his life than most of his remaining friends, with the exception of Red, perhaps.

"I didn't think he ever saw the abuse."

"Oh, he saw it and knew it. He just couldn't say it. It was years after you were gone. He was married to 'Manda. They had more problems than you had, and he said he couldn't ever figure out why they were married. He said they had absolutely nothing in common, and he didn't know why he ever went home to 'the warpath' day in and day out. Aside from nightly fights and sex, they hardly knew each other."

"I thought that was a prerequisite with him. If you wanted to survive, you took the sex and ignored the rest."

"He was sick."

"Oh, very."

"After you left, he got worse."

"I didn't think that was possible."

"It wasn't the way you might think. It was more like he got lost. He once told me that he went to you to refuel. Long after you were gone, he said it occurred to him that he had taken so much from you that you probably didn't have anything left to give. He had so much bad in him that he just kept using up all your good."

"All my what?"

"All your love, your strength. But he didn't know it at the time. He didn't understand marriage, or at least healthy marriage. He had no idea that it was supposed to be give and take, that you supplied him and he supplied you and it kept the whole thing going. When he realized what happened, he just felt terrible."

"Not nearly as terrible as I felt. Worthless, stupid, empty, emotionally drained, with this little kid and nowhere to go, no one to turn to … "

"But neither did he. And by then, it was too late to turn anything around. He knew he needed help, but he was so stubborn and proud. He just figured he'd get the same thing from his friends that he'd gotten from you. Only it wasn't the same. So he just modified everything a bit and hung on to what you'd left him with. He said sometimes he'd refuse to talk to Amanda because every time he opened his mouth the words that came out were yours."

"I'll bet that was a real hoot."

"He couldn't stop it. Sometimes, he'd get really upset with his friends, not because they'd done anything, but because he'd spent so much time with them and lost all that time with you. He just kept adding more and more of these guys, like he was collecting them, feeding on their lives and their experiences, trying to get up to where he was when he'd been with you. After a while, he knew it wouldn't work. Couldn't work. He always said you were the keel."

"The what?"

"The keel, the center of all things balanced."

"Fuck him."

Suzi reached over. "It's okay … to be angry with him, Elizabeth. It's all part of everything."

"I spent two or three years in hell because of him, because of his sickness. I lost most of my heart and all of my soul to his sickness. I salvaged what little bit of emotional strength I had to pick up and start over and fought every day of my life to keep memories of what he'd done away from me and mine. Now, in respect for the dead, I've returned to pay my dues. Everything I've denied and refused for twenty years has come forward to claim what little I have left. I just can't do this again. Everything I struggled to do, be, buy, see, or feel, he managed to destroy. Every dream I ever dreamt, he left shredded, every hope I ever had, he annihilated, and every wish, he wasted. Everything."

"Except your son."

"Except *our* son. People always seem to forget that Dieks is *our* son, not just mine. His mother died trying to protect her son, the son that only she claimed. I'd already resolved that history wouldn't get a chance to repeat itself. He never got the chance to plant one seed of hate in our son. He never got the opportunity for that one precious out-of-control moment where he could reignite that sick cycle of abuse and humiliation."

"Liz, he knew that. In fact, he said almost every word of what you've said. He knew he couldn't correct it. Eventually, he did learn to control it, with Nicki, but he never again trusted himself to be half of something."

"He had a third wife."

"No, he probably had a second mother. Freud would've loved it. Even up until a few years ago, she'd come back, hole up with him for a few days, and then go home to her husband. They just used up each other's sexual tension. They'd casually converse, go out to dinner in a very removed, civilized manner, and then go their separate ways again. He was practicing for the time when you'd come home."

"Get serious. There was absolutely no comparison."

"Oh, he knew that. But it didn't make any difference to him."

"I nearly died, more than once, at his hands. There was nothing he could've done to convince me to entrust my life to him again. Zero. He was Jekyll and Hyde, and I was an experiment at Auschwitz, with Mengele in charge. Our marriage was a study in graduated lessons. Movement and Survival With Lower Forms of Life."

"You know better than that."

"Do I? And even if I thought I knew, what then? What does it matter now? He's dead. Stone cold dead. Any evil he left in his wake will have to remain unaltered for all time. That's just the way it is. His people say death neutralizes everything, everybody."

"I think you need to come to terms with what he did to you. He loved you--"

"God forbid if I'd ever been around when he disliked me."

"You were too strong for him, Liz. He spent his whole life looking for someone to love and admire, someone he could do things for and be worthy of, someone who needed him as desperately as he needed them, someone who tried to understand all the sickness in his past, and tried to get beyond it. He thought that someone was you. But you never faltered or fell. You never needed him. You never reached out for him to rescue you. He was needy, jealous and insecure. But through you, for you, he felt proud and important.

"After you, he worked harder than he'd ever worked at creating all kinds of things, art, sculpture, show cars, second-to-none marvels. He'd win all kinds of prizes, and everybody'd shower him with praise. For that moment he'd feel pretty good about himself. But afterwards, it was always the same. You didn't come home. What he did was never good enough to get you and his sons back. Excellence in things he knew how to do better than anyone else never corrected the mountains of mistakes he'd made. He just kept backing himself into a corner where he was little more than a lonely, detached, unreachable misfit."

"Aren't we all? Look at us here. All of us are retrofits."

"But Dieks thought it was just him. Richard never gave him any self-confidence. His mother died too early in his life. He needed someone to encourage, support, and assure him that we all have problems. We get over them and move on. All he knew was conquering women. But even that became painful as he got older. They were just another distraction."

Suzi stopped talking as Alan moved closer to her from where he'd been standing off to one side.

"Finish this thought, Alan, honey. 'Women were always praising all Dieks Shaunessy knew how to do and that made him feel better, but as he got older, even that became too painful. Everything was too much for him until … '"

Alan searched my face to see my reaction to her sentence. I simply listened without response.

He pointed the bottle at me, and said, "Until he saw her again." He took a drink. "Twice, in fact. Once was on his birthday a couple years back. Nicole was in Texas. By the time she got back, Dieks said he knew he couldn't keep taking up any more time in her life. Best woman he ever dated. The next time was … last year?" He's looking at Suzi and she nods. "On the main drag in Eldon. He had his car there … "

"For your bicentennial or some celebration, and I was in town for my brother-in-law's kid's wedding. All of my brothers and sisters and their wives and husbands, including mine, went down to the loop for the festivities after the wedding reception. We were pretty wasted by then, none of us being heavy drinkers. Sam spotted Dieks and the T-Bird and we all went over. My God, he shook Sam's hand like he was the deliverer, and then he grabbed me."

"Dieks said he was on his absolute best behavior that night. He said he tried to get you to come over and get acquainted with us, but you were pressed for time. He confided in us that he was pretty sure you were thinking about coming home."

"M'God, there's that word again. I have no home. He won it in the great war, all tribal lands south of Interstate eighty. I was given hunting, fishing and camping rights on the lands of the northern tundra, everything in, on and around Cedar Falls and Waterloo. All that fine cold, barren land, mine, mine, mine."

"But then he'd bought your mother's house. One more marker, and he just knew that you'd come home to that. Each year had a Liz B marker, you see. One was when you stopped by on his birthday. The next was when you came to see the Bird displayed downtown. Another was when you called to tell him that the grandbabies were born, and again, when your mother passed away, and you'd told him how you'd help him get the house. Finally, when you stopped in town to do some legal work and you left a message on his machine. He retaped your voice onto a cassette and kept it."

"This just gets sicker and sicker."

"He'd decided that for the rest of his life, he'd focus on only one thing, that you'd remarry him. He never once accepted the fact that his Liz B'd never come back home. He said several couples in your family had divorced and remarried. It really wasn't all that strange.

"He was so relieved when your husband got involved with that old barmaid. It knocked him down a few pegs. Then he too was vulnerable, no longer perfect, and Dieks felt that he was circling, closing in for the kill. He'd been on this long hunting expedition as far as he was concerned. That was all."

"He was working on his vocabulary. He'd slimmed down, quit chasing women, and was getting near retirement. Of everything he'd planned in his life, this was his cleanest and most complete. He was ready."

"Except for Sally," I added.

"We never met her," they said at the same time, looking at each other.

"Nicki was the last one he cared about as far as we knew. But even then, he was so sure you were close to needing him, that he just let her go. He said he sensed it and everything was in order."

I shook my head. "He may've sensed something, but I couldn't have imagined taking the risk again. And now, all I want is peace. Just a clean break where I get to recover my emotions and examine the hurt, go through the layers and layers of heartache and then just let go, affixing some official stamp to it, saying, 'DEATH PAYS ALL DEBTS IN FULL, DEEDEE.'

"His death is my final freedom, of sorts. I've held all his sadness in my heart for so long, and now I can finally begin to let go. I've been the assigned keeper of all his sick, sad, hurtful memories, keeping them caged and away from his life so he wouldn't ever have to relive them. I don't regret having taken on his grief. I won't ever regret having loved him so completely.

"In fact, I give thanks for a once-in-a-lifetime experience, before all his sickness took over. I knew a love that was unlike anything I'd ever seen or heard. However briefly, it was sincerely reciprocated. Lots of people go a lifetime without knowing such love. I have the early times of unparalleled and intense passion. From that I've a wonderful son and two beautiful grandchildren. I've seen the cycle of abuse broken and a rebirth of hope in the lineage of a family where all hope had died. For that I'm thankful.

"But finally, at the site of all that sickness and sorrow, the land is cleared. Only the ghosts serve as monuments to the hell that Delly managed to outlive. For that, I guess we should all give thanks."

After we left the gathering, I agreed to follow my son Dieks through town to the motel. I couldn't merge with the moment, couldn't get past my anger or Suzi's niceness. Tread softly, the voice kept saying. The memories you're messing with are dangerous and deceptive. I held tight to the wheel and continued to follow my son's lead. But I found out all too soon that the memories were headed in the other direction, back to Harrow's Branch, where I'm cramped and immobile, with eyes wide open, staring into darkness and seeing nothing.

In the Garden

I have my whole body wrapped tightly around the naked, grey-primered steering column of a '29 Ford Sedan. It's probably quite a sight with the sweeping, baby blue flannel gown draped across the filthy floor, but I'm not concerned with anything except staying hidden. I crouch further down, pushing my back against the prodding metal of clutch and brake.

The car is garaged at Harrow's Branch in the make-do shell of a dirt-floor building that leans ever so slightly toward Tacey Owens' house to the west. I've stopped breathing, because I hear Dieks fumbling with the lock on the door outside. He's unaware that the storage building behind the garage is unlocked and I've come through the crawl space.

He abandons the padlock, and light darts about the room as he makes a quick sweep from front to back through the filthy window. He's decided that I'm not there. It's probably occurred to him that I couldn't have padlocked the door from the inside, so his visit is brief. Since he had to get his jeans on, I had a pretty good head start, but he knows I'm in my nightgown and wouldn't go too far.

Something dark and deadly had set him off, and he'd started swinging, wildly at first, almost as though I wasn't even in the room. As the punches landed firmly in the small of my back, he began pounding relentlessly with the sole purpose of inflicting pain, causing injury. The baby's crib sets just beyond the end of our bed, with Delly sleeping soundly, oblivious to the stifled screams that accompanied each thud of his father's fists.

Just beyond the kitchen, through the two closed bathroom doors, at the end of the house, Bobbi and Red are sleeping in Dieks' boyhood bedroom with faded wallpaper and a cotton mattress with sleeping bag bedding. Dieks was sure the distance was out of hearing range, for Lucy always swore that she couldn't hear Dick beating him "clear back there" at night.

He continued to hit every part of my body, my back, legs, arms and sides -- while pulling and prying first one arm, then the other. As I managed to keep them secure around my ears and head, he paused and continued to swear through gritted teeth as he pried my legs down from where they were locked in place at my chest.

Just as he thought he had them down, and could body drop on top of me, I rolled over. He lunged and missed, unwittingly bouncing me into a spring-loaded upright position where I hit the floor running. Through the living room, dining room, and kitchen I ran with breakneck speed, never looking back as I brushed past tables and cabinets, knocking things to the floor in my wake. He must've stopped at the back porch and then returned to the bedroom for his jeans, giving me the thirty seconds I needed to sprint from the house with my floor-length nightgown pulled up to my thighs. Across the front yard, and then on to the back, I stood momentarily behind the old oak next to the tracks and watched him sidewind down the embankment. As he came to the north, I headed south and west to the storage building, depending on the shadows of the trees to conceal me.

I've moved from the car, slinking across the garage floor and back to the opening at the end of the crawl space, like a cat. But a full moon hovers overhead and I think the two boys night-raiding Tacey's harvest of watermelons will see me as I struggle to stay down and inch out of the crawl space at the back of the storage shed. The garden's in full bloom, and now I've taken refuge in the standing vines of the pole beans, staked several feet high, enough to give me the coverage of leaf and shadow.

I realize that a ghost, or even a ghostly presence, would move them out quickly and their movement might be a helpful deterrent. If Dieks sees them running or hears them, he'll stay up near the house, where he's returned after his sweep of the area. With my toes curling in the cool, moist topsoil, I whistle low and menacing, like a foreboding autumn wind.

"Was that you?" one whispers.

"No! Let's get the hell out of here!" Each struggles to escape with a huge watermelon, refusing to let even the ghosts share their bounty. They head off to the empty backside of the lot, away from Richard's, the garage, and Harrow's Branch streetlights.

Dieks watches them from the back porch steps, turning, slowly surveying the northwest end of the lot one more time. He steps down to the weathered remains of the doghouse under the apple tree and gets down on his hands and knees, waving a stick back and forth into the emptiness. He looks again toward the tracks, running over to them as if something had moved there. As he emerges again from the bank by the tracks, he looks first to the sky, then out into the stillness.

He has become his father now, to my version of the terrorized little boy Dieks. He's checked every place he'd ever had to run, every hiding niche he'd ever known or made. Just as Richard searched for him, he was coming after me. By experience and instinct, he knew that the runner never runs far, just far enough to escape the assault. Wherever they stop, they simply wait and watch, thinking the beast will cool down, wear out, or sober up, and control will return. Then they can come out from hiding and go quietly back to bed. But I was not a child, and felt no need or obligation to make my position known. I was layin' in the weeds for the long haul.

I've moved back ever so carefully to the tangled cornstalks in Tacey's garden. I continued watching the back porch, where a single bare bulb night-light kept the steps dimly lit. If he went back up them, I'd see him. But he didn't. He must've gone back in through the front door. I inch slowly down, stretching my gown down around my feet, binding my knees together tightly with gathered fabric, folding my arms across them, and resting my head. I felt the pound of pulse at my temples and in my neck, and I heard the release of every racing heartbeat in my chest.

If I could wait another hour or so, just before sunrise, I thought, I could make my way back across the yard and into the house before the baby's first bottle. But I fell asleep. A car rattled the rails as it crossed the tracks and woke me with a start. The birds were already warming up with morning songs. I tried to stand, but my legs fought back stiffly as I straightened, so I leaned back down, giving them a moment to adjust. I had to try to get across the yard without being seen, I remembered thinking. After all, what would the neighbors say?

As I stood to look around, I saw the Nelson woman across the street taking milk in from the insulated metal box on their front porch. I had just glanced toward the house, but my heart began to race wildly in the split second that I saw movement on the back porch.

He was there at the window, watching me, still standing in the garden among the beans. He cradled Baby Delly, feeding him his bottle. I began to walk toward the house, no longer concerned with being seen by the neighbors, as my feet chilled in the morning dew. My back and neck throbbed and my legs still cramped. My eyes burned from lack of sleep and the glare of the sun. Though I walked with purpose, there was no one in that nightgown.

I opened the screen door at the top of the steps and walked past him standing just inside. I walked through the kitchen without stopping to pick up the pieces of a broken sugar bowl, or to sweep the scattered sugar up off the floor. I walked through the front rooms stepping over and around the remains of a picture frame and scattered dried flowers. I went directly to the bedroom where everything that had been on dresser, table, or chair now littered the floor. No one seemed to be awake as I glanced at the bedside clock. It was six-thirty; Richard was always up and around by then. Even he knew something was to be avoided.

No one stirred as I slipped out of my gown and into denim cutoffs and a T-shirt. Dieks had not moved from the back porch where I'd walked past him at the door. He was burping the baby and a half-full bottle waited on a filthy tool chest that had served forever as a backdoor catchall.

I walked up, taking Delly from him, whisking away the bottle in the same movement. Back through the spilled sugar, the toppled chair, past the half-torn drapery between living room and bedroom, I moved out to the front porch glider, resting there in the morning stillness, fed the baby the rest of his bottle.

My eyes looked to the street but saw little more than heartache beyond the porch. Though the sun was shining brilliantly and the day appeared full of promise, I began to cry as I tried to remember tenderness, stroking the pink cheeks and plump hands of the baby. I tried to recall the warmth of Dieks' kisses, the way he touched my hair and snuggled my neck, and held my heart in his hands, protecting every ounce of love I gave him. But it was miles away, beyond my reach, beyond belief.

He's at the door watching me. I feel his eyes on the back of my neck. I've got Delly up on my shoulder, patting his diapered bottom, then, cradling him, I cradle my own needs as well.

Dieks opens the door and moves quietly behind me, up against the house. At a whisper almost, he says, "He will always know how much you love him."

I nodded distantly.

"You will always know he loves you, too."

I nodded again.

He paused and bounced against the wall like a child with a confession that he was too embarrassed to say. "You won't remember that I loved you, though. You'll probably remember that I hurt you."

I didn't move.

"Someday you'll look back on all this and say, 'Why'd I stay with that mean sonofabitch?' I don't know when, but I do know you will. Someday you'll run out the back door and you'll just keep running."

I sat Delly on my lap and ran my hand over the fine blonde down that glistened in the morning light. His eyes examined my face, searching for the reason I'm not talking to him as I always did when we sat, curiously reaching for my mouth with pudgy baby fingers.

"No. You'll never run without him, will you."

I shook my head.

"Are you ever going to talk to me again?"

I shook my head no again.

"I don't know why, Liz B, I swear I don't. Somethin' just snaps. It's somethin' I can't explain. It just … snaps."

I looked out to the street again, feeling deceived and hollow, cheated and empty. I didn't want that stranger using my intimate, loving nickname. I wanted that creature to leave. I wanted back the man I knew, the one who'd been missing for so long, since just before the baby was born. I wanted my lover, my friend. But the stranger just kept standing there and the stranger just kept talking.

"It's nothin' you've done. You're really all I want, all I've ever wanted. But it's like I gotta go. I gotta keep lookin' for somethin' - - maybe somethin' I lost, and it causes me to act like that. Like I gotta get away from the baby, to protect him. I have to protect him from something … dark," he said, his voice fading.

I looked up at him, wondering if the thing he tried to protect the baby from was what had caused all this heartache.

He bent down before me, on one knee and put his arms at the sides of my thighs, his hands at my waist. As he looked directly into my eyes, I looked purposefully away.

"Liz B, it's not you!" he whispered intensely. "I hate being away from you! Something pulls me away. All the time I wanna be with you, in your arms, watching the baby grow, seeing you with him, but part of me keeps sayin' 'No, don't go there, she don' need you like you need her.'"

I'm shaking my head. "What rot."

"I can't expect you to understand. I can't understand it myself. But it's like if I wait to come home, you'll want me more. You'll only need me more and love me more if you can't have me with you all the time. Then, honey, you'll crave me like I do you. You'll cherish me like I do you and the baby."

I turned to stare at him in disbelief.

"You've always got the baby! I've got no one," he said with a whimper.

"You're a selfish, insecure, dangerous child. Where you had one, you have two, and that's not enough love for you?"

"I know, I know. Please, please help me. I love you so much. I just don't know, I just don't."

I hear water running inside and know that Red and Bobbi are probably up.

"They won't stay long," he said. They'll probably head out pretty quick. Be nice, for a little bit, okay? Please? I'll make it up to you. Really."

He reaches over and squeezes my shoulder. I jerk back in pain from one of many of the night's bruises and shake my head in disgust. Red was throwing a duffle bag into the trunk of their car, along with a small overnight case and a pillow.

"How's that boy?" he yelled from the drive.

"Gettin' bigger," I answered, holding him up on display.

He walked up to the side of the porch draping his arms over the rails, a safe distance from having to actually touch the baby.

"He's sure ... a boy," he grinned.

"You're pretty good with words, there, Reddick. Now, try it again."

"He's sure ... a helluva nice big boy!" he offered.

"Well, that's better, but not much."

Bobbi came out the front door with a slice of toast. She threw the crust out to the lawn and reached down for Delly.

"Hey!" Red yelled. "Don't you touch that kid! You'll catch something!"

"Like pregnancy?" I laughed.

But he was too late. She was baby-talking and cooing and cuddling Delly before Red could motion her over to the car.

"Now, look what you've done," he said, turning to me.

"Yeah, just look. She'll make a good Mommy," I teased.

"Let's go. C'mon, now, cut that out! I don' need this." He's walking back to the car, and she turns Delly over to me.

As she picks up her purse, she whispers, "He paced the floor the rest of the night, you know. It's not like we're all deaf or somethin' … see ya," and she waved as she bounced down the steps and walked out to the car. Dieks never came out of the house.

He took me to Ottumwa that day, and we spent the whole day together. He held my hand and carried the baby while I pushed the empty stroller. We bought new baby clothes and window-shopped at the jewelers. He waved to passing friends, like this was the most common and natural thing. But his undivided attention was ours.

As we stood in the baby department at Spurgeon's, he said, "Maybe he needs a little sister."

"No, what he really needs is a full-time father."

"Well, he's got that." Cradling Baby Dieks at his shoulder, he turned so the baby was looking straight into the saleslady's eyes.

"Wouldn't you say this is about the nicest baby you ever saw?"

"Yes," she answered, smiling. "I believe he may be just that."

He turned back around to me and said, "See, Liz B? Who else would know that? Just a dad, that's who," and he put him into his stroller.

That was then. Three days later, the baby and I were alone again. I was back to afternoons with Richard, nights with the TV, the stench of exhaled stale beer and the smell of secondhand smoke surrounding me at two or three every morning. Yet I waited for "the pull" to release him; I waited for the day he'd return.

I watched everyday as he'd get up late, eat, and leave, gone more hours during layoff than when he worked straight eights. I waited, watched, and stayed, night and day, thinking about the past when I had his undivided attention, unwilling to pay the price he thought he needed for him to give it again. When, on occasion, he was willing to give more of an explanation, I was usually ill prepared, unaware of the impact his confidentialities would have.

The pliers were once offered as a truce, I think. Instead, over time, they came to symbolize all that I hoped to avoid in the world. *All.*

Waking Nightmares

He hated pliers. In his toolboxes, they were used the least. He had several -- just your standard, run-of-the-mill pliers, but I never saw him use them. Sometimes, he'd use two or three things to get something loose, or stabilized, or turned. I found it interesting that I noticed what he didn't use. I had no reason to keep track, but I definitely knew what he never touched.

Once, when it seemed terribly apparent to me that it'd be far more efficient to use pliers, I tapped him on the shoulder and handed him a small pair of yellow rubber-handled pliers.

He glanced over his shoulder and jumped back, dropping everything that had precariously held together the round glass of the odometer casing. All parts hit the floor in succession, shattering first the glass, then the pieces of glass into yet smaller pieces.

His eyes flashed and lips quivered as he rasped, "Don't *ever* do that again."

"What? Do what?"

"Don't ever pull that sonofabitch out of the toolbox. He grabbed the pliers from the floor and pitched them against the back wall of the garage.

I couldn't understand what I'd done that was so terribly wrong. I thought I was helping. I thought I recognized something I could do to assist him without causing too much ruckus. But I knew I shouldn't ask, at least not right then.

He kicked the tire and spun around, grabbing a whisk broom, and began to furiously sweep the pieces of glass off the floor and out the door of the skeletal roadster. "That was stock, I hope you know. I sure as hell won't find another one. Maybe I can get something cut down from some vintage glass, or if I have to … " and his mumblings rang with disgust. He was speaking to the floor of the car, I figured.

It didn't appear that he expected me to be listening or responding, and I was just as happy not to.

My feet were firmly planted next to the car, just behind him, but I couldn't move, not away, not toward, not at all.

He finally lifted his head and looked at me.

"What d'ya want?" he asked, sounding very serious.

I shook my head. "Nothin'."

"Then you better move it or lose it." He was smiling again and pinched my bottom as he walked around me.

Nothing ever happened here, I was thinking. We simply never had the exchange. He didn't throw the pliers. I didn't see him jump or his lip quiver. Surely he's not afraid of pliers. I shook my head.

He was standing on the other side of the car, watching me work my way through it, looking at the toolbox, at the empty odometer hole, at the pliers where he'd thrown them, then at him.

"Later," he said, pointing a screwdriver at me. "I'll tell ya later."

But it was not mentioned again that day.

...

"Later" turned out to be a month or more. I'd pulled a bean bag chair out onto the grass next to where he was working on an inside door panel, trying to get the window and door lock to work in unison.

Delly was in his playpen, rolling around, with his feet up. It was too early to eat, or for his nap, and he seemed content to just lay in the shade of the oak tree in the side yard. I thought how we looked just like a blue ribbon, all-American, middle-class family.

Dieks'd been chit-chatting about nothing in particular, and we had a pretty good day going when Richard banged on the window and motioned for him to come to the back porch. He seemed to drag his feet, but went up to the window as Richard yelled through the glass.

Dieks nodded and walked back to the car beating something into the palm of his hand. The great news Richard had told him was that he'd made some of his famous potato salad, and it'd be ready in a couple of hours. But he didn't tell me that.

"What'd he want?" I asked.

"Nothin'."

"Then why'd he knock?"

"I said, 'nothin' … can't you hear? Maybe he's jus' lookin' for trouble. That's why."

I shut up and picked up the rattle Delly had just fumbled at the side of the net playpen where he was practicing his nearly perfect 'roll over left, roll over right, stop and drop the rattle' game. I said nothing for a long time, making only baby whispers and clicking noises, not so much to keep our child's attention as to divert his dad's away from me.

Then the someone I'd come to hate and fear began talking inside Dieks, kind of low and angry. It wasn't to me, or even toward me, exactly. It was, however, clearly *for* me. The tone was laced with an undercurrent of danger, or threat, -- something not quite human.

"Hey, boy." It was throaty, whispery and dark. "'Tato salad'll be done soon. Don't be gettin' too far, boy. Supper'll be on and yer ass'll be grass."

"Then he started." Dieks' voice was back to his own. "Once the bottle came out, though, there was no turnin' back.

"He swore at the TV, shook his fists at the neighbors, slammed chairs against the table or the floor as he went by. He'd get his cigar box out of the stand next to his chair, and from there I knew it'd all go to hell."

Dieks kept talking without encouragement or question. He wandered back in time where it was invariably tense and always painful for both of us. Sometimes, I wished he'd just drop it, and maybe the pain wouldn't crest out of control.

But that didn't happen very often.

"Hey, rat," he sneered, spitting out words covered with tobacco juice and acid. "Hey, you dirty rat-faced fucker, food's on.

"He'd beat on the porch window until I thought it'd break, but it never did. Sharp, fast raps with a spoon sometimes, or a fork, ladle, whatever he'd been working with. Anything metal, anything that sounded hard, menacing.

"'Come 'n git it, you rat-faced, good-fer-nothin' piece of bastard shit!' He'd always have a string of 'em that he could throw together in the split seconds of a drunken rage. I don't think he even remembered my name most of the time. I always thought that maybe Mom gave me her name, thinking it'd slow down his hatred, like a boil to a simmer. But, by then, I don't think he remembered her name, either.

"Anyway, it never helped me. He never used my name, and when he seemed to recall hers, he only remembered rage. It was never his fault that she died; it was mine. He wanted to save her, but somebody caused her to die. It sure as hell seemed to be me. After years of beatings, I sure hoped it was me, so I'd be gettin' pulverized for some good reason."

The man reverting to the boy was wrenching on a lug nut, each turn a little harder, a little faster, with adrenaline force that was quickly getting violent as old anger turned the threads.

"I sat on the doghouse, just behind the apple tree, where I could look straight across to the kitchen window where he was cooking. He'd slosh a bit o' beer into whatever he was doing and take a swig himself. Then he'd get into the refrigerator and throw back a shot of whiskey. I always pretended that by watching every single movement, I could slow down the episode, change the inevitable, that it would pass like a storm. All the while I knew that it was there, waiting for me just behind the kitchen door, something savage and hideous.

"I'd finally get brave enough to walk through the door, and there was always something waiting for me. I'd get slapped in the head or hit with a pan or poked with a fork. He'd always get me, no matter how hard I tried to slide through small and unseen. Cold, calculating, one way or the other, he'd get me.

"Some days were worse than others. He'd slap the back of my head, or trip me and I'd fall to the floor, knowing that something else was sure to follow. I knew I wasn't able to protect everything, so I'd put my hands and arms up over my head, but he'd be kicking me in the back, yelling, 'Fuckin' moron, clumsy oaf, can't you ever git it right? Sprawlin' out there where people have to trip over ya to git anywhere,' and he'd pretend he was walking across the room, and he'd stumble, managing to kick me again with his steel toed work shoes, or he'd stomp on one of my legs as I tried to get out of his way.

"He'd scream, 'It's your own goddam fault! You can't even stand up, layin' around on the floor like some goddam whinin' baby,' and he'd dump some beer on me as I kept rolled up so my head wouldn't get kicked. That was pretty much the scheme of things. Not just every now and then, but most every night. Every time I had to go in and eat, there would be a price to pay to stay alive, in his house, eating his food. I paid for my mother dying. I paid for Lucy running away. I paid because I was there and they weren't.

"'Git yer ass in here, rat!' He yelled, then pounded on the window again.

"So I slid down off the roof of the doghouse, like I had a choice." Dieks turned slowly and motioned toward the apple tree out back of the house. "I slid down, and took a big gulp of air, and headed to the kitchen. But that wasn't enough. Before I even got to the first back step, he'd reached down and grabbed me by my neck. I knew in that instant, it'd be worse, worse than anything ever. I knew that the rat-tat-tats on the window had been louder. I knew the grip he had on my neck was tighter. I was choking and gasping for air as he dragged me up the stairs and the screen door slammed shut with a sharp warning, like a gunshot.

"I stopped choking when he threw me from the back porch to the kitchen floor. But it was only a split second before he was on top of me, screaming in my ear, 'On the floor again? You fuckin' clumsy river rat,' and his words were only a little slurred, warning me that he was just warming up. Over his head, he was swinging something like a cowboy'd swing a lasso, but it was shiny and metal. I thought it was a fork. Before I could pull my knees up, he kicked me in the guts. I started crying and that really set him off.

"'Crybaby river rat,' he was yelling. 'Git the fuck out o' the way,' and he kicked me again, and then he was on top of me."

Dieks had stopped working on the car and leaned back against it, his arms crossed, staring out toward the tracks, hypnotized by his recurring nightmare.

"He rolled me over, and I kept holding my stomach where he'd kicked me, and I was getting sick. I remember my teeth were sticking out, like they were real big, too far out, it felt like. I was squinting in pain, I think, and he had these ... pliers ... "

As Dieks struggled with the words, his left hand was squeezing together like pliers clamping down. "And he locked the pliers ... onto my front teeth, and I was screaming and choking back down the puke that kept retching up. I kept screaming and screaming for help, but nobody came. The screaming just seemed to keep echoing on and on in my head, and he was yanking on these pliers, and the nerves in my teeth were shooting knives of pain through my ears and my eyes and into my head, and I heard a click, or a snap, and I was sure he had ripped my teeth out, 'cause he was getting up.

"But he hadn't, 'cause I could feel them with my tongue. Just when I thought I'd made it through, when I felt the end was close and I could take a breath, he was standin' over the top of me. He was just 'fixin' my buck rat teeth,' he said, and the tears just kept runnin' down my face. No matter how hard I tried to stop, they wouldn't, and he just kept laughing. 'Look at the lit'l ole rat cry. Cry, you rat-faced fuck, you tit-suckin' baby.' I never saw such hate on anyone's face. And then, for the bawlin' sissy, he said, he had somethin' I could use, and he unzipped his pants … and pissed all over my head.

"So, there I was, stuck to the kitchen floor with beer and tears and piss and blood. Just about what I'm made of now. Jerad Richard Shaunessy's son, remodeled and redefined in his image, and turned over to the world. But, most especially to you, Liz B."

Dieks had moved back to working on the metal inside the door panel. He was talking calmly and quietly now, but the tears are streaming down my cheeks. I tried to keep the sniffling to a minimum, but there is no end to the grief, and something in my chest is aching. It must be my heart. I think it's busy breaking, for the little boy who grew up in the devil's house, without an advocate or a prayer.

"So, now you know. All those questions you ask. You think you want to know, but you really don't. Ain' it better sometimes to just not know? To just let time roll on by, and not tell anybody the things they think they need to know when they really don't?"

He threw the rag on the ground and shut the car door. Then, he rolled up the window, opened and closed the door again, then locked it from the inside, and pulled the key out of his pocket.

He tossed it to me and said, "Here, give it a try."

I got up from where I'd been sitting and moved toward the car, but my head felt light, like I was going to fall over, and I wasn't sure I could work the key into the lock without scratching the new paint. Still sniffling and wiping my nose with the front of my shirt, I tried saying I probably needed to know those things, the things that he reacted to without apparent rhyme or reason.

But all that came out was a couple of hiccupping sniffles that accompanied, "I think … I mean, I prob'ly need to know." But I just couldn't say anything else.

"Why? Why in the hell would you or anyone else need to know something that sick fuck did fifteen years ago?" he asked.

"'Cause, 'cause," and I choked and sobbed, and jerked to a stop.

He got out of the car and put his arms around me, patting my back and stroking my hair. "Shhh, it's okay. Forget it. Shhhh. You're okay. It's okay. It's over and done with. I shouldn't've told you. Shhh ... "

I was shaking my head back and forth, saying that it wasn't okay. "It's something I have to remember, when you ... get mean, when you get drunk ... and act like we're insects or rats--"

"Don't ever say that to me!" He moved me in front of his face, shook me, and glared into my eyes. "Don't ever say that to me! Don't ever say that anything I do or have or am is anything like a rat. He hated me my whole life with those words. For fifteen years and no one will again, ever! Do you understand?"

"Yes," I said, nodding, wiping away tears and sniffles. I understood more than I ever dreamed I could, and as he said, more than I ever really wanted to. I understood when he slept with his mouth open and he covered his teeth with a fist. I understood his avoidance and loathing of the pliers. I understood his rage and how he handled it, capturing, tackling, seizing throats of demons that waged wars in his memory, disarming ghosts that tapped at him from the porch window, or devils that waved spoons.

The biggest problem, I realized that day, had to do with the fact that the delusions and nightmares became entangled with the reality of our lives whenever he drank too much. Then, I became all the players in his macabre nightmare: the victim, the father, the sister, neighbors, aunts, teachers, police, everyone who should have intervened and saved a young boy from a childhood hell. Instead, they all looked away.

...

I had become the mirror of the past and to the past. With his memories becoming so horribly real, it appeared to me that the only means of escape may well have been to jump headlong into the nightmare with him, to see if together we couldn't alter some of the horror that had oozed into our once nearly normal lives.

As I sat staring at the side of the Super 8 where Dieks and Debby had led me, I realized that my son was rapping on the window of my car. It wasn't Richard at all. It wasn't his stirring spoon. I wasn't the frightened child.

"C'mon, hurry up and get changed. If you're going down to meet Red, you'd better get a move on."

I looked up at him blankly, surprised that he looked so much like me, surprised that I'd moved across twenty years in a heartbeat. I unbuckled my seat belt and let it flip back to place. As I wiped away fresh old tears, I had a sneaking suspicion that I'd need all the safety the belt provided, and then some, when I thought about where I was headed that night.

Son of The Rat, Grandson of The Bat

Because he had my archless lips and looked a lot like me,
I believed that we were free and we would always be.
Because I loved him most, his eyes resembled not the ghost,
but those of faded memories, and the memories were me.

But he aged, as children do, and took on the looks of you.
And when his winsome smile stretched thin,
it became, instead, your winning grin.
And I squirmed a bit within,
and hoped it wouldn't show.

For it was I who'd loved him so and it was I who'd let him go -
to grow, to think, to be ... and he no longer looked like me.
He bore a close resemblance to his ancestral semblance:
the wise, the kind, the dead ...
Wokinih.

A Brew at Sundown

Just before eight that evening, my son and I crossed Veteran's Bridge and headed down Main Street to the less-traveled end of town. There, nestled in the overhang of a weather-beaten brick building, was the entrance to the infamous Sundown, legendary saloon for lost souls and lousy lovers. We went there for only one reason, and it had little to do with anything tangible.

Back at the Valley of the Shepherd, as he'd stood gazing into a distant sea of headstones, Red had said that he wouldn't be going anywhere for ham sandwiches, cordial conversation or niceties. Bloodshot blue eyes stared past the people, past their tidy funereal garb and their prim and proper stance. He especially wanted to avoid the relatives and didn't think he could bear being in close proximity.

"Besides," he'd added, "the only people relative to Dieks' life will be lost in the brew at Sundown."

I then realized that of all those people, the one constant, whether questionably sane as had been implied, or reasonably strained as I suspected, had always been, and would always be, Big Red. He knew Dieks end to end -- past, present, and with all certainty, his future.

I asked him why Sundown.

"Johnny Yuma," he said matter-of-factly.

"The rebel? I didn't know he was out." I laughed.

It was an old joke with a sick twist, but Red would understand. I was taking liberty with the memory of Dieks' familiarity, not mine. I knew Yuma was out. I'd seen him several times between visitation and the cemetery. There was no confusing Jim Yuma with anyone else in the world. He seemed drawn from a strange concoction – two parts Genghis Khan, one part Quasimoto. But he'd been in and out of the joint the entire time I'd known him. Dieks said that same line every time someone'd mention Yuma's name.

Red looked at me and then smiled weakly, just a little amused. I could see the pain of losing Dieks lingering behind his eyes.

"Besides, since when can felons get a liquor license?"

"His sister owns the bar. He and his girlfriend just run it. They've been together a long time, and she might be one of the reasons he's managed to stay a couple steps ahead of the law this time around."

He rolled the paper up that he'd carried out with him from the service and lightly knighted my shoulders. "See you there?"

"If I do venture out and manage to get dead drunk and obnoxious, you'll carry me home?"

"To your doorstep, just like the ol' man."

"It's a deal."

I watched him as he ambled blindly away from the crowd. From his gait and carriage, I knew only about half of the pistons were firing. As thinning blonde hair blew back from his face, he tucked his head down, as if preparing for the storm that was forming on the distant horizon.

So there we sat, my son and I, across the street from Sundown, on the evening of his funeral. In the shadow of night, we nervously discussed who might frequent such a place, trying to build the bravado to go in. It was a dismal hole -- two stories of peeling paint and crumbling mortar that seemed spewed into the darkness at random, thankfully camouflaged by night. I wondered out loud if people voluntarily went through the door, or if they were sucked in when they got too close.

Dieks offered his own option. "We could just leave, and no one would even know we were ever here."

"That's precisely why we're going in," I said, opening my driver side door.

Shoulder to shoulder we crossed the street, determined to take in stride whatever the underside of the town offered. A "NO FEAR" bumper sticker warned us from the back window of an old pickup truck in the parking lot. Right, I thought, and still I wondered why I was here.

Once inside, I understood clearly when Yuma appeared. Just as he was at the funeral, salt and pepper shoulder-length hair, bloodshot black eyes struggling to focus straight and center, sinewy arms that seemed fashioned after those of the legendary village blacksmith.

Without provocation, they rested, folded across his barreled chest, as he stood guard to every patron's well-being. This was clearly his charge.

Red was just inside the door at the first booth, though the crowd required a few minutes of maneuvering to get that far. I was surprised to see so many old familiar faces -- most recognizable even after fifteen or twenty years. With some, mannerisms immediately gave them away. With others, it took a while before their voices broke through the barrier of forgetfulness and time.

I finally got to the far side of the booth and plopped down next to Red. He patted my shoulder and introduced me to his friend, Andy. "This here's Liz B, Elizabeth Shaunes –" He stopped and turned to me for help.

"Wilson," I offered. "Liz Wilson." I shook his waiting hand. "Pleased to meet you, Andy."

Just then, an uninvited Yuma set his beer down on the table and scrunched his wide body in next to Andy. Directly across from me, he leaned forward on his elbows, trying hard to focus on my face, and finally managed to say, "So ... ya come back. I figured ya would. I heard 'em say you was there t'day and I'm real glad I got t'see ya."

He slurred an apology for not speaking to me at the visitation, and for missing me again at the cemetery. I was impressed that he knew or cared, one way or the other. But with his words, there was little doubt that he had loved the man whose friendship had extended beyond juvie hall and Westwood's walls, the man who'd voluntarily stayed in Yuma's misbegotten life on the outside. Now, I thought, Dieks' kindness can no longer reach him. It was quite clear that Yuma's heart was good and his grief genuine where the late, great Dieks Shaunessy was concerned.

He hadn't cried in over twenty years, he said shamelessly. But this day, he'd cried all day, one continuous tear. His black Harley T-shirt was as mean and clean as it was when he'd resolutely raised the casket to his shoulder and marched out in unison with the rest of the best. It was as clean as it had ever been, I figured, and probably cleaner than it'd ever be again.

"This is who I am," he said to my son, holding out the front of his shirt. "This is who Dieks would expect to see."

I knew it. And he meant it.

I felt a twinge in my heart for him. Thirty years after the fact, and now, what could, he hit, hurt, beat, or burn that would decrease this pain? What could he possibly do to recapture the importance of one good, irretrievably lost, long-time true friend?

He watched with detached amusement as his main squeeze, whom he'd just introduced to me as "Me Shell," tried to light a single strand of braid hanging down the back of the bar's lone black patron. Clearly, Eldon in general, Sundown specifically, is unaccustomed to people of color, any color. Bert and Ernie would have a tough time here. Renegade bikers wearin' colors might not. It has been said that they frequent the town and this bar, not only because it hails them, but because it welcomes fools and compadres with equal respect, especially those who roar empty warnings from one nowhere man to another.

Mishelle's getting frustrated. It looked like a candlewick, and she said it all but invited her over. It should have fired up like a wick, but it didn't. Not even the trusty flick of her BIC could eke out a spark, much less the slow, rolling flame she'd hoped for.

"That sum'bitch," she said, throwing her lighter to the floor. She stomped out the door and disappeared to what I guessed was their upstairs apartment. Yuma never batted an eye. Her behavior was her problem. His was his.

"Nine kids," he announced. Between drinks, on his fingers, he counted and named them, pausing, looking up at the ceiling, ending the roster loudly and proudly with his and Missy's two youngest, ages three and six. Enough to field a baseball team, I thought. A real scrappy baseball team.

He talked to Dieks for a while, breaking periodically to socialize and work the crowd like the proud managing host that he was. His presence provided a permanent, in-house bouncer, though he showed no apparent care for the upkeep or cleanliness of the joint. But the safety of the patrons, at least, was assured. Jim Yuma would always be the greatest threat they'd ever be confronted with.

I was impressed with the number of people who offered him their condolences, nodding, patting, fearlessly hugging him as he continued on through the crowd, shamelessly wiping away escaped tears, one after another. Just as I glanced at Dieks standing next to the bar, he pointed gingerly and nodded toward the door.

Before I could stop my words, they rolled out. "If you hear something that cracks sharply like the sound of a gun, it is. Hit the floor."

Missy had returned from their upstairs apartment and was inching her way through the crowd with her intentions clearly set again on the brazen black braid at the end of the bar. Only this time, she had on her head a white pillowcase, with two holes cut out for eyes. They were uneven, and when combined with slits for nose and mouth, the end result more closely resembled a jack-o'-lantern. But the crude spirit of her charade was obvious. The prominent pointed end of the pillowcase waved just above the heads of those standing bar side. It slithered past patrons in dangerously slow motion, like a shark fin weaving in for the kill. I felt my chest begin to tighten and had time to glance over at Dieks as he watched me. Our eyes agreed - - we saw it, but simply couldn't believe it.

Yuma was moving toward her slowly and stealthily, like a cat about to pounce on its prey. Just as the black man turned, I jumped to the inside of the booth, nearly on top of Red, not daring to look.

Inches from his face, I yelled over the noise, "Where we come from, she'd be shot dead now, along with a few innocent bystanders."

A bit crowded, he shrugged and took another drink. "You come from here. D'ya know how long it's been since I had a woman?"

He smiled and continued to look me straight in the eyes. I quickly moved back over, putting respectable space between us again.

What a piece of work, I thought. Here, twenty years later, he's just as he was. Though they tell me this isn't so. They say Big Red's a little off-center now, then shake their heads and look away. They say his wife of fifteen years left him and headed south, taking with her the only kid still at home. I'd seen her earlier, in the parking lot at the funeral home, and was amazed at how well she looked. In a brilliant, flowing, blue silk chiffon, she was absolutely gorgeous, and as she glanced briefly over at Red, I saw "love you" written all over her face. As soon as their eyes met, he jerked quickly away, as if he'd had all he could handle for a day, or a week, or a life. He knew I saw the exchange and it would only be a matter of time before I started asking questions. I knew I could get away with it and he knew I'd try.

I'd heard the whispers that he hadn't held a steady job for longer than most could remember. Then, they'd add, of course, this doesn't help. His best friend, ever. Forty years … just buried.

But it was Vietnam, they said, that still blasted through both waking and sleeping hours without warning. It was the element of surprise that kept him on edge, always looking over his shoulder, always ready for hand-to-hand combat, crouched and waiting. No, I s'pose he seems as he was, but I'd guess he is most assuredly different now. Perhaps that would explain why he finds some degree of comfort in a crowd of lost souls and lousy lovers.

Out of the blue I asked him how he felt about everything.

"Bitter. I got fucked," he answered.

"Oh? How so?"

He shrugged. "She left. Took everything."

"Why? Why would she leave after so long?" I pried.

"Because, I ... " He stopped, making mental lists for a while. "Because I did everything wrong." The answer seemed clearly stilted, programmed and processed.

"Like what?" The armchair analyst had escaped, and I couldn't reel her back in.

"Lie, cheat, steal, you know, the normal everything."

"And then what?" I hit my forehead. "Surprise me, she left? Why, the audacity of that bitch."

"Yeah," he said smiling and nodded knowingly. He knew what I meant. He knew I remembered how hard Bobbi had worked at making everything just right for him. And only him. I was among the first to meet her when Red brought her home to Iowa, right out of the pages of Petticoat Junction and a lazy little Louisiana town where she'd met him at the Army base. She was so fresh and pretty, with her peaches and cream skin, emerald green eyes and brown hair that seemed to float down around her waist.

She had ample hips and an equal serving of breasts that seemed to enter every room before she did. But it was the hot pants that turned their heads. Electrically charged cheeks, I'd always teased her. And she'd always laughed and say, "Oh, huh ... "

But it didn't take much imagination to see that Red was forever stepping in between her and hands that seemed to be drawn to her from every direction. Young and sexy, almost more than his low-key, lackluster personality could handle, she kept the fires in him stoked. It was no secret that he had a helluva time keeping up with her sexual appetite. But he was the envy of every man in town, and there was no doubt that she had eyes only for him. He knew I'd been there, remembered them "back when," and that I'd always liked her energy, spunk, and panache.

"You're right, kind of. And, well, not kind of. She left me with nothin'. I had nothin' to go on, nothin' to work with."

"Red, she only took what she'd brought to the relationship to begin with. If she left nothin', it seems to me it's a wake up call. You had nothin' left to give. If she's gone with everything, you were probably contributing nothin'. Now you wanna blame her for your emptiness? Does that make sense? Tell me something, where is it that you guys get off thinkin' you only need to love people when it's convenient? When it's a little work, or proves to be a bit more difficult than you might've planned, when these people turn out to be normal and flawed, these very people you claim to love and cherish are the first ones you turn your backs on and neglect, or abuse. Then you whine about 'em not being there for you. They're s'pose to come back, time after time, year in and year out, without ever gettin' a refill, without gettin' somethin' they can draw on to run their own weary lives. That's a little arrogant, don't you think? I'm sorry, but this is one of those areas I've had a good twenty years to mull over."

I was climbing up to my pedestal, just right of my soapbox.

"Why did I go? Why was Dieks shocked that I left him, knowin' how much I loved him? Don't you people ever stop and look at life goin' on around you -- beyond the end of your nose, I mean. It's like this whole area's stuck in some mucked up quagmire. Some primitive mentality tells you conquered captives mercilessly abused will love you more. Magic will transform them into airheads that will remain forever submissive, just waitin' at your feet for a pat on the head or a good game of chase. Talk about gettin' fucked. Bobbi could probably write volumes on it after fifteen years."

"Hey, she worked. She got out. We had stuff."

"Red, to this day, I've never met anyone tighter with a buck than you, and that's only 'cause I never met yer ol' man."

"It's how he was. That's how we were raised."

"An' you couldn't figure that out? You resented him for being like that. Why'd you think it'd be any more endearing coming from you, to your wife and kids, huh? I remember you bitching about Verlene twenty years after your dad died. 'Member? She dated a doctor, and he gave her everything she'd ever need and promised her everything she'd ever want. But you and your brother, two grown men, acting like selfish, mean-spirited shitheels, you guys insisted that she stay alone, with next to nothing, to honor the memory of your dear ole mean, dead dad.

"Yet you laughed at her turnin' off lights by six, religiously savin' her green stamps, cuttin' out coupons, shoppin' at the day old store and takin' in ironing to make ends meet. It's a wonder that you could share your life, no, your goods, with anyone. Imagine what your kids must've thought."

He shrugged, "That's just the way it is."

"No, that's the way it *was*! Now it's nothing at all."

"Why's it have to be that way?" he quietly wondered out loud.

"Don't you get it? It can't be that way. We just can't keep perpetuating these cycles that are given to us without question. Your dad was a stolid, removed, cold-hearted bigot, everything that made a good German soldier great, and he was rewarded for it. It reinforced that behavior, and, however inappropriately, he brought it home and passed it on to you. You took some of it to heart. How could you help it? I don't think kids move too far away from things they learn early on. The acorn doesn't fall far from the tree and all that shit. But short of growin' up and becomin' a skinhead, I don' think those lessons are goin' to do ya much good ... "

As I paused and took another drink of Berry Berry someone had handed me, Red turned directly to me and changed the subject, saying, "So, why're you here?"

"For the funeral? For Dieks," I said, and I nodded to the bar where my son stood talking to his newly-acquainted blood brother. "To protect him, maybe. To keep him from being influenced by some potentially ugly situations, to deflect nasty comments or inferences. I don't trust too many people. Thanks to Dieks Shaunessy, the dead. I worked a long time getting this kid to understand that he was okay as he was, that he was a good kid and it was his dad that lost out in their situation, not him. I fought for years to convince him that we all have opportunities and choices. Once we size them or seize them, we have to live with them or die by them, but we never have to choose to be victims -- especially when we have so little control over other people's actions."

"You think it helps?"

"What?"

"That you're here, that he knows. D'ya think it helps you as much as you want it to help him?"

"Maybe, maybe not. Certainly not the way most people would like to think."

Almost on cue, Dieks plopped down next to me in the booth.

"What? A light beer?" I said, tapping my forehead. "That's sacrilege here. They'll point and make jokes behind your back you know, call you a wuss, a lightweight. Dieks always said a light beer tasted little better than dog piss," and   I shrugged. But, then again, who'd dispute it? He may've been the only man to ever drink dog piss to have a means of comparison."

Red laughed, and Dieks top-ended his bottle of dog piss, holding it high enough for Callahan to see that it was empty. In moments, he was handed another.

"We're a sick, sick pair," I said, looking at him, shaking my head. "What kind of mean-hearted mother would lead her poor, sweet, studious son astray, taking him away from his loving wife and babies, out on the perilous town? Who'd believe that they ventured down to these catacombs to try and drink away their torment and grief on the very evening of the day they buried his dearly departed dad?"

Red ignored the last part. "Hey, where are those kids and your ol'," but he stopped and changed course abruptly, " ... wife, anyway?"

"Super 8?" He looked at me. I nodded.

"We had to make a choice. So, I told 'em, 'I'm shallyin' on to Sundown with Red. Period. I'm going to get blasted 'cause I haven't for a long time, and Red said he'd carry me home if he had to.' Every five or six years, do or die, I unwind and get absolutely potted, and I am well overdue."

My voice had been getting louder, carrying further than I wanted it to, so I leaned over to Red, and added quietly, "Dieks here had the option of stayin' or goin' and he pretty much decided that someone responsible had better come along and watch out for the Bitch BziL – my alter ego, y'know. Shows up," I snapped my fingers, "just like that when there's spirits about."

I nodded toward my son. "So he came, just in case I might need help. But, I don' think so ... "

He's shaking his head in disagreement. "This is how Dad says she gets when she's drunk ... disgusting. But, if you can handle her, I'm leaving." He slid out of the booth and turned to me as he stood up. "Y'know where Paradise is?"

"No, but if you listen to a lot o' guys around here, they'll try to convince you they can take you there. Does that count?"

He rolled his eyes and stood on his toes to scan the crowd. "Hey, Callahan, where's Paradise?"

"Down by Waterway," he yelled back through the noise and smoke.

"Waterway," Dieks said to me. "When you're done here, come to Paradise on Waterway. Y'know where that is?"

"Yeah, go'way." I waved him away. "I grew up here, 'member? Shoo, and I'll catch up with you later."

I turned back to the booth. Andy was agreeing with Red that Dieks the younger seemed to be a good kid.

"You can see a lot of the ol' man in 'im," Red said. "Doesn't look a lot like 'im, but he acts like 'im. I remember 'im in that first day in the hospital."

. . .

They were gone. Dieks and Red had been in Sterling for some time. Six or seven weeks, maybe, but I refused to count after a while. That morning, on the day that became different than all other days, I slept in. When I finally crawled out of bed, I couldn't stand the thought of food. I just wanted to get everything clean.

I started in the bedroom and worked my way through the house, ending with centuries of grime on the back porch. Everything always looked filthy at Richard's. It was as if a thin layer of dust and grime permanently resided on every surface, from ceiling to floor, furniture to pictures, and walls to windows -- nothing ever seemed clean. No matter how long or hard I worked, the house always looked and smelled as musty, dirty, and dreary as when I started.

By six, labor pains had begun. There was no mistaking them. I called Rush Baker and asked her if she might find somebody who could round up Dieks in Sterling, Illinois. She called Abbie down at the bar, and Abbie called everyone she knew that might have had an idea where either one of the guys were. Dieks had never told me how to reach him. In fact, he'd not written in weeks.

Early in the evening, I called my mother and told her I was driving myself to the Wapello County Hospital. I didn't know if anyone knew where to find Dieks in Illinois or, whether or not he'd make it home in time. She said she and Dad would meet me as soon as they could.

Doc Morgan admitted me and checked me over. He said it'd be hours before I was ready. But by midnight, I was ready. The baby, however, was not. My mother sat with me well into the early morning hours, letting me clutch her arm every time the pains started. After a while, I never let go. The labor just went on and on throughout the night, with moments too small to measure between contractions. At about four in the morning, Dieks burst through the door, with Red close behind. As he pulled up a chair, I let go of my mother's arm. When they traded places, I saw the imprints on her forearm were turning to bruises.

"No saddle block," was all I heard her whisper to Dieks. "They said he didn't believe it'd be necessary."

"Do you think it's necessary?" he asked her, pleading.

She nodded yes.

He quickly left the room, only to return a few minutes later, saying the nurses wouldn't call Doc Morgan until at least six. Dieks then assumed my mother's position where I could now cut off his circulation, and my mother just stayed to blot the beads of perspiration from my forehead for the next few hours. At six, when the doctor was finally called, it was too late for a saddle block, or anything else. The baby was on the way.

They called him a nature doctor, as if that was a good thing. But I was eighteen, and all I knew for sure was that someone didn't seem to understand that a baby's head moving through the birth canal feels a lot like being involved in an earthquake. The idea of a fault line kept reverberating through my pelvis. As I thought about whose "fault" this was, I heard the responsible party saying "it" would heal faster and much better that way. I offered to let him personally experience the wonder of his decision, but I don't remember my words being that well chosen as they echoed off the walls.

...

I float effortlessly back across the years and casually return to the conversation as Red's leaning toward Andy, setting down his beer to explain.

"He was about this big," spreading his hands apart like he was telling a good fish story. "Wrinkled and red. Never said, 'boo.' Didn't bawl er nothin'."

He laughed and shook his head. "Damnedest thing you ever saw. Had him in a little glass box, kinda downhill toward his head, said he had to drain or somethin' and Dieks's standin' there on his ear, watchin' 'im, sayin', 'Hey, lookit here. Lookit my kid, you know, lookit this, lookit that.' That baby'd be scootin' on his belly, like them damned Cong in Nam, scootin' down this glass box with one eye open, and the other squeezed shut like Popeye, these little fists just goin' along 'til he got to the end and then he'd bang his head, and Shaunessy'd say, 'He's sure gonna be a scrapper, ain' he?'"

"The nurse'd come and pull 'im back and bundle 'im a little tighter. In ten or twenty minutes, he'd be right back down there again, beatin' his head against the wall, jus' like his ole man."

My head jerked up with a warning. "Not a helluva lot like 'im, I hope. Debby sure won't need to deal with that crap. She'll be beatin' her head and his against the wall if they get to the point we did."

"Did you have it so bad, really?" he asked, turning to face me.

I nodded. "Yeah, I had it so bad, *really*. And what makes it worse is the fact that all you guys knew what was going on and did nothing to stop him. I have memories that'd make people puke. And you know what? Until today, when we turned off the main road, and then came back home from Eldon on the tar road, I've managed to keep most of 'em at bay. Twenty years I've fought off the likes of the thoughts I've had all day. Twenty damned years and then today ... "

"I'll bet every other car on that road had someone saying, 'I never thought I'd be on this road like this.' I sure knew I was saying' it, an' Ed, an' Jimmy an' ... "

Red's words were getting slower and slower. I couldn't figure out if it was because we were both getting drunker, or if reality was beginning to take a foothold. We wouldn't be looking up to see Dieks waltzing through the door and up to the bar like he owned the joint. We'd never again see him turn, resting nonchalantly on one elbow to survey the crowd, smiling, nodding to the first set of eyes he met with, "How's it goin'," or raising his beer bottle to someone else and winking, "Hey there."

"You know, his first wife took everything from toilet paper and light bulbs to the bed, the blankets, and the steaks in the freezer. I left with our son, our clothes, and his crib in my sister's car. I never asked for anything, and he sure as hell never offered. I wanna whine about this for awhile."

"What'd you just tell me? If you got nothin', it's 'cause you never had a thing anyway, or somethin' like that?"

"Somethin' like that. But not exactly that," I said.

"Oh, I see. It's not like that when you're the one left holdin' the bag."

"No, it is like that, but not exactly, I said. We -- you, me, him, Bobbi -- we all became victims of our own choosing. We knew things were wrong, but we never did anything about 'em. We became victims of our own abuse, neglect, stupidity, whatever. You can't say you didn't know what you were doin' or not doin', what was wrong, or out of your control. Anymore than I could say Dieks' abuse of me was okay for a while, and then one day it wasn't okay anymore.

"I knew it was wrong from the get-go. But I think we're all pathetically lonely, somehow. We're so damned lonely, in fact, that we accept the absolute worst in people, instead of demanding their absolute best. Then we add insult to our own injuries by seekin' out the worst people to wrap ourselves up with, so we don't have to look at all the things that could've been, should've been, might've been.

"When someone isn't wreaking havoc with our hearts, we go out and dredge up our own garbage and grief. We just drape it over our sorry-assed shoulders and carry on. Or, we simply create some new from the leftovers of ache and anger. It might not look like much to a stranger, but it's comfortable 'cause it's ours, forgettin' the fact that familiarity breeds contempt.

"I can find emptiness in my own living room, surrounded by all the old familiar signs of material security. I've got a paper that says I'm married into perpetuity, babies that have the ol' boys' eyes, a dog that won't die, and an unpaid mortgage. You name it. I got it. You manage to find death and mayhem in your own mind, litterin' all your good, grey matter with blood-splattered remains you were s'posed to've left in Nam. Dear sweet Dieks, bless him, finally found peace. No more searchin', no more need to enshroud himself with all the shit detail we clamber after in life. It was all done for him. Oh, I think he fought to the end trying to put off his journey down The Hangin' Road. All things considered, it was a valiant fight by an unarmed man in a state of limbo. But a couple months is about as much as you can expect from a weak, sick man who's starved and dehydrated.

"You wanna talked screwed? His so-called family has offered to *sell* his things to his sons. If they could've cremated 'im without an Indian uprising, they would've offered 'em the ashes as well, for a price. If they couldn't sell 'em, they'd scatter 'em across the fields and avoid the burial expense. Or, better yet, they'd just stick 'im in a tree house and set it on fire and say it was the Injun way. I tell ya, there's a real education here for the takin' if you're willin' to see things through the ol' eyes of the clan … "

I paused while Red laughed, covered his face in disbelief, and then looked up and said, "But they say they care." He cupped his hand over his heart and rubbed his thumb back and forth across his fingers, like he did when he spoke of the ever-elusive money, money, money.

I raced ahead. "All the while they're carrying on about losin' his companionship, grieved by their loss and their pain, they've chosen to assuage this horrible emptiness and grief by looting and stripping everything like hordes of house locusts."

Red looked at me with his mouth open and jaw dropped. "Me an' Fortier wondered what would happen to everything."

"Hey, when they said everything was stolen by the "robbers" in an *alleged* break-in, they meant it. Granted, it was a little premature, 'cause they really hadn't stolen a lot at that point. But their slip of the tongue was sincere. The break-in, and the explanations that followed, went so well that every time someone asked about something, anything, the answer was, 'It musta bin taked in the robbry.'

"Since the boys had always been designated as beneficiaries on his life insurance, there was nothin' the clan could do about that and it just served to piss 'em off. Why, in clan lands to the west, the penalty for the crime of 'Wrong Beneficiary' is death, preferably No Fault Death. Ideally, Death by Dissociation. If responsibility falls into the hands of the clan, and they become the Legal Guardian in a dilemma where there's money at stake, all concerned parties should automatically consider and expect them to act in their own best interests as judge, jury, and executioner.

"So, with a little guidance from some backwoods Southern lawyer, the legal work was done posthaste. I can't even begin to imagine the revelry that followed. Within the month, disability checks went straight to clan central. Titles to the most expensive pieces in his estate were transferred without fanfare. The most sentimental possessions were boxed up for auction, and the obviously expensive things disappeared into the night with worker ants and pack rats, darting in and out, from one truck to another. All the while, standing in the wings are dozens of bosom buddies that thought themselves close enough to be brothers, they said. But, strangest thing, not one of these lifetime friends opened their mouths to defend his kids and their legacy while it was being ransacked.

"After having depended on each other and trusted each other through thick and thin for more years than anyone knows, not one of those good friends that he might've thought would come forward, ever did. Not one person openly said, 'Hey, this is all wrong," or, 'Hey, put that back, you slime bucket!' No one could even mouth the words, 'My God, they're taking his life! They're taking everything! This is too outrageous for belief.'"

"Who were we going to say it to?" Red said, trying to defend himself. "Each other? You? We couldn't do a thing and neither could you, so it never made a shittin' bitta difference that nobody said a word. The clan sure as hell didn't care what we thought about any of it."

Red's shifting uneasily, refusing to look at me, the way he always did when he had to take a stand. He isn't necessarily mad, but he's not going to let me get away with blaming somebody for being helpless when all of us were basket cases.

"Maybe that's what I'm upset about," I said. "We weren't helpless. We were people. Regular run o' the mill people who should've at least let the clan know that it was all wrong, that what they did was wrong, and that each and every one of us was watching them, and their every move. We should've said something to let them know that this wasn't going to be forgotten -- that it was wrong from the beginning, it was wrong in the middle, and it's most definitely wrong now. We were all that he ever had. Any one of us close enough to know him well knew that we were folding on him. The time it took and the turns along the way could've been disputed. But not one of us ever stood up and demanded to be listened to.

"In the midst of this frenetic pace, the Legal Guardian and Most Benevolent Order of Shaman and Witch Doctors agreed that all medical attempts to restore his health would be considered heroic or without reasonable hope for recovery. Between the two factions, an order was issued ceasing all food, water and medication, as well as skilled nursing services. This just happened to occur a month or so before his health insurance would expire.

"I knew it. And I can't believe that most of you guys didn't know it, too. But I was just 'the ex-ol' lady' to you. And I hesitated to become involved because it might look bad. So, along with all the rest of you, I just sat back and watched while the really ugly horror show ran its course, as if I had nothing to do with the man whose life was wasting away in front of me. Every one of us has an excuse; and in every excuse, there's some feeble line that goes something like, 'What could I have done?'

"You could've said, I could've said, any one of us could've said, 'If you don't hook that thing back up, I'm going to bring lawyers in here, all day, every day, until you think they're crawlin' up your ass, and I'm going to sue you for depriving my son of the company of his father. I'm going to bring charges against every medical person and every institution that bears an ounce of responsibility for starving this man to death, because he once meant as much to me as the sun and the moon and the stars.' But I didn't, and you didn't, and none of us who claimed to have loved him as much as a brother, not one of us, stood up and said, 'This is not acceptable.' That's really about all it would've taken.

"And I don't know that he would've ever recovered at all. I don't know that he would've regained any of his faculties. I don't know that he would've wanted us to stay out of it. But I know this, through sheer willpower, he kept himself alive on nothing for nearly six weeks. I don't know if he was waiting for me in particular to step forward, but I do know that I'll probably take that question and a dozen others like it to my grave.

"As for the clan, I think there are fewer relevant questions. If anyone were to have any hope of turning the remains of his estate into a respectable amount, it would have had to've been done before the insurance ran out. Once that ran out, one of two things would've had to happen. Either the clan would've had to bear the responsibility of Dieks' care, or all of his assets would've had to be liquidated in order to cover the considerable expenses of a rehab center for the rest of his life. We just buried the results of their decision.

"Everything he owned has now been declared a free-for-all, limited of course, to the clan. His sons have never been offered so much as a leftover letter, picture, or pair of socks for memorabilia.

"There is no will. He had no intention of dying. To get a will drawn up was tempting fate in his mind. Even though, when Mom died, he said we were real lucky to have everything so cut and dried. With his dad's estate, he and Lucy faced a terrible mess, until one fortunate day that Richard briefly came to his senses long enough for them to get him to sign a living will, just days before he died. No, he wouldn't have prescribed this scenario. But destitution and ignorance can pull any decent person into a slagheap, and that's a pretty big assumption on my part -- that there was ever a shred of decency in the teeming throng of backwoods clan that took turns hovering over his bedside.

"Both sons got shoved aside. Lucy collected his checks, picked up his mail, paid his bills, and managed to get all the necessary legal papers filed.

"She got vehicles licensed in her name, bank accounts turned over, keys to lock boxes and vaults, and, of course, they parked their beloved sixty-two Ramblaire Extraordinaire. They took to driving a few of the many immaculate collector's cars that he'd kept in mint condition, under lock and key, in storage garages throughout the county.

"By winter, a short six weeks after the incident, she held the sullied gloves of the clan up in a victory dance. Her 'brother's stuff,' as she called it, was all, all, all meant for her. Because, she emphatically repeated, he loved her so very, very much, more, it seems, than he could ever have loved his own children."

I took a breath, shaking my head. "I think she struggles very hard to believe that. Moreover, she truly wants us to believe it."

"No shit?" Red's words dripped with disbelief. They were more than idle comments, because we both knew that Dieks had only one great fear, and it was spinning into reality -- the one and only person in the whole world that Dell Collins Shaunessy would've refused any benefit to was his brother-in-law, GI Joe Bergen.

Even if this meant that his sister and their children had to live in cardboard box for the rest of their days, so be it. Joe Bergen was directly responsible for Lucy leaving her brother in the hands of a monster. He would never, ever be welcome to anything Dieks would have to leave behind. Dieks would've burned it first.

"Red, she said, 'Hey, make me an offer,' when Dieks' own sons asked her about his early artwork. She knows that neither one of them had a dime to spare, but neither did she. Her own brother always said she'd never have a pot to piss in or a window to pitch it out of. He never would've guessed that she'd have something some day and it'd all be his, that those friends he'd trusted all his life to intervene wouldn't know where to start or what to say. He's probably already turning over in his grave.

"When my son asked about the beechwood greyhound that Dieks had always kept carefully under lock and key, the one his mother gave to him, Lucy said, 'Well, hey, Bud, what's that ol' critter worth to ya?'

"I mentioned one thing, an eggshell jewelry box, that I'd hoped to get back for a keepsake and lo and behold, she said, 'You jus' won' believe this, but that was the onliest thing smashed to smithereens' ... of course, in the break-in.

"Meanwhile, everything else that was in Dieks' house is being used to furnish her sons' apartments, and that includes the woven basket of silk wildflowers I'd sent to the funeral home. Nothing was offered to his own children or grandchildren. To me, that's beyond ignorance and greed. I'd call it balls the size of pickle jars, and thing like that just have a way of comin' back around and bitin' ya in the ass."

Red sat stunned, immobile. "I've known 'em 'most all my life. I coulda seen this comin', but I still wouldn't've believed it."

Gold and Silver Lies

"And the wind shall say,
'Here were decent, godless people;
Their only monument the asphalt road
And a thousand lost golf balls.'"
The Rock
T. S. Eliot

On my way to the bathroom, I stopped and talked to an old neighbor. It could've been more than ten minutes, but when I sat back down, Red seemed edgy.

"I restore toys," he volunteered.

I hadn't asked because I wasn't sure I wanted to know what he ended of doing with his wounded life. Since everyone I'd talked to that day said Reddick had taken the events of the last year badly, I didn't want to push him to tell me what he did or didn't do to occupy his time or put food on his table. Not that it mattered to me. He didn't have to say or do anything as far as I was concerned. For the time being, breathing and being conscious met my requirements.

"Twenties, thirties, forties. D'you know a man, what's his name, Bryce? Ken? Ken Bryce?" He turned to Andy, clicking his fingers, trying to remember, "You 'member?"

Andy shook his head. He seemed to be assigned the job of helping Red keep his sanity in check for the evening. But I couldn't be sure. I didn't ask, but it looked like the veteran's buddy system -- for posttraumatic stress assistance.

"Hmmmm," he went on, letting the name escape him. "Anyway, he buys and sells 'em for me, all over the country, at flea markets and swap meets. I drive up and get 'em from him sometimes, up there right by where you live. Full VA, you know," and he tapped the side of his head.

"I go to Knoxville once a week. See an advisor ... "

That was the second or third time he'd said it. I'd been warned, I figured. Maybe he was fragile. Or, maybe he was accustomed to being treated as though he was fragile, as if he had been or easily could be again. Recognizing the possibility was half the battle.

"Anyway, it's something to do. What d'you do, Liz B?"

I could never decide if this term of endearment transferred intimacy rights. I was always Liz B to Dieks, Libby to some, Liz to others, and only Elizabeth formally. But Red had already taken liberty and I couldn't rightly recall if he hadn't always called me Liz B. In fact, I was fast approaching the point where I was having trouble remembering a lot of things. Worse, I was having trouble forgetting a lot of things. Then I understood why he volunteered what he did. I was expected to trade words for words.

"Nothin'," I finally answered.

"Didn't you go to college? You said you were leavin' this goddamn town and you were gonna get educated and make sixty thousand dollars a year when you got done. Yuma makes sixty thou' a year, easy. Ain't that right, Missy?"

She smiles. "Did'n take no goddamn college, that's fer sure. We got better things to do with our time." She closed her eyes as a well-practiced, perfectly round smoke ring floated up and joined forces with the thoroughly polluted blue grey haze that drifted in layers across the top of the room.

"Hell," Red said, "I seen Jimmy holdin' sixty grand in a paper bag behind the bar, sometimes a helluva lot more 'n that."

"You gotta take the good with the bad," I said. "If they ever catch him, if some cop decides they're tired of bustin' ass for a measly twenty grand a year and wants ta even a score, they'll look up Jimmy and one of those paper bags. Sixty in a bag smells a lot like a conviction in a few circles. If not a conviction, at the very least, an IRS heyday with owners, managers, records, and inquisitions for such a profitable little down-home saloon."

He ignored me and continued on. "So? What do you make?"

"Zero. Zip. Nada, personally."

"Didn't you go away to school, get a shitload of degrees, make your ma happy and all that bull?"

Red wasn't really asking me about what I did with my life after Dieks. What he was actually doing was challenging me to defend the walkaway. To say, in essence, that I went in search of something better than Dieks, better than their lives and his friendships, better than this town and all it represented. What I was supposed to say was that I never found it and I was back, and all was clear, and I should just 'fess up. I quickly realized it wouldn't matter how I responded. Whatever I said in return would sound the same to him - - I left, didn't find the proverbial pot of gold, and returned neither rich nor famous, and probably was responsible for Dieks' downfall somehow. I would've been just as well off to have stayed in Eldon and partied hearty, saving myself time and money, and saving their good, dead friend. I refused the bait and ducked out the back door of the question instead.

"Sort of. Isn't that how you answer these questions? Sort of. Yes, I went away to school. Eventually, I made my mother happy, and finally, after being banished from southern to northern Iowa, I finally finished college up at UNI."

"In what?" he interrupted. "Business?"

"Nope, pleasure. English, actually, with speech and psychology on the side. That was nearly twenty years ago. And then, some seven, eight years back, I went and got another one in ... computer applications. I used 'em a couple times, didn't seem to be what I had in mind. So, one day I decided what I really liked was golfing. It made as much sense as anything else I'd done up to that point.

"And, on any given day, I could feel as good as I'd ever felt working and making a few bucks, or as bad as I felt on any given day when I realized I'd made about two-thirds of what my male counterparts took home, working in my area with less education, less experience. That was when I figured out I'd always be more satisfied as a bad golfer than I'd ever be as a good worker."

My words had slowed to about half speed. Red was just looking at me, trying to decide if I was bullshitting or serious. Missy seemed interested, but I couldn't understand why.

"What's yer ol' man do?" she asked, with her eyes suspicious and squinting, fishing for a secret.

Then I knew.

"He's a carpet layer and a tile setter. Owns and runs his own business."

"An' he don' care if you don' work?"

"Nope. He don' care."

Red was recapping it all in his head and finally said, "You mean to say you went to college, spent all that money, and got degrees in all that shit--"

"An' I stay home. I don't use fifty thousand dollars' worth of lectures, learning, and literacy. I spend my free time golfing. Oh, don' get me wrong. I do understand and I do have responsibilities. I do the wash, the dishes, the lawn. I vacuum the carpets, dust the cobwebs, keep books for his business, and write a little in the wee hours of the morning to placate the beast within, but not much else, really. For a long time I worked real hard at trying to do everything and be everything for everybody. And then one day I realized a pretty fundamental truth. The kids didn't give a shit what I did, as long as they had food in their mouths, clothes on their backs, and somebody to taxi 'em all over town. Sam didn't give a shit what I did, as long as he didn't have to do his own wash, cut a half a yard of grass, shop for groceries, or stand over a sink full of dishes.

"But what really frosted me was when I realized that most of the people you work for don't give a shit what you do, either. They don't care what you know or how well you do your job. They only care if your performance, or lack thereof, will help or run interference with whatever it is they've got their sights set on achieving through you.

"I didn't spend six years in college to support my local sponge. If no one else in the world had any respect for a college education and all the work it took to get, I still did. I figured I owed the notion something. If education can't be put to honorable use, or at the very least, good use, then it shouldn't be used at all. We should all just roll over and go on the dole. Anyway, that's when I quit. Just walked away from working and never looked back. It seemed far more reasonable to say, 'Piss on it,' and skate. That was, maybe, five, six years ago.

"So, when the president tells you how he's going to reeducate and retrain all of us poor, out-of-work, out-of-touch know-nothings so we can do our fair share and carry some dumb fuck's dead weight, you just smile and shuffle, nod and remember, 'Yes sir, no sir, you are the boss.' If you can repeat those words over and over, salute, bow, stand on your head, and spit nickels, you'll have a pretty fair idea where I stand on reality, life, and the labor market."

"Don' you get bored?" Missy's been thinkin' about all this for quite a while. It's all pretty deep stuff for the proud working mother and serious daytime manager of the somewhat-sullied Sundown.

"Sometimes I get absolutely bored to death. Then I just take a nap. But, I don't indulge in illusions or delusions. I just am. Everything that used to be important enough to conceal is gone. Now, there's no depth to who I am and what I do, and I move effortlessly through life from one role to another without ever faltering."

"Tell you what, Liz B, you can come stay with me anytime." Red's patting my poor, bored hand.

"No, thanks. Sweet ole Sam might not take kindly to that. After all, who'd do his dishes, wash his clothes, and spend his hard-earned money with as much conviction as I do? Nobody, that's who."

"Aw, c'mon, what's he got that I ain't got?"

"Oh, he's hung like a horse."

Red reared back and his hand pounds his heart. "I can't believe you said that."

"I can't believe you asked," I laughed and shoved an empty wine bottle away, reaching for the next Berry Berry something or other.

Red put his hand over mine and said softly, seriously, "But, do you love him?"

I stopped and pulled back. "What kind of a question is that? Or, in the words of the ever-famous Tina Turner, 'What's love got to do with it?'"

"Well … do you?" Insistent. Hmmmmm.

"No, now that you mention it, I don't believe I do, just love him, that is. But after twenty years, the notion seems so shallow 'cause love and dependency get tangled up in the course of time. I'm use to seein' his face when I wake up. Miss him when he's not there. He gets up in the middle of the night and goes all the way downstairs and lets the dog out so I don't have to. I'm accustomed to his careful driving and his taste for the strangest movies. He doesn't let the soap waste away on the shower floor, and he fixes a real mean omelette. You know, all those things that you don't normally think about. They're just there, standin' beside ya or watchin' over ya all the time. It gets really hard to separate one from another 'cause all our concerns just seem to rise and fall in each other's lives, like those old lava lamps we all used to have. You know, the tide moves in and then out again, and the kids are important, then the house, the car, the neighbors, the various relatives that make you crazy … "

"Wow," he said, propping his head up. "Then, why'd you stay?"

"I thought that was obvious. Where else would I go? I'm not lost. I figure I got it pretty good and wherever I'd go, I'd just have to start gettin' used to somebody all over again."

"That's what I'm thinkin'," Missy mumbled, without raisin' her head from her arm, half asleep, or half stoned.

"For twenty years, he's been there. He's never raised a hand in anger, never asked me to defend my actions. He's never laid down a rule or shouted to the rafters what he expected me to do for him, to him, or with him. He's really smart, pretty responsible, and fairly reliable. Up until a few years ago, he'd never cheated on me. Then, he did."

Missy's eyes ignited. There was the flaw she'd been waiting for. "Ain't you afraid of disease?"

"That was a long time ago. One woman, and never again."

"I never knowed any cheat to stop at one woman."

"Well, this one did. Ripped me apart. And in someone else's words, here's where," I looked at Red, "I got real cold. When I left this fuckin' town, I was burned out, and every nerve ending was worn to a frazzle and singed black as coal. It took me nearly ten years to figure out how to go about trusting a man. Then, in one night out with the girls, I learned how to let go," I said, snapping my fingers. "That fast. The same way I'd let go with Dieks. You just raise your hands, and you take a real good look, and you say, 'Whoa, fuck this noise. I'm outta here. History. Don't even touch me.'"

"That sounds like somethin' I faintly remember," Red said, looking at the ceiling and soakin' up the words. It looks like he's just coasting. Andy listens, watching Red, then turns back to me and waits.

"So, you see, we're all pretty much the same, us misfits. We carry our stinkin' rotten garbage on our backs in these big, heavy bags, year to year, and life to life. Even though we know all the heavy shit inside 'em threatens us at every turn, we just keep hangin' on to 'em, 'cause this pathetic load's all we got to call our own.

"You strike out at your wife, your kids, your own personal war that won't go 'way, and sure 'nough, war's the winner. The wife and kids leave just like I did. At first, you think you got a real bargain 'cause you couldn't download Nam anyway. It wakes you up every morning, taunts you in the bathroom mirror, salutes you at the breakfast table, and then it just kinda creeps into all the voids that open up in your days. You give and give and give, and in return, you get kicked right in your old … vulnerabilities.

"Me, too. 'Cept I work at keeping the residue of the really shallow shit alive. You know the stuff, where you get to smile for a split-second because recall's so sweet and then you start sliding, and you sink lower and lower 'cause you realize it's all you got left. Whatever you thought living was s'pose to be has become an old, dead dream. I don't mind most o' the time. Remember me? No depth, I'm learning to exist on the surface, skittering across life like one of those long-legged bugs you see on pond scum.

"This way, I figure nobody ever gets to fuck me over again. And, when I'm feeling really brave or particularly defiant, I venture out and open up an old gunnysack of garbage. I examine all the rot and call it, voila! Conversation and camaraderie with old friends. Ain't it great?

"Our intended lives have long been abandoned. We've all settled for something less, anything to pretend we're still moving forward, when we know for a fact that we've hit bottom. We're just slogging around in the sludge with the rest of life's dregs. No one escapes alive. Dieks showed us the only out: Death by denial, under watchful eyes of friends and relatives, starvation, dehydration, and morphine, the holy grail of the misbegotten. That should've been a real kick-ass he served up for the masses. He defied everyone who thought they'd cut short his stay, grab his shit, and run.

"Only they forgot the grisly past. Maybe they never knew that he was once left to survive life with Father. And he did, by God. So, finally, after thirty years, what better way to give them something as guilt-laden as they deserved. With ancient powers that the rest of the world forgot, he found at the end of his life, Eureka! You don't think there were some outside forces operating here? I'm surprised Cheyenne and the whole Indian nation didn't rise up, stage a revolt, step in, and stomp 'em."

"You really believe that shit?"

"Oh, yeah, Red. I've lived that shit. You've had a couple brushes with destiny, gotten your feet put to the fire a few times. What'd'you think? You get singled out and singed, and everyone stops to watch, become believers. In the end, we'll all believe that shit, too. I'm here to tell you there's a way in from the other side. Quite frankly, I'd be shaking in my boots if I were responsible for all the underhanded and devious shit that's going on now. If anybody thinks that cheatin' his sons out of their due'll go without notice, they got another think acomin'. He'll get 'em from the other side, and when the shit hits the fan, it ain't gonna be evenly distributed."

"You seem pretty sure of yourself." Red's barely holding up his end of the table talk, and he takes a gulp.

"Sounds like a goddam threat to me," Missy snorts. "I don' think them boys got a leg to stand on."

"Then you don't think at all. You got a couple kids. D'you think you'd forget whose blood runs through their veins? D'you think that you'd die and say, 'Fuck them kids. I want my reprehensible, illiterate, white trash kin to have everything I've ever worked for 'cause they're stupid and greedy and don' know squat. Go ahead and tell me that's what you'd do. That's what I thought! It's not right, and they know it, I know it, and you know it. "

Missy was tapping out the end of yet another cigarette, when she blew a perfect smoke ring, and said, "Liz, there ain't one of us ever been tight with family."

"My point exactly. Neither was Shaunessy. He recognized two of his children legally, but he stood back and let other people bear the responsibility of their childhoods. But, he hated his in-laws with a deep and abiding passion. Called 'em The Clan, separated them by their differences, and wasn't exactly subtle when he did it. The Big Clan, the Dumb Clan, the Shit Can Clan, the Fuckin' Clan, or any combination thereof. Later, he got clever with The Lucy Clean Clan.

"He was ashamed that his sister was so desperate that she ran away with trash. She was too fuckin' stupid to save her own life, just repeated the mistake. GI Joe was a jobless hick that finished the destitution, despair, and violence that Richard started. They were both too pathetic to ever escape the poverty they wallowed in. Dieks never forgot and never even considered the word forgive when it came to those responsible for destroying his life. She made his every waking moment sheer hell when she left. He gave most of his excess to strangers, and financed a series of nameless bimbos. He never once gave thought to Joe and Lucy Bergen or their condition.

"Somebody's been blowin' smoke up somebody's ass. All Shaunessy was ever concerned with was his art and antiques, his cars, houses and tools, and whether or not he could get laid on a continuous basis without having to commit to some woman that he just knew he'd regret waking up to. The last thing he had in mind was providing for a clan family of misfits with the IQ's of kumquats.

"Ask Red. He's been kickin' around for forty years or so. How many times, Red, did you hear Dieks say that 'son'bitch better not touch a goddamn thing, or I'll blow his ass away' and he meant it?"

Red's smiling. "Yep, that's about the way he put it. Spent most of his life thinkin' 'bout defending everything that was his from Bergen and his bunch. Figured they'd come to blows over it, sooner or later. He said Lucy kept Joe alive by keepin' his ass out of there when they had to sort Richard's estate. Dieks and 'Manda did most of the work and made all the arrangements."

"I'll bet that was a real square deal," I said, shoving another empty to the middle of the table."

He didn't answer, just kept going. "I was there most of the time, from when Richard went into the hospital. When he finally died, Dieks just took most of the stuff that had been in the garage and the old store, and that old army footlocker the old man guarded. 'Member that? Said it had twenty-dollar gold pieces and a derringer in it, and Cheyenne's prescriptions from the Pet Doctor, and he said that all the bottles had skull and crossbones drawn on them. There was a bunch of dirty books and pictures of naked women in all different poses, and the deed to the house and the land."

"All the important stuff, cherished family heirlooms and such, right?"

"No, no, I don't think so ... "

"That's a joke, son." I said it to no one in particular.

Red hesitated a moment. "Oh, but Lucille took most everything else. Then they just hired an auction company to come in, mark it, and unload it. Dieks hated what was left. He refused to look at any of it, tried to forget it, the furniture, house, land, just got rid of it. No feeling at all."

"Oh, no feeling at all might be a bit of an understatement. There were plenty of feelings about that place. All bad. Once, when Delly was about two or three, we visited Richard. I sent Dieks a picture of Delly sittin' on Richard's lap, in the living room of the house down at Harrow's Branch. A few years later, he remembered getting the picture in the mail and said he'd got gut sick and started shaking, thinking how no one could imagine the horrible things Richard could do to a little kid. He wanted the baby off that man's lap and as far away from that monster as he could get. Now, that's feeling."

I think Missy's passed out. Her eyes are open, and she's upright, but she hasn't moved for quite awhile.

Just as I'm sure she's no longer with us, she says, "I gotta pee."

Andy scoots over and stands, letting her slide out of the booth. She gets up, but seems to have forgotten where she was headed.

"To the can," Red says, pointing to the back, and she nods and weaves slowly through the crowd, pausing to rest at the closest corner of the pool table.

"I don't think Dieks ever knew what was important," Red said. "Not 'til clear at the end, anyway. He never let much of anybody see little Dieks when he came to town, just Adams sometimes, and me." Stopped by a few times. Always said, 'You 'member Little Dieks?' He was big as him. They'd just be out runnin' around like ol' buddies that'd been doin' it for years."

"Only they hadn't."

"Oh, we all knew that. We were there. We knew who was in and who was out, who he didn't care about. But, damn, he was proud of them boys. He'd just grin ear to ear when he'd be uptown and someone'd ask about Callahan or mention his big promotion. He'd go on and on about Dieks and his grades, his family, and their future. Like he was the one responsible for it. We knew, an' he knew we knew. It was a big game we all played, an' everybody played along.

"He'd probably been smart enough hisself to go right on to college outta high school. Only no one ever said nothin' to him about it. Then, him an' Carolyn had a kid, and well, you know the rest. Couldn't ever get far enough away from what Richard had done. I mean, I think he wanted to be different. He kept tryin' to be different, gettin' married, havin' kids, gettin' divorced. He knew life worked like that somehow. He just couldn't get the middle part right. He just never had anything to go on. All us guys were single. Then, we started gettin' married, and not much changed.

"Only he couldn't see the way things were behind our doors. They probably weren't much different than his, but we never had to say, 'Okay, this kid can go with that man, and this kid can go with that man,' cause, sorry," and he glanced at me, "every time a wife left him, he lost the kids, too. In the end, I think he felt pretty bad about that."

"A little late, I'd say."

"Yeah, well, maybe better late than never," Red defended.

"I'm not so sure late and never aren't the same in this case. I think this was pretty hard on both Dieks and Callahan. It was like saying, 'Hey, we got good news, and bad news. The good news is, your biological father really loved you, even if he never had the time of day for you for twenty years, or so. The bad news is, your biological father really loves you and he'd like to spend the rest of his life with you. But, it's five-forty-five and he'll be checkin' out around six.'

"'Can you drop what you're doin' and rush right over? Oh, and by the way, don't get too close just 'cause you're sons, 'cause y'ain't no son o' mine. An' don' be gettin' any funny ideas, anything you might 'member as warm and fuzzy you better shitcan 'cause you're just here to watch him die.'"

"Hey, Liz B, don't mince your words, now, okay?"

"Yeah, right. Like now's when I need to gloss over everything. I spent a lot of time dragging my kid out of the skids. I'll be damned if they sucker him back in just long enough to say, 'Oh by the way, you were the son, but now he's dead, and you ain't really the son, well, at least not where cash and carry's concerned. And, oh, by the way, just 'cause you eked by, living poor as a church mouse, and he spent his money on good times, wine, women and song, that's no reason to believe that either one of you's gonna have any reason to get righteous come sundown.'

"And they'll say, 'It's, well, to be perfectly truthful, it's all ours.' Then a heavy sigh'll accompany the speech, and a few woe is me's, and maybe even a 'boy, do I feel real bad 'bout this.' But you know how it is, 'if you gots a dirty lawyer and keys to the house, well, possession *is* ninety percent of the law' or something like that."

"Life sucks, don' it."

"Always has, Red."

Andy's talking, and I almost feel bad that I'm not listening, but my head is somewhere in the early seventies, I think. I've told Dieks that life sucks, and I'm disgusted with everything. He writes me a long, elaborate letter telling me not to worry, 'cause he'll always be there, my sun, moon, and stars. We'll always be together. And at the end, there's a poem, but I can't quite reach it.

Lazy Liz B? No. Frizzledy Lizzledy? Naw, Liz B's Memories? What was it that he'd written to me that day?

When we were married, he promised me gold
and all the furs my arms could hold.
I have a gold filling, third molar I think,
and a purring ole cat with fur soft as mink.

The silver he promised shines only at night,
and he polishes pearls with my Ultra Brite.
Star clusters and diamonds clutter my lawn
when I look out at morning and find that he's gone.

He's given me all that he promised and soon,
I'll have what I wanted: my son and his moon ...

It has faded into the aged pages of my memories. It was playful
and funny and amused me for many years. But it died inside spent
anger and unused kisses and empty, lonely arms where I rested my
head on the kitchen table, waiting well into the night for him to come
home from some other woman's company.

Timing is Everything

Five or six years after graduating from high school, Dieks decided to go to college. This was a real dilemma for him, since he'd spent half his life pretending to be a veteran of everything. He'd spent the other half drinking away deficits. To face the fact that he really didn't know all there was to know was a real kick in the ass. But he went anyway. Instead of drinking himself into a dither every night with the reprobates downtown, he went to evening classes at the Area Ten Community College just outside town. After class, he'd show up at my house to study. We'd review that night's notes and then we'd go over and over the most mundane facts from the rest of his mostly general courses. He was always afraid that he'd be embarrassed by not knowing the answer when he was called on.

I wrote his papers and tutored him for tests. It was an efficient system that seemed to help both of us understand the effort required in education. I once complained that I just couldn't produce papers of the quality he wanted on my old Adler manual typewriter. He listened quietly while I groused, but said nothing, just stood up, grabbed his coat, and left.

Just over an hour later, I heard him fidgeting with the front door. I ran through the dining room to help him open the doors as he tried to balance a large case of macaroni, or so I thought. He pulled the towel off and tossed it aside, proudly displaying the box's contents on the coffee table. There before me, with the telltale, conservative, matte grey finish, was a new ball element IBM electric typewriter. He pulled two boxes of ribbon from his coat pocket and tossed them to me, asking if it would now be easier to do the quality of paper he wanted.

I said yes, and having learned not to ask for any of the particulars, I told him it was very nice and let it go at that. However, a few months later, when the type was getting too light, I had to change the ribbon for the first time. When I flipped up the top, I found serial numbers and a property tag identifying the college as the rightful owner.

The week following our IBM acquisition, we struggled for several days trying to write a critique of an oil painting by Titian, called *The Rape of Europa*. After several days of research, a few days of working through a preliminary rough draft, and a final day of editing, rewriting, and typing the final draft, we got hung up on three lines at the end of the paper.

Dieks was arguing content, saying it just didn't belong. I defended style and form, insisting that it was incomplete without the lines that tied it to the beginning. Finally, he just shook his head and said, "Whatever," as he stopped pacing and sat down, waiting for the final page so he could leave.

A week or two later, I stopped by his house and saw that the paper had been returned. Folded in half and laying at one end of the bar, he'd never mentioned it to me. I picked it up and opened the cover page, immediately recognizing the scrawl of his art instructor. We'd managed an A-. Just under the grade was a single comment, "Excellent research and observations," with her initials.

I turned to the last page, where we'd had our war. In both margins there were brackets, singling out the three lines. In the right margin the teacher had written simply, "These really don't work, do they?"

He never mentioned it to me.

. . .

I wrote him long, elaborate letters, and he returned long, elaborate replies. I'd write him lovely, gooey poetry, and he'd politely reply in kind. Sometimes I'd find a dandelion, sometimes a rose. Both smelled as sweet to me.

He taught me to drive a stick shift "like I meant it," and he was just as thrilled as I was when I finally got the feel for it. I could pop the clutch and pull a wheelie and hold it for quite a ways before the old '29 sedan would slam down and jerk to a halt. It scared the hell out of his friends, but he'd stand off to one side in the street with an all-knowing smirk and motion for me to ease off, shift, or brake.

While they'd be haulin' ass to jump up to the parking, off the street and out of harm's way, just in case I forgot the ground rules and decided I might want to turn and run over them, he'd stand proud, supportive, and trusting, close enough to touch me as I passed them by. Braced by clutch and gas in tandem, I hung on to the wheel for dear life as the beast reined back like a stallion on hindquarters, or a well-balanced hound on haunches, precariously pawing midair.

Every other year he had a project car. Seasons were designated for segments of each section of something or other to be completed: glass and gauges, gaskets and hoses, stripping the paint, beating out bumps and dings from body parts, sending metal away to be chromed, seats and door panels to be upholstered. Tearing down the engine, replacing or rebuilding parts that were no longer available anywhere. From glass, steel and chrome to engine and interior, he was driven by a nearly fanatical obsession for perfection.

In the off years, he spent his free time frequenting galleries and ferreting out rare antiques from rural roadside shops. He hauled every item home like some would a stray animal, and viewed each piece as though it would ultimately be the priceless treasure of the century. Always, though, they just needed a little this, a little that. Between the shop-hopping and the restoration of neglected wonders, he still found time to sculpt and paint. He was never empty-handed, and the more time I spent watching him keep busy, the more I realized that I would've been the next project if he'd ever been able to figure out where to start.

I never thought I could allow him to renovate me personally. But, I believe to this day that he felt, somewhere in his bag of tricks, he had the wherewithal to fix my faulty parts. I think that alone was the reason he'd always felt I'd come back -- if there was ever anyone in need of total renovation, it most assuredly would've been me.

For all our near-death episodes with each other, he was always receptive to new ideas, trusting that my true heart would run the show and I wouldn't lead him astray. I found him particularly malleable when he was sober. One day, as we drove around town doing nothing in particular, we went past a little bungalow that I used to daydream about in Mr. Franklin's ninth grade science class at the Eldon High School.

I pointed out the "For Sale" sign in the window and proceeded to convince him that he needed to get out of rentals and into something he could call his own. The little place on Cortland just fit the bill. It was a slab building, originally designed as a two-car garage. The owner lived in the house next door and had converted it some twenty years before into a bungalow where her elderly parents could live with minimal care. There were no stairs to climb to a second story, and no attic, closet, or cabinets that couldn't be accessed with a ladder.

As the old joke goes, we got it for a song. We also got tunnels of termites, poorly designed plumbing, wiring, and heating systems, dry rot and walls that leaned in to meet and greet the sagging ceilings. He lived there, but I never did.

Because I was indirectly responsible for the success of this investment, I'd been recruited to help with its remodeling. We tore down walls and ripped out termite-tormented floors. The infestation was so bad that one of the local pest control businesses stopped by and offered to treat the ground at no charge if he could have select pieces of infested floor joist to use in his window display. In bold red lettering, two feet high, his banner said, "DON'T LET THIS HAPPEN TO YOUR LOVELY HOME!"

We worked side by side, day and night. Delly would be playing or sleeping in his bassinet or playpen outside with the little girl down the street as his unofficial caretaker. One day, lo and behold, it was finally complete.

I fought and argued to no avail when he did the bedroom in period piece hippy style, with forty strands of red beads in six-foot lengths hanging from ceiling to floor. Harlequin-red shag carpet graced both living room and bedroom, saluting each unsuspecting visitor with a pulsating sexual tension alert. An oversized bar, with cheap wood paneling and padded black vinyl sides, ran the length of the living room. Behind it, heavy garish red and black brocade draperies, framed by hideous red and gold-flocked wallpaper, covered a span of nothing on a windowless, cinder block wall.

He glued Woolworth's best gold-flecked marbled mirrors on the bottom three feet of the wall divider that stood at the end of his bed, while an old, weatherworn porch post from some dilapidated farmhouse became the frame for the left side of the doorway. He became artsy and innovative with red, opaque plastic inserts that served as the top four or five feet of the room divider, between the living room and the next room's sea of king-size waterbed and lone chest of drawers.

On one wall of the living room, he hung heavy, fake Spanish sconces on cheap walnut paneling. Between them, he displayed a large, pastoral oil painting by someone named Whittier that he'd stolen from an unsuspecting, unprotected gallery outside St. Paul. He mounted a fluorescent grow lamp above it, and left it on both day and night.

Finished, he stood back and marveled at the beautiful rooms he'd created. I stood back and predicted that the baby would become color-blind, confused, cross-eyed, or criminally adept if he spent a great deal of time there, and I pledged my dead-level best to protect him from the influence of bad taste and no class. It had all the earmarkings of a bordello.

"From a sow's ear to a sow's ass," I told him, but he just flashed his proud, teethy smile, and refused to change a thing.

It was then all too clear to me. It had never been his intention to create a cozy home for the three of us. He wanted instead to provide an atmosphere of acultural tawdriness, where guys could drag in their most recent conquests from local bars and do with them what they could.

I grew to hate The Bordello with a deep, enduring passion. I hated the cars that frequented it day and night. I hated hearing people talk about droppin' in at Shaunessy's. I hated becoming a private eye with a baby sleeping in his carseat, while I'd sit and take note of each slut's arrival and subsequent departure. I'd purse my lips and tell him through gritted teeth, "I saw them." But he'd just laugh, and still, he wouldn't change a thing.

The guys would fill his bar with all the booze and dope they'd ever need, wasting days, nights, and women in rapid succession. They'd leave for a few hours, then they'd all come back, and the tokin', jokin', and smokin' would start all over. I'd stand in the doorway, like the self-designated house police, with Delly on my hip or sound asleep on my shoulder. Dieks called me the pow-wow party crasher as I stood by helplessly fuming, and his good-better-best friends patted my less-than-threatening shoulders and said, "Cool down, Lizzie B," as they'd walk cautiously around me to take another hit, hold another breath, and exhale exuberantly, adding to the thick blue haze that raced out the door with me while they pointed and laughed.

As they took turns using the Voyeur Room with the marbled mirrors, I buckled the baby in his car seat and took him home to an antiseptic house that knew no visitors. We slept in beds where we didn't have to wait our turn, and breathed freely in our clean, lonely air.

Just after his spring finals, Dieks said he'd have to go in search of work again. Unemployment benefits had run out, and there was simply nothing left for him in town. It was the longest he'd ever been laid off at the packing plant, and he wasn't alone. A lot of experienced people beat the bushes for work; there just wasn't any to be found.

As before, knowing I couldn't stop him, I simply waved good-bye. Being understandably agreeable made me appear to be more secure, more sympathetic, a better person, I told myself. But I didn't like it any more than I had the first time he left. Only this time, at least, I wasn't a month away from having a baby.

With that, he was gone. For weeks, I heard nothing. Then I started getting long, lonely letters, reminiscent of those in my college days. In mournful, pleading lines, he wrote of past wrongs, of hopes and dreams, promises for our future, and of our son.

"Our future, our son, we three, when I get back," graced every letter, every card. And for the first time in a long time, I thought that, at last, the misery of loneliness would finally turn our sad state of affairs around, and our sorry existence would eventually improve as well.

It was not to be. One day, I ran into Stan Brooks at the bank, an old friend who'd never hesitated to say anything that needed to be said.

"I figured you'd be getting' divorced as soon as that prick headed to St. Paul with Leila to have the baby."

I felt weak, and knew I was in trouble, like I was falling and there was no one to catch me. In fact, there was no one to notice the plummet.

"Huh?" That was all I could get to come out of my mouth.

"Oh, my God. I'm so sorry. You didn't know, did you."

I shook my head and focused on his mouth and his teeth and his very green eyes boring holes in my head.

"Her parents are pretty well-heeled, you know. When they found out she was pregnant and the father was married, hell, they wrapped up her little ass and shipped her out, right now." He snapped his fingers matter-of-factly.

"Her sister says she's heartbroken, pretty close to suicidal, in fact. But her folks wouldn't give in. Said her life'd be ruined if she had a kid now. She's too young, always been protected, wouldn't know where to turn."

I felt my heart collapsing, seeping down, down into my wobbling weak legs, past my gelatin knees, into my gooshy shoes. It felt as if my innards were seizing up in protest and hardening in resolve -- something I'd never felt before, something I've never allowed since. Some parts went numb, while some died quickly. Yet others briefly fluttered, then flew away, leaving me completely void, unable to retrieve the remains of an emotional ghost.

"I should've known," I finally mumbled.

"I can't believe you didn't." His thin, pale lips replied.

I never recovered what was lost in that moment. From that point in time to this, I've always known that interminable stretch of minutes stripped me of something that set me apart from the rest of humanity. It cast aside promises, hopes and dreams, leaving in their place the lifeless shells of marriage might've and could've beens.

Dieks, however, recovered quite nicely. Eventually, he returned to his house on Cortland and came crawling back. Literally. On his hands and knees, with his head down in submission, he begged for forgiveness and prayed that I would once again provide the love and approval he needed so badly. He swore he'd die if I left him, that he'd rip his own heart out if he ever made the same foolish mistake.

I forgave him, though I've since come to refuse the notion that any human has the right to requital for another's alleged injuries. I did what I needed to, and stayed because I had nothing better to do. I gave great thought to what I had to do; I needed only to follow through. Execute with exactitude -- although timing is everything after the thinking, planning, and scheming have been completed.

So, while I thought, planned, and schemed, I lived simply and less violently across town, away from him and "his shame." I was still serviced with great regularity. His lovemaking was a sweet, splendid jaunt down memory lane, but it was servicing, just the same. He worked hard at getting back into my good graces. And, as a kept woman, I retained a certain amount of freedom and latitude. Big deal, I thought. Big, fucking deal.

I figured I could always maintain my independence. After St. Paul, the big lie, and my equally false forgiveness, I'd determined that anything was possible. I continued on with my life and studies in pursuit of a distant dream. Just beyond the commute and each morning's radiant sunrise, I was certain a brass ring was beckoning. Each morning I'd wake and find it was another day, not unlike the day before. Each night, I'd go to bed never quite sure the midnight raids he'd made for so long were now in the past.

Part IV

Fragments

The grieving half brothers, Dieks and Callahan, barely knew each other, but handily made their way through an hour or two at Sundown, had since left the Levy, and were headed to Pair O' Dice. Through the amber eyes of Old Milwaukee, they'd maneuvered their way through more than twenty years of unfamiliar waters and on to the state of camaraderie within family.

In our roles, as the grieving Vietnam syndrome buddy and the grieving second ex-wife, Red and I were getting rip-snorting drunk, reviewing caches of past lives and pitiful loves over at Sundown. Yuma the Rebel and his lovely significant other were high, wide and teetering on the edge, when they decided we all might want to move on -- across town to The Fool's Pair O' Dice -- while we were still mobile.

As I approached the front door, I recognized a large, tasteless pair of fuzzy black and dingy white dice hanging in the window, and realized it was the place Dieks brought me, back in the summer of '91.

"We closed this place once," I said to no one in particular as the screen door slammed behind us.

. . .

I'd driven down to Eldon to visit my mother up on Mockingbird Hill. Dieks and Debby, my son and newly acquired daughter-in-law, had driven down to meet me from Iowa City, where they were between semesters at the University of Iowa. By the time I arrived, Mom said they'd already gone across the tracks to see Dieks Shaunessy.

After they'd been gone a couple of hours, the phone rang and Mom handed it to me. My son was asking ever so nonchalantly if I couldn't come over and visit Big Dieks.

Thoughts scrambled in my head while a mix of emotions formed an answer.

"I don't think that's a good idea.

But, he hemmed and hawed, stalled and whispered that dear ol' Dad had just told them that he hadn't seen me in years and would be so pleased.

"Twelve, in fact, and there's a reason for that. Just tell him I'm pretty sure I haven't changed, and I'm less than receptive."

"Mom, I don't think that will work. It happens to be his birthday, you know. I kinda promised I'd come through."

"Really? And what did you tell him you were going to do to convince me there was a compelling need to come over there and subject myself to his scrutiny?"

"Well, we did remember that you guys used to be married. Then there's Debby. She might want to see what you're like together, uh, I mean, what you might've been like together, or what kind of relationship it was that produced me, your wonderful son."

I paused a moment. "I know who you are. You don't have to remind me who's responsible." Strange feeling, I couldn't decide.

"You told me that anybody can endure anything for a few hours. That's all you gotta do, just endure this for a few hours. Endeavor to persevere, you say. Anyway, it's late, and that'd be a good excuse for you to leave after a little bit if you wanted to."

My mother was watching me from her rocker in front of the TV. I thought she was biting her tongue.

"What the hell," I said. "Give me ten minutes."

I walked out into the night air, down the street, through an empty field of black-eyed Susans and buttonweed, then up and over the tracks. As I stepped onto his porch, I smiled at the old slat swing hanging there. It was one of the normal things he'd promised me, when he was into promising normal, standard run-of-the-mill shit. 'A white picket fence, a wrap-around porch with a creaky old swing, a couple o' half-breeds, along with dog, cat, station wagon, dishwasher, and more lovin' than any white woman's heart could stand,' he'd said.

I was always amused that he defined his ethnicity for me by noting my lily-white, washed-out nothingness. I always figured he was about as full-blood Indian as I was any one strain of melting-pot-mixed German, French, Irish, Polish, who knows what Heinz 57 ancestry. But he did seem to have Cheyenne's dominant genes: deep brown eyes characteristic of the Cherokee on her mother's side, sun-darkened skin and high cheekbones of Sioux warriors, like her father and his father before him.

Just inside the front door, the surroundings were at once strangely familiar as well as mildly uncomfortable. I recognized many things I'd given him and more we'd bought together. I was quickly reminded that I'd left them all behind when I'd abandoned his promises, taking with me the only remaining truth of the love we'd known, our son.

Unlike me, the relics in the room were untouched by time, unaffected by the passage of years. There was little evidence of the number of times Dieks had remarried, or the endless stream of women who'd flowed in and out of his life. I'd left him everything, and he'd kept it all -- even our blue-speckled dishes in the drainer, I noted, while passing through the kitchen. In our first month, we'd bought them on a shopping trip to Des Moines.

In an alcove, just off the kitchen, I spied a glass curio cabinet. There, side by side, in either the hall of honor or the wall of shame, sat his two most prized possessions: the sleek, beechwood carving of a racing whippet, and a three-tiered, round jewelry box made in Bangladesh from molded, crushed eggshells dyed black and gold.

The dog was stretched in stride, with finger grooves across its midsection. It looked like a handle that was missing its armoire. His mother had secretly given it to him shortly before she died. At the time, he knew little of its significance, other than she demanded that he take it and hide it. She told him to keep it forever, and to never let Richard know that he had it. It was years before he learned that it was all she'd ever had of his father's -- the hand-carved grip of an ancestral bow, missing all parts including its history.

The delicate black and gold jewelry box had been a Christmas gift from me, the second year we were married. I found it in the basement of Hoffman Drugstore in downtown Ottumwa where a little import shop bought crafts from all over the world. I was too poor to buy anything else, and it was only three dollars. But it was the only gift he got that year.

I smiled and made a conscious attempt to breathe again as I headed out the back door, stepping down to an intimate little sundeck -- most inviting in the night light of an old fashioned street lamp standing next to the garage. As I opened the garage door, he hurried over to me, embracing me for much longer than I was comfortable with.

"I've missed you," he whispered in my ear, and clasped my hand as he walked with me across to where our son sat with his new wife.

He reclaimed everyone he'd ever known that way. Hugs, smiles, and handshakes that reestablished links, were to me both frightening and unsettling.

He suddenly clapped his hands together, and said, "Why don't we close up here and go inside for a drink. A cola for you, Missy," as he pointed to his son's very pregnant wife. "It's not as humid in the house," and he hit the button on the automatic garage door control as he passed by.

We stood and single-filed up the back door steps, past the inviting glow of streetlight and intimate deck, and into the house. As I held the back door, waiting for Dieks and Debby to get in, he put his hand on my bottom, as if to give me support, much the same as he'd done back when.

"Don't fall back, now."

"I don't think there's much worry there, DC. I found that a lot begins to settle around forty. Falling isn't the problem. It's getting it up, or getting up, I mean."

He deserved both of the zaps he got on that one. I was one of the few who called him DC. It was an intimacy, a familiarity held on reserve that allowed him to be chided without anyone else knowing the inference. We both knew what he was doing. Whys and wherefores weren't needed. The fact was he simply never could keep his hands to himself, or his parts in his pants, where I was concerned.

We talked 'til midnight, though I can't remember the content of the conversation. Debby kept dozing off, falling sideways as she struggled to stay awake. When we finally rose to leave, I saw his eyes pleading with me, much the same as he had years before: Don't go, they begged. Oh, please, please, don't go.

So I stayed.

I suspected why. Part of it was because I knew he wouldn't expect me to, partly because I knew Sam wouldn't care. But more than either of those reasons was because it was his birthday. What no one else ever realized was that there were two things that died with his mother back in the fifties -- the kindness of a human touch, and a little boy's birthday.

After her death, for the rest of his childhood, he was never once hugged or touched lovingly again. His birth was never celebrated by the man who called him "The Rat," and the date went by for years, unnoticed and without mention. Now, only someone in the know would see fit to note the passing of the day, and I was the only one there.

That was when we went to The Fool's Pair O' Dice.

It was there, after champagne at his house and countless beers throughout the evening, that he stood up that night, on the top of a barstool and announced to people that only one of us obviously knew -- night stragglers and living leftovers -- that he was truly sorry.

This was, he told them, a public "pile o' gee" for having been a lousy husband, a rotten father, and one bad Injun. Then he grinned.

But," he added, pointing a finger to the ceiling as he stepped down from the barstool, " ... I was a helluva lover! Even she," and he raised his beer and pointed it at me in the first booth, "will tell you that!"

. . .

Sitting there, next to Red, in the same booth just two short years later, I saw Dieks' teeth shining in the dim light and Dieks' eyes dancing in the dark. I heard Dieks' voice asking if I couldn't come back home now, as if I'd proved whatever it was that I'd set out to prove. The great warrior was conceding defeat in some old battle of an ancient war that no longer mattered. He was serious.

"I been waitin'," he said, " ... just puttin' in time. Seems I always get back to that with you, waitin' for that ol' someday, and I guess it finally got here. Hey, I can say it out loud. You wanna hear it again?"

I pulled him down as he started to get up on the barstool.

No, I told him. By default, home was where I lived. Cedar Falls had become my designated area. It had been good to me, good for a family, good for raising children. Sam was good for me -- reliable, predictable, dependable, quiet. He said Sam sounded like a lawn mower, and he began pouting.

"I've changed," he said. I reminded him that it couldn't have been an awful lot. As I'd passed through his kitchen that night I'd noticed an envelope on the table. "Big Tears," somewhere in Texas, was the return address, where Debby had said his friend Nicki was.

"Dieks told me this is the longest relationship you've ever had. He thought that was a good sign."

"How many times can you read even a great novel, like *War and Peace?*" he asked.

"That depends, on which one I was, the war or the piece."

"Neither. You're the writer. There aren't even any chapters in my life without you."

"Right. Even I can't imagine your life without volumes of stories to tell and embellish."

"It's true. You're the whole library. You're the shelves. You're the--"

"Dewey Decimal System." I interrupted. "I wanna be the Dewey."

"Huh? Okay, then, you can be 'the Dewey.' But not just a book. Not just a story read once and then put back forever."

I smiled at the memory - how he'd appease me, and try so hard to please, knowing all the while that it was little more than a child's chase, endless and futile. The chase was the guts of the matter.

It wasn't 'til much later, after beers, cheers, threats, and tears, that he reminded me he'd kept his promise that he'd never marry anyone with children. He wouldn't raise someone else's child when he couldn't find the time or technique to raise his own.

I felt smug then; it's more numbing now. Nicole loved him as much as I had and probably more than I could, and she loved her son as much as I loved mine. But she allowed Dieks to separate their worlds. He could have one, but not the other. If she got too far from Dieks or too close to his nightmares, the result would be the same. It was a tenuous balancing act. In the end, her son was safe at home in his mother's arms, while her lover lay cold in a casket.

Where I had once felt honored that Dieks had the decency to respect that fundamental promise, I felt ashamed when I realized it was just one more contingency placed on his life. It was another one of the obstacles preventing him from being a regular guy, somebody's husband, somebody's dad. He would never know the warmth and comfort that comes with all the years it takes to establish an identity that sounds like somebody's lawn mower.

My worse thought, though, was that his refusal to commit to her may have meant his life. As a nurse, Nicki would have seen the signs, recognized the significance, and acted with immediacy. The golden hour would never have been squandered struggling with him, trying to clothe him, waiting for someone to help him to the car. His stubborn vanity would have been ignored, 911 would have been called, and the hour that determines life or death wouldn't have passed him by. They wouldn't have bothered trying to lift him, or spent precious moments bickering about embarrassments. In short, he wouldn't have realized too late that the time spent deliberating was the rest of his life.

. . .

At the hospital, each of the players repeated their version of the drama of the night's horrific events as my mind surged with cluttered refuse from the past. Thin-as-a-rail Lisa had struggled to keep me on my feet while transferring Baby Dieks from my locked arms to her mother-in-law, Rush, who was calling the hospital.

The last movement of our tragedy had sent me reeling and crashing, just before he passed out unharmed in a drunken stupor on the living room floor. My fingers spread open wide, reaching up, and I'd tried to deflect the fringed brown cowboy boot with the silver and turquoise circle, but it flew through the air and jumped and jiggled on impact, catching me solidly at my right temple. I wondered if the pain he felt that night was as horrible as mine when I regained consciousness after the calamity at Harrow's Branch back in seventy.

Dieks was in his crib crying, and my head felt locked in the jaws of a vise as I struggled to hold on to him, wrapped in blankets and stuffed down inside his bunting. We stumbled out the back door, through the snow, to the old red pickup parked in the icy ruts of the side yard at Richard's. I put him on the floor, thinking he wouldn't roll off there, and he shouldn't be there long enough to get chilled, though I could see snow through the holes in the floorboards.

I coaxed the old cold engine to start and finally managed to get it bucking and jumping along, though it fought me all the way across town. I left the engine running to light the icy path to Lisa Baker's back door and stood there, barefoot, in pajamas, without coat or hat, pounding with my fists and head in unison, watching the wonderful kaleidoscope of colors when the back porch light came on. And then, there was no color at all. I saw one skinny Lisa, and then many skinny Lisas, all in pulsating pink cotton gowns, all looking at me sad and knowingly, having once traveled the same road I'd come down. Little more than that made its way back through the haze.

. . .

Red listened as my drunken memories continued to unwind. He said he saw the Veterans' shrink each week and lamented that he came home so cold. Ever since Nam, he said, he'd always been so cold.

"What did you expect," I said.

"Bodies," he reminisced, "piled higher than this room." The words strung along by themselves without lead. " ... one right on top of the other, like bloody rag dolls with eyes that never blink ... they just keep staring and staring."

"You shot Boing Boing," I said, remembering out loud.

"He was a dog," he snapped back in disbelief. Then he reiterated quietly, "He was a dog. I ain't thought about that mutt in years. What's a dog anyway, after all them people?"

"Maybe what keeps us human, or nearly so. Maybe that's what separates us from the other animals, you know, the opposable thumb, the use of tools, and an understanding of compassion. Although I think Mark Twain said something else about blushing, that 'we're the only animal that blushes, or needs to.' Maybe we're the only ones who know we have an option to exercise compassion and sympathy instead of blind indifference.

"That stupid dog belonged to you. He trusted you, depended on you. In return, you neglected him, left him alone for days on a four-foot chain with a bowl of food to share with the ants, a rain barrel full of water that he could drink or drown in, and heat that could fry an egg on the sidewalk. You let him loose in the woods when he'd only known confinement in a cage and on a chain. He barely knew how to walk, he only knew how to jump in and out of a goddamn rain barrel. In the two months you owned him, his only treat was to go for a walk in the woods. Such a deal. After turning him loose - allowing him freedom for the first time, he actually came back to you, all he knew and all he had in the whole world. And guess what? You shot him. And then you walked away and left the lifeless heap to rot."

"He was a dog," Red repeated flatly. But it was clear that his mind was wandering away, maybe to the tangled briars and brambles in the woods by the tracks, across the road from where they lived just south of the old hotel. Maybe he was back in the hollow where he'd shot Boing Boing as he jumped forward and sideways, confused at just how to go about getting back through the thicket to the hand and face of his friend.

Maybe he'd returned to Nam, where he just followed orders and fired on the villagers, cutting them down, one after the other: women with infants, young children, old men waving pieces of white cloth with their meatless arms and stick legs, barely seeing the soldiers through ancient eyes. He told the story only once, just after he'd returned, but lived it every day in his mind he said.

"You know, that might've been the kindest thing you could've done," I said, thinking of Richard. "You only got to kill 'im once. And he sure couldn't be expected to come back and lick your hand."

Red's looking at me as though he's absorbing things he never intended, thinking thoughts he'd long forgotten.

"Remember Yuri?" I asked.

"Who?"

"Yuri, you know, the little black dog we brought back from Arizona. Ornery, high-spirited, feisty little spitfire. I'd just read *Zhivago* and named 'im after one of the characters. He was just a puppy. We got him from the travel agent I'd been working for in Phoenix. Brought 'im all the way back, under the seat in the Nova. He was great company for me, with little black eyes and needle sharp teeth. A smart little runt, learned to do his business outside within just a few days of coming back.

"One cold day, I let him out to pee. After a couple of minutes, I called and whistled my special whistle, but he never came. You pulled up and stopped where I stood in the middle of the road, just beyond the railroad tracks. You were driving the 'Vette, the same one you drove to Illinois, I think. Anyway, I didn't move when you came flying in from the tar road. You threw open the passenger side door, and said, 'Get in,' so I did. I didn't even know who you were through the tears. All I saw was a little rug of bloodied black fur.

"I sat as you drove for what seemed an eternity, and you never said one word to me. Then the door opened, and Dieks was standing there, searching my face and then yours, and I said, 'He's dead.' He thought I meant Richard, and he looked over at you.

"You made a circular movement with your finger at the side of your head like I was crazy, and said, 'The dog.' Then you just rolled your eyes and shook your head as you walked away from me. By then you were probably accustomed to death, numbed by it. Dieks might've been too, he'd lost his mother and Butch by then. But I'd never lost anything or anyone before. Neither one of you had the slightest idea what you might do to comfort me. I was treated with the same disregard as the dead dog."

"So what?"

"So you shot your dog on purpose, without remorse or second thought 'cause he pissed you off. Yuri was run over and left to rot on the road. I didn't want him to die. He was my only friend, and nobody cared. It wasn't enough to just leave me each day with a mean old man. I had to be left completely alone, without even the company of a dog. You were both so callous and inconsiderate. I learned something that day -- a valuable lesson about property and disrespect, human kindness and the insignificance of life.

"Just when I expected Dieks to console me and soothe away the pain, he grabbed me. As you closed the garage door, he jerked me out of the car, screaming over and over, 'Did he touch you? Did he touch you?' Startled, I asked him, 'Who?' sniffling and trying to make sense of it, and he just kept yelling, 'Red. Did he touch you?'

"I said, 'No, no, I don't think so. I think he just opened the door, and I got in, and he drove ... here.' He slammed me down on an empty five-gallon drum, and walked away while I sat there stunned and alone in the cold. He went back into the garage with his buddies, back to whatever he'd been doing, and I became a minor inconvenience, a passing interruption. He never looked back, never checked on me, even though I was over eight months pregnant. When my face had turned numb, and my fingers and toes had started stinging, I got up and walked my fat round body the twenty blocks back across town to Harrow's Branch.

"I was trying to dig a hole to bury Yuri in when he finally came home. I'd only gotten down through a few inches of the frozen ground when he slammed the car door and marched over, pushing me out of the way. He grabbed the spade out of my hand and the blood-soaked potato sack Yuri was in, and he heaved 'em under the apple tree. As the wind whipped across my cheeks, he was yelling at me and the words were so simple, yet so cruel, 'He was a fuckin' dog,' and he dragged me by the hood of my coat into the house."

That night, I struggled through my sadness by writing a poem. It was a sad little ditty, written in defiance, about negligence, about a hard lesson learned. No child of mine, I vowed, would ever get too far away, because I feared no tears would fall with the loss. Life was cheap in Harrow's Branch and someone might say, "He was just a kid," and shrug their shoulders, "a fuckin' little nobody." I shuddered at the possibility.

I gathered his chew bones and bowl, blanket and box, and set them by the backdoor -- thinking I'd pack Yuri and all his worldly stuff together to be buried like an Egyptian -- after Dieks left the next day. But by the time I got up, the stack had already been moved from under the apple tree to the curb with the garbage can. As the truck creaked and screeched, lurching to a halt at the end of the driveway, I watched as the guy tossed a frozen Yuri in a blood soaked bag on top of potato peels, emptied cereal boxes, and the grey-green garbage bags of neighbors. His bones and the bowl bounced to the back and his blanket rested with the compact collage of crushed nothingness.

. . .

Yuri

can a pen press the pity
of your death to my heart?

mangled,
muddied,
twisted head,
wet,
blood red.

collar to corral you
paws in sad repose
stiffly, you are frozen there
in autumn air
refusing to disclose

. your name .

unfair!
unfair!
i claim
in pining whine

too little ...
too young ...
too soon ...

too mine.

...

I've stood back and watched quietly as Jimmy Yuma's made his way through the evening. He hangs on to Mishelle sometimes like he's rudderless, afloat and alone at sea, and only she can know what he's going through and only she can guide him away from the rocks. There are gestures one makes in great pain, and body movements that can't be mistaken for anything but grief. I believe a few of us look like we're copying each other's moves. Just a few people, just a few moves. But we're feeling things like Yuma, and some of us are feeling other things, too.

. . .

Dieks told me once that calling Yuma a rebel was a compliment. A rebel, he said, knows the difference between what he's s'pose to be and what he chooses to be. Yuma never had a clue. The fact of the matter was that Jim Yuma was absolutely vile, but he didn't elaborate, other than saying that he might have been the only human being with more evil runnin' through his veins than the ol' man. I gave it some thought, and asked why he even associated with Yuma.

"Wouldn't you? Who would you rather have as your friend, someone who could do you good, or someone who could do you dirt?"

"Someone who could do me good," I answered emphatically.

"Wrong. That might work in the movies, but in the real world, you want someone really bad on your side. It's worth a helluva lot more than a handshake or a name on your door or a few bucks in your pocket. If you got someone really bad, the worst you know, and they're your friend, that's more than one worry you can put to rest."

On a creeper, under a brilliant, cardinal red MG, Dieks is doing something with the exhaust, I think. In the last couple of weeks, he's taken the car completely apart and fixed all the rust. The seats were out to Jenny's being reupholstered, while he tore out the old floorboards and replaced the metal, recarpeting everything. The parts that had been rechromed were waiting to be put back on, and all the scratches on the dash had been sanded and repainted. It looked showroom new. With new tires and hubcaps, he'd probably triple his investment.

He's sliding out toward my feet on the creeper and looks up at me from just under one side. He's waving a ratchet and I think he's going to use it as a pointer. I'm about to get a lesson. I hate lessons. They don't always hurt, but invariably I learned things I probably needed to know but wished I didn't in the end.

"Say someone tells you about how they go around casing different joints. A hardware store, or, a ... parts shop, or a little ol' lady's house. Say they tell you how every week, they watch and keep track of people comin' and goin' and whether or not there's a guard dog, or a harmless ol' cat. They know if there's timers on lights or alarms on doors and windows, or motion detectors. Let's say this person would know when someone goes to bed, or when the neighbors go to bed, or who closes their shades, or goes out on Sundays, or to card group on Thursdays.

"And to make it even clearer, let's just say this person can tell you what kind o' pills an old woman takes before bedtime, that she drinks a half a glass of water with three of 'em, that her cat sleeps on the pillow next to her, and she kisses a picture that sets on her nightstand just before she slides out of her pink slippers and swings her legs up into bed, just before she covers up with a sheet, a blanket, and a bedspread that has blue and purple flowers. That she sleeps on her side because she has trouble breathing on her back, and in the night, she whimpers a lot and calls to someone named Herbert, reaches out into the darkness to him.

"Let's just say this person don' know this ol' lady from Adam, this person's jus' tellin' ya this 'cause there just might be somethin' that this ol' lady might leave to her relatives, and it might just come your way instead. Maybe you'd be interested in buyin' it, if the price was right, say, dime's on the dollar. Then, in a week or so, this person just happens to stop by to shoot the shit. They bring in a couple things that are real old, like German watches or gold leaf vases, and a few weeks after that, a beautiful sapphire and ruby brooch, and a gold chain. Only you don' ask questions. You just look at the stuff and say, 'Wow.'

"A few weeks later, you're asked if you might be able to fence some stuff. If maybe you know someone who might fork out some bucks for stuff like this. You shrug and say, 'I don' know. Let me check it out.'

"You look around, see a couple pieces just like 'em at a ritzy antique store in Des Moines. They want $ 1300 for the lot. So, you go back home and offer this person a couple hundred bucks for the pieces they have. You say that your finder's fee, for knowin' where to unload them, is one of the pieces for free. The guy agrees and takes the deal, gives you one of the other pieces and you come out smellin' like a rose."

"That's grand theft, accessory, or somethin' like that."

"Yeah? You think somebody's goin' to say that to the person doin' the casin' and liftin' the goods? Hell, no," he says, waving the ratchet at me.

"Then, you're readin' the paper one night and you see where a little ol' blue hair calls the cops after a burglary. She got beat up when she got up to go to the can at midnight. Not killed, mind ya, just knocked around a bit. Bashed her head on floor, got herself bruised up, broke a hip when she fell.

"Then, what'd'ya think? You think, I sure don' wanna know the person who did that? Or, do ya think, I'm sure glad I got friends that leave my shit alone. So, it all comes down to ... do ya want criminal friends, or do ya want criminal enemies?

"You wanna open your eyes some night and see someone next to your bed, readin' your pill bottles, somebody that might have a knife, or a ball bat? You still confused about who you might want as your friend?"

"The bad guy."

"Bingo! She's comin' 'round, Lord."

He slid back under the MG, so I could just see the end of his legs and his feet. "Don't think about that story too long, Sweet Liz B, or maybe never. You don't need to know a lot to make a sound decision in a pinch."

Howdy, Doody

Red's hand is clamped tightly over my mouth and he's dragging me backwards, away from Yuma. In my drunkenness I see his eyes flashing fire, and his tightly clenched fists next to his sides. Missy's holding him back, bobbing and weaving, distracting, running interference.

I'm yelling, "It's a joke, you shit! Don't take yourself so goddamn seriously! It's a fuckin' joke!"

Missy's pulling him away to one end of the bar while Red's dragging me in the opposite direction. The tequila's beginning to talk for me, bold, brash, and daring, not at all controlled like a purebred.

Red's yelling in my ear, "Shut up, damn it! He's just looking for a body to blame this pain on! Anyone's! He don' care! He'll kill you in a heartbeat!"

"I doubt it," I mumbled. "It's been attempted by the likes of a helluva lot better than him." I start flailing and swinging in every direction. "It don' take, I'm a no-keeper, you fuckheads! Do I look like Doody to you?"

They don't understand the words. They don't remember the sirens and the remains of an old friend scraped off the highway. They never knew about the kitchen table or the pet or turtle soup. They never absorbed the story or the pain or the threat of remembrance.

They've managed to move Yuma to the end of the bar, and my son is draped over him, unknowingly filling his head with stories. Yuma seems receptive and I know why. It's the smile, the flashy, teethy, thin-lipped, best friends, good buds for life smile. It's the smile of the son, calling on the good graces of his father's protection. Don't hurt this child of mine. Yes, hers too, but also mine.

"One of these days Missy won't be able to intervene, and Yuma'll kill some poor sonofabitch," I said.

"Yeah," Red said, not letting go of my arm.

Just then, Dieks came over to our table, saying, "He's just an over-grown teddy bear," and he flashed another grin.

Not likely, I thought to myself, and another shot of tequila screamed down my throat to add insult to the injury of an already overloaded brain and bloodstream.

. . .

In Cedar Falls, Iowa, at the Pheasant Ridge Golf Course, just beyond the men's tee box at Hole No. 6, and slightly to the right, there lies a large pond that awaits every unsuspecting mis-hit drive. After the men have teed off and we set out on the cart path to the women's tee box some hundred yards ahead, I'm always temporarily recharged and alert. For it's there, under the menacing branches of a large weeping willow, that I scan the reeds where flat rocks, nestled at the edge of the water, are camouflaged.

On mostly sunny days, a lone, medium-size turtle lies warming himself, and I find when he's there, all's right with the world. I call him Yertle, and believe he exists in that spot of the universe to help settle me. He is the reincarnation of Doody, the replacement for a lonely little boy's only pet, and Doody's existence in this world, some thirty years or more after the fact, soothes my heart. It's a simple, unexplained phenomenon. But Yertle lifts my spirits, gives me hope. He is evidence of justice for things I could never change.

. . .

Beautiful, downtown Eldon, 1972. The physical fitness and health craze had finally made its way from the coast to the most remote areas of the Midwest. It was novel, a different slant on living. In response to an ad that said I could take charge of my life and health while making money, I hired on part-time at the Fit and Trim Health Spa, located just across from the Post Office, next door to the A & P.

Since we always had more than our share of observers, instructors could not afford to be self-conscious in any way. Barbie Allen insisted that we leave the drapes open so those who merely appeared to be voyeurs could become exercise enthusiasts, without feeling they didn't know the program or that they wouldn't be welcome as paying members.

Getting more exercise than any three people needed, I headed up aerobics at ten in the morning and two in the afternoon. After each session, I did intermittent weigh-ins and measurements for client progress charts. The 'various other duties' included in the job description translated to washing windows, dusting floors, and keeping the equipment cleaned and oiled. The work wasn't exactly my idea of a challenge, but I decided minimum wage was better than nothing.

By four in the afternoon, when my shift ended, I was so wired with adrenaline that I often tried to get downtown to the Fitz Inn Lounge where I could usually find Dieks holding up his end of the bar. There, with all the rest of the town reprobates, we'd unwind in the privacy and comfort of the thick, blue haze that hung over the bar -- not a particularly healthy environment for someone who was paid to push the benefits of regular exercise from ten 'til four. But it was unlikely that anyone from the spa would darken the doorway.

Fitz made sure his patrons felt welcome, greeting each by name, making it a point of knowing current concerns, lives and histories. In return, they frequented his bar with great regularity. It was always crowded, but Fridays were the best, or worst, with every table full and people packed elbow-to-elbow at the bar. Fortunately, no one seemed to take particular interest in my get-up.

With long black leotards and ballet slippers, a brilliant chartreuse, three-quarter length coverall, with an oversized Peter Pan collar, all flopped over my tights, I had all the earmarks of someone straight out of a Green Giant commercial. With a beer in one hand and a cigarette in the other, I didn't have to worry about giving the health spa a bad name. No one would've ever guessed I was affiliated with anything normal or healthy.

That afternoon, Dieks was obligingly rubbing down the taut muscles in my legs that were perched across the barstools next to me. Most of the regulars hadn't arrived, so we had the four or five spots at the end of the L-shaped bar to ourselves. This allowed his foreign parts to wander at will, the Russian hands and Roman fingers that he laughingly called royal blue blood leftovers. I told him he was lucky if that's all the blue bloods left him. The less fortunate of the royals ended up with lunatics and hemophiliacs when they'd tried to keep their lineage free of commoners. But it involved a little inbreeding, too. He just laughed and carried on.

As the place began to fill, Dieks patted my leg and I moved it down so he could slide onto the stool next to me. He watched them take seats around us, while they glanced at him, silently nodding. In a small town, where no one's a stranger, there are always doors that swing both ways. On one side, they're smug, content with knowing so much about their neighbors. On the other, they're often uncomfortable with intimacies over which they have no influence. While I'm with him, they won't interfere. But when I leave, they'll move in for his attention, and he'll comply as expected.

I couldn't justify paying for a sitter beyond six, so I never planned on any big drunks. For an hour or two I got to relax with a few beers, and knew I'd be on my way home in good time. There wasn't a lot of diversity in my nights. Options were limited to motherly duties, activities with a baby. Supper, dishes, TV, bath, book, and bed, for both of us. Whether Dieks showed up or not had long ceased to be an issue. If he did, he did. If he didn't, I got more sleep.

Just as I turned, slipping off the barstool to go, I saw Jens Hansen making his way through the crowd, pausing with every other person, saying something, and moving on. The closer he got to us, the more I heard. Some just gasped, "Oh my God." or, "No, no."

As I looked at those near the front door where he'd come in, heads were bowed and hands covered faces in his wake.

The muscles in my legs retightened in anticipation. Teeth clenched and shoulders pulled together, I braced for whatever would fill the air next. One more person between us and then it was him. All who stood behind him looked like dominoes, collapsing into each other. Then he was there, moving between the two of us, facing the bartenders, holding his beer with both hands woven together. I moved quietly back onto my seat.

"Dud's dead." He didn't look at either one of us. He just continued to stare into the half empty mug. He straightened and looked to the back of the bar where row after row of bottles stood without response. Then, in what seemed to be an emotionless statement of disbelief, he repeated it for the umpteenth time, as a bearer of bad news, as confirmation.

"Yep. Dud's dead."

"What?" With one word, grasping Hansen by the arm, Dieks was demanding that he take back what he said.

He shook his head. We were the end of the line, and it was all that he could do to maintain his macho posture.

"Missed the curve at the interchange, got hit head on, slid ... " and his voice faded to a whisper, "sixty, maybe eighty feet on his face. Nothin' left to see ... part of an ear ... "

"When? Where's he at now?" Dieks demanded.

"'Bout an hour ago. Prob'ly down at the morgue by now, I s'pose. Wasn't nothin' anybody could do. Nothin' 'cause they said he was dead as a stone when they got to what was left of him. Bloody pulp and the Harley's a box o'bolts, what they could find of it to haul away. Took Carleen to the hospital. That's 'bout all I know."

Knots were forming in my calves. I jumped back down and tried working them out. Dieks saw the problem and immediately dropped to my side, rubbing fast and furious on first my calves, then my thighs.

Hansen just stared at us in disbelief.

"Exercise classes. Cramps, charlie horse, whatever the hell they call 'em. She tenses up and they take over," Dieks offered.

Hansen seemed relieved. It took some of the tension from the room as the tragedy unfolded end to end.

I still couldn't find my voice, couldn't find any words. And then, they rose and blurted out, "He was only twenty years old! That baby's not even goin' to remember his face!"

Dieks pulled me to his chest and patted my back as I finally took in and released breaths.

"It coulda been any one of us," Hansen said, taking another drink.

"But it wasn't. It was Dudikopf." Dieks sighed.

Hansen held up his beer and motioned for Fitz to fill ours as well. I put my hand up and shook my head.

"I gotta get home. My sitter's gonna be gone in a minute."

"It's a five-minute drive, Liz B. You got a half an hour or more. Another won't hurt." Dieks held my glass up again and motioned to Fitz.

I closed my eyes for a moment, hoping it would all go away. When I opened them, another full mug was before me. I hated beer. Always had hated it. It tasted bad goin' down, stayed bad throughout the night, and generally, worsened by morning. But oh, how it soothed tight muscles, toning down the screams of a couple of workouts, and the nonstop beatings life seemed to provide.

Hansen moved over to the guys motioning to him from a corner booth. Alone, we sat a full five minutes without a word. Then Dieks said something, but I couldn't quite hear him. The noise was picking up as bar life continued on, ignoring casualties. But, for us, normal conversation was no longer possible.

I turned to face him, looking at his mouth as he repeated the words. But he wasn't looking at me. He was looking at the top of the bar, drawing an imaginary line across the surface in the shape of a rectangle about a foot and a half long and a couple of inches wide. He retraced the line slowly and deliberately, saying something I still couldn't understand.

Then, he turned directly to me and said with finality, "Turtle soup."

His eyes squinted back tears, and he seemed caught somewhere in time, somewhere dormant that surfaced when he least needed it. My legs tensed up again. I knew the look. I knew the posture. I knew that he wasn't given to seizures, but that was about as close as it came to what he would be experiencing in a matter of moments.

I reached down for my satchel, saying, "I really gotta run."

But he clamped down on my arm. "Ten more minutes," he said, looking up at the bar clock.

I couldn't stop it and he couldn't stop it. When it started, it came like a freight train, and I would absorb without choice whatever it was that was about to unfold before us. Invariably, I would ache and cry about it later, unable to change the memory, incapable of altering the damage it brought with its unwelcome baggage. Dieks, however, would be cleansed somehow and relieved of the weight.

"He was this big." He made a semi-circle with his forefinger and thumb, about an inch and a half in diameter.

"I called him Doody. Like Howdy Doody. Me 'n' Red went down to the creek one Saturday morning. We found 'im there on the bank and took 'im over to Red's house. But his ol' man said he'd throw 'im back when Red wasn't lookin' so I took him home with me.

"We didn't have any pets, just an empty dog house. Maybe Mother had a dog once. But me 'n' Lucy never had anything. So I figured a turtle'd be good. Cheap. Didn't make noise, didn't take no space, didn't need a lotta care, couldn't cause any harm, like eatin' shoes or shreddin' the furniture or pissin' on the floor.

"I found a cigar box, poked some holes in the top, and put some grass and rocks in it with a jar lid full of water. Put some bugs 'n' peanut butter in it for food and spent the afternoon pushing ol' Doody around in the box, gettin' his head to pull back and then waitin' for 'im to poke it out again. Sometimes I'd just flip 'im over on his back and watch 'im squirm, tryin' to get right."

He held his empty glass up again, and again it was refilled. I glanced up at the clock. It was five forty-five. He looked at me, then at it, and kept going.

"By five-thirty, I'd picked up Doody and his box, and we'd moved into the kitchen. I knew the ol' man'd be home soon. I was so proud that I'd found somethin' for a pet that wouldn't be a pain in the ass. And Red couldn't keep it, so it was doubly good. When I took him out of the box and set him on the kitchen table, he'd try to swim first, and then he'd just sorta wait for his feet to settle on the surface or somethin' and then real slow, he'd go awobblin' and aweavin' across the table, 'bout this far." He traced the rectangle on the bar top again.

"Then, he'd turn, makin' this square turn, like this, and go right back to where he started. Stop, rest, and go again. Like he was already trained."

Dieks stopped and turned to look at me. It was strange the way he looked, proud and childlike, begging me to understand the significance of it all. A tear glistened, nestled at the bottom of one eye, and I reached over to touch his hand. But he pulled away from me and retraced the lines once again.

"I heard him pull up. And I was real excited, but I sat right there at the table and waited for him to come in the back door."

He took another drink and squinted, gazing off into the haze.

"When he opened the back door, I looked up and he stopped, and just stood there, staring at the turtle.

"'Me 'n' Red found this neat turtle down by the creek, and he's already got a trick. Wanna see it, Dad? Huh?' But he just grunted and headed to the refrigerator. A shot of whiskey raced down, passed his answer.

"'Where's your sister?' was all he said.

"'I don' know. She left with Jane a long time ago. Didn' see her all day.'

"'I named 'im Doody. That's a pretty good name for a turtle, ain't it? Like Howdy Doody. He won' be no trouble. He can live right here in this box an' eat bugs and flies and stuff, huh, Dad?'

"Another shot of whiskey fired to the back of his throat and an iron skillet slammed down on the stovetop behind me. He walked past me to the back porch and seemed to be looking out to the open field by the tracks. As he stood there, out the corner of my eye I thought I saw the toolbox open and close.

"He walked quietly back through the doorway, and I was careful not to raise my head so I wouldn't rile him. I just kept my face down by Doody, watchin' him slide and dawdle as I scooched him along the red tabletop with my finger. I thought it might help if I changed the subject, and I tried to be real quiet, askin' him, 'What we havin' for supper?'

"An arm in a grey cotton work shirt shot down with the speed and deadeye accuracy of a guillotine. At the end of the arm was a hand with grey-brown spriggles of hair and large, bony fingers wrapped around a black-handled hammer so tightly that the knuckles were white.

"I remember it like yesterday. The hammer whizzed by with partial yellow letters imprinted on the shaft, and it echoed with a crack when he bashed it down, splattering Doody on my face, and the table, and his grey work pants."

Dieks' closed fist slammed down in the middle of the rectangular track he'd drawn on the bar. I looked around, but no one seemed to notice the bashing.

"'Turtle soup, boy.' That's what he said. And then he threw back his head and laughed as I wiped Doody's guts from my face and scooped the pieces of his shell over to the edge of the table. I just kinda shoved all that was left into the cigar box, and I took it out back and buried it."

Dieks paused. Taking another drink, he edged his way back to Fitz' Inn from Richard's kitchen. I shoved my empty glass to the back of the bar.

"Yep," he said, emphasizing the p with a pop, "ol' Dud's a definite Doody. Just turtle soup."

He spun away from the bar as he gulped his last swallow, setting the glass down and standing up in one movement.

"Take your time." He patted my arm. "Have another. I'll take care of the Poopa today. Maybe pick up some of the Colonel. See ya t'home." He winked, grinned, and disappeared.

I turned and another beer set staring back at me. But it didn't matter. My legs were knotted, and my heart pumped wildly as I frantically tried to regain control. I chugged the beer without a second thought, glanced down the bar where most of the faces were grimaced, fighting back tears in disbelief of Dud's demise. The ones that weren't were buried in broad chests or were down, cradled in folded arms while shoulders jerked spasmodically with telltale sobs.

Since no one could bear to look at anyone else, my struggle to stand steady and find balance on shaky pins through blinding tears and stifled sniffles was not all that obvious. Even the screamin' Green Sprout suit failed to draw attention to me as I made my way to the door.

My Vega was sandwiched between somebody's rusted out pickup and a Subaru that eventually got nudged back a bit, allowing me to squeeze out. I had a feeling in the pit of my stomach, and I didn't like the translation -- wherever he was, great pain was draped over him like a heavy shroud.

However old or distant, helplessness invaded his thoughts, and the child he had been resurfaced, jeering at the man he'd become, not strong enough to forget or smart enough to ignore the onslaught of memories.

As his friend and confidante, it was my privilege to share in the most private reiterations of his life. To me, they were agonies whispered shamefully in the dark, only to reappear later in a form that more closely resembled a tasteless tabloid headline that someone else was tattling. By telling me each story as it was triggered in his memory, the frightened child was temporarily released from whatever grip a particular episode had. Terrors were minimized, neutralized, somehow rendered harmless by way of the conveyance.

Or so I thought. As the designated vessel for destructive images that emerged from the memories of his disjointed family, my once happy, nearly normal, non-violent childhood became forever-after tainted. His nightmares galloped in, bearing down on the innocence of my youth, and defied me to separate present from past, abstract from real, parent from child, him from me.

I made my way across town, looking down the road, straining to see the aftermath of the accident. Flashing lights barricaded the area where the sheriff, deputies, and investigators scoured the area for parts, reeling in measuring tapes and writing down numbers, then casting them out again like morbid fishermen. They were directing the curious to the outside lane where most simply pulled over to watch.

Turtle soup, I thought. Dead, destroyed, devastated, fleeting, as brief as a child's promise of friendship born in the morning and ending in violent shock at sunset.

As I rounded the corner, I saw Dieks walking slowly toward the front steps with the baby toddling along beside him, hanging onto one finger. A red and white box of chicken was wedged under one arm, and they seemed perfectly peaceful in their simple journey from the car to the house. Maybe we could hope for a nearly normal night with a quiet picnic on the porch. Maybe the night wouldn't seem as bad as it could have. Maybe we wouldn't complain 'cause we were alive, 'cause the baby was growing ... 'cause we weren't being served turtle soup.

Gomorrah

I was segregated to the end of the row of barstools where Yuma had been sitting before. It was a dream, lost somewhere in time, a shallow pool with clear water and deep under the surface was the key to everything I was and everything I'd ever be. I stared ahead, looking into the night.

Seeing nothing, I said, "I'd like to reclaim my life, I think. Whatever's left, anyway."

I was answering Red. He'd asked what I wanted, what I expected to find, by coming back. He'd asked me the same question several times in different ways. I'd answered them essentially the same each time -- I need to protect my son from some unknown. I need to support whatever he feels, however he reacts, I'd said. He doesn't know these people, or, at best, he may have vague memories of a few.

"But, more than that?" He's returned to the question again. "What do you think you'll get from all this?"

"My life back," I answered wistfully. "Either that or I'll turn into a pillar of salt."

He just stared and me and shook his head again.

Our conversation is fragmented and only sporadically connects. As we look at each other, we think a dozen thoughts, but only one surfaces. Behind it, another blurts out, and yet another before we can control which one is a thought and which one escapes as words. But every now and then, we seem to zone in on a right question and an appropriate answer. It may've been moments before, with a smattering of things in between. But that didn't matter. Red and I were equal in our disparities.

"I always thought I could lock it all out, you know? I could just shove it all back into some deep, dark recess of my mind so I could get on with my life. But it just wouldn't stay put. Even with another life, another man, another child, I still couldn't bury it deep enough to keep it safely silent. Nothing protects my heart from the knowledge of the gap, the huge, looming gap that exists in all my memories. It begins with the summer of sixty-nine and ends with the summer of seventy-four.

"No matter how hard I slam the door, it's always there. If I look at it, it scares the hell out of me, so I've conditioned myself to not look, or to look the other way, or to look, but not see. But I get caught sometimes, like when I stumble onto something that seems innocent enough, like a baby picture taken at his house and two young, naive parents in the background. Or, I'll open a book I haven't looked at for years, and there'll be an ancient love note, or a picture of a car we owned, or vacation plans scribbled on the back of a bill. Stupid things that should trigger nothing, and then, wham! Before I can take another breath, memories fill the open slots. Before I know it, one slides in and a sweet, simple memory looks like something that got run over by a Mack truck and becomes a wrestling match that I have to deal with for weeks."

Red's squirming, clearly uncomfortable. "Boy, do I know that feeling. They told me over at the center to just let it all hang out. Only thing is, sometimes you think you'll just get it over with, so you square off and get ready to duke it out. But, the minute you just 'let it all hang out,' shit rolls over you like a tank and there ain't even time to put up your fists. You're on the floor for the count."

"Some men's wars are some women's marriages."

"You think so?" he asked.

"From what you say? Absolutely. Oh, yeah, sounds same-o same-o. I have night sweats where I think I'm awake and running, always running, dodging, and hiding. As I turn around, I find this nameless hurt towering over me, breathing fire on my head, melting my brain, choking me as I try to swallow.

"It's like when you're in Nam all over again. You run and run, and all of a sudden, you're in your own front yard, surrounded by napalmed children and bullet-riddled old men, screaming women with their clothes burned off, carrying limp babies with missing limbs. There's no escape. We take no prisoners. Just us. For our own protection, we've encased ourselves in bulletproof nightmares.

"They're fragile nightmares to the casual observer. We're looking through a one-way glass, able to see, but unable to touch the heart of the world. Our terrors stand just outside, making obscene gestures, daring us to try to be a part of something we can no longer reach. We've limited the outcome by limiting the number of players and redefining the playing field. Nobody can get in to help and nobody can get out to a demilitarized zone.

"Just when we think we pulled one over on the beast, 'cause we survived, the beast gets up. It was just playin' possum.

"Every time it gets up, we go down. Oh, we say we're gonna win. If it don't kill us, it'll make us stronger, and all that shit. But, the fact of the matter is, it's killin' me. Oh sure, I'm getting so it's kind of diluted. I can face the past, and I can keep on going. Every time somebody bets I'll stay down, I come a little closer to not gettin' up. But, here, this time, I can't ignore the beast. I mean, take a good look around. They're all here, each friend, holding evidence of memories like valentines. Some just glance at me with curiosity, some of them glare with caustic hate. And why? What'd I ever do to them? I loved and married their friend whose name I borrowed and returned unsullied. I accepted and shared his love while weathering his abuse longer than any sane person should have.

"The nightmares were all mine to bear, or to be consumed by. I assumed the yoke for him, otherwise he'd never have moved on at all. I became his surrogate of sorts, carrying and enduring, delivering him from his pain. A fuckin' martyr, huh?

"Dieks put his childhood lessons in power and evil to work. He surrounded himself with people who protected him, buffers from that unknown, unseen something that bore down on him after dark. Whenever he was alone, the fear that gnawed at him every night as a child had a death grip on him as a man."

"Who knew?" Red said.

"Butch. You. Me. Maybe Nicki. A few. He trusted very few people with the guts of his life. Butch died with secrets intact. You came back from Nam with your own crazies. I moved away with the secrets locked in a box with old love letters and cute cards. Nicki got close to knowing everything, to discovering that awful secret he kept so well guarded, that at the heart of the man there cowered a child who'd been so abused, stomped, burned, beaten, betrayed, and so lonely. Convinced that he was forever doomed as an inveterate and miserable misanthrope without redeeming value, he settled for a helluva lot less than he should've.

"So, he solved the only problem left, and threw Nicki away. If she was outcast and refused, she'd never have any need to mention anything to anyone. His secret would be safe again. He traded her in for wanna be's, the women who'd put out, but couldn't figure out the answers 'cause they never knew the questions. The only other people left standing who might've suspected that he lived on the edge of sanity were Aunt Cher, Marvelle, Daniella, and Lucy. They've always been too ashamed to admit having known anything about the hideous events that made up Dieks' life. They'd never tell. He was safe. So safe, in fact, that he'd be allowed to die without question.

"In short, this man died because he had no one left who stood on equal footing with him. No one else knew that the headaches were the same as his mother's had been. No one would admit knowing how he'd borne the penalty kicks to the head as a child, had been mercilessly thrown to the floor, tortured, and terrorized at every turn. There was simply no one who dared or cared enough to tell him he needed immediate help.

"That golden, critical hour was entrusted to his current lover, an insecure, on-again, off-again shot at romance who wanted very badly to believe that she'd be the one of great, true worth to him. In the end, I guess she was. He's dead.

"With that, I've resolved that I did no more than what I was allowed to do, told no more than I was allowed to tell. My reward, of sorts, is that I get to keep my sanity, such as it is. Now, I get to regather my wits, my life, my son's scant memories, and I'll be allowed to carry on and try to make things seem acceptable, so *he* doesn't drag with him the seeds of regret for a lifetime of irreversible pain.

"I have to leave this town with the knowledge that I gave and got in kind. The brief passion-filled years Dieks and I shared were rewarding. We managed to pull from the ruins a really good kid, born of fire and ice. I figure I'm all that's left to make his few memories of the man who helped create him somewhat dignified and honorable.

"I can and will do this because this kid deserves it. If nothing else came from our futile marriage, it will at last get through to these alleged friends and pathetic relatives that our son and I survived. We took with us something that not one of them will ever know, Dieks' confidence and irrefutable love.

"They can plunder and deny anything of value ever existed, but they can never, ever take back the promise of his words, the memories of his ancestors, and his laughter still shining in the eyes of his children and grandchildren."

Fool's Pair O' Dice

We've taken up permanent residency at the Fool's Pair O' Dice, for no other reason, I believe, than the fact that we've all descended to a like level of sotted sentimentality. I've often found a barren but crowded room can sound a lot like the soothing "sssshhhh" that often preceded my mother's comforting pat and, "Don't cry."

Sally's standing next to me in the waiting line for the can. We've both been drinking too long, and I have no inhibitions whatsoever after all the wine, tequilas, and beer chasers. I'm not real sure I had many to start with. My old self keeps taunting me by chanting, "CAT FIGHT! CAT FIGHT!" inside my head, but my life's only been threatened once tonight, and I've only fallen down a few times, so there's really no need to pretend I have any reason to be alert. Since Dieks and Callahan made off with my car keys ages ago, no one's bothered to ask if I'm driving, and I'm beyond the response they might expect.

Sally's valiantly struggled to maintain her composure, such as it is -- a bereaved, hail-Oprah girlfriend, mourning her very dead ex-lover. In her state of mourning, she has become a walking, grieving shroud, draping her dark and brooding bulk like a death mantle over the frame of her current companion.

We must all acknowledge her great loss and feel her great grief, for she was wailing great rivers of tears in her beer. When she turned the faucets off at last and did her flighty girlfriend thing with Missy, she drank a little more, hung a little looser, and became increasingly friendly with the enemy.

Didn't the Trojans do this? The certifiably drunk alter ego, BziL, is pestering denyingly drunk Liz B. Yes, I believe so, Liz counters. Just look at that black hair, those dark, sinister eyes. *Beware Greeks bearing gifts,* BziL warns. But she's not gifted, Liz thinks, confused.

"Oh, don't mind me. Excuse me, 'scuse me, pardon me. She's creeping up through Burnham Wood. *Is this Shakespeare?* The drunk BziL asks. No, but she's trying to infiltrate the enemy camp. It won't be a surprise though, 'cause her cologne's going to bludgeon the sentries. Say, is she disguised as a horse? *That's no disguise*, BziL answers.

Smile. Smile. Smile. "Excuse me ... exCUSE ... "

You think that's possible? BziL quips.

I'm becoming uncomfortable and begin easing back away from where she inches along the wall. I now fear that someone else has died this day, for the one stall door never opens. The space between Sally and me has become terribly close, and I'm feeling both nauseous and claustrophobic.

Her eyes are dead level with mine, less than a foot apart. "I truly loved him, you know. I mean I really loved him," she declares.

"Uh huh." The drunk BziL says, *excuse me?* and Steve Martin says, *Well, excuuuuuoooze mee ...*

"You can ask anybody."

I've turned my back to the door, away from her, but she pivots with me. I say nothing and keep telling myself to say nothing, knowing full well that my drunk self BziL isn't a nice person like I am. *Oh huh*, the drunk snorts.

"We talked about marriage. Nobody knew that, but we did. And we'd just been to see all our best friends that last weekend. He said he'd been feeling something, like it was time."

Prob'ly gas, BziL snickers.

She's in my face throughout this chatty monologue that she so carefully, so distinctly, enunciates. I raise my eyebrows which she reads as a go ahead, and all the while BziL's behind me carrying on brazenly. We talked about marriage. *... let me see ... and he said, it's a great institution, if you like living in an institution.* Ssshhhhh, I said to the drunk, shaking my head.

"He really thought it was time to get married, I think."

I shrugged. It was nothing to me. *Oh bullshit*, BziL countered. Ssshhhhhh, I said to the drunk.

"Why don't you say something?"

"I have nothing to say," I replied politely, remembering my mom telling me that if you can't say something nice, don't say anything. *I have nothing to say*, BziL sneered, repeating the nice nothing anything but nicely. Ssshhh, I said sharply to the drunk.

"It seems you talk to everybody else ... Jimmy, Red. Well, you've been talking to Red for hours."

"We had a lot to remember." *Go ahead,* BziL rudely shoved me forward. *Tell her that good ol' Jimmy wanted to kill you, Elizabeth Anne ... just for old time's sake. What a hoot!*

"I got a lot to remember, too. We could be friends, you know," and she reached for my arm.

I recoiled and shuddered at the gesture, thinking, not in this life. *Ah c'mon, let her take you by the arm, chickenshit. CAT FIGHT!* The drunk BziL smiles knowingly behind my quiet control. I'm doing my best here. Gimme a break, please!

Somebody's trying to get out, but the door's stuck, or they're too drunk to work the latch. Sally knocks, "Rita? That you, Rita?"

"Uh-huh."

"You done?"

"Noooo," she groans from the other side, "I'm sick."

Oh, great. Confined quarters in a one-holer and puke to boot, the drunk says, and I moved back, thinking I could hold it. But Sally grabs my arm again.

"We were going to get married, Libby. Maybe in the fall ... " and she doesn't let go.

I'm moving steadily down the wall, safely away from Rita and the puke behind the locked door, but Sally's moving with me. The worst part is that BziL's leading the way, and I'm not sure I trust BziL's drunk sense of direction at this point.

"I s'pose you think that's bull."

I believe I said that already. Shut up, I said to BziL, and then in my nice voice, "No. No, fall is good. It worked for me." *I'm impressed. There's a heart of a true diplomat in there,* the bad BziL observed.

"Well, *I* wasn't pregnant. He would have chosen to get married this time."

Uh-oh. BziL's got 'er dukes up. *Uh-oh. That was uncalled for,* she said, shaking her sotted head. *Wrong button.* "Excuse me?" I turned and all three of us were eye-to-eye-to-eye.

"Well, I know he got married several times, and a few of them were simply because he had to," she says with great authority.

"Really? I didn't know that. Who made him do that?" The drunk's poking me from the back, egging me on, as my mother would say.

"Why, his first wife, of course, and then you," she said, proud to be so knowledgeable.

I didn't need to hear whatever she'd added. I heard the someone hit the bell. BziL, I bet, and the first round was over, or maybe it was just begun. I turned to see and sure enough, my trainer and coach was a belligerent drunk, motioning me on. Before I could stop her, I found myself interrupting the sentence I'd already tuned out. I pulled my arm back, away from her, and poked my finger into her chest.

"You wanna talk, Sweetie? You need to talk real bad? We'll talk."

Instead of saying the warranted and customary, "Fuck you," and walking away as I was given to do, I took her shirt between my thumb and forefinger and led her like dripping garbage to the first booth against the wall. "Let's talk," I whispered between clenched teeth. *All right,* BziL cheered, *now we're getting somewhere.* "Now."

She sat down and then got up. "I, I gotta drink over here," she said, moving sideways to the bar. "You want one?"

"I don' need any more," I said, waving away the offer. *No! No!* BziL cried. *You need more, really!* I'm shaking my head, fighting with the drunk while Red's motioning to me from the front of the room, DO YOU … NEED … HELP? SHOULD … I … COME? No, I nodded to him and to the very insistent drunk behind me. No, no help, no more, and I turned to Sally.

"So," I continued, "I, that is, the late, great Dieks Shaunessy and I, had to get married. Let's see, that'd be about twenty-three years and ten months ago" BziL's thinking. *Really? Has it been that long? Time flies when you're drunk.*

"Well, Dieks was born less than six months after you got married. That's all I meant."

"That's not what you meant, for starters, but I applaud your efforts for doing your homework. No pun intended. You're pretty good. Actually, it was less than five months after we got married. But that's not all you meant, was it, dearie." *All right! Uppercut, poke 'er in the ole jaw, give 'er a titty-twister, jab 'er eyes!* Would you shut up! I scream silently at the drunk.

I'm trying to be as patronizing as possible, but I think it was wasted on her. She read my words as familiar, or sharing. *Maybe you've lost your touch … Hmmmmmmmm?* Great. Now BziL's become Yoda, my true and wise advisor. Stop it, I said to Yoda BziL.

"And that's not all you meant about Callahan, either, was it? So, why don't we just cut through the chase and get straight to the shit. You think you're entitled to all that remains of Dieks' life and leftovers. You think that he would've been ... what? Less than receptive to my presence, or, maybe, to his sons' presence? He would've praised your ... what? How should we put this? Praised your, um, persistence, ambition, blind faith? Hope without foundation?" *That's a little wordy,* BziL says. *Sounds more like H. R. Haldeman, or Ollie Liz B North. Now that's funny.*

"Because, let's see, because he 'had to get married' as you put it?"

Sally's squirming. See Sally squirm. Squirm, squirm, squirm. The very rude derelict has begun to inch forward. The vindictive bitch can't be far behind. BziL's grinning, though her hands are hiding her eyes, and Sally has no idea what she's close to releasing. She's blindsided, hadn't planned on this. Sometimes, when you're not informed about the enemy, you overreact.

"Look, all I know is that I've known Dicky for well over a year. But we'd been doin' serious dating for several months. We were very--"

"Dicky? You called him Dicky?" I interrupted her first run as rudely and quickly as I could while the drunk was holding her sides, laughing. "You called him the same name his sadistic father went by? What a fucking moron. Perhaps I'm being a little presumptuous here, but I wouldn't plead my case in front of very many people if you're always leading the grand march with a cha-cha. Is that the best you've got to show?" *That wasn't a very nice thing to say,* BziL chides, shaking her finger at me. *That was something a pompous bitch would say.* Oh, shut up!

"Here, let me wrap all this up for ya. You were close, i.e., you got laid often. Um, you talked about marriage, as in he listened and didn't disagree. You didn't get the chance to get married 'cause he up and died. You went to see him every moment you could. You put in a lot of time, tears, and miles that ended up being wasted on a dead man. Now, you think you should be compensated for all the inconvenience." *In a nutshell,* said the staggering derelict who poses as my alter ego.

"It's true that he died, and it's true that you tried. But you weren't married. Your name is not and never has been Shaunessy, unlike some of the misbegotten. Your efforts were noble, but your legal rights are shit. There. Did I miss anything?" *No. No, I don't believe you did,* BziL says, shaking her head knowingly. Thank you. Now go away. *And miss this? Not on your life!* My two selves are bickering.

Sally's staring daggers at me. "I didn't say that."

"Dollface, you didn't need to. Do you even know who I am?" *I do, I do!* Now, cut that shit out.

"Well, of course I do!" *See, I told you so.*

"Then you know that I divorced Dieks over twenty years ago."

"Yes."

"And you also know that he's quite dead?" *I can vouch for that. I saw him earlier, layin' in a casket across town ... Go away!*

"Yes."

"Then what the fuck does all this have to do with me?"

"Well, he talked about you and thought a lot of you and Dieks."

"And you thought that meant he didn't like us anymore?"

"No, no, no. I just thought you needed to know--"

"Oh, I needed to know he remembered us and you thought it would be important to remind me that our son was born too soon?"

"It's not like that."

"What is it like, then? Is it like your first husband who ignores that you and your son even exist? Or, is it more like your second husband who moved out without so much as a word while you were at work?" *Now that was completely uncalled for.*

"I just thought you might want to know that he talked about you, and Dieks Junior, of course."

"Dieks, Junior? Give me a fucking break. Even when he *was* a Shaunessy he *wasn't* a junior. You'd better walk softly and find yourself a big stick. I got a sneakin' suspicion you're goin' to be needing one here real soon." *Yeah! CAT FIGHT! CAT FIGHT!* Are you doing this? 'Cause if you are, there's going to be hell to pay in the morning. Now, cut it out! "And you thought we might want to know that he talked about us? Why would we care about what he said to you when we kept in touch with him and knew what he said to us?"

"I don't know."

"Precisely. You don't know. I'm glad that's clear to you now. I'd have a real problem with someone thinking they needed to interpret Dieks Shaunessy for me. 'Cause you see, I've always known that he thought the sun rose and set over Dieks and Callahan. If you knew Shaunessy at all, you'd know beyond a doubt that his only loyalty in the whole world rested with his boys. I was down the line, but I didn't mind 'cause I had other things on my agenda. My dance card was full with a husband and all."

Her head jerked around.

"Yes, me. He told me. I didn't have to have anyone tell me. To the day he died, he called me his Sweet Liz B, never once accepting the fact that I left and never looked back. No, thanks, I don't need a post mortem translator. Least of all, one of his multitudes of nameless service wenches."

She rose in exaggerated indignation, but I grabbed her sleeve, pulling her back down to wallow with me. BziL's off in the corner, filing her nails, and looking at the songs on the jukebox. She knows I'm not going to do anything now. I might have, but she just couldn't get me to take that next drink. *Oh, huh!* she snorts from the corner.

"Look, sweetie, you wanted to talk. We're talking, and we'll talk until neither one of us ever wants to talk again. Now, where was I? Oh, I remember, I admired my ex-husband for a lot of things. First and foremost, of course, were his tremendous creative talents. I also admired his sensitivity, his ability to not only withstand adversity, but to thrive on it, and I marveled at his survival skills throughout a childhood hell. But I most admired his good sense of judgment where marriage was concerned, his honor, after the fact, of course, and his word." *You're getting downright nasty again,* BziL says to me confidentially. I waved her away with a queenly flip of my wrist.

"Hey, he knew he was slipping. He'd laugh and cover the bases with, 'We're all getting' older…' But, the fact was, he'd begun to settle for a lot less than he ever would've before."

She looked away as if the words couldn't touch her if she didn't see my mouth move. *The enemy camp's an ugly place to be, full of venom, and vipers, and bears, oh my.*

"His promise to me remained unbroken, 'to death.' He said it. He said he wouldn't ever marry anyone with kids. Never. Not so much because he had an aversion to them, but because he never kept his own. And there were many to think about not keeping, believe me." *Me too,* the quiet BziL nodded in her corner. "I was the only person he'd ever been close enough to for long enough to feel obligated. We were soul mates, if you will."

Sally rolls her eyes at the trite bite of the words.

"Look, Doll, you wanted talk. I'm talkin'. We'll just say this'll last both of us a lifetime, so bear with me.

"Dieks Shaunessy and I had what no one before or after could have. I shared with him a strength that pulled him up and out and allowed him to get through life. He had absolutely nothing without it, and understood no facets of a relationship. He understood only hurt and pain and people taking things away from him, of always giving and never getting. He just couldn't get the hang of a partner. He certainly couldn't imagine the notion of something that endured a lifetime. He'd seen lifetimes come and go. In the Shaunessy household, nothing withstood time. So, if you wanted to be a Shaunessy, you've had to be something really outstanding. D'you think you were that outstanding?" *Well, I'm thinking NOT*, said BziL, shaking her drunk head back and forth slowly.

"And now, for his boy. Ah, Deedee the Sweetie, or Poopa, or Shorty, or Shorty the Judge, or, Mad Face, or any of the names he called him. Dieks the son was something else. Callahan looked a lot like Dieks, the father. But Little Dieks, as others called him, Little Dieks looked just like me. He was built just like his dad, but he looked like his mom.

"That was frightening to Shaunessy. As a child, he looked a lot like Cheyenne, like the dark, wild Indians of his mother's side. He looked nothing like J. Richard. So he was disowned by the Dickhead, as he referred to him later. His father called him an orphan rat, a filthy bastard, and a piece of shit, among other things, and said he belonged to the cocksucker down the street. In time, Dieks' own son became a real curiosity to him, and he couldn't decide if he might eat him up, or try to be him, 'cause the baby got so much attention. At the very least, he might've tried to get the mother-love away from him. But he had no role model. He'd never seen love given by a father, so he had no idea how it worked. Am I boring you with all this detail?"

She shook her head no and wiped one eye with her napkin.

"Ultimately, after losing two sons, he knew he'd better turn over the rights to someone who at least had an inkling. Oh sure, he got a kick in the ass from Amanda to get the ball rolling. But in the end, I think he felt it worked out. Unfortunately, any woman with a child would never know marriage to Dieks. That, my dear, includes you.

"Now, to add a little intrigue to the story, let's talk time. We've established an October marriage and a March birth. What we failed to mention was that our first date, over twenty-four years ago, was this very week. Janis Joplin was in concert at the Vet's Auditorium in

Des Moines, and by the last week of July in sixty-nine, three weeks after our first date, while we lay on a blanket in an isolated camping area at Lake Wapello, he slipped a full carat diamond on my finger. I had no idea. He never asked me if I wanted it. He never 'talked of marriage,' as you put it.

"He never proposed. One day he said, 'Let's get dressed and go down to the Missouri line.' I thought he meant we'd go camping down at the dam. But we went to Lancaster, 'cause I was only seventeen and wouldn't need my parents' consent there. We got blood tests, went to the courthouse, grabbed a couple of strangers standing in line for their car licenses to be our witnesses, and it was done.

"He never once said, thought, or questioned anything. It was a done deal. With Dieks, you knew 'cause he knew. So sweetheart, you better save the guts of your discussion for people like you who never knew him. The rest of us just aren't believers."

She's dabbing the bar napkin at her eyes. So's the drunk. *That's really beautiful ... BziL's getting sloppy now. Condescending as hell, but really ... Oh, shut up. Jesus, we better get her outta here while we're still functional, or, at least, mobile.*

"There. I'm done. Now it's your turn, sweet cheeks. Talk t'me. How big was your diamond? What? No diamond? Okay, then, how 'bout ... let's see, your first vacation? Oh? No vacation? Hmmm ... how 'bout his best friend? You never met him? Oh my. How 'bout his horrible year at Westwood? Oops, another mystery? Oh, dear, dear. The things you learn at day camp. Well, I guess I gotta run. It's been real swell talkin' to ya. Give my best to your current umm, what? Significant Other? Big boy?" *Now that was really mean. Talk about kickin' a woman when she's down.* She asked for it. No, sir!

I wanted a CATFIGHT! You know how I love a CATFIGHT! BziL's pouting. BziL, the bitch, BziL, the incorrigible, brazen bitch. Wait, wait! I got it! BziL, the winner and still reigning champion of lousy lovers and lost souls, she declares.

I walked back up to the front of the bar where Red stood, nursin' the same beer he'd had when I left. Andy's laid back and easy, and Red's close to sleep.

He's shaking his ahead again. "Yer lookin' to git dead 'fore the night's over."

"Naw, Reddick, I'm jus' getting' even. Like I said before, I come outta the gates on borrowed time to reclaim what's mine, no more, no less. Come on out here and dance the ancestor's ghost dance with me. We owe it to each other. We owe it to him." *And to me*, BziL says dreamily.

I pulled him up, and we fell into each other's arms, swaying to the sounds of Garth-in-a-box, the din of the night, and the smokey haze of a room lonely lovers knew no better than to call Pair O' Dice.

The Devil's Kin

We had breakfast at McDonald's and sat quietly outside with the babies, half-dazed and amazed that we'd survived visitation, service and interment without collapse. I managed to finish my food without giving much thought to the bit of hangover that persisted from the night before. Somewhat resolutely, I rose and went to the car with Dieks and Debby to help get the babies strapped into their car seats and to say my good-byes.

As they drove off to the north, I decided to have a last look at Hell's Homestead down in Harrow's Branch. I wasn't in a hurry, had no commitments, and was still more tangled in memories than I cared to be. Since they'd failed to correct themselves with a good drunk and hearty commiseration, I decided I'd try to help them along by revisiting the scene of the crime. Driving through the town, and seeing little that would inspire me to return, I struggled to maintain objectivity and focus as I pulled into the yard and sat staring into the emptiness of the once-cluttered lot.

Nothing was left of the house. It had been bulldozed years before. The unpainted doghouse stood as straight and vacant as it had for over fifty years, and the rusted T-posts of clothesline saluted each other like crosses poised for a shoot-out. Everything was grown over with grass: sidewalks that led to the garage and around the side of the house, Tacey's once-cleared garden plot, and the half-dug hole that I still knew to be there, carved out of the frozen ground for a dead puppy. I dropped to my knees and knelt there, eyes closed and teeth clenched.

When I finally looked up, I saw an old man watching me from his front window, across the empty lot to the east. I looked away, but when I glanced back he was still watching me. A few minutes later, he approached from the empty lot to the back. He walked with a pronounced limp, as though one side of his body no longer took instructions from his brain. A black cane, wedged between his foot and right hand, against the bum leg, seemed to keep it moving, but the forward movement itself was a curious sight.

I thought of getting up to go, but chose to stay as he neared and raised a crooked forefinger on his left hand to keep me in place.

"We saw you at the cemetery," he announced loudly, as if I were as deaf as he probably was.

I nodded.

"You knew 'im?"

I nodded again.

"How? How'd you know 'im?" His finger's quivering sideways now as he points just over my head and looks across the street with rheumy blue eyes, searching through his memories.

I didn't bother to get up. A hundred responses came to mind at once, like "Up close and personal," or, "Down and dirty," or, "Naked coming and going." But not one of them seemed to be an appropriate answer for an old man. I settled on the most kind and least-telling.

"He was an old friend."

"Hmmm. I'm thinkin' he was more'n that."

The finger had dropped down to the cane, clutching it as his body seemed propped in that direction.

"He was once my husband," I added. Though I loved him much more than that, more like one loves an innocent child with an incurable disease, I thought.

"Hmmm. I thought so. He was once my nephew. No use sittin' here in the sun. Y'oughta come over to the porch in the shade."

He turned and headed back in the direction of the house, resting periodically. He continued on until he reached the front porch steps, where he struggled to turn and sit, lowering himself onto a step, leaving the cane to rest against the railing. He then motioned for me to come over and sit next to him.

Everybody's got their nose wedged in where it don't belong. My mother was adding her two cents to my thoughts. Always pokin' around in somebody else's business, always takin' it upon themselves to get involved in somebody else's somethin' they got no business messin' with. Mind your own business. Keep your nose to the grindstone. Yeah, right.

Part of me wants to get up, but most of me wants to get out. Some of me would like to just sit real still and be invisible. No, what

I'd really like to be is vacuumed out. I smile and shake my head. No, not really. I'd just like to get all the particulars under control, so when I think about things I know, I can put together some kind of theory that would explain what happened in those years so I'd feel like I did what I could. I'd like assurance now that it wasn't my fault, and eventually, the correcting forces of the universe will right these wrongs. But something told me that was not possible. The wrongs were so terrible, so horribly, unspeakably wrong.

The old man is watching me ever so patiently. He doesn't know this is the last time I will voluntarily address this issue. What's more, he has no idea that I was in the empty backyard because I'm bent on summoning the gods to intervene. I smile. Everyone has something to say. Sooner or later, someone would have to summarize the whole damned thing, and the congealed information might be just what I need. To bring the world to a state of centered right and balance again, I have become the designated gatherer, the historical catchall of backward glances. My insides are numb, and my heart's been battered by the rush of memories in the last few days. The fact that I'm relatively upright and cognizant of my whereabouts is nothing short of shocking to me. I'm only human, I whine to myself, "a reasonable facsimile, anyway," I say out loud.

A distant train sounds its warning as I head across the lot. So, this is Roy, the brother whose hair Richard had pulled out by the roots by winding up an alarm clock and setting off the alarm and holding it to his long tresses 'til it wound his hair right out of his head. Left a big bare hole, he said, and he just laughed. Oh, Christ, the things I remember. But I'm a sucker for a story, even if it only serves to add miseries to memories. And invariably …

"He was the poorest excuse for a human being I ever saw," he said before I even sat down.

Without moving an inch from where he'd collapsed on the second step, he continued. His story proved to be among the best, providing some of the most ancient parts to the puzzle that few had enough pieces of to construct a picture in its entirety.

"He brought that young girl here from up north and never once treated her like anything but a punchin' bag."

He pulled the cane over to him and propped it at an angle on the sidewalk so he could rest on it. His manner was matter-of-fact, but he spoke with clarity, his aged voice laced with disgust.

"She was the prettiest little thing we'd ever seen. When she spoke, it was like a tiny nightingale visiting a flock of screechin' ravens. Aside from her sisters and Old Doc, she never had a friend, never went anywhere 'cept Old Doc's without 'im. He treated her with pure contempt, and never once allowed her to be anything other than somethin' he'd bought and paid for. As far's we could tell, she only had one thing to call her own and that was a skinny ol' hound of a dog.

"She'd gone to visit her sisters one weekend and the next, that one big, teeterin' sister came back by with that dog. Damnedes' dog you ever did see. Looked like it'd been starved, carved out of bone with bare 'nough flesh to cover it. A whippet, they said it was. Come from England, I's told. Lordy, how she loved that dog.

"She'd sit on the porch, waitin' for that mean son'bitch to come home, and that dog'd just sit there without movin' a muscle, with them bug eyes fixed on her face, as if his life depended on a single word from her lips. If'n she was hangin' out clothes, that dog'd trot 'side her. Every time she'd stop, he'd stop. And he'd stay sit, 'til ever' last piece was hangin', an' then he'd be prancin' right proud next to her, headin' into the house, never once thinkin' t'run. It seemed to me that dog was the only bein' that poor woman ever had in the whole wide world.

"Some said it was an Injun dog. Had its name, Black Sky's Thunder, tattooed in one of its ears. It was sorta brownish, with big black eyes, sleek head, boney body, looked fragile. But I s'pect it was built for racin' speed, not comfort. Fast and smart, prob'ly a thoroughbred.

He paused and looked away to the tracks, either rejuvenating or regenerating, I wasn't sure.

"Surely was one nice dog, real nice li'l dog. She called him Blackie. Loved her more'n its own life. I only say that 'cause it's so, don't ya know. Pissed the ol' man off, that dog an' her bein' so close. Mighta been what set 'im off that night. When all hell broke loose and we didn't think it was possible for the ol' man to get much meaner, well, he did. He was always beatin' on 'er an' we kept awaitin' for 'er to leave, but she never did. One of them nights, when he'd beat 'er 'most to death and left her there, she called to that li'l Blackie, and that li'l dog went to her there, layin' on the kitchen floor. He crouched down beside her and licked the blood from her face, and she finally got 'round to gettin' up.

"Now the ol' man's told us this. So, I know, and you'll know, that I ain't storyin' ya. He told anybody'd listen. Two babies in the other room, always hearin' them screams, cryin' theirselves t'sleep each night. He beat 'er aknowin' that. Anyways, where was I ...

"Oh, where she got beat and her li'l dog helped her to get up and the ol' man came and kicked the dog 'cross the room.

"Well, that was that. That li'l woman come straight back at 'im with a rollin' pin, mind ya. Just a damned ol' rollin' pin. He plucked it from 'er hand and commenced to beat her half to death with it. She screamed for that li'l Blackie and he leapt up, but din't do no harm. No good neither. He was a poor excuse for helpin' anything. Anyways, Chey passed out cold, and all we heard was a single gunshot – blew its head clean off.

"Nex' mornin', there't was, hangin' from the apple tree, dead as a doornail. She was never the same after that. Never."

He shook his head. "Never knew an animal as mean as that man, or a human bein' as sorry an excuse and still called a man. He left that dog hangin' there throughout the winter and used it to shoot at, to hurt her so'more, more'n likely. Piece by piece, he shot it t'hell until there was nothin' left but mangled bones and weathered raw hide danglin' at the end of a rope. Sometimes, after he'd drink himself dead drunk, we'd hear her out back singin' old Indian songs. Kneelin' near the apple tree in the dead o'winter, callin' for some Mister t'come and take 'er away to the Hangin' Road with Walkin' Knee.

"They say them Cheyenne forgives all sins and sinners at death, and that's surely what she was lookin' for, I think. Still hear them songs at night sometimes, knowin' that Mister Ghost musta finally took her to The Hangin' Road so's she could meet up with that Walkin' Knee at the Milky Way. Now, like she was beggin' for, we s'pose her spirit's Tasoom and his soul's Tasoom and maybe they're all Tasoomin' t'gether, and maybe the ole man's clean as a newborn.

"Only we can't forget, prob'ly won't e'er forget. Yeh, they mighta got alt'gether, and they might be happy as bugs in a rug, but not me. To this day, it scares the b'Jeezus right outta me, to think that I grew side b'side with a monster, that he's my brother and we prob'ly got the same blood and all our kids give it t'all their kids and their kids on down the line. And we're all runnin' 'round with that vile blood. Makes a grown man shudder to think it. Dell's done gone to his ma now, and he won't have nothin' to worry 'bout no more. The ole man

and all that bad blood's gone, and nobody's goin' t'be ahurtin' hisself
or nobody else no more no how."

Not to speak of, or that anyone'd notice, my clenched thoughts
muttered.

"You got his sons?" he asked.

"A couple," I answered, standing to leave.

"Sorry."

"Don't be. Wokinih watches over him and his, from just beyond
The Milky Way."

The last words sealed shut another chapter as I walked across
the field, reminding myself to take one step and then another. Three
and then four, and each one added to the one before, and at last, I
felt secure that there was enough distance between the man and his
brother, me and mine.

Aces and Eights

We'd managed to get off another round of three or four months before I found myself surrounded one more time with people past their prime, weeping for someone gone too soon. As I stood there amongst them in the funeral home, the thought occurred to me that I should consider doing this sort of thing for a living somehow. I'd gotten so very good at it. Touching people's arms, embracing strangers that were intimately linked to a bygone friend from some other lifetime. Bobbi had been just one of such a long line of many. And the deaths just kept happening.

My son mentioned it one day -- quietly, curiously. "Has it ever occurred to you that most of the people you know, or have known well in the last twenty years, are all dying? Just dropping like flies."

Yes, I'd said. It had occurred to me. And I just couldn't believe that it wouldn't soon be my turn to stand up and come forward, to meet my come-uppance, as my mother might've said. But it wasn't to be. I was pretty much in the middle of the old Sartre play again. For me, there was *No Exit*. Whatever your greatest fear was, that would become your hell. For me, I figured, it must be that I would be left alone to turn out the lights after everyone else was gone. Because they sure as hell were leaving me, month after month, year in and year out, friend after friend, without rhyme or reason. I determined that it must be the season, the autumn of my life, come too soon.

My friend, Sara, had always told me that I lived my life sooner than most. This must've been what she was thinking about when she said it. I found out about everything too soon. When most people retired and took to reading obits on a daily basis, and then planning their weekly activities around them, they were in their sixties or seventies. I'd become an expert at making fast getaways -- helping out at a funeral here and a wake there, for one friend or another, thirty years too soon. I was beginning to grow weary of the pattern.

I looked at her, so peaceful, so serene. Just sleeping, my young brain assured me. But I knew worse.

"She was so young," an old woman whispered.

Her friend nodded. "And so pretty."

I nodded to myself and then walked back and sat down, alone.

. . .

One afternoon, in a long, dry spell where money seemed a little scarcer than usual, Dieks came in and started running bath water.

"Start gettin' ready. We're goin' to Reddick's tonight."

We never went anywhere in Eldon. He all but lived at any one of Baker's garages by day, and one of several bars most nights. People knew who we were, that Dieks had family somewhere down there at Harrow's Branch, but no one ever had the time nor inclination to stop by. Dieks was my only contact with the outside world. For better or worse, in Eldon, I was completely isolated.

We got ready with sponge baths and changed clothes. I applied a full face of makeup, curled my hair, grabbed a sandwich, and reheated a bowl of soup. He never once complained about the food or the time and seemed to have an unstated agenda that kept him preoccupied as I struggled to get myself and the baby ready. We went down the street a few blocks and headed north to Natalie and Russell's -- Red's older brother's house.

Both Natalie and Bobbi cooed and cuddled with Delly while both of the tightfisted Reddick brothers cringed at the thought.

"Don' need no rug rats," they'd say. "Not now," Red'd add. "Not ever," Russell echoed.

"Thought you were gonna play some cards," Red said to Bobbi.

"Dieks never told me he played cards," I said.

"Oh, he don't. You an' Nat an' Bobbi Jo's gonna play. What ya'll gonna play?" he asked Bobbi.

"Poker," Natalie said.

Natalie brought out a change jar and asked how much I needed. I shrugged. I didn't know I needed any, and didn't have any money to change anyway. Dieks handed her a five, and she dumped quarters, dimes, and nickels out on the kitchen table, counting out piles of each.

"I've never played poker," I said.

"Oh, you'll learn, hon', don't worry." Dieks patted me on the back with great confidence. "You guys just tell her what to do."

So they did. As the three of us sat in the kitchen playing poker, Dieks sat with Russell and Red in the living room and watched TV while the baby kicked and squirmed and banged a rattle on his rocking seat.

I'd never socialized in Eldon before, but I was pretty sure this wasn't how it was done. He brought the baby in to me to be fed, but changed his mind, warmed the bottle, and fed Delly himself. Then he picked him up, along with a clean diaper from the bag, and left the room to change him. No questions asked.

By midnight, I'd pretty much figured the game out. I had all of their dollars and all but a few of their quarters. I figured I'd been pretty lucky with the cards.

Dieks came in and stood quietly behind me, whispering, "Hey, you guys, come look at this."

We all got up and went into the living room where he'd motioned, and there, in front of the TV, in his car seat, between the two baby-shy Reddicks, Delly slept soundly while thunderous snores echoed around him from both sides.

Bobbi laughed, and Natalie ran and got the camera, taking a picture. For "evidence," they said.

Dieks glanced in at the table and then at the clock. "Oh boy, I'm bushed," he said rather loudly. "We really gotta run."

He walked over to the table with the baby's diaper bag and started shoving all the money piled up at my place into the bag. I thought we were playing for fun, and the money would be returned to everybody. But Dieks closed the flap on the bag, and just winked and smiled at Natalie and Bobbi. "Nice doin' business with ya ladies. I wouldn't wanna wake up those two real soon after this."

"Maybe we can get together again sometime," I said, but he was pulling me out the side door, carrying Delly in his car seat and the jingling diaper bag, sagging with all the loot from the table.

Then we were gone. He'd bet my ability to learn and play poker against the Reddick wives. We'd started out with a measly five bucks each, but they'd pushed and pushed to win it back until the fifteen became fifty-two by the time we went home.

Natalie and Bobbi didn't talk to me for months. I might not've known the difference except in the grocery store, when Bobbi looked straight at me, then walked past me without sayin' a word -- not even to the baby.

"What's wrong?" I asked, catching up with her in the next aisle.

"We got in a lotta trouble that night 'cause o' you an' that poker money. We thought we'd get our money back by the time we was done."

"I did, too." I said exasperated.

"But you took mine and Nat's. We all been fightin' about it for months."

"Geez, Bobbi, if it's a big problem, I'll get you guys' money back."

"Fergit it," she said firmly. "It's done. What's done's done."

"Then why're you still mad at me?"

"'Cause I got in a lotta trouble," she repeated.

"I didn't do it. Look at me. We didn't do it," I said, pointing to her, the baby and myself. "They did it. We didn't bet on each other. We thought we were playing a damned game. At least, that's what I thought."

"Maybe so," she said, biting her lip. "But I got in a lotta trouble with Red."

. . .

The years that followed my great northern escape were the same years that composed of the wax and wane that made up Bobbi's life. Mine, too, I s'pose. The babies that came after I left, her work in the fiberglass factory, Red's bouts with the syndrome, became the stuff life was made of.

Her ever-smiling face and soft, Southern drawl were woven through my memories as fragments of youthful innocence, goodness and simple pleasantries. And then ... she too was gone.

I'd never even tracked her down that day I saw her in the parking lot at Dieks' funeral. I'd seen the old familiar love for Red flash across her face, and watched her lithe body glide to her car with sea foam scarves of silken furies flapping about her in alarm like recalcitrant children, which she gathered and calmed, held to her as if to be seen and not heard. And then ... she too was gone.

Tragically, unexpectedly, just weeks after Dieks' funeral, she'd been examined, diagnosed, and condemned. Red gathered his scattered strengths and sat in stunned disbelief at her bedside, waiting for the day when she'd rise above it all like she always did. But he sat waiting in vain. They remembered together their years of sharing love and life and, between the horror and the pain, they shared slight smiles at what had been, and they shared measured tears for what would never be again. And then … she too was gone.

With his own hands, and his only son's help, they dug the grave together, and together they made peace within their mutual loss. They buried her in the little cemetery across the road from their home, and when it was all said and done, I could only think to regret the money I'd won after she'd taught me how to play poker, and that I'd never returned any of it to her or Nat, and how it meant so much more to either of them than it ever did to me.

And then …

Cherokee Maiden

The harmless autumn breeze picked up force and shifted into winter gear. Gusts of cold air rushed up from the grove at the edge of the cemetery, but I sat unmoved, content to be still with the dead. It was often my preference. I'd come to believe that I belonged there, with them, rather than cast back -- unfit for either world.

Frail leaves somersaulted about me. Pausing periodically, then raising themselves on alert stem toes, they saluted and continued on with cartwheels across the apparent flatlands. They dipped and dived and plunged along, parading their skills, feigning some small degree of artistic control. I knew it to be a hoax and felt no pity. Most of us have no more than that -- blown along by the prevailing direction of the wind.

Disconnected, praying hands of marble rise reverently majestic, from a sea of pristine nothingness. Neatly trimmed hedges provide sharp demarcation for the resting shepherds, sanguine saints and ascenders. As the breeze took a particularly nasty turn to frigid, I returned to sensibility and to living, to the world of the walking wounded.

Sliding my sleeve back, I glanced down at my watch and stood, brushing the grass clippings from my palms. Leisure lines, imprints leftover from leaning, had obscured my lifeline and heartline; the line of destiny had become entangled with intuition, and at my wrist, only the bracelets of health and wealth remained. Happiness had disappeared with the morning's sitspell.

"Libby Anne here, you guys. I just want y'all t'know, I still think a serious error has been made, and, the offer stands. If any one of you want to change places, let me know. I'm receptive to new ideas, always seeking to unfold the mysteries of the universe and all that shit. Hawking, and me you know. Oh, and don't send the damn screech owl again. That damn owl gives me the creeps. Anyway, I'm outta here. Just thought I'd swing by, stop and drop for a while. And, oh, you know how it is. Big mistake wasn't it? All those 'I won't forget you' promises, and not one of you said you'd remember any one of us, you just take off, and it's s'posed to be cool. I know, I know. You'll live. So you say."

I bent down, picking up the grass clippers, the emptied water jug, Windex, and wadded up leftover greenwrap from the florist. "But it's real lonely and all that, better than what's in second place, huh? So I've been told. What say ye? I thought so. Hasta la vista mi madre, mi padre, mi hermano."

I walked across a sea of flat bronze markers to the car and sat for some time before I finally headed back up the narrow trail to the highway. I thought about driving over past our old house, or our even older house, or on to the street where my childhood home once stood, demolished for the old folks' hightower that looked over the middle-class two stories. Subconsciously, I voted for none of the above.

What, then? *For sentimental reasons,* I hummed. Nope. More like, *"Nothing but the dead and dying back in my little town ... "*

No, no, no.

"Slipslidin' away, slipslidin' away. You know the nearer your destination, the more you're slipslidin' away. I knew a man, he came from my hometown. He wore his passion for his woman like a thorny crown." I sang Simon, or was it Garfunkel, at the top of my lungs.

"He said, 'Delores, I live in fear. You know my love's so overpowerin', I'm afraid that I might disappear.' Slipslidin' away, slipslidin' away. You know the nearer your destination, the more you're slipslidin' away."

I'd turned toward the fairgrounds. Gone, gone, gone gone gone. All gone. No one left. No mother, father, sister, brother, cousin, aunt or uncle. Thoroughly, completely, gone.

Johnny Rivers provided the midday serenade. *"So welcome back, baby, to the poor side of town. I can't blame you for tryin' ... I'm tryin' to make it too. I got one little hang up, baby. I just can't make it without you. So tell me, girl, are you gonna stay now?"*

I shook my head no and continued,

"Will you stand by me, girl, all the way now?"

Again, I shook my head, no, and kept going,

"For me, you were the greatest thing this boy had ever found and girl, it's hard to find nice things on the poor side of town."

And I stopped.

The little white vinyl-sided bungalow had not changed in thirty years?

I hadn't thought about her in all that time. At least, not any more than I'd thought of any of the pitiful people and painful pieces of my/ our pathetic pasts. I'd fluttered through repressed memories the week of Dieks' funeral (Memories 1, 2 & 3, Memories 4, 5 & 6) and tried to remain open to suggestion. I'd kept in touch with Red (Memories 7, 8 & 9), supported my son in his legal warfare, took pictures of the old neighborhood (Memories 10 and 11), even ventured up north and got a dose of good, old-fashioned native mysticism (12).

But I wasn't, what? Fulfilled?

No. Convinced.

No. At peace (13).

I sat on her couch, aware that she was perched in her chair, staring at me expectantly, not knowing what to say. In front of me, there stretched the most handsome coffee table, longer in length than the couch itself. The busily burled wood, with perfectly precise dove tailed joints, and a sea of poured, gleaming glaze, drank the light and flaunted layered depths.

It was one of his early pieces, dating back to when they told him he'd have to demonstrate some mighty outstanding qualities, something to display skills that would refute the counselor's notion otherwise, to show that his hopelessly miserable excuse for a life was remotely salvageable. But there was method to his efforts. When he told his Aunt Cher that he was making something special for her, he was looking for refuge, somewhere to live while he finished high school, somewhere safe, somewhere sane. She took him in.

The leather shop and all it had been was gone. He'd been able to retrieve and save only the smallest of pieces, key chains, belts and billfolds, apron, backpack, tobacco pouches, all etched and carved with designs that he'd never been able to identify. Glyphs that came to him when his hands worked the supple leathers, or grasped the chisels, awls, and burning brushes. But even the most intricate of these were not enough to showcase his talents. He had watercolors and oils, but they were catalogued and stacked in storage, little more than pigmented pages of the turmoil and tumult of angry years, the victim years. Thunderous darkness descended with each creation and all became smoke and mirrors with blacks, greys, blood reds and maroon splattering each canvas, making each unveiling for casual observers a moribund and wearying experience.

The painstakingly-hammered bronze and sterling filigree pieces of jewelry had all been bartered or sold to allow him, at first, safety within the walls and, at last, the luxury of clothing that blended with the masses. Cash brought him a degree of normalcy in a strange town, with strange people, and an equal footing on otherwise shaky ground with those who approached and challenged his difference, defied his acceptability.

I couldn't help but stare, lost in the depths that he'd purposefully left for all of us to contemplate. It was a smooth, flowing, kidney-shaped table that seemed somehow to hover just above the carpet. He'd always said he never planned the design, it just came to him when he touched the wood, a massive slab of walnut, gnarled to beauty through generations of disease. Perhaps he knew creativity was born of the continual twisted fear he'd known as childhood, or of the confinement he'd suffered while at the training school. Like coal that cannot help but become a diamond after an infinite passage of time, with suppression or compression, it just happens. No one knows why. But it's known, nonetheless, that it will.

It was of little consequence now, some thirty years beyond it all. It remained a splendid one-of-a-kind piece, magnificent and perhaps priceless. Wasted that it was here. Worse that it was hers.

It was one of the first things I'd ever seen of his, and that was the first time I'd ever seen the curious engravings that crawled up and down the legs, across the frame and bracing. When I'd asked him what they were, what they stood for, he shrugged and shook his head back and forth, "Just things," he said.

There seemed to be no repetition, no two marks alike, yet they tumbled down in a proper sequence as if they told a story, like the mysteries of hieroglyphics or runes. He'd never seemed to ascribe to beliefs that might mean the etchings were anything but happenstance. Sitting there, gazing vacantly at the letterless symbols, once again I felt that these somethings meant more -- a lineage, perhaps, a progression from some historically significant creation to an unknown, insignificant vanishing point.

It intrigued me still, and of all he'd ever done, with perhaps the exception of Green-Eyed Lady, I envied the owner of the wonderful work that he'd created in his own defense. It was a labor of love that ended with his freedom. It was a trial of worth, judged by those least qualified, having never understood the drive, the motivation, nor the well from which genius drew breath.

"I was just in town to tend to the graves. I drive down and visit them from time to time, but I usually just turn around and drive back up north. I don't really have anyone left to visit now. My friends are either dead and buried or gone to greener pastures."

Feeling restless, and realizing I was trapped, I shifted and squirmed in place. An unsuspecting captive, caught. His ancient aunt continued to stare at me, a hint of menace in her eyes. Cushioned from care by the uncomfortable quiet of the room, I finally cleared my throat and swallowed, breaking through the barrier of silence.

"I didn't know if you'd care for company, or maybe I interrupted something. I'll just ... " I reached down for my purse as I inched toward the edge of the couch to make ready my escape.

"Company's always welcome," she said abruptly. "Put your purse down. Have some coffee. It's in on the counter." She motioned in the direction of the kitchen with a nod of her head.

More recent visions came to mind. Not exactly kind, I thought. If cruel laughter were added, it wouldn't be unlike Jabba the Hut, only I wasn't a guest, hadn't been bountied, sought, captured, or chained. I was anchored only by idle curiosity and decided to accept the casual coffee as a peace offering.

I moved past her through the dining room to a kitchenette of bright florals, blues, reds, yellows. But everything seemed miniaturized, as if Thumbelina might've once lived there instead of this aged bulky, faded Indian maid. Her eyes squinted at me through leftover lines of spent laughter. I couldn't help but think the remains were especially cruel residue for one who'd since forgotten how to smile.

Returning to my designated place, she said, "I get caught sometimes and forget myself when I get to thinking. No one comes over anymore, and I don't realize I'm being rude when I simply don't remember anyone being here besides me."

"Oh, no big deal. I just thought I might've come in the middle of something."

"No," she interrupted quickly, "I'm afraid you're the only something that's been anywhere near here today, or for this week, I imagine. Prob'ly since Dieks' funeral, for that matter."

"Well, like I said, I don't get to town much anymore. When I do, it's usually straight over to the Valley of the Shepherd. We've got several of the family in the Garden of the Ascension. Anyway, my sisters and I take turns tending the graves, changing the flowers, or just visiting when we need to talk to Mom."

"Isn't the Garden the one with the flat stones?"

"Yes, but it's really beautiful. So serene on the back side of the hill. When you drive down to it, it's not like a cemetery at all, it's more like a quiet, private glade, with little wrought iron seats for sitting and thinking, scattered here and there. And, of course, there's a gorgeous grove of evergreens that runs clear across the bottom of the hill with all kinds of wildflowers growing everywhere. It's very peaceful. At least I think so. Soothing and healing sometimes, sometimes just thought provoking. The markers are all flat to allow the groundskeepers easy mowing, I imagine. I doubt that any of the inhabitants care.

"At any rate, sometimes, most times actually, after I've been down in the Valley, I'm not likely to be fit company for anyone, or anything, so I just go home. I'm getting better, though. It's been three years since Mom died, and that was the absolute worst. Didn't think I'd ever crawl out of the darkness on that one."

She's nodding and gazes out the picture window, but I think that time and cataracts have taken their toll, and she no longer sees distant images at all. It's just as well. The view wasn't so hot, anyway. Grey asphalt siding on the house across the street blended with the maze of various junk piles around it, a rusted stove with gaping oven, exhausted junk cars parked and packed with junk parts, branches waiting to be cut into firewood -- not much of anything worth seeing.

She took a deep breath and sighed endlessly. "She was too young to die," she said loudly.

"Sixty-eight," I said. "I guess I just thought she'd live forever 'cause I wanted her to. She'd always been there; she'd always be there. The others were hard, my dad, my brother, but losing Mom was devastating."

It was still hard to talk about it, no matter what kind of clichés people offer. Time doesn't heal heartbreak. I didn't forget the grief. I never found other interests to busy myself into forgetfulness. In fact, every day, I remembered. Every single day of my life, I'd remembered clearly. And when I'd walked away from their graves, the visions walked with me. Everything was the same, the heartache, emptiness, the profound sense of absolute loss. The only new thing

I learned was the brave face, the mask that became an extension of some internal coping mechanism.

"She was forty-two," she said quietly this time, and closed her eyes without moving a muscle, with hands still clasped at her lap.

"Oh," was all I could offer. Self-absorbed shit that I am, so damned lost in my own life that I forget the endless stream of archives, ancient nooks and crannies, concealed and sealed, in other people's vaults, by other people's coping masks.

"I'm forty-two." Again, without thinking.

"It was just a number. Could've been any number. Time didn't take any notice of her. Chey was always fourteen in her heart and happiness. In her carelessness, too." Aunt Cher settled back into the folds of the overstuffed couch.

Stop. Danger. Run. Too late.

"No matter what, our troubles, the struggles, despair, all of it. All that mattered was of no matter to her. She was never affected by any of it. Never resisted, just went along and happened. She just existed. The river flowed and the sun rose and set and the world went 'round and Cheyenne Lucy was at its center."

I'm startled to realize that time had taken notice of this sole surviving child of Lucy Fields Smith. I remember as well that she sat immobile at the funeral, like a great pyramid of weight and worry. I've forgotten that thirty years is eternity at the end of time. Cherokee Lynn, born before the turn of the century, had seen ninety years of struggle and loss in her own family, sisters, mother, others.

"You must miss her," I said, trying to be sympathetic.

"No," she snapped. "I never missed her. We, that is, Sioux Ann an' me, never did. Mother might've, but not us. We hardly knew her well enough to miss her. She was like a ghost. An interfering, interrupting ghost. Always there, but not really there at all. Gone, yet, never gone. We were older and knew enough to put our selfishness on a back burner. But not her. We were tired of work and always hungry, but we were poor and had to work, hungry or not. But not her. Not Missy Cheyenne, Mama's baby girl.

"She was too little. Protected from the start, from our Indian coarseness and poverty, we watched while she grew beautiful and careless and worked ourselves bent and cautious. We spent our lives being careful, making do, and doing without. She spent hers being careless, looking for trouble, and creating heartaches."

Cherokee stopped abruptly and looked back at me. I thought I was supposed to respond, but I couldn't find any words that fit the thoughts going through my head. Like, at the end of all time, there always seem to be ancient injuries that surface in one form or another. We can't be responsible for each other's injuries. Taken to its furthest end, I could not possibly hold her accountable for my litany of woes because she was Dieks' blood relative.

"I see what you're thinking. I know what you'll say when you leave. But I'm an old woman with more than a foot and a half in the grave. And I've offered on more than one occasion in my life to have you walk in my mocs, and not one of you or your kind came forward."

Which kind was she referring to -- the ex-wives and their various relatives, those who unduly judge, criticize? Parents, maybe? Dieks was shaking his head in my subconsciousness. You idiot. You, with your perfect pale face, delicate freckles, sky blue eyes and honey blonde hair. Oh, I grimaced.

"I don't waste my time with chitchat because those who are left to visit me are thin-skinned and sickening. Those who left town were a pain in the keester anyway. I might have a cup of that now if you'd fetch one for me." She motioned toward Thumbelina's kitchen and coffee, again with a nod.

"Sure," I answered and quickly escaped my own friendly misfortune.

"Everybody thinks they know everything, and most of 'em know just about nothin'. Damn busybodies is all they amount to, anyway."

She's still talking in the living room, knowing I'm a stone's throw away and that I have no intention of making a getaway without my purse.

"She was headstrong and dangerous, to herself and to everybody around her. But beautiful. Oh, was she beautiful. Her father was one of the most handsome men ever seen at the Nations. But he had many women, and there were other children. She was just one of them. Not with us, though. Mother made sure we all knew she was a princess.

"Sure, he was fond of her, and he was fond of Mother, but he never loved 'em. They all just used each other. The men, I mean. They just used the lonely women to satisfy their lust. Then they'd say silly things, like, in the old days, she woulda been his main woman, just one of many, anyway. But he left another child with us, and then he left all of us for good, and we just kept getting harder and harder to take care of.

"Nobody kept track of anything. Never a ceremony, or wedding, and nobody knew who was born to who, and nobody cared or noticed when any of us died. Nobody ever loved my mother 'cept Redbird Smith, I don't s'pose. And nobody cried when they finally figured out he'd died. Nobody noticed that the babies and the children were starving, and whole families were wiped out by disease, and there were no blankets, no medicines, no doctors.

"Who'd ever care for us? 'Half animals,' they saw us as. Widows took relief where they could find it. I never begrudged her that.

"When we moved to Iowa, we thought we'd have half a chance, but Cheyenne turned out to be just like her father, always causin' trouble and makin' problems for the rest of us. Runnin' 'round like a reckless whore. Just when we knew we couldn't stand it anymore, she turned up pregnant. Fourteen years old and pregnant. And proud, by God, that one was proud of it. It was the child of Black Sky, Wokinih's Grandson--"

"Who? The warrior Wokinih?"

"Yeah, the great Wokinih, the great warrior. We just kept workin' and worryin', and she just kept on like she didn't even notice the fuss."

Cherokee shifted, sipping what had to be cold coffee, but didn't seem to notice or care. I'd begun to realize that I'd probably been her only visitor in as long as she'd said, and I also understood why. She rested the cup back in its saucer and took another deep breath.

"I know you think I just go on and on with an old woman's regrets like this. Maybe it's jealousy. Maybe it's 'cause we lived long, old lives and never got back the short young lives she took from us. She lived inside every moment of her days. Those moments were all we had for life, and she took 'em along with hers, and after she'd used everybody's up, she went and died."

"I doubt that she meant to. What happened to her ... guy, that Black Sky?"

"Oh, him. He came. Came to take her back with him. And we was relieved, I'm here to tell you. Me an' Sioux was both countin' our lucky stars that day. But she set to cryin' and hollerin' and carryin' on and threw herself, actually up and threw herself at Mother's feet and begged to stay. She knew she'd have to work. She'd have to grow up if she went with Sky. Mother patted her beautiful head and held her close and just told Sky to go away. She drove him away. Not ever and ever, but away in shame, and that was worse, I think. 'Cause everybody knew that baby Chey was carryin' was his, and he wasn't man enough to get her away from her mother. Mother asked him what the hell he had to offer her with his Indian life, with his dogs and tar paper shack and not havin' any job to speak of.

"When we had to leave the reservation, she had one more big worry and that one more big worry became mine and Sioux's and Yellow Robe's, but certainly nothin' for Cheyenne to think about. The baby came, and she still didn't change her ways. Rogues just sniffed the air it seemed, and they all followed her, and trouble followed all of us."

I was shaking my head, thinking of all of the sorrow that had trudged alongside their family from as far back as anyone could remember. Cher took my silence to mean I didn't think what she said was right.

"What? You think I don't know why you're here? You think we didn't try? How he said how you knew? Oh, we knew. Believe you me. Like the others, we heard it all. We spent our lives with it. She was the baby, and we should've helped her. Well, we tried to help. We put our lives on hold for her. We did all the things for her she should've done for herself, and we all ended up paying a price for her, for her beauty and her greed and her selfishness.

"She never even cared for Coochee. She never even bothered to name him! Del Collins was who named him. Took us all in, gave us food and shelter, and gave that baby his father's name, William Collins. That poor little Coochee was almost a year old by then. Chauncey ended up taking him away, raised him on the run, like he was his own son, and it was a damned sight better than the big nothing Chey had ever offered that baby.

"She ran off with the bastard SOB who came with his bootleg cash and the big car and free dope and liquor. He let her be all that she never could be if she'd had to stay sober. All she had to do for him was act like he was really somethin' of a big stud lover in front of all his gangster friends. Here's this beautiful young woman always fawning over him, stuck to him like the cheap Indian trinket that she was. And all we had to do was wait. 'Cause time after time, he'd beat her up and dump her out front, half-dead at our doorstep, and we'd have to haul her carcass in again, and again … and again."

She paused and clutched her chest. "I'm so tired."

"Can I get you something? Or, I could just go. Maybe I should. I can go, really. I probably oughta head back out anyway--"

"No, you wait," she said, pointing at me in the middle of a heavy sigh. "We gotta get this taken care of. Once and for all. Now, where was I?"

"He beat her up and she came home," I answered quickly.

"Yeah. He did that a lot. And she ruined just about every life she'd ever touched. And then, one day, she went away to stay, and we were glad. We were all glad. And it went on for almost ten years, maybe more. I'd gotten married, and Sioux eloped, and Mother just hung on to hope and the songs of her youth and her memories of Father. She never cried, never talked about it, but never said her name again, either.

"Finally, we all got rest, found a little hope. The Collins Brothers of Zenetta got themselves company and cooks, gardeners, and washerwomen. Mother knew the ways of her husband's family. Red Bird Smith was from a long line of Cherokee farmers, and when we all helped out, we were pretty much set, even after she drove Chauncey Yellow Robe away, and that sweet baby child. Even after she'd damned near cost us all everything.

"And while we paid in heartache and hurt, she never seemed to pay at all, but we were free of her and had started to recover. Then, we got the call from Doc Petti. He said Cheyenne could use a bit of family company. We went down there, thinking that she'd finally grown up, come to her senses and all. Me an' Sioux went, thinking it would help us all find our way, make amends, maybe. So we got there, and there she was, waitin' with her suitcase packed and ready to go. Whittled away at, with her beauty saggin' under all the weight of drugs and booze and beatings and loneliness. She used us to escape and then raced back to what she knew best, whoring and using, and deceiving and cheating. She went back to Delmonico Collins, used her old leverage with him and seduced him. Right there in front of all of us. Defied us to interfere, to point to his foolhardy trust, to dispute that she'd left the sinister wrath of a madman at home. So, we didn't say a word. But we watched Mother slip away from any care.

"When I had my child, my only child, Mother said she'd be a good worker, like a slave with good teeth or a mule with a strong back for carrying straw and water, a short trade with no horses, no dowry. And I named her Marvelle, because she was splendid and perfectly marvelous. With all her little fingers and toes and plump, red cheeks. And Mother said she hoped she'd be clever and learn to settle for less.

"When Daniella was born, Sioux Ann nearly died in childbirth. Mother turned away in disgust and said birthing was natural unless, of course, the union or the result was cursed. We both cried and held each other through the night and considered ourselves damned lucky to have managed childbirth in our forties, when we were closer to the end than the beginning.

"When the girls were toddlers and we'd settled for our lives as they were, Black Sky returned. He had plenty of money and drove a big, black Cadillac that looked just like a hearse. He said he'd come to talk to Mother, to show her that he'd finally mastered the white man's ways, and he said with authority this time that he'd come to get his Lovely Cheyenne Lucy. But all we could do was take him to the field at the edge of the corn where Lucy Smith'd spent every waking moment of her ancient years, rockin' the pain and waitin' for Yellow Robe and Coochee to come back. We told him where to find Chey and he did, along with a little yellow-skinned, towhead girl who walked like a porcupine, he told us later.

"He loved her as he'd always loved her. He'd done his dead level best to convince her to leave Shaunessy. But Cheyenne was stubborn and selfish and stupid. She saw only what she had in that house, with her fur coats and her dresses and her liquor and them heavy drugs that Doc Petti kept her supplied with. She'd never leave it. Never.

"Sky never went back, I don't think. He married some sweet young thing from Ottumwa and set her up in a big spread near Albia. He kept on raisin' those half-dead lookin' hounds, scrawny racin' dogs, and fancy wolfhounds, and he messed around and ruined the good name of every white woman he ever met, and then left 'em in the lurch. Just like he'd been left. Heartbroken and wonderin' what hit 'em.

"Oh, he was a real success, that one. Like every life she'd ever touched, I say again. Every single one. She destroyed 'em. Only man she never made worse couldn't a'been worsened."

"Why ya s'pose she stayed?"

"Where in the hell d'ya think she'd go? She'd worn out her welcome everywhere she'd ever been. She was born the belle of the ball and queen of the hop, and thought the whole world was hers to direct. She never worked a day of her life and never once attended school anywhere she ever lived."

"Never?" I interrupted.

"Never," Cherokee confirmed, shaking her ancient grey head. "Not a day. She never did a thing 'cept parade around like a tramp and tease men into giving her anything she could think of."

"Could she read, or write?"

"Don't think so, no. I never saw her, anyway. Mother knew both alphabets, taught me an' Chauncey Yellow Robe. Too tired to teach Sioux Ann, I think. But that one, nobody ever expected a thing from her. Nobody ever asked for anything that required effort on her part."

"She couldn't read? Not even a children's book?"

"Nope. I don't think she ever even wrote a check or a letter or signed her name to anything I'd ever seen."

I'm thinking there must be something that would dispute or refute this. But I can't remember having seen a thing. Always thought that was because Richard had thrown everything away, but he must've been the only one to know what was stated in the bible that the kids found. If all of her relatives were listed, and he lineage traced back to the Cherokees, Cheyenne, and Sioux, Richard knew for sure and Dieks' mother knew next to nothing.

"She didn't have to learn nothin' 'bout nothin'. Shaunessy'd keep her in cash, and she'd just stick it in her purse and use it when she needed it. At first I thought it was from the guns and the mob and the booze and then it was from somewhere else. But I'll tell ya what I know for sure. It wasn't ever legal."

"Wait. Wait, wait. What about a marriage license or tax forms?"

Cherokee shook her head. "Nothin' there and 'sides, she never said she ever got married. We never found anything in her stuff that ever said she did either."

"Oh, m'God."

"I'm tellin' ya, Dick Shaunessy was a racketeer and a mobster his whole life. Never gave a two bits about anybody, and sure as hell wasn't goin' to try to make an Indian girl decent by gettin' married when he didn't have to. Never did an honest thing in his life. Day didn't go by when he wasn't up to something no good.

"You couldn't get within a mile of 'im without knowin' that. He'd half kill her and beat the hell out of them little kids, and then he'd bribe the Sheriff or threaten 'im and nobody ever brought charges. If ya got close when he was drunk, he'd pull out his guns and invite you a step closer.

"You think we didn't know this? You think we weren't figurin' how to make off with them babies like we said we'd do? Hell, they'd be with us just for the weekend and we'd find dead rats in our mailboxes. Once, Sioux found a couple puppies with their heads cut off in her dairy delivery box on the front porch. Milkman dropped her from his route. Said she was crazy, and he wouldn't deliver anymore. Oh, we knew. We knew all 'bout what Shaunessy could do to us."

"The SOB was s'pose to run a sporting goods store, but the whole back room was stocked high to the ceiling with nothin' but guns and ammunition. We knew and everybody else knew. But you don't just step in and stop evil. It covers you like boiling oil, and if you escape alive, you think you're damned lucky to sport the scars. You help each other bind wounds and you keep your mouths shut."

I shuddered, remembering Dieks telling stories that confirmed everything she said, only his always ended with, "Why didn't somebody ever say somethin'? Why didn't anybody help us?"

"We watched those kids from a distance, and we made a pact to each other that we wouldn't stick our necks out and get ruined again by what she'd done or not done, or left behind. What she'd begged us to do when she was gone was a death sentence. If you knew anything about Shaunessy, you knew that. She never did anything for herself or for them when she was able, and we couldn't cross his path when she was dead 'cause we had kids of own to take care of. The kids figured it out and took care of themselves--"

"That's not how they remembered it. All they remembered was that there was a whole town of people watchin' two little kids get the hell beat out of 'em every night, and no one cared. No care was given to them and no care was taken for them."

"Wasn't our fault. She did it. She left us to our own and used us every time she could. We had lives to live, and we worked hard to have our own lives. We didn't have to be destroyed by her or her droppings."

"By her droppings … " I thought. So that was it. After all, after everything was said and done, Cheyenne'd shoved them over the line, and the only way they'd be sucked in to help was to have her extend a hand of humanity. But she had nothing to work with and they had nothing to feel obligated to, and the circle kept spiraling around and around. In the end, everybody was bound too tightly to move.

"There, it's said, and I don't regret one bit of it." The black eyes, heavy with fat and exhaustion, are drooping a bit, though firmly fixed on me, on my face.

"You think we were, what? Cruel? Heartless? Not that I care, nor anybody else now, for that matter. You got the answers? You know it all? What d'you think we were?" she asked.

My heart is so heavy. That was what I was thinking. My heart's parts are shifting and moving quietly about in their chambers. Victims, it whispers quietly. We're all victims, and victims of victims, ad nauseam. That's what we are. It's so sad, so very sad.

"So I thought," she continued, "like we all thought, that these self-righteous critics were passing judgment on people who did no more than what they could do, no more than what any sane person would do under the same circumstances. And God knows what we did, under the circumstances, Mother, Chauncey, Sioux Ann, Billy Cohoe, you--"

"Billy Cohoe?"

"Yes, him too. Comin' 'round after the war -- like we owed him, too. We didn't owe anybody anything. We paid our own way from the beginning, got nothin' from nobody for our effort."

"I don't know Billy Cohoe."

"He's just an old man now, and lucky to be an old man since just about everything else she touched shriveled and died. But Billy Cohoe lived. He's the babychild Cheyenne bore and Chauncey Yellow Robe took away up north. Not that it matters. Nothin' ever did. He was the first son of Black Sky."

"The first?" I raised my head from the back of the couch where I'd been staring at the ceiling, seeing flatlands, gravestones, dates, names, and grass clippings scattered around markers, large ivory praying hands reaching together toward the sky.

For the first time, the tables turned, and she squirmed in her chair. Ever so slightly, the mountain rumbled.

"Yes. He had other children. Billy Cohoe, or Coochee, as we called him, was just one of a long line. Like many of them who roamed the Indian Nations and the reservations back then, he was an irresponsible sort. He might've been a year older than Cheyenne when they ... when she dropped that baby like a shameless hussy."

"Why do you say 'dropped' and 'droppings' like they're a litter of pups, or, worse?"

"With her, they were. Most people, hell, most animals even, at least turn and clean and nudge their young along to breathe. Make sure they take food, stand up, live long enough to survive before they leave. Not her. It was missing in her, never existed, most likely never would in any form. So, they were more like excrement. Shit detail that we'd have to deal with for all of our lives, not hers. And we did. Chauncey with Billy, me an' Delly and Sioux and Lucy Junior--"

"Lucy Junior?"

"That's what we called her back then. Not to her face, mind you."

"When?"

"Started when she ran away. It was the whole thing all over again and worse. Much worse. She was fifteen and that SOB told her to run."

"Richard?"

"No, Joe Bergen. He had ninety-three cents on him when Sioux found 'em. Met 'em somewhere. Kansas City, I think. She was pregnant, sick, puffed up and fat."

"What?"

"Mother an' daughter, front an' back, same cheap gunny sack--"

"Fifteen?"

"And pregnant, a runaway drop out. No job, no skills, and a worthless sonofabitch claimin' ownership, proud to claim her, made 'im a property owner accordin' to rules of the clan down that way. Makes a body shudder to think of it."

"What'd they do?"

"They said she had to have an abortion. Said that her dad had raped her. And that sounded pretty bad."

"Sounds worse than pretty bad. Sounds criminal."

"First of all, it wasn't her dad. Del Collins was her dad. But she didn't know that we knew that. Second of all, she was saying that Richard raped her, and we knew that he couldn't. Only she didn't know that, either."

"Huh?"

"It's an old family secret. He couldn't have done it. Let's just leave it at that, with the rest of the ugly secrets. So, anyways, it was just like old times. We had a liar and a whore and a user, a cheat, a thief, whatever name you want to plaster on 'er."

"Ya think that's fair?"

"No?"

"Well, her life wasn't exactly a picture of good examples up to that point. I mean, she saw a lot and learned to survive and get by with whatever means were necessary, I think. If that meant lying--"

"She didn't get by on her own. What're you talkin' about? She did exactly what her mother did. She just existed and waited for everybody else to clean up the mess behind her.

"Maybe you don't 'member, but abortion was illegal back then. 'Back alley butchers' they called 'em' when they caught up with 'em. Anything illegal costs more. Illegal abortions were just as dangerous to them that had as to them that did. What's more, Lucy didn't have a clue where to begin and what to do, who to call and how to pay. Somebody had to take charge, hoping against hope one more time that her life might get right after a cleanup. So, there we went again, and for what?

"For that no good sonofabitch she ran away with. So he didn't have to get a job, raise a kid, the same sickening shit right down the line. Only we're s'posed to be the stupid aunts, mind you. Believin' all these stories these two's conjured up, to help this poor innocent lamb of our late beloved, beautiful sister. And we were both workin' and raisin' our kids and payin' our bills and livin' decent lives, and we had to do what we knew was wrong, all over again.

"Well, Kansas City's a pretty rough place and an expensive place, but we did it. I made all the necessary arrangements, and Sioux lost a day's pay and took her down and we'd scraped together the money to get her taken care of. Then she took off, left her aunt there, sittin' all night in a hallway, waitin' for the word that it was over, that she was okay and they could go back home. But Lucy Junior'd taken off with Bergen and the hundred dollars, and they left Sioux Ann stranded there, to try and explain to those hoodlums why she didn't have the money and how she'd get it and what they'd hold until she did. So, she got docked another day's pay and had to take a Greyhound Bus back up north, and then back down, and pay those guys who said they had ways of dealing with welshers.

"Three months later, Lucy surfaces, back at the clan's lands, and within a year, drops her first kid. The same year that we'd covered her and cared for her and bought her an abortion and paid twice. So, that was that. We all learned a good lesson, and we didn't forget it too soon."

"And Dieks?"

"More of the same. Sent down the river, violent, irresponsible, no common sense, was just too ... "

I looked down at the walnut table that stretched before me and finished her sentence in my mind. Creative, gifted, talented, too twisted up inside himself to ever be anything but a victim in a long line of many. He figured it all out somehow. How to harness it. Like this, I thought as ran my hand across the sleek sheen of varnish that filled the chamfered edges.

"Dell was a huckster," Cher said, struggling to get the word out while her dentures whistled a hiss in the last syllable.

"Not bad. Could've been worse, I s'pose, given the options that lay before him. Given his 'circumstances,'" I parroted back to her, "he could just as easily have been a murderer."

"And nearly was," she said promptly.

"Self-defense. Justifiably. Indisputably."

"Never had a lick o' sense, that one. Peed on the football once when the girls just went down to play one weekend."

Oh, Christ, not the fucking football again. "Yeah, Delly had a lot of good, solid role models to choose from. He sure turned out well, considering his circumstances."

"He was the best of the lot. I'll say that much, and that's not much, mind ya."

"I know I might be out of line here, and maybe off the beaten path a bit. But I get the distinct impression you're mad at something way different than what's been said. And, I know you're real pissed off at Cheyenne, but something's--"

"For what? Why would I? The damage is done. I'm an old woman, and my life, our lives, were all ruined. The whole family destroyed each other and all that's left is the rot of regret and grief and death stands waiting behind every door."

"You have grandchildren and great-grandchildren who enjoy the promise of a future that's better than yours. That's something. I have children and grandchildren who have come to live beyond the effects of these tragic lives of senseless violence. Our children and their children have family love and support. They have a sense of morals and values that show them the way. They have and can depend on each other. They have a sense of control, and know that no one has to go through life as victim without recourse, that no one will allow it to happen ever again."

Cherokee interrupted. "She took everything. First, our mother's love and attention, then our youth. She cost us our brother's companionship and after that, our respectability and dreams, and finally, our will to change. In return, she gave us guilt and shame. And when she died, we were left to contend with all her burdens in lives that had become too long to enjoy any kind remembrance. Condemned to live on and on. There. Now you have it all. Go away and leave me alone like the rest of 'em."

I jumped up. She didn't have to say it twice.

"Your purse," she reminded me, looking down.

"If there ever comes a time, when you think better of any of us, I'd like to visit again."

"Visit?" she asked, emphasizing the "V" with dentures tightly pressing her lower lip. "Visit? This was no visit. This was a bloodletting."

"At any rate ... "

"Yes," she nodded. "I agree. At any rate, I'll leave the damn table to him in my will. Your son, that is."

"*His* son."

"Yes."

At any rate, and after all, when bitterness hardens and life becomes limbo, love turns to loss and faith curls up into futility, at that rate.

"I want to thank you."

"I'm sure you do. I've confirmed what you thought all along. We killed him. You think it should've been any one of the rest of us. But this is probably just as well. Get it over with. There's no escaping fate.

"I'm an old, fat woman condemned to live alone, and suffer the humility of being hoisted and hauled by strangers from bed to bath, TV to table and back again, with several strong men comin' in to wield hoists and cranks, straps and gears, and we all squeak and creak and groan 'til it's done. Humiliating end. No worse than his, I guess. Don't you think?"

No Exit, Sartre. No answer, Liz B.

Then I was out the door, and her team of hoisters and haulers pulled up in their Happy Hearts and Healthy Hands van. I was relieved that I didn't have to witness the embarrassment of it all. But, I'm sure she'd timed it that way.

On and on, like she'd said, I pulled slowly away and back down the street, out of town, to the north, to home, to my own life, condemned to live on and on.

A Quarter Century

Twenty-five years. If I'd known I was gonna live this long, I would've taken better care of myself. Not funny anymore. By the time I was twenty, I'd known feelings most people go whole lifetimes without experiencing: near suffocation, drowning, loaded guns held to my head. My teeth had been loosened, my eyes had been gouged, my face sliced, bruised, and burned. Lit cigarettes had been crushed in and on my hands and arms. My hair had been pulled out, my feet, back, and head had been stomped, and a week after childbirth, my legs were forced apart and every stitch carefully placed had been kicked cleanly out.

I had toast, jam, eggs, pancakes, and mashed potatoes smeared in my face, shoved up my nose, in my hair, ears and eyes, and I'd been used as a human mop for a floor strewn with hot spaghetti sauce and noodles. My face had been shoved in a tub of butter, a bowl of cereal, and a pan of strawberry Jell-O with bananas. My head had been bashed through sheetrocked walls, and paneled doors. It had broken the passenger side window in a '68 VW, as well as stood on to "teach me a lesson." I'd been abandoned in the dead of night and broad daylight on more in town streets and country back-roads than I could count. I'd been embarrassed to tears in more stores and shops than I could remember, and I'd been knocked off bar stools, slapped, pinched, punched, and jabbed in restaurants, bars, and theatres, at home and away.

Indeed, I would've taken better care of myself if I'd only known. But after a short while, it didn't matter. I didn't remember who I was, nor what I'd ever been, much less what I'd ever planned to be.

The most fundamental and rudimentary rules for living simply disappeared from memory. Every incident I survived was stored away subconsciously, and every mental summary of the event ended with a postscript that read, "At least he didn't kill me."

He ripped to shreds every piece of clothing I'd owned before we were married -- every sweater, blouse, dress, skirt, and pair of slacks. I lived for two years in jeans, T-shirts, and sweatshirts. If the occasion warranted other, I couldn't go.

In those brief years of marriage, my loving husband made somewhere in the area of sixty or seventy thousand dollars, not including benefits and profits from various pieces of artwork or antiques, in addition to proceeds from the restoration of vintage cars and fencing stolen property.

In all that time, we lived together only eleven months. For four of those years, I cared for the son that bore his name, and for that, he gave me exactly two hundred and thirty-five dollars and couldn't understand why he should have to share what he'd "busted his ass for." The baby and I lived on one hundred and fifty-one dollars a month from Aid to Dependent Children. For just over four years, we lived on a total of seventy-four hundred dollars. For those same months, he lived on an average of just under twenty times as much.

In spite of all that, we survived in those conditions up until the day that we drove away in a rented U-Haul truck crammed full of all I could pack, lift, and lug from the shabby house I rented on the poor side of town. We went north without a plan, except defiance.

From the night he'd shoved me out of bed, and told me to put his jeans on, and I did, I knew someday it would all end like this. The famous LEVI scene, where I put on the jeans that were supposed to show me "who wore the pants in the family," fell through. The pants fit perfectly, and after that night, I always wore "his jeans."

The money was never mine to touch, much less spend. The child was always mine to provide for, to love, and protect. The oppression, denial, negligence, and humiliation were always mine. The nightlife and all that it stood for was always his.

And he left me in charge of the stories -- ghostly, ghastly, horrid tales of children beaten and battered, burned and bruised, shot at, neglected, defeated, abused. But I didn't know where they stopped and he started, or where I stopped and they started, or where we picked up when they never ended. And even though I ran and ran from the visions and horrors, from the memories of the stories, the children kept pace, right alongside of me. They screamed and cried and hid and prayed and became little more than extensions of the monsters that threatened their days and destroyed their nights.

Years and years away now, I still hear him say, "My fingers are melting and still, he pushes down. I smell the dead dog outside, but it's really just me with my burning fingers, and she stands back and says quietly, so he won't notice, 'Don't, Daddy. No, Daddy, please don't, Daddy. Oh, Daddy, don't... '

"And he pushes harder, and his knee is in my back as he pins me to the front of the stove and knobs on the burners are choking me and poking my throat shut as he holds my hand on the coil, and burns the skin off my fingers. He's burning my fingers off for a dollar fifty that Lucy took from his nightstand. And she won't say that it was her that did it, and she won't say it wasn't me, so he just keeps burning me and burning me. I don't have any more tears, and I don't have any more words, and I can't breathe. He finally lets go of me, and I pass out from the pain, and fall to the floor. He left me there and went to watch TV."

Twenty-five years. I would've taken better care of myself if I'd only known I was going to live this long. But what will become of the children? They are grown now and look what they've become. Dead. Each one's no better than the last one, and for what? For what did I pay? What good did it do to hold in check the horror of their childhood? So they could share and see and say this is what he did to me while everyone was watching and this is what he did to me and no one ever cared ... I cared.

And they never understood, never comprehended my abject horror at seeing him buried next to them for eternity. Twenty-five years, and somehow, it must end here. I have to think how to make it stop, say every single one of the words, repeat all of the heinous events that no one ever recalled or mentioned knowing, relive the memories for the battered and bruised, for the starving, and the desperate hopelessness that went on and on, for those who bear scars as wide as rivers in the wake of their existence and passing.

Catharsis

Can you see through my eyes?
Only sometimes, when you cry.
Can you see how hard I tried?
I always saw, until I died.

It didn't matter then, I guess.
I was mortal, more or less,
and being hollow,
couldn't know, that
that was not the way to go.

Now I cannot touch the tears
nor even feel to change the years,
and still, I can't let go.

I know.

How can you be so much with me,
Yet more, with him, and then, with them?
It's different now, my dear.
For now, it's all so clear,
except for how you're here
and I'm there,
and I'm gone and still care.

I know.
Let go.

Wokinih's Medicine

"Most people are other people.
Their thoughts are someone else's opinions,
their lives a mimicry, their passions a quotation."
DeProfundis
Oscar Wilde

In the end, I was he and he was me. We'd never planned it that way, but that is most definitely how it ended. Then I ran away.

Somehow, at some time, I determined that the only way to exist was selfishly, wholly, and solely for me. At last, I understood that to be something for my son, I had to be something for myself. I set myself free and pledged certainty to him, to me. After that time, there was never room for tepid or lukewarm response. My life, along with every part and parcel, was hot or cold. There was no political mugwumping, I was vibrantly radical or totally indifferent.

I said what I meant and meant what I said, and the devil could suffer the consequences. I could not exist without total immersion. I couldn't go half the distance when the end of the line was just beyond the next horizon, beckoning to me at every turn. I loved with abandon and hated with venom. When I went down, it was to the depths of hell. When I soared, it was with eagles.

It seemed only fitting that we became each other and ceased to differentiate between our disconnected and damaged souls. Having mingled so often with such white-hot intensity, we melded without warning or option. If I'd been warned, I wouldn't have believed it anyway. But when it became a way of life -- completely and unalterably immersed -- I couldn't remember it having been any other way.

When he died, layers of life, stored safely away for years, were addressed and old scores were settled. One by one, they withered away to dust. At last, I came to reclaim lifelong debts, promises made in moments of passion, pledges made in gasps of uncontrolled ecstasy. All were returned to me with his final sighs. The Shaunessy shadows passed me by in the night, and I realized too late that I no longer wanted back what I'd willingly surrendered years before. The markers had been connecting threads to all other parts of my life. Without them, I had no access to the black hole that had become my soul. I was back to the fundamentals of simplicity, though somehow disparate. My life. My family. My memories to rediscover. My heart to reopen. New connections had to be woven.

At first, I was relieved it was over. It was good that at least one unfinished thing had ended. But the spaces that opened where his memories had been brought a loneliness I'd never known. With my brother's death, I lost unparalleled truth; with my mother's, I lost unconditional love. With Dieks' death, I lost the passion and beauty of youth in one pass. The pieces of life that remained were fragments of dreams and common lots of middle age maladies that consisted of anger and boredom, leaving a wounded heart fluttering along with little more than evolution to keep it going. Back at the black hole, unfamiliar and long-forgotten mismatched pieces were glued together, then grafted over the battle scars that constituted love, life, and property rights.

Untethered, I went back up north, feeling worse than I'd felt in many years -- detached, foreign, abandoned, and empty. I tried to summarize the reasons, but all I could think of were words that should've been said and stories that should've been shared. But I couldn't, and others didn't. I simply couldn't part with what was never meant for the masses. I couldn't find relief, and had long refused tears for a life that was beyond reach.

Each day I went through the motions, I saw my husband watching me, looking for signs of life beyond the graves. He offered what he could, and waited for my return. I stared out the window with every sun's rise and set, and never stopped wondering why. After months of searching, I became consumed with the only constant -- in life, we're never allowed to know why. As with my brother and my parents, the reasons went to the grave with Dieks.

There's someone at the front door. I glance up at the clock. It's two-thirty in the afternoon. Too late for the mail. Too early for the paper. I peer around the curtain. An elderly gentleman is standing on the steps, looking straight ahead. He appears to be in his sixties, maybe seventies. Just above the windows, I see jet black hair with silver streaks, pulled tightly back in a long, singular braid. I think this is very strange, given his apparent age. He's not Jehovah's Witness. He's no one I've ever seen or known.

I open the inside wooden door before the metal storm, mentally preparing an impromptu speech designed to send most any unwanted visitor away unharmed. With one hand on the doorframe and one on the handle, I find myself clutching both when I look up and choke on unspoken words.

The deep, black eyes are eyes I've known forever. The high, rounded cheeks are reminiscent of Cheyenne or Sioux. The aquiline nose hails the proud lineage of ancient braves.

"I've come," he said with finality.

I swallow and try to remember how to speak. But neither word nor fundamental movement seem able to accommodate the need.

"You've waited," he added, as an introduction, a definition. Who he was. Who I was.

I look past him to the Volvo parked behind my truck. All I can think in that moment is how I'm going to explain this to my husband, how all things are circular, all worlds eventually overlap and merge, how I know in my bones who he is. I simply don't know where he came from, or how he came to me, or why, or who showed him the way. It occurs to me that he knew with certainty all of these things, as well as what I was thinking.

Osmosis, I thought, without flinching, challenging.

"Wokinih," he answered, off-handedly, as a matter-of-fact.

I nodded. Of course.

A rush of relief releases my hand from the door handle and the other from the frame.

"Do you wish that I leave?"

I shook my head, no.

"Do you need a few moments to consort with your heart?"

Words came to my rescue from somewhere, "No. Come in. Please."

I opened the outer door and leaned back to allow him passage through the front porch.

"Thank you."

He walked past me, through the porch to the living room and into the kitchen. Glancing up at the cabinets, he opened the door of the one closest to the sink and took a mug out, moving over and pouring himself a cup of coffee at the counter.

"Would you like one?" he asked, as if he were host and I the uninvited messenger.

"I'll get it."

I backed up and retrieved my empty mug from a living room table, filled it at the coffee maker, and walked back across the kitchen to where the man sat perched on a barstool at the island table of oak and white ceramic tile. He was running his hand along the beveled edge and looking underneath at the construction.

"He does nice work."

"Yes."

"You must be proud."

"I am."

"You are very patient."

"It hasn't always been that way."

"It rarely is."

"Will you be comfortable there?" I asked, motioning to the seat.

"We'll see," he answered, taking a brief drink.

He cleared his throat and loosened his tie, as if he were getting prepared for a delivery, or the beginning of a deposition.

"Where do you want to start?"

"In the beginning."

He smiled. "In the beginning, we were happy. We had nothing, but we had each other. That isn't saying we didn't know sorrow. It was all around us, a widowed Indian woman with too many mouths to feed. It was poverty and denial, never knowing who we were or where we fit, or if we fit at all.

"Lucy Smith was extraordinary. But I suspect you knew that. She met each challenge head on and never once flinched at the demands life made on her. Some saw her differently, careless, promiscuous, and stubborn. She was. All that and more. In the twenties, when she moved us to farm with the Collins brothers, up around here somewhere, she was nearly fifty years old. Yet, she worked side by side with her grown children and the men in the fields. At the end of the day, she worked in the house and never once complained. She was always terribly grateful that someone extended a hand to her and our family.

"She showed them farming techniques in the way of the Cherokee, as she'd learned from Red Bird and the Tennessee clan.

She taught my aunts how to care for a family, how to love each other, how important it was.

"Shortly after they'd settled in with the farmers, I was born to Cheyenne, Lucy's youngest. All I remember of living there was being happy and being with people who loved me. The last thing I remember about being with the family was being up on Yellow Robe's shoulders and waving happily to my grandmother as we walked though rows and rows of corn. But that's ahead of myself. We were happy, and then Prohibition caught up with us.

"After several years of Prohibition, it seemed that nothin' but trouble came to the countryside. If it wasn't Sak and Fox firewater, it was the Irish whiskey, and if not them, it was German tempers or Danish farmers. Someone was always upsettin' the applecart, someone owing someone else for something long gone. Lucy's brood managed to stay clear of the gin mills, never indulged, and were never beholden in any way to the 'leggers.

"However, that didn't stop Delmonico Collins. He was the farmer that took 'em in after they were pushed off the reservation. His brother, Lucas, was a real sober and serious sort. Del was not. He took to the whiskey that the Chicago runners brought around and got to owing quite a sum. When the boys stopped by to collect, they roughed young Del up a bit and said the next time it wouldn't be so clean. We tried to stay out of it without looking ungrateful.

"Lucas kept the books, and he said they didn't have any money to give the men so they'd better figure out what to do the next time they came. That didn't go so well. The next time they came and the brothers still didn't have the money, this 'legger named Shaunessy turned some thugs loose, and they left Del in pretty rough shape. Nearly broke the hearts of Lucy and Sioux, Cherokee, and my mother. But most of all, it brought out the absolute worst in Uncle Yellow Robe.

"He'd spent a long time being quiet and hardworking. Like Lucy and the others, he had no property, no rights, nothing really, except a good heart and a strong back. He felt he owed everything they had to the Collins brothers. There were lots of people in pretty bad shape in those days, and Indians were at the very bottom of the heap. It didn't seem right to Yellow Robe that a man could get hooked on something illegal anyway, and then end up in so much debt that he couldn't possibly meet their demands. To boot, Del was beaten so viciously that he could hardly move for a week after they left.

"To make a long story short, after a few times, Lucas and Del decided they'd have to do something. They didn't have any money to give this guy Shaunessy. But liquor was illegal, so they figured they had the law on their side. They thought they could just run a bluff and threaten these guys with bringing the law in on the deal.

"That was probably the worst thing they could've done 'cause Shaunessy provided the whole area with liquor, and that included the local sheriff and deputies who were involved with the 'leggers, so they looked the other way. Just when the Collinses thought they were free, Shaunessy came back with some strong arms out of Chicago, and they set to beating both brothers to bloody pulp.

This was more than Yellow Robe could stand, and he got involved in the fray. My uncle was a big man, and normally, a quiet man, but he was also proud and intense, like Lucy. Once he got in the middle of the violence, there was no stopping him. When it was over, there was a lot of blood and knife wounds, but everyone was alive, and they all understood each other completely. My Grandmother Lucy patched 'em up and sent 'em on their way.

"The next day, this Shaunessy comes back with the Grundy County Sheriff, and he says they're looking for a dangerous renegade that attacked this white man for no reason. Yellow Robe hid in the fruit cellar 'til the authorities left. But they'd told Delmonico Collins that they'd be back for the Indian, and he'd better be there when they returned.

"The next week came and went, and nobody showed up looking for Uncle Yellow Robe. But Cheyenne come up missing. Lucy was half-mad with suspicions and finally saw little Chey dragging herself up the road. She'd been beaten pretty badly, and her clothes were half gone. She could barely walk and wouldn't talk to anyone for days. When she finally did, she said she'd have to go away, but none would be comin' for Yellow Robe anymore.

"A couple days later, that bootlegger pulls up to the gate in his fancy car, and he just sits there. Doesn't get out. Just sits there and smokes cigarettes. After a while, Cheyenne comes out, all cleaned up, and she leaves with him.

"Like clockwork, in a few days, the same car comes flyin' up the front road, throwin' gravel and dust all over the place, and skids to a halt. The door flops open, and Cheyenne gets shoved out on the ground. This time, she's in even worse shape than before.

"They should've known it'd be too much for Yellow Robe. Maybe that's what they planned. He come on a dead run from the barn, and even before they got Chey to the house, he's jumped on the runnin' board, draggin' Shaunessy out of the car, leaving it to sputter off to a standstill into the fence. He commences to pound him mercilessly until the brothers finally get him pulled off. They take this Shaunessy to the house, and they have to doctor him right along with Cheyenne 'til he's strong enough to leave. They first thought they should let him die there, like the no-count cur he was, but they cared for him instead. By the time he left, he promised them he'd be back, and one way or the other, he'd see to it that Yellow Robe would go down.

"Cheyenne runs to the car as he's leaving and begs him to make a deal, but all Dick Shaunessy wants is revenge. He pushes her aside like a rag doll and takes off. By mid-afternoon, the sheriff's back to collect Yellow Robe again. And again, he hid, this time out in the fields until the sheriff left.

"Again Cheyenne disappeared, and again she came back, half-dead. Only this time, it's Del that vows revenge. The old cash debt had been forgiven, and the Collinses were free and clear of any trouble with Shaunessy. But there's a new problem, Cheyenne's with child again, and Del thought he was responsible for the pregnancy. He was determined to defend her.

"When Shaunessy came to the gate, it was Del Collins that met the car and exchanged the words. Then Del and Shaunessy set to fighting. Every time he showed up, disaster followed. It was like he came looking for trouble, like he needed to be in a brawl, needed a reason to hate the world and everyone in it. Lucas managed to pull them apart, and Cheyenne came out, got in the car without a word, and left. That time, they didn't hear from her for months.

"Then, late one night, she came back. As she pulled open the screen door, she collapsed, and Del rushed over and picked her up, carried her to his bed. She was pale, like she'd lost a lot of blood, and she was too weak to talk. Didn't seem to care if she lived or died. For a month, they took turns nursing her, sitting the night, feeding her, watching, wondering if she'd ever get her strength back. Half delirious, Cheyenne told them of being beaten and going into labor too soon. Said she'd been taken to an empty house in Cicero, just outside Chicago somewhere, and there, she had a baby girl who came too soon. She was very small, like a little bird, she said, but she seemed to be okay, 'til Shaunessy took her to the kitchen and held her under a sink full of water.

"She told the broken story in segments, like it had happened to someone else. She repeated the words like it was a dream and somebody else's baby was drowned, not hers. She went over and over how the baby was wrapped in newspaper, and the newspaper was put in a grocery sack, and somebody carried the sack out the door. How she started hemorrhaging and they wrapped a big black coat around her, and stuffed her in the trunk of a car. It drove and drove, and then she was back at the farm outside Zenetta, layin' in the dust and then crawlin' up to the porch steps and restin' before she finally got to the door.

"Lucy had to leave the house. From the fields, they heard her wail into the night sky, and from the front porch, they heard her weep 'til morning. Wracking sobs, the sounds a grandmother makes while her heart breaks, and she wishes to turn back the clock, or die in exchange.

"Yellow Robe went to Chicago after Shaunessy. Tried to kill him, and damned near did. Left 'im for dead. But all he'd managed to do was break a couple ribs, a collarbone, and a jaw. Blinded him in one eye and left him deaf in one ear. But Shaunessy survived, and a warrant was issued for Yellow Robe's arrest for attempted murder. That time, when the sheriff came to the farm, he and his men sat and waited. Staked out the whole place and stayed for weeks. But Lucy'd had enough. After she cleaned him up and took a slug out of his back, she sent Yellow Robe away. She said to go north, to take me with him to Minnesota, and find a man called Chebona Bula, son of Red Horse. 'Tell him Mother Lucy sent you. He'll know what to do.'

"We found him working the quarry at Pipestone, and though he'd become a pretty good craftsman, there wasn't much need of pipes by then. He put us up for a few weeks, got Yellow Robe lined up with a man near Red Wing who did painting and sculptures and the like. So then Chauncey Yellow Robe went to school to become an artist like him. But, in Red Wing, he was just an assistant.

"He worked with that man for thirty years, became almost as well known in oils, and some twenty, twenty-five years ago, he left this world. All that he owned, including his collection of most-favored names, he left to me, William Collins Cohoe, who he'd raised and cared for like a father, instead of an uncle."

"And your mother? The stone that marks her grave, it's pipestone, isn't it."

"Straight from the quarry where we'd met with her half brother, Chebona Bula. He was one of the best that ever was. He never knew her, never met her. But it just tore him up when she died. Uncle Yellow Robe never did get over it, either. Always felt responsible for the whole thing, you know. He thought she never would've been involved with that mean sonofabitch if he hadn't lost his temper. For the rest of his life, he regretted that mistake.

"Said bad judgment destroyed our lives. But I never thought so. I always thought it was a matter of white man tryin' to kill white man, and when no one took responsibility, they put it on him. If he'd kept in his place, and stayed completely out of the whole thing, it probably would've taken care of itself.

"Did you ever see her again?"

"Mother? Once, just after the war. I came back to the states feeling mighty big, a man who could survive a round with the Bismarck could sure as hell muster up the courage to introduce himself to his mother."

"And?"

"And, I found a frail and sickly shell of a woman that I couldn't bring myself to approach. I stayed in town for days, had a room at the old hotel next to the tracks. Every day I'd watch and wait for hours, hoping to get a glimpse of her on the street, and when I did, I couldn't bear for her to see me. I'd dreamed of touching the soft, bronze face I remembered smiling down at me. I longed to press her hands between mine and simply thank her for the gift of life. But I saw her, and couldn't.

"I was shocked to silence and shame. From all accounts I'd ever heard, she'd been one of the most beautiful young women in all of southern Iowa, and here was this faded and brittle-looking, birdlike creature that seemed dazed or drugged.

"I was no more than ten, twenty feet away from her when she came out of that store. But I said nothing, reasoning that I'd give her a heart attack if I approached her. Years later, I realized my heart's truth. I feared my own mother would not remember me."

"Were you Cojo?"

"No, I was Coochee. Cowacoochee, the Wildcat. By the time I was two, Grandma Lucy said I should go with Sequoya Chauncey up north. He would need such a fierce wildcat to protect him there. I was proud to be that big of a boy. But to them, she said I'd be safer with Yellow Robe on the run than I'd ever be anywhere near the bad blood of that Shaunessy. She was probably right. Given half a chance, he would've destroyed me, too.

"And Cojo, like Cohoe, my name, it's what her people called those who limped. Lucille's probably the one she called Cojo. Her Daddy had that limp she was born with, you know."

I spun around to search his face. "What?"

"You never knew this?"

"What?"

"Lucille Colleen Shaunessy was, no, is Del Collins' daughter, the man for whom she was named. The limp was a little less pronounced in him 'cause he was a big strappin' man. But it was of his family, had to do with calcium absorption or some such thing, and the difference showed in the uneven growth rate of bones, generally affecting length of arms and legs. Just kept passing it on from generation to generation."

"No shit? Oh, God, I'm sorry. But, it was Dieks that always got beat for being the bastard son. Said he belonged to the man down the street. Shaunessy just destroyed his life, victimized the kid from the time Cheyenne died 'til, forever, I guess."

"He was my brother. He did not belong 'to the man down the street.' We had a common father, Black Sky of the Sioux. Sky and Cheyenne Lucy were childhood playmates at the Reservation. They were nearly the same age, grew together, and loved each other from the beginning of time. Nobody could keep 'em apart.

"Grandma Lucy simply said she wouldn't, no, couldn't, allow Cheyenne to marry a Sioux. She was, after all, the child of a noble and brave family, adored and envied by all who knew. The promise of privilege and status would occur only through marriage to a white man, only that would be good enough for Cheyenne Lucy Collins.

Although they knew, everyone did, and no one ever mentioned the greater concern, the taboo of the Sioux and the Cheyenne, and of the white man, too, for that matter.

Cohoe turned slowly off the barstool and went back to the coffee maker. He filled his cup and without looking back at me, he continued, standing perfectly still, gazing out the kitchen window. My kitchen window.

"Black Sky was also the child of a brave and noble family. His mother was Agigau, the most beautiful and beloved of all women.

Lucy Smith might've been jealous, when Agi stole the attention of her lover, John Sauts. She may have refused to accept the birth of Black Sky, Son of Sauts and Agigau. But I don't think so. I think she knew who he was and knew with certainty that Cheyenne and Black Sky must never be man and wife, they were half brother and sister. Although that never stopped them from being drawn to each other, it never prevented my birth, or my brother's.

He turned back around to face me, leaning up against the counter, pausing to sip his coffee.

"My God, what could anyone do?"

"Cheyenne did what she was expected to do. She went away with Shaunessy and fulfilled her destiny by marrying the privilege that comes with the white man, at least in appearance. Twenty-two years later, Sky went and found her. By then he was a very successful man and probably could've made as honest woman of her, a pillar of the community. No one knew her background. But she wouldn't go. She couldn't help but love him, but she was steadfast in her decision. She would stay with the white man. It was right for her children.

"Sky swore he'd kill Shaunessy for her, but she just sent him away. The ol' man was impotent, anyway. Probably always was, or who knows, maybe Chauncey Yellow Robe did more damage than he thought. No one ever cared. It probably made her decision that much easier, I'd think. Cheyenne never let on that there was a problem. In fact, she was probably relieved. Shaunessy knew that Dieks wasn't his, just as he knew Lucy wasn't his. The incident at Cicero was because the girl was Del's, but it was Chauncey that ended up paying the price. Mother once told Yellow Robe that the heart has to have what the heart has to have. I don't know what that means, but I know she managed to get back to two different men long after she'd moved away with Shaunessy. Neither one was her husband, yet she bore children to both. Only she learned a lesson when one of Del's was drowned, and she made sure that both of Black Sky's survived.

"She had her kids, and they all had the name and privilege of the white man's ways. I think she knew that Father was never an option. She also knew he could never live the white lie, the life her kids would have to have and keep. But he'd always be in her heart and in our hearts. When the crime of loving Sky became apparent, her decision to go with Shaunessy was sealed, more even than her need to buy Yellow Robe's freedom. She became her own judge, jury, and executioner when she sentenced herself to death by choosing life with Shaunessy. The only thing was, she sentenced Dieks as well when she died, leaving his welfare to Lucille."

"What else? What happened to Lucy Smith?"

"Died during the war. Broken heart, they say. That'd be hard to believe, but she'd been through an awful lot. She was the only one who stayed on the farm with Lucas and his wife, Mathilde. They adopted a couple of boys, but she never once saw Cheyenne Lucy's kids. They buried her out back, next to the old path Yellow Robe took when he hoisted me up on his shoulders and headed north. Said she spent most of her rockin' chair days out there under the shade of that ancient elm, just staring off into the fields to the north, and waiting.

"Del Collins married late in life, moved to Zenetta with his wife, Lucinda. He left farming not long after that and worked in town at the post office there for five or ten years before finally retiring. Early in forty-four, February or March, maybe, Lucille Colleen was born to Cheyenne in Eldon and in the next month, Delinda Lucy was born in Zenetta. Both were big-boned girls with sky-blue eyes and tilt legs. You'd think they were The Weebles Sisters if you ever saw 'em together." He chuckled to himself and looked back to me. But neither one ever saw the other one.

"You mean to say that Lucy's really not Dieks' sister?"

"Not full-blood, if that's what you're askin'. Half. Some had the same mother, some the same father. Lucille and Delinda were both Del's, Dieks and me, of course, were the taboo products of parents who were half brother and sister. Gets rather complicated, but nobody cares when everybody's dead, or nearly so."

"And how'd you know where to find me, what to say once you got here?"

"I didn't, exactly. That was Sarah's doing. My wife is a great observer of the human race. In our many years, she's been the soothing salve for most of my emotional wounds. She's my lover, my best friend, my mother, father, brother, all I've lost along the way.

"Though you say you were married only briefly to my brother, Sarah said your eyes shared an enduring length of life with him. At the funeral, she said it was your eyes that were too painful to peer into, and though you weren't aware of it, many people turned away and wept when they saw the grief in your eyes. She said she looked closely and was silenced by the cry for grace and mercy from within you. You did not cry, she said, as a man does not weep for his own passing. He stands in wonder at the mystery of it all, but does not succumb to the challenge of the finale."

"That's very, humbling. But I must admit that I don't remember you or her. I can usually spot significant others, and I knew your face immediately when I opened the door today. I can't imagine having missed you at the visitation or the funeral."

"My brother must've have found your honesty empowering." He paused. "We saw you briefly the night of the visitation, though we didn't stay long. We saw you at a distance in the funeral home and stood directly behind you at the cemetery. Sometimes, we choose to be a less than memorable presence."

"But I usually ... " my voice led me away and dropped the thought.

"Do you know the story behind the ghost dance?"

"Basics, I s'pose. Why do you ask?"

"For those who believe, sometimes unexplained physical invisibility is little more than a mental unreality. Tell me what you know of Wovoka's religion."

"I don't know a lot. It seems that it was a promise of a return to, something, the old ways, Indian ways. Those who truly believed and fervently practiced Wovoka's Ghost Dance religion would be saved from the inevitable decimation of their race. White men would leave, the buffalo would return, the dead would rise, the living would never die, lands would be cleansed, and all would be as it was. Those who wore the Ghost Dance chamois would be invisible to bullets of white men, immortal. I guess that's all I know."

"And, when you address Wokinih, do you know to whom you appeal?"

"No. It was a name Dieks used when he was being reverent. At least as reverent as he was capable of being."

"Wokinih, the man, would've been his great-grandfather. Twice over, we now know. However, it's doubtful that he could've known that. He probably just repeated words he'd heard Mother say, because Wokinih came to mean all ancestors who'd traveled The Hanging Road and had gone on to the Great Beyond to become Tasoom. Grandfather Wokinih was a legend in his own time, truly powerful and valiant. Memories made him even greater as time passed. But he never practiced the ghost dance. It wasn't brought to the tribes from the West 'til after his death. But he did claim to have a magic war headdress that stopped bullets, they say. Then again, I believe he was felled by a bullet.

"His son, Sauts, was conceived the night before he died. Sauts' mother was supposed to be the only woman Wokinih ever had. Many think the woman seduced him somehow and stole the magic powers of his invulnerability to create her child. They say that's the reason he went into battle powerless the next day. He died, but another legend was born. They called the child Roman Nose, and Sauts, The Bat. When I was young, I was often told that I resembled him. However, from pictures I've seen, my brother Dieks was as close to his twin as two generations would allow.

"The child called John Sauts had at least two sons, both born to Sioux women in Oklahoma. Agigau was one of the women, and Morning Dance of the Oglala was another, I believe. Cheyenne Lucy was his only daughter as far as I know, and Grandma Lucy Fields Smith was, of course, Cherokee and Cheyenne herself. Black Sky was the lesser known of the two sons, and until his death a few years ago, chose to live in seclusion, just outside Ottumwa. When he was younger, his operation was among the largest, most reputable of hound breeders in the nation, greyhounds, whippets, afghans, elkhounds, and the like."

"Did you ever meet him?"

"I tried. He refused to hear me. I told him who I was and he did not believe."

"When was that?"

"Oh, sixty-five, maybe sixty-six, I s'pose. I'd gone to his kennels and posed as a buyer. He was outside with the dogs. He was old, and angry, I think. He didn't look at me, though I stood right next to him at the fence, watching the dogs.

"I said to him, 'Black Sky of the Sioux, I am your son and the son of Cheyenne Lucy.' After a while, all he said back was, 'Who is Thunder?'"

"Did you know?"

"What?"

"Did you know who Thunder was?"

"No. I thought he was forgetful, senile, maybe."

"What did you say? How did you answer him?"

"I told him that I'd never met Thunder, that I'd been sent to the lands up north with Sequoya Chauncey Yellow Robe when I was a child."

"And?"

"He walked away without looking back. So I let go the hope that I'd ever know him."

"I know the answer."

"I don't know the question."

"Who is Thunder?"

"Is someone Thunder?"

"No. A man told me, though, just after Dieks' funeral, when I stopped back at Harrow's Branch. He said that Cheyenne once had a little dog she loved more than anything. It was a whippet she called Blackie. He said it had a tattoo in its ear, and it was the dog's name, Black Sky's Thunder. She must've gotten it from him."

"Black Sky's Thunder," he repeated sadly. "I didn't know ... "

"No, I don't s'pose. I hope Dieks is happy now. I hope they watch over him. He deserved better than he got in this world."

"Dieks? He was always out o' synch here."

I nodded.

He was still thinking about the dog, and like me, about being too late.

"He's looked after. You can rest assured that he's well cared for. If ever there was one who would come to guard the sanctity of a child's soul, it would be Wokinih. Since this child is grandchild and great-grandchild of two Wokinihs, he must be truly coveted. And you should be feeling twice blessed, in the exchange of love and in the acknowledged care and comfort."

"I don't exactly feel blessed. In fact, I'd say I feel a lot closer to cursed. I have this worldly excursion to complete, and I have this huge hole in my heart, with an empty soul on the side. It's not a lot to work with, if you know what I mean. I have a man to whom I owe a great deal, who stands by me, believes in me, and trusts that some day I'll emerge from this mirage completely healed. I'd like very much to believe that great notion as well. So far, though, I'm not exactly impressed with the leftovers I've had to work with."

"I am here and the circle is concentric, as you've noticed. You prayed to the powers of your beloved brother, Liz B. You openly lamented that you could not know, did not understand. He responded to your pleas and sent you the last of those who would know. It was your brother who appealed to Wokinih. It was Wokinih who appealed to me. So I've come to you an old man. But I alone am equipped with the truth and the knowledge necessary to assuage your grief and provide you with answers at last. I would say that you have all you need to free yourself and get on with your life, if that is truly your wish. You have the means and you know the way."

"So, William Collins Cohoe, how do I get back to the beginning?"

"Do you want to retrace your steps? That would seem to be a lot of useless travel to me. I'd think you might want to lay down your burdens and look to your heart. This man with whom you share life, you say he's good, and you've seen many years together. This would seem to be a significant allegiance. I think he'll help you find the way. I think he's guided many steps you are unaware of today."

"And Wokinih?"

"To his infinite wisdom, I yield. I'm here at Sarah's bidding, for she speaks in many tongues. Wokinih confers in many tongues. Who am I to question these things when results speak for themselves? I am here, and you have answers. That would seem sufficient."

"And you? What have you found?"

"The blood of the lamb."

- The Beginning -

Wise and kind Wokinih,
Why do the willows weep?

A child, his youth.

Why do the shadows shiver so?

Aged ancestors,
anguished souls,
those who can't let go.

Oh, Wise Wokinih,
sacred spirit of the dead,
I implore you,
remove these memories that mock my humanity,
calm the child's cries,
the garnered grief that spawned this grave.

But he walks with his mother now,
where the red dust of the pipestone
dances across the gelid quarry floor.
The blood of his ancestors blends
with that of the lamb.

He will not return.
What fear you now?

That I cannot go with him.